# W.A. HARBINSON

# STRYKER'S KINGDOM

ISBN: 0-931773-79-2

Manufactured in the United States of America

FOR SHAUN

*The idealist is incorrigible: if he be thrown out of his
Heaven, he makes himself a suitable ideal out of Hell.*
NIETZSCHE, *Miscellaneous Maxims and Opinions*

*I take it that what all men are really after is some form
or perhaps only some formula of peace.*

JOSEPH CONRAD, *Under Western Eyes*

# STRYKER'S KINGDOM

# STRYKER'S KINGDOM

# PART ONE: GARDEN

# CHAPTER ONE

STRYKER was going hunting. He opened his foot locker and pulled out the SS dagger and slid it down between his boot and the stiff army gaiter. Stryker liked that knife; it was one of his prized possessions. He had taken it from a Nazi SS officer who had walked out of a house in Agrigento with his hands held hopefully above his head. Stryker had shot him. The German's head had disappeared. Stryker had taken the knife and all the *Geld* he could find, then he had kicked the corpse once in the guts and moved along to the next house. He had been with Patton's 7th Army then. They had fought their way to Palermo. Now Stryker was in a Nissen hut in a camp run by the Limeys, and he felt the old tightening in his gut, the need for some action.

'Three days in London,' Stryker said. 'I'm gonna fucking enjoy them.'

He straightened up. He was chewing some Wrigley's. He had a deeply-tanned truck-driver's face, with very dark, un-revealing eyes. Also, he was big: tall and very broad. His belly was flat, and his muscles bulged beneath the green fatigues.

'Hey, you,' he said. 'Move your ass over here.'

Stryker snapped his fingers and more than one man looked around. They were all a little frightened of Stryker, and Stryker wanted it that way. He snapped his fingers again. He had a grin on his face. He was looking at the private on the bed nearest to him, his brown eyes strangely bright and com-manding. The private blinked. His head was shaved and he wore spectacles. He was dressed in vest and trousers, his feet were bare, and he had the raw, gangling body of an adolescent. He walked over to Stryker, flushed a little and smiled. His eyes behind the spectacles were blue and not all that intelligent. He seemed small next to Stryker.

'Yes, Stryker,' he said.

'Staff-sergeant,' Stryker said. 'This is the 7th Army Corps, Kantaylis, and don't fucking forget it.'

'Sorry, staff-sergeant.'

'Right, kid. Now I want you to get that box beneath my bed and pull out all the Hershey bars you can find. When you've done that, I want you to put the fuckers in my bag. Got it?'

'Yes, staff-sergeant.'

'Good. I also want you to go to the PX and pick me up a couple of dozen packs of Chesterfields. Don't buy them. See that fat slob Boletti, who's supposed to fucking work there, and tell him they're for me and you'll get them. Okay?'

'Okay, staff-sergeant.'

'Good. Put the Chesterfields in the bag with the Hershey bars, then, when you've done that, zip the bag up and come and tap me lightly on the shoulder. I won't be far away.'

'You got a pass, staff-sergeant?'

'Yeah, kid, I got a pass. That's what you get for being a good boy. Now start shaking your ass.'

Kantaylis grinned and knelt down by the bed. While he was pulling out the square wooden box that Stryker always kept there, Stryker glanced casually around the Nissen hut. The hut was long and gloomy, filled with iron-framed beds. There was a stove in the middle and it cast a red glow over the men playing cards around the table. These men were mostly veterans: they had muscles and were scarred. They were smoking and slugging bottles of beer and quietly cursing and scratching themselves. It was getting dark outside. A grey light came through the windows. It fell on the beds, on the men reading and writing, some naked and some half undressed, most of them looking exhausted. It had been a rough day. They had just run an assault course. Stryker had pushed them hard and now he grinned at the thought of them stewing the whole weekend in this hut. There were two million men like this. They were camped along the English coastline. They couldn't get passes because the invasion was imminent, and only specialists like Stryker could escape by bending some elbows. Thinking this, Stryker grinned and chewed his gum.

'Hey, kid,' Stryker said to Kantaylis, 'don't steal no Hershey bars.'

'My mouth's watering at the thought of it,' Kantaylis said. 'Just let me have one, staff.'

'Okay,' Stryker said with a grin. 'Just one. And I don't want no thanks, kid.'

Kantaylis was still on his knees. He had opened the wooden box. It was packed with Hershey bars and bottles of Scotch and other luxury items. Kantaylis unwrapped a Hershey bar. He grinned up at Stryker. Stryker slapped him on the shoulder and then walked across the hut to the card table. The air was thick with cigarette smoke. The stove cast its red glow. The men were covered in sweat and the table was covered in dollar bills.

'You got a pass?' Kline said.

'Yeah,' Stryker said. 'I got a pass. I think of you poor bastards, I could bleed, but I got me a pass.'

Kline didn't look up. He was studying his cards. He had a flush of hearts and his lean face was totally expressionless.

'Oh, yeah?' he said. 'And who's ass did you slip into for that?'

Stryker snorted, chewed his gum and grinned. Kline had been with him when they'd hit the beach at Gela, when they'd beaten back the massed tanks of the Hermann Goering Division and pushed up to the hills that formed the backbone of Sicily. Kline was a good ole boy. He could handle himself. He was one of the few men in the hut that Stryker respected. Now he shifted in his chair, glanced lazily around him. Stryker looked at him and then thought of Sicily; of the white beach, the brazen sun, the chaos. They had taken the beach. They had annihilated the fucking wops. *'Ci rendiamo!'* the wops had cried, coming out of the swirling dust, their hands above their heads, their faces grimy, the world exploding around them. And Kline had cut them down. He had done it coldly, professionally. He had not displayed that thick-throated lust that Stryker felt when he killed.

Yet Stryker respected him. He did not take any chances. Later, fighting their way northwards through the hilly country above Palma di Montechiaro, moving forward under the umbrella of a heavy naval bombardment, Kline had saved Stryker's life. Stryker had been stupid. His sense of humour had made him stupid. He had found four sleeping wops bare-assed naked in their pillbox, and had sprayed them while they still had their pants down. It was just too funny. They were spinning around bare-assed. Their hands were outflung and he saw their swinging cocks just before their bodies started pumping blood. Stryker had laughed. He had laughed as he wiped them out. He was so amused by the scene that he forgot to look around him, so he didn't see the wop to his left. Two shots rang out at once. The wop slammed into the wall. Stryker turned to see Kline just behind him, his gun barrel still smoking.

'You're gittin' careless in your old age,' Kline had said. 'He almost had you for dinner.'

Stryker hadn't forgotten that. He wouldn't forget it in the future. Observation and control were all that mattered, and they mattered a lot. Now he looked at Kline. Kline put down his flush in hearts. Cassavetes put an ace on the table, and Kline softly cursed.

'That's it,' Kline said. 'Go fuck yourself.'

Cassavetes chuckled. Kline lit up a Camel. Cassavetes started shuffling the cards while Kline looked up at Stryker.

'I lost,' Kline said.

'Yeah,' Stryker said. 'You lost. I ain't never seen you win that fucking game. You ain't got the instincts.'

Kline shrugged. 'It passes the time,' he said. 'We don't all get passes every weekend.'

'You wanna come with me?'

'No, I fucking don't.'

'Why?'

'Because you're fucking mad, that's why. I don't want no part of it.'

Stryker snorted. He thought Kline was a good ole boy. They

had seen a few rough times together, and that counted for something.

'I'll get you a blow job,' Stryker said.

'I don't want a fucking blow job. I want to get on a Limey ship and go to Europe. I want something to do.'

'It won't be long now.'

'Oh? Who's ear *you* got?'

'I got ears all over this goddam place, and it won't be long now.'

Kline shrugged, his face wreathed in cigarette smoke. The muscles bulged beneath his white vest, and his right arm was scarred.

'Does it hurt?' Stryker asked.

'No, it don't hurt.'

'It must be glamorous to the ladies, that war wound.'

'Oh, yeah,' Kline said. 'It sure is at that. They start comin' the minute I take my shirt off. You oughta try it yourself.'

Stryker snorted again. His lips cracked in a crooked grin. He ran his fingers through his hair and glanced around him in a vague, restless manner. He didn't like the Nissen hut. It was cold and pretty dark. It made him think of all the prisons he'd been in, of the cell bars, the long hours. Stryker often felt trapped in here. That's why he liked to get out a lot. He liked to move with the sky above his head, with no dog soldiers watching him. You got like that in the army. You developed an itch for privacy. You got so you couldn't stand the presence of the other men, the constant movement and noise all around you, the sweat and the stench. Now Stryker glanced around him. These sad sacks were all trapped. They were writing and reading and playing cards, and the air stank of beer.

'Jesus Christ,' Stryker said in a loud and ringing manner, 'you fuckers sure are a sad sight. You oughta be in a pig stye.'

A few eyes glanced up. Someone offered a nervous giggle. Kline looked up at Stryker with a small, knowing grin, well aware of what Stryker was after. Stryker was feeling high. He was fixing for some action. He wanted someone to forget just who he was, but no one made that mistake.

'A bunch of fucking pigs,' Stryker said. 'You eat shit and you look it.'

15

No one replied. Someone coughed and someone giggled. A couple of men close to Stryker started inching away, licking their lips and glancing warily around them. Stryker spat on the floor.

'Filthy,' Stryker said. 'This fucking place is filthy. I oughta run you sonsofbitches ragged. Just look at this fucking floor.'

Stryker looked down at the floor. The spit had landed near his boot. Stryker raised his head and looked at Cassavetes, who had his cards in his hand.

'The floor,' Cassavetes said.

'Yeah,' Stryker said. 'The floor. Where the hell do you get off, Cassavetes? This fucking floor's filthy.'

Cassavetes smiled nervously. He was fat and unshaven. He rubbed at the stubble on his chin and glanced desperately around him.

'Well?' Stryker said.

'Okay, Stryker, I get it.'

'Staff-sergeant, Cassavetes. *Staff-sergeant*. And don't fucking forget it.'

'Sorry, staff-sergeant. Now all I wanna do's play fucking cards. I didn't spit on the floor.'

'It don't matter who spit on the floor,' Stryker said. 'What fucking matters is that it's there. Now clean this spit up.'

Cassavetes rubbed his jaw. He was red with humiliation. He glanced across at Kline and Kline gave a little smile, and Cassavetes heaved a sigh and stood up. He picked a rag off the table.

'Okay, staff-sergeant,' he said. 'I'll clean up the spit.'

Stryker grinned and turned away. He glanced across at Kantaylis. The kid was finishing off his Hershey bar and grinning broadly at Stryker.

'Okay, kid,' Stryker said. 'You've had your fucking dinner. Now move your ass over to the PX and see that bastard Boletti.'

The kid waved his hand and jumped. He walked out of the hut. The door slammed behind him and Stryker looked down at Cassavetes. The fat slob was on his knees, wiping up Stryker's spit. He was breathing heavily and muttering under his breath and that made Stryker feel good.

'You're too fat,' Stryker said to Cassavetes. 'I oughta work you some more. Maybe once or twice around that fucking field with a pack on your back. How'd you like that, Cassavetes? It might do you some good. You're supposed to be a fucking GI and you look like a pansy. That's some gut you got on you.'

Cassavetes sighed, finished wiping the spit up, climbed to his feet and looked at Stryker, his brown eyes evasive.

'Okay, Stryker,' he said. 'Knock it off. I just wanna play cards.'

Stryker chewed his gum. He grinned at Cassavetes. He looked at Kline and ole Kline just sat there smoking, watching them both.

'What I like about these guys,' Stryker said, 'is that they're all full of shit. I mean, you call them fucking pigs and they all just sit silent and you can't see their eyeballs for the sweat. A real tough bunch of GIs.' He grinned at Kline, studied the men at the card table. They were silent and they didn't look at Stryker for fear he might pounce on them. 'A bunch of fucking wimmen. All hot air and farts. And all of them frightened of ole Stryker. Isn't that right, Kline?'

Kline smoked his cigarette. He took his time exhaling. He blew out the smoke and looked at Stryker with a small, nerveless smile.

'Yes, Stryker,' he said. 'I suppose so.'

'But not you, Kline, eh?'

'No, Stryker, not me.'

'You want to mess with me, Kline?'

'No, Stryker,' Kline said softly. 'I don't want to mess with you. It'd bore me to have to kick your nuts off. And who'd get me my free beers?'

Stryker snorted with mirth. He knew Kline wasn't frightened of him. He knew Kline was the only guy in the barracks who didn't piss in his presence. That's why Stryker liked him. Kline didn't knuckle under. He was a fucking good soldier and he knew how to handle himself. You couldn't say that for many of them.

'Talking about beer,' Stryker said. 'I've got a thirst coming on. You want a beer, Kline?'

'Sure,' Kline said. 'I'll have a beer.'

Kline got to his feet with a lazy, graceful movement while Cassavetes, heaving a soft sigh of relief, went back to the table and sat down again. He picked up his cards. His hands were shaking. Stryker saw this and snorted and then glanced across the room at Corporal Bliss. The corporal was on his bed. He was sitting upright and smoking. His lower lip was cut and the right side of his face had been bruised. Stryker had done it. He had worked the corporal over two days ago. He had gone on a bender and come back in a high mood, and decided to have himself some fun. He didn't like Bliss; he thought Bliss was too soft. He had made Bliss get out of his bed and put up his fists. Bliss hadn't refused. No one refused Stryker. They had fought with bare fists and Stryker hadn't relaxed until he saw the blood smearing Bliss's face. Bliss hadn't uttered a sound. He had taken his beating quietly. He had stayed on his feet until Stryker knocked him senseless and picked him up and threw him on his bed. Now Stryker looked at Bliss. The corporal had blond hair and blue eyes. He was smoking a cigarette and he glanced across at Stryker and painfully, unconsciously, licked his cut lip.

'Hey, Bliss,' Stryker said. 'You got some beer?'

'Beer?' Bliss said carefully.

'Yeah,' Stryker said. 'Fucking beer. You suddenly gone deaf or something, Bliss?'

'Yes, staff-sergeant, I've got some beer.'

'That's right, Bliss, you got some beer in your footlocker. You got half a dozen cans to be exact, so bring a couple over here.'

'That beer's got to last me all weekend, staff.'

'Hard shit,' Stryker said. 'I said I want a couple of cans. Now get your ass off that fucking bed and bring the beer over here.'

'You pay me for the cans, staff, and I can go and get myself some more. That's only fair, staff.'

'You Jewish prick,' Stryker said. 'Who the fuck do you think you're talking to? You want some fucking money, come take it. I'm ready and waiting.'

Bliss sat there on the bed. He seemed frail in the vest and

shorts. His face was pale and rather delicate, undeniably handsome, and only marred by the bruise around his left eye. The swollen lip was going down. His blue eyes were very clear. He flicked the blond hair from his forehead, looked thoughtfully at Stryker, then slowly swung his legs off the bed. Some of the other men watched him. Some preferred not to know. He opened his foot locker and picked up two cans and walked steadily across the wooden floor and held the cans out to Stryker.

'Always obey your sergeant,' he said quietly. 'Every good GI knows that, staff.'

Stryker stopped chewing his gum, stared steadily at Bliss. His eyes darkened and then he reached out for the cans and started grinning again.

'What's the matter, kid?' he said. 'Donja *like* the army?'

'No, staff, not particularly.'

'You fucking draftees.'

'That's right, staff.'

'You scared of getting shot, kid? You scared of getting your circumcized prick blown off in Europe?'

'Maybe.'

'It's you fuckers we're fighting for,' Stryker said.

'Really?'

'Yeah, really. We're fighting this fucking war to save the Jews. Now isn't that something?'

'I didn't know you cared,' Corporal Bliss said.

Stryker looked at him. Stryker slowly chewed his gum. His eyes narrowed, but the grin stayed on his face while he studied the kid. The kid stared straight at him.

'How the fuck did you ever get to be a corporal?' Stryker said, holding the beer cans in his huge hands.

'I don't know, staff. I thought you recommended me.'

'Recommend you, shit. I put my trash in the trash can. I don't elevate it to something it ain't with a pair of fucking stripes.'

'I'll try to remember that, staff.'

Stryker stared at Corporal Bliss. The fucking kid was a smart ass. Stryker thought he might kick him in the nuts, but then he thought better of it. He didn't want to victimize any-one; they could all take their turn.

'You got a mouth,' Stryker said. 'I'll give you that, kid. You're a smart ass and you ain't learnt your lesson, so you might need some more. I'll bear it in mind.'

The kid didn't move. Stryker turned and walked away. He sat on his bed and cracked open a can and had a drink while Kline walked up to the kid and gave him a dollar. The kid took it, surprised.

'Fuck it,' Kline said. 'Go get yourself a couple of cans.'

The kid nodded and walked away. He climbed back onto his bed. He put his head back and closed his eyes and inhaled on his cigarette. Then Kline walked up to Stryker. He sat down on the bed beside him. He picked up the other can, stubbed out his Camel and looked at Stryker.

'You're a soft touch, Sergeant Kline,' Stryker said. 'You got a heart of pure gold.'

Kline shrugged. He cracked open the can. 'What the fuck,' he said. 'I don't need to steal from a fucking kid.'

'I don't steal,' Stryker said. 'I take what's mine.'

'And this beer's yours?'

'Yeah, it's mine. If I want it, it's mine. Anything I want from these fuckers, I'll just go and take. This whole god-damned Nissen hut is mine. I won't let them forget it.'

'Well, you sure have an influence, Stryker.'

'Yeah, I got an influence. I run this fucking hut. They don't shit without they come and see me first. And they pay for the privilege.'

'Oh, yeah,' Kline said. 'They sure do that.'

Kline knew all about Stryker. He had known him a long time. He knew that Stryker was in rackets, that he bought and sold goods, that he organized crap games and arranged for weekend passes and peddled food and other luxuries to civilians. Stryker was a fixer. He worked for and by himself. He ruled half the camp and he beat down all resistance, and he knew how to work around the Book without getting his ass burned. People were frightened of Stryker. They had seen what he could do They had seen more than one guy spitting out his front teeth after Stryker had had a bit of sport.

There was a demon in Stryker. Kline knew this and was wary of it. He knew that Stryker needed violence, excitement, the thrill of challenge, needed to dominate everyone around him, wanted total submission. Stryker rarely relaxed. His imprisoned energy tormented him. Brooding, calculating, intensely secretive and mysterious, he moved restlessly through a world that was entirely his own, dispensing cruelty or kindness at a whim, smashing down all resistance.

Yes, Kline knew him. He had known him since Sicily. Stryker had fought through Sicily with a bright, ferocious pleasure, and had, when not fighting, gone his own rapacious way, trading in booze and cigarettes, stealing souvenirs from the dead, selling the souvenirs to journalists and then sending the journalists, mostly inexperienced men, vain and in love with the romance of war, walking down into empty fields where the gunfire of German snipers would cut them down while Stryker chortled with pleasure. All that and more: the whispered rumours about Stryker, the tales of his exploits in the conquered white-walled towns, Niscemi, Campobello, Caltanissetta, Agrigento, bizarre tales of looting, of black marketeering, of obscure acts of violence and unbelievable sexual practices, the hungry child-women of Palermo, the Nazi playmates of Marsela, the rumours and the legends passing down through the ranks, whispered in awe, often whispered in fear, too fantastic to be true, fantastic enough to be possible, while all the time Stryker, with his obsessed, demonic energy, kept his own knowledge of the truth hidden away, used the legends for leverage.

Now Kline drank his beer. He wiped his lips with one hand. He remembered the bleached hills of Sicily, the trucks on the dusty roads, the shouts of 'Viva America!' in the liberated towns, the thousands of prisoners being marched into the compounds with relief in their eyes. Stryker had been right in there. He had traded in cigarettes and booze. There were rumours that he had been slipping whores into the compounds for prices way beyond what they were worth. Other deals were also rumoured: collaborators had been released; a lot of favours had been granted; local dignitaries who had spent the war licking German boots had been seen in whispered negotiations with the staff-sergeant. Stryker was investigated. Heads fell all around him. He continued laughing and he never lacked for money, and they never could touch him. Now Stryker was in England, was waiting for the invasion. He wanted to go to Europe, to France and then to Germany, to straddle the whirlwind when the Reich started crumbling and the pickings would be easy and plentiful ... Stryker wanted more action.

'Fuck it,' he said. 'Just let me outa here. Just let me get going.'

'What're you waiting for?' Kline said. 'They ain't about to blow taps.'

Stryker grinned. 'I want them Chesterfields,' he said. 'I gotta get a little action going, so I need me some cigarettes.' He looked at Kline. There was no response from Kline. Ole Kline just had a slug of beer and stared at him with flat eyes. 'Well?' Stryker said, chewing his gum and grinning crookedly. 'Why donja ask me what the action is? I'd tell you. You know that, Kline.'

'No, you wouldn't,' Kline said. 'You'd just like me to ask. Just like you'd like me to say I wanna come to town. You'd turn me down on both counts.'

'Jesus, Kline, what'ya think I am? A fucking sadist or something?'

'Might be,' Kline said, lighting up another Camel. 'You sure got a pretty peculiar sense of humour. Not nice, as they say.'

Stryker snorted, put his beer can to his lips. He drank and wiped his lips with one hand, glanced across the dark billet.

'That fucking yid,' he said, looking directly at Corporal Bliss. 'I might have to cut that piss-ass down, put my boot in his nuts.'

'He's alright,' Kline said. 'He's a pretty decent kid. Just because he ain't a regular soljer don't mean he's a piss-ass. You just hate the Jews.'

'Right,' Stryker said. 'I hate the fucking jews. I hate yids and micks and beaners and niggers and krauts and decent white Americans. I hate *every* fucker.'

'A man of the world,' Kline said.

22

'Yeah. Fucking right.' Stryker had a drink of beer. 'I been around too long to fall asleep. I keep my ass tight.'

'All them Hershey bars,' Kline said. 'You sure must know a lot of hungry Limeys.'

'Yeah,' Stryker said. 'They're running out of sweet things. I like to keep my little ladies happy. I give 'em chocolate and cigarettes.'

'Glad to know you at least like the ladies. They should think themselves privileged.'

'Oh, I like them,' Stryker said. 'Old Stryker likes his piece of cunt. He likes 'em with their legs wide apart and their stupid mouths shut.' Stryker grinned at Kline, a crooked grin, mocking. 'Why donja come with me?' he said. 'Take a bite of the action. We'll have ourselves a regular field day: some cold beer and hot pussy.'

'No, thanks,' Kline said.

'Why not?' Stryker asked.

'Because you're fucking mad, is why. Because I don't want any trouble. Because I've seen you when you're drinking and I don't want to land up in the brig. I'll just stay here and beat myself.'

'I always thought myself a quiet man,' Stryker said.

'Oh, sure,' Kline said. 'You're a quiet man alright. You're as quiet as a fucking Sherman tank smashing through a brick wall. I've seen you in action, Stryker. I've made the mistake of drinking with you. I've woken up in too many wrecked bars with my fucking head splitting. No thanks; I'm retired now.'

Stryker snorted with mirth. He drank some more beer. He wiped his lips with the back of his hand and had a good look around him.

'Where's that fucking Kantaylis?' he said. 'I wanna get out of here.'

'He's probably arguing with Boletti,' Kline said.

'No he isn't,' Stryker said. 'There'll be no argument from Boletti. That slob's too in love with his few remaining teeth to go and pick a fight with good ole Stryker. He'll hand over the cigarettes.'

'The word's out on Boletti,' Kline said. 'The MPs have

let it be known that he's under suspicion for graft, that the PX books have been checked and found wanting, that too many crates of cigarettes and booze and other items have been disappearing over the past few months. They put the word out deliberately. They wanna give Boletti a chance. They want him to knock it off before they're forced to grab him – and Boletti knows this. He's pretty fucking scared. He sweats all the time. He knows that if they grab him it won't be a minor charge, that it'll be the Stockade, and he knows what they do to guys in the Stockade. But Boletti won't stop. The MPs just can't figure it. He's scared shitless, but he won't stop the stealing, he just goes right on doing it.'

Stryker snorted. It was a snort of mirth and mockery. He drank some beer, and his brown eyes fixed intently on Kline.

'Poor Boletti,' he said. 'That poor slob. He just ain't got no sense.'

'He's got sense,' Kline said. 'He's just scared, that's all. He's scared of the Stockade, but obviously he's even more scared of something else – something or someone.'

'You suggesting something, Kline?'

'No, I'm not suggesting nothing. I'm just thinking that it would be a pretty lousy deal if Boletti went in there, that he's not cut out for that, that the Stockade would break him in two, and he doesn't deserve that. There's tricks and there's tricks, Stryker. A guy's gotta look after himself. But it's one thing to put a bit of pressure on a guy, and another to let him go to the Stockade. No GI deserves that, Stryker.'

'And what's so fucking special about GIs?'

'You know what I mean, Stryker.'

'Fuck Boletti,' Stryker said. 'Let him go to the Stockade. He won't be the first and he won't be the last. It might even be good for him.'

'We all *know* you've been in the Stockade, Stryker.'

'Yeah, I've fucking been in there. It taught me a thing or two. It turned me into a rough, tough GI. Boletti oughta be grateful. Anyway,' he added, glancing sideways at Kline, wiping his lips with one hand and grinning crookedly, 'what the fuck are you telling me all this for? I just want some cigarettes.'

24

'Okay, Stryker, forget it. Forget I mentioned it.'

'Fucking right. I'll do that.'

Stryker was restless. He really wanted to get moving. He wanted to get on a train and disembark at Paddington and lose himself in the night life of London, in those thriving, blacked-out streets. The urge was growing stronger. It was starting to play at his nerves. He felt the old familiar lust, the churning need, the awesome hunger for action. Stryker licked his lips. He closed his eyes for a moment. He saw the darkness, the whites of their eyes, the opened mouths and the throttled fear. It was always like that. In the depths there was freedom: in the darkness, in the moonlight, under cold, remorseless stars, the Ack-Ack guns hammering away in the distance, the planes rumbling overhead. Stryker wanted to experience it. He had to enter that garden. He had to plunge down to the stench and come up to where the bright light was freedom. A fierce lust swept through him. He shivered slightly and opened his eyes. He saw Kline and he grinned and drank his beer, took control of himself.

'Where's that fucking Kantaylis?'

Kantaylis returned. He was carrying a few cartons. They were wrapped in brown paper and he brought them straight across the hut to Stryker, stopped in front of the bed.

'Okay, staff,' he said, 'here's your cigarettes.'

'About time,' Stryker said. 'I thought you'd gone to fucking Chicago. You have any trouble with Boletti?'

'No, staff. No trouble. He took them out of the warehouse. He sort of groaned and he sweated a lot, but he didn't say much. He seemed a bit worried though.'

Stryker grinned. 'Oh, he's worried alright. Now put the cigarettes in that fucking bag and go back to your bed. Go jerk yourself off, kid.'

Kantaylis grinned in a dopey manner. The light flashed off his glasses. He knelt down by the bed and carefully put the cigarettes in Stryker's bag. Then he stood up again. He grinned and scratched his shaved head. He glanced from Stryker to Kline, and then shrugged, and walked across to his bed. Stryker kept his eyes on him.

'A pretty good kid,' Stryker said. 'A bit dumb, but obedient.'

'Yeah,' Kline said softly. 'Just your type.'

Stryker stared at him. Kline was grinning a little. The cigarette was dangling from his lips and his grey eyes were squinting.

'Don't push it,' Stryker said. 'Don't fucking push it. I might just get annoyed.'

He climbed to his feet, buttoned up his tunic, took the bag in his right hand and just stood there, looking around him.

'Fuck you,' he said in a loud and ringing tone. 'Fuck the lot of you.'

Then he walked from the Nissen hut.

# CHAPTER TWO

WANDERING slowly through Brewer Street market, feeling vaguely self-conscious as he always did in his uniform, David Holmyard kept his eyes at a modest level. Released from the camp near Lympstone on a weekend pass, he was now looking forward to a quiet evening with Katherine, with the added luxury of some fruit and a good wine. The wine had been supplied by his father-in-law, the major-general, also of the Royal Marine Division, who had sent the bottle to Lympstone with an accompanying note in which he had expressed his hopes of seeing David soon. David smiled at this thought, a gently cynical smile, and stopped to look down at some pineapples. Since a weekend pass had become something of a luxury, the self-indulgence of a pineapple seemed a small sin.

'How much are they?' David asked.

'Five guineas each, guvnor,' the man behind the stall said. 'All fresh in this mornin' an' so juicy they'd melt in yer mouth.'

'That's rather expensive,' David said.

'I wouldn't argue that, guvnor. They're too expensive for the likes o' me. I'd only eat one if I won at the dogs – but that's what they cost me.'

The pineapples were piled up in woven baskets, as were the grapes at 16 shillings a pound. David fingered the grapes with a certain amused longing, but decided to settle for half a dozen peaches: at two shillings each they were cheaper and would last longer ... and would not upset Katherine's sense of propriety. David picked out six peaches, handed them to the man, and watched him put them into a paper bag and spin the bag over expertly.

"'Ere you are, guvnor,' the man said. 'Enjoy 'em. They're more than *I* can afford.'

David blushed and took the bag. He handed the man six two-shilling pieces. The man thanked him and David nodded and walked away, still feeling embarrassed. The privilege of class, he thought. The war hasn't changed that much. He put the peaches in his bag with the cheese and the wine, and walked along the middle of the road between the vegetable carts. The market was busy, the hawkers shouting above the noise, the people a grey mass of movement that spoke of hardship and poverty. David always felt embarrassed in such surroundings.

It seemed a long way from Oxford, from the large room in Meadow Buildings, from the long nights when the students discussed Homer and Euripides, smoking pipes and drinking cheap Algerian wine, their voices mocking, opinionated. Now, walking towards Shaftesbury Avenue and the busy rumble of its traffic, he thought rather guiltily of how, frequently bored, probably spoilt to the point of ignorance, he had gone to read Law, discussed Spain and the Rise of Fascism, submitted highly derivative poetry to the vain pages of the *Cherwell*, and fallen in love with a young lady at Somerville, a major-general's daughter. Much less an education than a romantic diversion, divorced from real experience and the actuality of the times, it had nevertheless encouraged him to look beyond Christ Church with an ever increasing sense of guilt. He was reminded of that guilt now. It would not let him go. He always felt it when he thought of a world of class divisions, of privilege based on wealth and family ties, of the poor who supported it.

He had not thought of it before. Spain and Germany had forced the issue. And perhaps that was why he had not gone directly into law, but had instead decided to enlist before the war had been won. It hadn't helped him much, had merely pleased his father-in-law. Ill at ease in a uniform, convinced he was no soldier, he could never think of himself as a man trained to lead men without feeling a sort of shameful amusement, an irrevocable self-mockery.

David felt almost foreign in Shaftesbury Avenue. The pavements were a solid mass of American GIs, of Canadian Commandoes and French paratroopers, of Australian diggers and Hungarian exiles and sailors and pilots and WACs, all heading for Soho or Mayfair or the Strand, looking forward to the evening, to some laughter and love, before the blackout took hold and the planes rumbled above and the bombs fell and the incendiaries started exploding. David was enthralled. It never ceased to amaze him. He felt lost and temporarily dislocated from the world he had known. There was an Ack-Ack battery at the corner of Rupert Street, the crew shining its barrels and blowing good-natured kisses at the whores who were getting ready for the evening. Across the road some shops were in ruins, their fronts blown away, the walls turned to rubble, the interiors exposed, complete with upper floors and furniture, like a set in a theatre of nightmare.

The crowds shuffled past them, oblivious. They were heading for home, or for the bars and the brothels, each in his own way preparing for the evening with its excitement and carnality and death. The barrage balloons floated above, grey in the waning light. Tonight that same sky would be pierced by the searchlights, torn by the gunfire, rent asunder by the howl of the planes, the deeper rumble of bombers. There was nothing permanent anymore. Each night brought its revelations. Carnal lust would be appeased, fleeting love would pass in darkness, while the English would quietly die in their homes, their bodies on fire.

It never ceased to amaze David. It made him feel very old. He saw the violence and the need to deny it as one and the same. Yet he also felt grief, a generalized sense of loss. He saw the guidelines of his past, the ancient buildings, his whole culture, disintegrating with an awesome consistency. The past was being obliterated. A new world was in the making. It was a world that would be built on the bones of the dead, a harsh and more realistic world, a world of shifting allegiances.

Brought up in Harrow, in more genteel days, his father an academic of considerable standing, his mother a glittering product of the secluded middle-classes, David was very aware of these changes. The raft of history was sinking. The old life-belts were disappearing. The moral support of the Empire, with its constants and possibilities, was being broken on the rack of expediency and would never recover. He saw it now. He saw it all in Shaftesbury Avenue. He saw the Americans and the Canadians and the French and the Australians, the men drawn from the farms and the factories and the streets, out of prisons and flophouses and defiant, stately mansions, to join together in hope and some fear for the liberation of Europe. And over there, across the Channel, behind the gun emplacements and the armoured divisions, the men of the Third Reich, that eternal dream now made redundant, were waiting for that final and most bloody of all confrontations. David had to go there. It was something he now needed. As if removed from himself, dissolved into the larger issues, untied from his old harbours and cast adrift in turbulent seas, he had to swim into darkness and danger for the hope of a new dawn.

He caught a bus to Knightsbridge, saw the barrage balloons above, looked down at Piccadilly, at the fields of Green Park, saw the grey sweep of Wellington Arch with the Ack-Ack guns around it. The war permeated everything. It cast its shadow on ancient dreams. David felt as if his past had been a mere preparation for the singular reality to come. He had thought a lot about the war. It was a secret obsession. Over the past few years, emerging tentatively into manhood, hampered by youthful passions and attempting to break from those same passions, he had felt himself no more than a shadow, without substance or motive. His father had encouraged him to go to Oxford, had wanted him to read Law. He had complied, but his heart had not been in it; it had seemed a bit unreal. Now, thinking of Oxford, of the comfortable, smokey rooms, of the ringing conversations, of Catullus and Justinian and Beardsley and Firbank, of long nights with cheap wine and politics and Verdi, of punting down the river and eating good meals in the George, of playing tennis with virgin girls and dreaming of secret pleasures, David felt a strange contempt for it, a slow building shame ... Halcyon days indeed. The most sublime ignorance rampant . . . He had come out of Oxford with a quick war degree and the knowledge that he was no longer at peace, that his whole world seemed hollow. He had also married Katherine. He had found that love was not enough. After one year of marriage, linked by love, torn by confusion, they no longer knew where they stood, nor what the future might offer. Thus the war had become an obsession. It both repelled and fascinated him. It represented the destruction of the world he had known, and the hope of some larger committment.

It represented escape.

Katherine heard him come in. She looked up from her newspaper. He was standing in the doorway of the lounge with a bag in his right hand. His eyes were a dark, reflective brown, highly intelligent, rather tentative, glancing at her and moving away while he offered a nervous smile. She put her newspaper down, a hint of tension shooting through her. She had missed him, but now she felt defensive, almost frightened; as if, with his return, in the actuality of his presence, she was stricken again by the confusion that had troubled their marriage.

'Well,' he said quietly, 'I'm home again.'

'Yes,' she said. 'I can see that.'

She smiled gently at him, rose gracefully to greet him. She straightened out her skirt and he saw her white fingers, a delicate web over her thighs, tugging lightly, uneasily. Her eyes were dark like his. Her hair tumbled across her forehead. He was struck once again by her beauty, by her slim, fragile strength. Then she stepped forward to embrace him, held him lightly and kissed his lips. She was soft and her warmth poured around him, making him fearful.

'Oh, Lord,' he said, stepping back and looking at her, 'you *do* look nice.'

'Thank you,' she replied, brushing the hair back from her eyes, smiling shyly and with a certain dark radiance. 'You don't look bad yourself.'

'It's the uniform,' he said. 'The ladies can't resist a uniform. I'm no longer an ordinary man – I'm a glamorous figure.'

'And how's the glamorous figure enjoying Lympstone?'

'Well, I've had easier times.'

'No matter. I'm sure father's proud of you.'

'Yes, I'm sure he is. And you?'

'As you said: a lady can't resist a uniform.'

'I feel uncomfortable in it,' he said. 'A bit of an imposter, actually. I don't think I'll ever get used to it.'

'Really?'

'Yes.'

She smiled. 'You've been wearing it long enough. And a 1st lieutenant, no less. You *should* feel natural by now.'

'Well, I don't.'

He glanced around the lounge. It was large and well furnished; the bright white of the walls was off-set by the brown of the carpets. It was his father-in-law's apartment. They simply couldn't afford their own. The major-general stared at him from a picture on the mantelpiece, reminding him of debts that were owed, of his shameful dependence. David stared at the photograph. The major-general's lips were tight. His eyes had the cold dry intelligence of a singular arrogance. Katherine didn't look like him. She lacked that singular arrogance. At times, as she had confessed to David, she did not even like him.

'Sit down,' Katherine said. 'Take your shoes off. Relax. I'll get you a drink.'

'Lovely. Any gin?'

'Yes.'

'We are privileged.'

'Now don't start, David.'

He smiled and sat down on the sofa, placing the paper bag by his side and following her with his eyes as she went to the walnut cabinet, pulled the doors open and withdrew an untouched bottle of gin.

'You've been leading a pure life in my absence,' he said.

'Yes,' she said. 'I never drink alone. I usually only drink with the girls at the end of the week.'

'That's today.'

'*You're* back today.'

He watched her pouring the gin, feeling a little embarrassed by his remark, by his insistence on reminding her of their privileged position, their dependence on her father's financial security. A crass imposter, he would bite the hand that fed him, would cherish his dreams of equality and justice while surrendering to his father-in-law's assistance: to the comforts denied others. Katherine was devoid of such hypocrisy; she accepted what she had been born to. She did not understand his disillusionment with Oxford, his increasing dissatisfactions, his reluctance to live in her father's apartment until he could settle down to a career when the war had been won. Doubtless, since he himself did not quite understand it, her feminine reasoning was sound.

'That's a large gin you're pouring,' he said.

'Well,' she said, 'I thought you might need it.'

'I do. I feel totally exhausted. The Royal Marines might make men out of boys, but this evening I feel very old indeed.'

Katherine smiled as she poured the tonic. She did not add any ice. She stirred the drinks and came over and sat beside him and gave him a glass.

'There you are. That should make you feel younger.'

They touched glasses and drank, smiling hesitantly at one another, both feeling a shyness, an uneasiness that should not have existed.

'Yes,' David said, 'that's good.'

'Well, I thought you might need it, but not *that* much. Do you *really* feel old?'

'Yes. After two weeks without a break I feel old.'

'You don't *look* old. In fact, you look extremely healthy. You used to look like an academic, but now your cheeks are all flushed and you positively *radiate* masculinity.'

'It's the drill field. I spend hours on the drill field. I also climb cliffs, go on route marches, clamber across rope bridges, go swimming with a pack on my back, crawl through mud pits, practise self-defence, inspect resentful platoons in the noon-day sun, and have more target practice than I can handle. I get lots of fresh air. I get even more exercise. It's more strenuous than punting, and doubtless good for me, but it does make me feel rather old.'

33

'You look wonderful.'

'Thank you. Do you think I'm as fit as the average German?'

'Anyone's as fit as a German. At least that's what they tell us.'

'Good. I'm glad to hear it. I can't wait to get over there and show them how healthy I am.'

'But you still don't like it.'

'The army?'

'Don't call it the army. My father would *hate* it if you called the Royal Marine Division *the army*.'

'My God, yes, he certainly would.'

Katherine smiled. 'So,' she said, sipping her drink, 'you don't like the Marines.'

David shrugged. 'I don't know,' he said. 'It's not so much a question of not liking it, but rather that I feel uncomfortable with it.' He sipped his drink, glancing idly at the window, noticing that the afternoon's grey light had darkened considerably. 'Truthfully,' he continued, 'I feel a little false – like a schoolboy pretending to be a soldier. Perhaps I'm just not cut out for it.'

'Father thinks differently. He says you're a natural. He says you have all the ingredients for a very fine soldier.'

'Well, that's gratifying to hear. But then your father would like me to *remain* a soldier.'

'Is that so terrible of him? After all, it's a family tradition.'

'It's *his* family tradition, not mine.'

Katherine nodded, smiling over her glass, the light reflecting out of her brown eyes, making them luminous.

'True,' she said. 'But you're now his son-in-law. And I know that he wanted a son much more than a daughter.'

'Of course. To carry on the family tradition.'

'And that also,' Katherine said, 'is understandable.'

'I'm not denying it,' David said, 'I just suspect I'm not suited for it. I feel like an imposter in this uniform. Like I'm out of my depth.'

'Then why did you enlist?'

'Ah, ha! There's the mystery!'

'It's not a mystery,' she said quietly. 'It's just something you refuse to discuss.'

34

She was looking directly at him, her brown eyes reflecting the light; they were dark and they drew in the light and turned it back towards him. He was fascinated by her face. He had always dearly loved it. Romantic, intelligent, almost mature beyond its years, it radiated that honesty which could well become its own hapless victim. Now he studied her eyes, was drawn into their depths, felt himself cast adrift in those questions that their young love had raised. He wanted to reach out and touch her. He wanted to soothe his mounting fears. He wanted to cleave to her body, to her pale, secret flesh, to explore her and thereby find himself: to let her know what he was. Yet he didn't dare think about it. The pain of failure was too great. As lovers, like children, they had yielded to one another and found only despair in the union, an inadmissable shame. They loved one another. They had found that love was not enough. They had touched, and in this touching was an ice that had left them both speechless.

'I don't refuse to discuss it,' he said. 'I just don't find it easy.'

'Why not?' she said. 'You're a perfectly good conversationalist. You believe in logic and reason and honesty; you *should* be able to discuss it.'

'What we believe in and what we can do are two different things.'

'Are they?'

'Yes.'

'You didn't learn *that* at Oxford.'

'No. I didn't learn it at Oxford. It just slowly crept up on me.'

Katherine sighed, leant back and glanced around her. She saw the richness of the decor, the paintings, and they gave her some comfort. Certainly she needed it. She no longer felt innocent. The bright simplicity of her adolescence, in her case a protected one, had given way to a sea of confusion and a complex uncertainty. She sipped her drink and glanced at David. She felt her love and her despair. Her emotions swam in search of release, but her reasoning stifled them. She closed her eyes, tapped her forehead with the glass, wanted David to reach out and undress her and help her to lose herself. It was a primal need, almost whorish in its intensity: she wanted to sink down and have him invade her, violate her, take the nerves of her flesh and stretch them out beyond the point of endurance. That's what she wanted. It made her open her eyes again. It was the dream of a consummation that had eluded them both and turned their marriage into a wilderness of silence and terror. Now she looked at him. Her love immediately turned into anguish. He looked at her with a love that was equal to her own, but the both of them were held in a vice of inexplicable panic. She couldn't understand it. Neither of them could. They had not made love until they were married, and then it was too late. How could they have anticipated it? Their love was too strong to even have imagined it. Yet the minute their bodies had touched, they had numbed one another. Katherine now looked at David. His face was gentle and evasive. He wanted to drink her in, to make them whole, but the secret eluded him.

'I wish you were more content,' she said. 'I wish you weren't so confused.'

'Confused?'

'Yes.' She looked down at the floor. 'You were more optimistic when I met you. You seemed more sure of yourself.'

'Student days,' he said, his smile gentle and much too old. 'The innocence and confidence of a spoilt brat. I daresay I was sure of myself.'

'So?' Katherine said. 'Is there anything wrong with that? Do you really think that being rather jaded is a sign of maturity? That's an old Oxford truism.'

'And is that what I am? Rather jaded?'

'I think that's what you would like to be.'

'Really?'

'Yes.'

'Suddenly I feel so cheap.'

'Oh, my God!'

She glanced at him and turned away. Night was falling beyond the window. She crossed the room, pulled the curtains and then came back and picked up their glasses.

'Let's have another,' she said.

36

David watched her pour the drinks, felt the twitching of his nerves. A desolation so complete it was ruinous took hold of his senses. They could no longer talk. They could talk, but it was silence. The silence was the void in between what they said and attempted. She poured the drinks with sharp gestures, brushed the hair back from her eyes. The muted light from the table cast its shadows on her face and enhanced the troubled beauty of her features: her dark eyes, her full lips. David stared at her, entranced. He saw her breasts, her outlined legs. He felt the tips of his fingers trailing over her skin, saw her pale, flowing body, touched her hollows and curves . . . died a sudden death. She came back towards him. He saw the glass in her hand. He took it and her body moved around him and sank down and reclined. He saw her brown eyes, the dark, troubled depths. Scarcely no more like a child (like himself, a mere child), she now floundered in the adult's more real world of sinking foundations. David wanted to help her, wanted desperately to help them both, wanted to take her naked body, to be blindingly inside her, to dissolve her and obliterate himself and find a singular freedom. Yet the thought itself was torture: it unearthed the buried memories, forcing him to acknowledge that their moments of passion had collapsed before murderous inhibition, an inexplicable fear.

'You enlisted,' she said. 'You didn't have to do that. You read Law and you got your degree and you went and enlisted. Now you say you're not happy.'

'No,' he said. 'I didn't quite say that.'

'Correction: you're not quite suited for it.'

'I just feel a bit ridiculous. I'm an officer and I give orders. I give orders from a position of authority that I can't really feel. What do I know of the army? What do I know of fighting? I might have to lead these men into battle – and that seems like a sour joke. Obviously they despise me. My officer's rank is a privilege of class. I give orders to men who fought at Dunkirk and in Africa, and they must look upon me as a fool, a privileged upstart.'

'That word *privilege*. My God, it's obsessed you!'

'Has it?' He thought about it. 'Yes, it probably has.'

'Privilege,' she said. 'You won't let that word go. Why on earth are you so ashamed of your background? You didn't invent it.'

'I'm not ashamed of it. I'm just more conscious of it. I just feel that the world has to change, and that I want to be part of it.'

'So you renounce your own class. You take pride in your guilt. Like the worst of the hypocrites of Oxford and Cambridge, you pretend that you can't stand your privileges, your inherited advantages.'

'I'm not pretending. I simply have a few doubts. I never thought about it before, but during my last year at Oxford it just quietly crept up upon me. I was reading a lot about Spain. It led on to other things. I finally realized that my world had been built on human suffering, and that those who had always been abused were now fighting for justice.'

'The working classes?'

'Yes, the working classes.'

'And you want to become one of them?'

David sighed, felt vaguely embarrassed. He studied the floor, glanced around the room, then had a sip of his gin.

'I don't know,' he finally said. 'You can't become what you aren't. I can't talk to them and they can't talk to me, but I sympathise with them.'

'There's nothing you can do,' Katherine said.

'Probably not. I think I realise that. I just can't get it out of my head. As you say, it's obsessed me.'

'You just need something,' Katherine said. 'You just don't know what you want to do. You need a focus for your life, and you think that this concern will fill the gap. Well, it won't. You're too divorced from it already. Your background, your education, your dreaded *privileges* have all put you beyond it. You'll have to find another cause, and it will have to come out of yourself. Not out of your reading.'

The rebuke was pertinent. It made David blush deeply. He had another drink and glanced at her, saw her dark, flashing eyes. Probably she was right. His brimming conscience was cowardice. He did not know himself, lacked direction, was devoid of motive, and he hoped to escape from this dilemma by finding a radical cause. The hypocrisy was real; the lack of justice was in himself. As a man he had lost himself, as a husband he had failed her, and in either case he wanted no more than escape from this truth. Thus his words were empty sounds, his principles mere protection. He talked of justice for the world while his only real thought was for the undiscovered mysteries of her body.

At that very moment, looking carefully at her, thinking shamefully of the vanity of his teeming dissatisfactions, he was struck by a vivid recollection of their first night together. Newly married, emotionally fraught, bound by love and childish fears, they had turned out the lights and pressed their bodies together in the hope of love's blinding revelations. Both had been virgins, breathing fear at one another: neither wanted to be the one to show an eagerness that might appear wanton. The act was tentative and fumbling. A puritanical world regaled them. In the darkness, in that torn, revealing silence they had joined and felt guilt. This breach was never filled. The wounds they carried could not be healed. They made love in the darkness, rarely saw themselves naked, and could not discuss the fact that an anguished inhibition had turned their love into a farce, an unyielding dilemma. Now David remembered this. It paralysed him with grief. He felt at odds with himself, with his principles, with his hopes, and he longed for the chance of escape in the invasion of Europe.

'No matter,' David said. 'Forget it. I don't want to discuss it.'

'No,' she said. 'You don't want to discuss it.'

'Please,' David said. 'I'm only home for the weekend. I'd just like to relax and forget it all. Just the two of us. Here.'

'Yes,' she said quietly. 'Of course.'

'Your father sent me a bottle of wine. I bought some cheese and peaches. I thought we might have a modest supper, preferably by candlelight.'

His hopes sank the minute he said it. He saw the flickering of her eyes. A slight flush was on her cheeks, and her fingers scratched nervously at her glass.

'I can't,' she said. 'At least not tonight. I'm working with the Women's Voluntary Service, over at Whitechapel. We run mobile laundries and baths, assist families left homeless, help the doctors and nurses, and so forth. We have to be there before the air-raids start and then we stay as long as we're needed. I'm sorry, but I can't call it off.'

She saw the hurt in his eyes, the hint of shock, the quick retreat, saw him look down at the floor and look away, his tongue licking his upper lip. He seemed defenceless at that moment, very young, strangely innocent, and it made her feel her own hurt more deeply, ashamed for them both. Yet she didn't want to stay. She had to make her escape. She knew that a supper by candlelight would force them to intimacy. She sensed that neither of them really wanted it. She knew they both would regret it, would both feel committed to acting out a relationship that had increasingly offered nothing but pain. She wanted him to fill her being, to set her free, but she knew that his inhibitions, which were equal to her own, would merely lead them both to further frustration, a gut-wrenching bewilderment. Perhaps she should take the initiative. She had often thought about it. She had thought to parade herself like a wanton, to make their coupling more natural. But she just could not do it. Instead, she tried to pretend: she closed her eyes and let him enter her body – and then their own tension throttled them . . . No, she couldn't stay. She couldn't go through it tonight. They loved each other, but their love was not enough to break down what constrained them.

'Well,' he said quietly, 'that's that, then.'

'I'm sorry,' she said. 'I really am.'

He put his glass down on the table, stroked his forehead abstractedly, glanced around him at the walls of the room, at the paintings, the antique lamps.

'Wine and candlelight,' he said. 'No matter. It was just an idea.'

And felt rotten immediately. Felt worse when she touched him. Felt her hand resting lightly on his wrist, standing in for unspoken words.

'I'm sorry,' she said again. 'Why not visit my father? I know he's looking forward to seeing you, and he's at home tonight.'

'Fine. And what about you?'

'Stay there until I'm finished. I'll join you there. We can come back together.'

David nodded, his smile disguising his disappointment.

Katherine stared steadily at him, her hand resting on his wrist, then she shrugged and gave a small, nervous smile and got to her feet.

'I better get ready,' she said. 'I don't want to be late.'

He didn't reply. There seemed little he could say. He watched her walk from the lounge, heard her moving about, and he knew that the ills of their marriage would not be cured this night.

David felt the hurt deeply. He also felt increasing shame. They had made love because they loved each other ... and something had died in them. He didn't know what it was, but felt the wrong was in himself, felt his sexual inhibition like a chain around his flesh, an unreasonable, overriding concern that made him stop at the gates. Katherine also possessed this weakness: she needed someone to lead the way. He understood this, but his own unyielding fears would not let him go.

The situation was ironic. The lack of logic sprang from thought. A civilized man, educated, articulate, he felt incarcerated in his own complex reasoning, divorced from his flesh.

Privileges, he thought, I am paying for my privileges. I live with my intellect while my body rebels against itself.

How pathetic it made him feel.

Katherine walked back to the lounge. She was buckling the belt of her overcoat. She saw him sitting on the sofa with his chin in his hands, his dark, rather sad, romantic eyes staring vaguely at nothing. She froze where she stood, couldn't take her eyes off him: he was suddenly like someone far away, someone close, disappearing. A fierce anguish shot through her; she felt bewildered, unreal. She started sinking, dissolving, where she stood, losing sight of herself.

Now she wanted to fall before him, wanted to lay down at his feet, wanted to have him take control and then wrack any havoc upon her. She closed her eyes, felt the melting of her loins. In that darkness, in that brief, light-flecked cosmos, she sensed the depth of her love. Then she opened her eyes again.

He looked at her and she smiled. She went over and kissed him lightly, her hands resting on his shoulders, then she picked up her bag and waved one hand and walked out of the room.

She felt relief after that.

# CHAPTER THREE

THE train crawled through the darkening English countryside, the wheels on the tracks making a harsh, metallic rumbling, while Staff-sergeant Stryker, feeling edgy and impatient, smoked a Chesterfield and contemplated the coming evening.

Stryker was going hunting. He reached down and stroked the knife. He gave a tight little smile and looked across at the GI corporal who was the only other person in the compartment. The corporal had a round, flushed, babyish face with red hair and large innocent eyes. He was reading a copy of *Men Only*, chuckling to himself, and occasionally slugging from a small silver flask. Stryker felt high, felt the need for communication. He leant forward and studied the corporal and kept the grin on his face.

'Hey, corporal,' he said, 'what you got there? In that neat silver flask.'

The corporal glanced up and blinked his blue eyes. They were the eyes of a Southerner, a redneck, a shitass from nowhere.

'Sergeant?'

'Staff-sergeant,' Stryker said, holding tight to his friendly grin.

'Oh ... yeah ... sorry, staff-sergeant. I didn't hear what you said.'

'I wanted to know what was in that silver flask, kid.'

The corporal blinked again, held the flask up and stared at it, then offered Stryker a sly, half bashful smile.

43

'This here,' he drawled in a voice not quite Southern, not quite New York, but somewhere in between, and pleasantly friendly, 'is genuine Johnny Walker Scotch whisky. You wanna try some, staff?'

'I sure would appreciate that,' Stryker said.

The wheels hammered on the railings, the darkening countryside whipped past, as Stryker took the silver flask, wiped the rim with his right hand, had a slug and then belched with satisfaction before handing it back.

'That's pretty good,' Stryker said in an uncanny imitation of the corporal's accent. 'I sure feel a lot better for that. You wanna Hershey bar, corporal?'

'No thanks, staff. I'm on a diet, you know? Like as not I'd blow up with that Hershey bar lining my guts.'

'You look pretty fit, kid.'

'Yeah, I am. And I wanna keep it that way. I think the army's doin' a little bit of good there. You know? Keep the belly down.'

The corporal had another drink. He grinned mildly at Stryker. His blue eyes were slightly tinged with crimson, were vague and benign.

'That magazine,' Stryker said. 'You can read that Limey shit? I never understood their goddamned humour. An' I just saw you giggling there.'

The corporal glanced at the magazine. It was lying across one knee. He stroked the bare ass of a lady in a coloured cartoon and grinned in a sublime, dopey manner, scratching his left ear.

'Well, I like it, you know? I mean, it's weird and pretty funny. It's not exactly *Yank*, but it sure does pass a few friendly hours.'

'Faggots,' Stryker said. 'These fucking Limeys are all faggots. I don't mind them, but I keep my ass tight when the bar's gettin' crowded.'

'Yeah,' the corporal said. 'I think I know what you mean. They don't always know where to put their cocks – but they sure are good fighters.'

'Shit,' Stryker said. 'That's all Limey propaganda. That

44

bunch of fucking faggots couldn't fight to save their asses. They just talk all around it.'

'You think so?' the corporal said.

'Yeah, I think so,' Stryker said.

'I don't know,' the corporal said. 'That's not what I heard. I heard they was beatin' back the Krauts when I sucked my first tit.'

'Them fucking Krauts,' Stryker said. 'They were just dumb, that's all. They're fucking mystics – you know? *superstition* – and they don't like the water.'

The corporal blinked. He seemed a little bewildered. He had a drink and then passed the flask to Stryker who had a stiff slug.

'Water?' the corporal said. 'I don't get it, staff.'

'The English Channel,' Stryker said. 'That's all the English had goin' for them. The Krauts had 'em in a box, but were scared of crossing the Channel, so they just sat there and let the Limeys boast about it. That's all there is to it. The rest is Limey propaganda. Without us these fucking faggots would just sit here and jerk themselves off.'

The corporal, who was obviously a little bit drunk, nodded in a philosphical manner and had a drink of his Scotch. He then wiped his lips with the back of one hand, grinned in that dopey fashion, and passed the flask over to Stryker.

'Here you are, staff,' he said. 'Line your stomach. It'll help pass the time.'

Stryker drank the Scotch, felt it burning down inside him. It made him feel bright and voluptuous, more aware of himself. He closed his eyes for a moment. The train rumbled all around him. He saw the streets of Chicago, saw the stockyards, smelt the blood, felt the knife between the gaiter and his ankle, knew that thick-throated lust. Stryker sighed, felt the tension working at him: he wanted to get off the train and find release, find the freedom of darkness.

He opened his eyes again. The corporal was leaning his head back. His blue eyes stared at nothing, and he smiled in a mild, distant manner. He then scratched at his balls.

'You got a pass?' Stryker said.

'Yes, staff, I got a pass. I got me one of them sweet mother-fuckers, and I sure will enjoy it.'

'How'd you manage it?' Stryker asked.

'What?'

'The pass. They ain't all that easy to get at this time of the year.'

'You mean the invasion?'

'Fucking right.'

The corporal giggled, a high, childish sound, his short body wriggling with mirth as Stryker passed the flask back.

'I did me some extra duties. I passed around a few bucks. You know? You get a little action going. It all helps on a Friday.'

'Jesus, kid,' Stryker said, leaning back and grinning broadly, 'you must be one loaded GI.'

The corporal nodded judiciously. 'Yeah, you might say that.' He had another drink of his Scotch. 'I got benevolent parents.'

'Your folks back home?'

'Yeah. In Richmond. We come from Charleston, but we all been up in Richmond for years. My ole man, he's in auto-mobiles.'

'That's pretty rich,' Stryker said.

'Yeah,' the corporal said, wiping his lips with one hand, passing the flask back to Stryker and grinning. 'It's rich, alright. And now that sonofabitch is making tanks and gettin' fatter each day.'

'So,' Stryker said, leaning forward, looking interested, 'they keep their little soljer boy in grease. They don't let him run dry.'

'That's right, staff-sergeant.' The corporal giggled again. His face was flushed and his grin was wide and innocent: a real pampered kid. 'I got a little bit of loot, and I got no hesi-tation in spending it.'

Stryker's eyes gleamed. He felt the itch and he had to scratch it. He glanced out the window and saw the grey, broken rooftops, the drab and impoverished stretches of Outer London. The wheels hammered on the tracks. The whole

46

train was shaking. The compartment was cold, and Stryker shivered and glanced back at the corporal.

'Yeah, kid,' Stryker said. 'Well, you might as well enjoy it. You get over to Europe, you'll have your ass on the line, so you might as well enjoy yourself now. Keep the pan on the cooker, kid.'

'Right,' the corporal said. 'That's exactly my sentiments. I'm gonna hit that fucking London, I'll drink Scotch and suck pussy, and they can bring me back to camp in a barrel. I just don't give a fuck.'

Stryker snorted. He thought the kid was pretty funny. He put the flask to his lips, let the Scotch burn down through him, then passed the flask back to the corporal, who also drank deeply.

'Hot damn,' the corporal said, wiping his lips with one hand, shaking his head and blinking crimson-blue eyes. 'I think I'm half canned already.'

'Swell,' Stryker said. 'That's a good way to start. Just start as you mean to go on and you won't have no problems.'

The corporal giggled, passed the flask back to Stryker. The staff-sergeant took it and drank deeply, feeling brighter each minute. The lust made him feel explosive. He felt the twanging of his nerves. He closed his eyes and saw the darkness, heard the sirens, the falling bombs, saw the blade of the knife glittering in the moonlight, knew the salt of their fear. He just couldn't wait. He was rising out of himself. The light streamed behind his eyes, the darkness swirled and beat at him, his heart pounded and his senses were on fire, obliterating his anguish. He opened his eyes again. The roofs of houses whipped past. The train was slowing, clanging over the tracks, coming into the station. Stryker passed back the flask.

'Hot damn,' Stryker said. 'That was good, kid.'

The corporal giggled, surveyed the outer world. 'I sure do feel excited,' he said, and put the flask to his lips.

Stryker needed to communicate. He had to keep the urge at bay. He had to entertain himself with something less demanding until he felt that the time was just right. He studied the flushed corporal. The kid was obviously drunk. He was dangling the silver flask before his face and looking forlorn.

47

'All gone,' he said.

Stryker got to his feet. He patted the corporal on the shoulder. 'Tell you what,' he said, instinctively picking up his bag, watching the platform of the station drifting past, the steel girders, the milling crowds. 'Why donja stick with me? I owe you a drink or two anyway. I know this town well, I could do with some company, and who knows? I just might fix you up with some rare English poontang.'

The corporal giggled. The train jolted to a halt. A whistle blew and they heard some men shouting, saw the crowds through the windows.

'Gee,' the corporal said. 'That's real swell, staff. If you really don't mind . . .'

'I don't mind,' Stryker said. 'I need some action myself. And a kid like you . . . well, I don't know, I just don't like to think about it.'

'Oh, I'm okay,' the corporal said, throwing his magazine on the floor and slipping his empty hip flask into a pocket. 'I been around. I can look after myself. I ain't no virgin boy.'

Stryker snorted. 'You always talk like that?' he said. 'I mean, coming from a family in automobiles; they just don't talk like that.'

The corporal grinned benignly. 'I just picked it up,' he said. 'I guess I got a good ear for dialects. I picked it up in the army.'

'Makes life easier, eh?'

'Yeah, that's right.'

'Okay, kid. Let's go.'

Stryker and the corporal got out of the train and pushed through the waiting crowds towards the terminal. Platforms six and seven had been hit by a bomb earlier in the month, and the ringing of pickaxes and shovels told the tale of destruction. Under the great arched domes of the station, the peaked hats and berets of a dozen nationalities moved back and forth around the arrival and departure gates. It was a bitch of a place. It was filthy and noisy. Stryker looked at the milling soldiers, at the drab, grey civilians, at the WACS and the voluntary workers and the whores, and felt the lust take a hold of him. Bomb them all, he thought. Burn the whole fucking lot of them. Let them blister and bleed and pour shit. It's just a fucking whorehouse. He grinned broadly at the corporal. The corporal was flushed and smiling benignly. He was looking at the debris of platforms six and seven while the crowds swarmed around him and pummelled him. Then Stryker waved his hand. The corporal wandered towards him. They left the station and turned into Praed Street and saw that darkness was falling. Stryker just kept on walking.

'Free,' he said softly. 'Free at last. I just can't fucking wait.'

'What was that, staff?'

'Nothing. What's your name, kid?'

'O'Hara,' the corporal said. 'Shaun O'Hara.'

'Irish, right?'

'Yeah, I suppose so. Sometime back. Long before I was born.'

'A fucking mick. Jesus Christ.'

'You don't like micks, staff-sergeant?'

'I don't like anyone,' Stryker said.

The corporal giggled. 'Well, all right,' he said. 'That makes *me* clean.'

Stryker snorted. He was walking towards Edgware Road. It was growing dark and the blackout would be in force inside of an hour. That's the time he liked most.

'Gee,' the corporal said, 'I feel thirsty. Where are we going, staff?'

'We're going to Edgware Road, then we're gonna get a cab, then we're going to Shaftesbury Avenue, then we're gonna have some beers. Then I'm gonna get my cock sucked and you can do what the fuck you like. You got any more questions?'

'No,' the corporal said. 'But I sure liked that last bit. That's what I'm in this town for. I'm told the girls here are cultured.'

Stryker actually laughed. He slapped the kid on the back. The kid was almost knocked off his feet, but he straightened up grinning.

'Staff,' he said, 'I think you been around.'

'Yeah, kid, I been around. I seen some action in my time. I've learnt a few tricks worth the knowing and I like satisfaction.'

49

'You got battle ribbons there. I can see that.'

'Yeah. Fucking Italy. A whorehouse.'

'Rough, eh?'

'It comes and it goes. Don't ask, kid: you'll learn soon enough. And you might learn too late for your own good. Make hay while the sun shines.'

The corporal giggled at that. They caught a cab near Norfolk Place. It went along Edgware Road, circled around Marble Arch, and then fell in with the traffic in Park Lane, heading towards Piccadilly. The corporal was agog. He said he hadn't been here before. He studied the green of Hyde Park, the grey walls of the buildings, the shops and the elegant citizens of Piccadilly, whistled low, his blue eyes wide. 'London!' he exclaimed. 'Oh my gawd! I can't believe that I'm here.' Stryker snorted. They passed the Royal Academy. They passed Fortnum and Mason's where the rich fuckers shopped, and then they reached Piccadilly Circus itself, now succumbing to darkness.

'It's not the same without the lights,' Stryker said, 'but I like it this way.'

He stopped the taxi at Rupert Street. The corporal climbed out in a daze. He hadn't thought about the fare, so Stryker paid it, then they both stared around them.

'Where's this?' the corporal asked.

'This is Shaftesbury Avenue, kid. There's more whores on these pavements than fucking soljers, but you need a fat billfold.'

'Oh, I got *that*, alright,' the corporal said. 'Gee, staff, this is great.'

The milling crowds moved back and forth, a dozen nationalities clashing, darkness falling on the black ruins, the Ack-Ack guns, the sandbags, on the taxis and the buses and the many army vehicles, on Stryker and the corporal as they pushed through the throng towards a nearby bar.

'Here you are, kid,' Stryker said. 'A Limey bar. You'll shit culture for breakfast.'

The bar was crowded. The air was thick with smoke. Various uniforms mingled with grey suits and drab dresses; and everyone seemed uninhibited, all shouting and laughing.

The blackout curtains had been drawn. The electric lights were subdued. The smoke swirled around flushed faces and red eyes, turned 'he air into purple haze. The corporal was agog, saw the breadth of English life: there were fruit-sellers and businessmen and shopkeepers and actors; the brassy whores were rubbing shoulders with Mayfair ladies; there were privates and captains. They were all drinking a lot, seemed oblivious to the war, and the cigarette smoke swirled around them and made them seem hazy.

'Oh boy!' said the corporal.

They both walked up to the bar. The corporal bought the first drinks. They decided that they didn't have a thirst after all, and that Scotch would be much more appropriate in this dense Limey atmosphere. The corporal, ordering doubles, pulled a note from a fat billfold. Stryker glanced at the billfold and licked his lips and then picked up his glass.

'Best of luck, kid,' he said.

They touched glasses and drank, glanced around them with pleasure. It was a plain pub with dark wooden tables and low, hardbacked chairs. All the chairs were occupied, the conversation was loud, and the tables were piled high with empty glasses and ash trays, the ash falling onto the floor and being tramped underfoot. Stryker liked it. The corporal obviously loved it. The whores were wandering lazily around the room and smiling at everyone. The smile, Stryker noticed, at least regarding the Forces, oftened widened in proportion to the rank of the hopeful receiver.

'Cultured cunt,' Stryker said. 'They always smell like a barber shop. They don't wash so they powder their asses and hope for the best.'

'I like 'em,' the corporal said. 'They're in skirts and they move. They can move beneath me any ole time. I'd be real fucking grateful.'

Stryker snorted, finished off his double Scotch. He ordered two more and they both knocked them back in one gulp. The cigarette smoke swirled. The conversations roared about them. Then the corporal ordered another couple of doubles and the night started glittering.

Stryker needed to communicate. He felt explosive and unreal. He leaned closer to the corporal, put one elbow on the bar, and said:

'I come from Chicago, kid. I grew up in the Northside. I been in and out of jail so many times I sometimes feel I was born there. I used to work in the stockyards. That's something you don't forget. The noise drives you insane, the machinery, the frightened cattle, and you can't ever wash away the stench of the blood and the tripe. That's all I remember, kid. The blood and the stench. They were hanging by their ankles and they moved past your head and the blood was pumping out of their cut throats and you slashed their guts open. You ever hear a stuck cow? You ever smell its spilling guts? Well, kid, I tell you, it's like nothing you've ever known; it's the beginning and the end of the world, a real fucking nightmare. No philosophy there, kid, just raw meat. And the stench is like vomit.'

The kid ordered two more doubles. They both knocked them back quickly. A whore with a handbag and bright-painted lips brushed the thigh of the corporal as she passed, making his eyes grow large.

'No,' Stryker said. 'I couldn't ever forget the stench. I couldn't wash the blood off my arms, off my face, off my chest. It was hot as hell in there. It was noisy and it was dark. You worked stripped to the waist and the cattle swung past and you slashed at their bellies and watched their insides pouring out. That fucking spew splashed all over you. It was grey slime filled with blood. It was greasy and it slid through your fingers and smeared your whole body. You were buried in shit, kid.'

Stryker ordered two more doubles. The pub swam in purple haze. He saw some men from the market in Brewer Street watching the whores.

'Fucking madness,' he said, drinking. 'The noise and stench drove you insane. There were niggers and wops and mexes and micks, and they were all a little crazy, driven mad by the place, and every day at least one of them, someone, would go off his head. You had to keep your ass tight. You never knew when it would happen. They'd just suddenly grab a knife or meat cleaver and start shrieking and swinging. You saw heads like pomegranates. You saw hands and arms chopped off.

You saw guys with their faces chopped to ribbons, with their bellies slit open. These guys would just explode. They'd start foaming and they'd attack. You want culture, kid? That's what culture is. It's the insides turned out.'

The corporal nodded understandingly. His blue eyes surveyed the pub. He saw sailors and pilots and soldiers and civilians, their faces flushed, their hands waving expressively while the whores moved between them. The corporal ordered two more doubles. He and Stryker drank them quickly. The noise was sharper, more vibrant with promise, exciting the senses.

'Blood,' Stryker said. 'It's what makes life and breaks it. You see blood and you know what life's about: you know it's nothing but dead meat. I was in the Stockade, kid. I saw blood there as well. I saw the MPs with clubs in their hands, and I knew what power was. You spill blood you have a victory. You break bones you have a loser. They broke noses and teeth in the Stockade, and they knew you'd obey them. That's what it's all about, kid. That's the beginning and end of it. We're all meat and the blood fills our insides, and we spill it and die.'

Stryker ordered two more doubles. He knew the corporal wasn't listening. The corporal was all flushed and his blue eyes were crimson, and he swayed and occasionally giggled like a man in a trance. Stryker didn't give a fuck: he just had to let it out. He felt explosive and the room swam around him and the noise flayed his nerves.

'I was in Italy,' he said. 'I couldn't wait to get there. I just had me the urge for some action and I went out and found it. You need to let it out, kid. You can't keep it all locked up. I had pressures and I had to release them and that's what this war's about. We slaughtered the fucking wops. We chopped them down like turnip greens. You squeezed the trigger and you watched them come apart and you knew what release was. There was a village in Italy. The SS had just been there. They had taken this old wop and strung him up by his feet and put a blow torch to his balls and his face. He was still alive when we found him. He'd been hanging there six hours. He was whimpering and he looked like fried turkey and he

53

begged us to kill him. I shot the old fucker. I pulled out his gold teeth. He was no more than a carcass on a hook, and I didn't feel nothing. That's what life's all about, kid.'

The kid blinked his eyes and grinned. He pointed through the smokey haze. 'Look,' he said. 'There's a couple of empty chairs. And there's two women there.' They walked across and sat down.

The women were both whores. They were painted and powdered. One had short-cropped brown hair and the other had her blonde hair in a head-scarf. Stryker grinned at them, a sharp, knowing grin. Behind the grin he burned with puritanical rage, with the need to avenge himself. The women smiled back. They were smoking and drinking gins. They studied Stryker and the corporal in turn, casually looking them up and down. The corporal giggled and drank his Scotch. His babyish face was very flushed. He glanced at Stryker and his blue eyes were filled with an innocent joy.

'Wallace,' Stryker said. 'Staff-sergeant. And this here's Corporal Smith.'

The corporal giggled. The whores looked at him and smiled. They knew an innocent abroad when they saw one, and they both licked their lips.

'I'm Marjorie,' said the blonde.

'I'm Harriet,' said the brunette.

'Are you two boys looking for comfort?' Marjorie said.

'That's it,' Stryker said.

Stryker bought them all more drinks. He started rapping with the whores. They both came from Whitechapel and they'd come into town to pick up on the mass of lonely warriors. Stryker just kept on talking. He felt lust and contempt. He talked about Italy, about the trucks on the dusty roads, about the blood and the ruin and the excitement, about the ragged wop whores. Stryker had been right in there. It had given him new life. It had taken him from the anonymity of the streets of Chicago and offered him a stunning awareness. He felt that awareness now: his head was bright and filled with phantoms. He wanted to hear the falling bombs, see the moonlight, watch the whites of their eyes. The whores appeared bewildered. The corporal grinned and licked his lips. The noise

54

of conversation richocheted all around them, and the smoke swirled and made them all hazy. Stryker just had to talk. He felt the need to communicate. He told them of the violence, of the bodies bought and sold, of the heat and the dust and the murderous lust that gave weak men new life. The blonde stroked Stryker's thigh. The brunette patted the corporal's cheek. Stryker snorted, slapped one hand on the table and then gazed all around him.

'A real whorehouse,' he said.

The young corporal was agog. He was drunk and disbelieving. They left the pub with the whores on their arms, felt the cool of the night. Shaftesbury Avenue was in darkness. The blackout was in force. The cars moved with dimmed headlights, torches shone down on the pavements, and the whores stood in black-shadowed doorways, their cigarettes glowing. Stryker loved it. He saw the Ack-Ack gun emplacements. He saw the sandbags and the barrage balloons, silvery tubes in the moonlight. They all made their way to Soho. They went along Old Compton Street. Light flashed on and off as doors opened and closed; voices roared out of pubs and were cut off, leaving footsteps and giggling. The young corporal was really drunk. He hardly made it up the stairs. The stairway stank of dirt and decay and led up to some rooms. One of the whores opened the door. She switched the light on. There were two ragged beds along the walls, some chairs, a brown table.

The corporal fell on the bed. He waved a bottle of Scotch. The brunette started taking off his clothes, and he didn't resist. Stryker took the bottle off him, drank and passed it to the blonde. She smiled and had a drink and put it down and started taking her clothes off. 'No,' Stryker said. Her fingers froze and she looked puzzled. They both looked at the corporal and the brunette who were writhing together. The corporal giggled and gasped. The woman on top of him was naked. She had raw, chubby hands, and they knew exactly what they were doing. The blonde just stood there, looked at Stryker with calm eyes. Stryker looked at the couple on the bed, a tight smile on his face. The corporal had stopped giggling. The whore was kneeling above him. Her white legs were spread and she lowered herself down and enveloped him. The corporal gasped loudly. His hands gripped her white flesh. Stryker unbuttoned his trousers, took himself in his hands, and then turned to the blonde and said, 'Okay. Down on your knees.' The blonde did as she was told. Her mouth worked its ways on Stryker. He stood there and looked down on her head and felt the back of her throat. A whorehouse, Stryker thought. It's nothing else; the whole world is a whorehouse. He kneaded the whore's blonde hair. He moved her head back and forth. They worked in silence as the couple on the bed suddenly threshed and were still. That was enough for Stryker. He heard the wail of the air-raid sirens. He clutched the head of the whore in desperation, then he shuddered and found release. The whore struggled to break free. The corporal gasped and then giggled. Stryker held the whore's head, would not let her escape, let the spasms whip his senses and drain him, leaving him spent. The corporal giggled again. The brunette looked on in amazement. The sirens wailed and Stryker pushed the blonde away and she spat on the floor.

'You rotten bastard,' she said.

Stryker kicked her. It was the only thing to do. He kicked her in the stomach and she jackknifed and slammed into the wall. The other whore screamed. The corporal gasped and jerked upright. The blonde fell to the side and her head thumped the floor and the brunette shrieked and grabbed at her clothes. Stryker kicked out again. The brunette threw out her arms. She spun around and slammed into the bed and slumped down to the floor.

'Oh, my God!' the corporal gasped. 'Jesus Christ!'

'Fucking whores,' Stryker said.

The corporal looked up at him. The corporal's baby face was white. His blue eyes were streaked with crimson, but the fear made them bright and very big. Stryker smiled and walked towards him. The corporal backed against the bed. He looked young, very frail and very frightened, and his hands waved before him.

'Oh, my God,' he said. 'Jesus Christ, staff, what the hell are . . .?'

Stryker swung at his head with a huge, white-ridged fist and the sharp crack of bone against bone stung the room's stricken silence. The corporal's face split open. His head slammed into the wall. He started sliding down the wall and Stryker grabbed him and hit him again. The corporal's body jerked sideways, toppled over and hit the floor. 'You fucking mick,' Stryker said. 'You stupid prick.' Then he kicked him again.

The corporal rolled onto his back, his face broken and bloody; his eyes flickered and rolled in their sockets and saw nothing but pain. Stryker listened to the distant sirens. He felt the pounding of his heart. He was sweating and his nerves were on fire and the bright light assailed him. The distant sirens continued wailing. The blonde whore groaned a little. Stryker grabbed the corporal's tunic and pulled out the fat billfold and put it into his pocket and picked his bag up. The blonde whore groaned again. Stryker walked across and kicked her. He kicked her head and she made no further sound as he walked from the room.

# CHAPTER FOUR

DAVID did not go immediately to his father-in-law's house, but instead got out of the taxi at Jack Straw's Castle and went in for a short, soothing drink. Tired, depressed, pained at Katherine's prompt departure, he gazed around the crowded bar, at the sophisticated clientele, and wished that he were somewhere in Europe, just a face in the larger flood.

Doubtless it would come soon enough. The whole country was talking about it. Various ports had become restricted areas, country roads were filled with troop carriers, and all along the coast the allied camps were filling up to the point where they could scarcely be managed. Also, there were rumours of great concrete embankments on the north side of the Thames, of strings of ammunition barges packed tightly end to end, and of shipping so thick in Weymouth Bay that no water was visible. Yes, the whole country was talking about it. The official silence bred speculation. David felt himself a small part of this drama -- and thus he also felt futile.

He left the bar after one drink, feeling even more depressed, and crossed the road to look over Hampstead Heath. Sirens wailed in the distance, searchlights webbed the night sky, and then he heard the far-off chatter of the Ack-Ack guns as the air-raid commenced. The full moon had waned. That always signified an attack. He stood above the sloping fields of the Heath and watched the bright, swaying searchlights. The Ack-Ack guns were hammering. The sky was filled with small explosions. Strings of red and yellow fire curved down towards earth, painting black sky and drifting cloud. Then he heard the German bombers. They made a single muffled rumbling. They flew high above the barrage balloons and were coming in lower.

David waited. He felt ashamed of his childish interest. He was ashamed, but he couldn't walk away until he heard the explosions. They came soon enough. Even the ground beneath him shook. It was almost imperceptible, but he felt it: a mild, rhythmic vibration. The wind whispered across the Heath. The trees were black within the darkness. Beyond the darkness were the searchlights and tracers, cutting swathes through the inky sky. Then the city began to glow: it glowed in red and yellow clouds. He heard the chatter of the Ack-Ack guns, the deep rumbling of the bombers, the sirens, the high-pitched whine of the Spitfires. He watched the probing searchlights, saw them weave and interlock. He saw the black speck of a plane where two beams of light met, and then it turned into a pulsing red cinder and started spinning towards earth. David was hypnotized. He saw the explosion of the plane. There was an uprush of orange and yellow, and then it receded.

Men are dying, he thought. I stand here while they die. They turn to flames in the aircraft while the women and children die in rubble . . . It doesn't seem real from here.

Nor did it. From where he stood it was a pageant: a spectacle of bright light and colour, a strange and terrible beauty. David turned away from it, walked towards the silent pond, saw shadows holding torches pointing downwards: people going their own way. It didn't seem real. The pain and death were far away. They were down there in the city where they wreaked their bloody havoc with a blind and indiscriminate fury. David passed the silent pond. Hints of light came off the water. He passed the pond and went along the High Street, down that dark, narrow road. People moved past him here. They often looked at the sky. They talked with that lack of inhibition which the war had encouraged. Thinking of this, he had to smile. The dying couldn't stop the living. The battle raged in the distance while the living went about their normal business . . . There was hope in that thought.

He turned off the High Street, went along a winding lane, and finally arrived at his father-in-law's house. No lights shone beyond the garden: the blackout curtains had been drawn. A silence reigned as he opened the gate and walked up to the front door. He stood there a moment. As usual he felt uneasy. He felt depressed and he knew that his father-in-law, the major-general, was not the man to make him feel much better. Still, he knocked. He didn't know where else to go. He heard footsteps in the hall behind the door and then the door opened.

The hallway was in darkness. The major-general seemed very tall. He had a torch in his hand, pointing downwards, shining down on his slippered feet.

'Ah, David!' the major-general said, his voice firm and thick-throated. 'What a pleasant surprise. I'm all alone. Quickly! Come in.'

The major-general stepped aside, David quickly brushed past him, then the general closed the door and they both walked into the brightly lit study. The walls were dark mahogany; the chairs were deep and made of leather. There was a desk with a well-polished top, now piled high with papers. The major-general saw David looking at it, and he smiled and waved one hand.

'Work,' he said. 'A major-general has no rest. It's the less glamorous part of our profession, though it has its importance.' He pointed at the nearest chair. 'Sit down, David,' he said. 'You look weary – or is that just the light? I'll fix you a drink.'

David sank into the chair, rubbed his eyes and glanced around him. The general was at the drinks cabinet, holding up a bottle of Scotch. David nodded his head.

'It's not the light,' David said. 'I'm rather tired. And a Scotch would be fine.'

'It's medicine,' the general said, pouring out two generous measures. 'A good Scotch is even better than brandy when you're feeling run down.'

He walked over to David, handed him the glass, then walked behind his desk and sat down. He raised his glass slightly. David raised his and they drank. The general put his glass down and sighed a little, a smile on his lips.

'That's good,' he said. 'And you're a good excuse for

having it. I don't like to drink when I'm alone. It would seem like a weakness.'

David smiled, but said nothing. The general's grey eyes washed over him. The eyes were calm and held a dry, sardonic intelligence, an unstated authority. The general was wearing a high-necked pull-over; his body bulged through the cotton. He had grey hair and his features were handsome, lined with age and experience.

'A weekend pass?' he said.

'Yes,' David said.

'Good. I'm delighted to see you. And I must say, you're looking well.' He sipped at his Scotch, studied David over the glass. He put the glass down and leant back and put his hands to his chin. 'And how is Katherine?' he said.

'She's fine,' David said. 'She seems to be keeping herself busy. Unfortunately, she had to go out tonight: the Women's Voluntary Service.'

'Ah, yes,' the general said. 'Very good. I'm glad to hear she's still at it.'

David said nothing. He didn't want to discuss it. He felt a tension that emanated not only from Katherine, but from the grey, arctic wastes of her father's eyes, now calmly surveying him.

'I think it's good,' the general said, 'that young ladies like Katherine should make themselves of use in these times. Surely better than wasting their time in unprofitable pursuits.'

'I shouldn't have thought that a job in the Ministry of Information would have been considered unprofitable by *you*.'

The general smiled bleakly. 'Ah, yes,' he said. 'But that's during the day. And, particularly regarding the ladies, it's the nights we should worry about.'

He might have been talking about anyone: his voice was soft and sardonic. There was a grey glint of amusement in his eyes, just the trace of contempt. It made David uncomfortable. It also made him feel embarrassed. The general talked about his daughter, David's wife, as he would talk of a stranger.

'I didn't think you would worry about Katherine's nights,' David said. 'It's not something I ever worried about myself.'

The general raised his eyebrows. 'Really?' he said. 'How

terribly romantic you are, David. Such trust is quite admirable.'

'I don't think so, sir. In fact, I think it's quite natural. And you know I've no reason to think otherwise. *Both* of us know that.'

The general chuckled. It was a politician's mirth. He picked his glass up, had a sip, put the glass down again. He stroked the rim with one finger.

'I'm sorry,' he said, smiling. 'I'm really just teasing you, David. I have the utmost respect for my daughter, as I'm sure you appreciate.' He lowered his head and raised his eyebrows, adopted a look of false contrition, continued stroking his glass with one finger, his eyes fixed on David. 'Naturally I'm happy for you and Katherine. You always seemed so well suited. And I'm pleased to see the marriage is working out.' He raised one eyebrow. 'It *is* working out?'

David shifted uncomfortably, felt the flushing of his cheeks. He glanced down at the floor and then looked back at the general, not wanting to give anything away, wondering what he might know.

'Yes,' he said quietly. 'No problems. We're just apart so much nowadays.'

The general raised his head, removed his finger from the glass. He started to tap the finger on the table as he gazed at the ceiling.

'Of course,' he said. 'This damnable war. It doesn't make things easier for any of us ... not even me.' He slapped his hand down on some papers, looked at them, then at David. 'I can't remember when I last went to bed without doing my homework.' He smiled at David, tapped his finger on the papers. 'There's a lot to be done yet,' he said, 'before the big push can start.'

They heard the low, far-off rumbling. The Ack-Ack guns broke through it. The general stood up and peered through the curtains, then sat down again.

'Jerry's worried,' he said. 'That's why they've stepped up the raids. But they're trying to do too much far too late. We'll soon be in France, David.'

'How soon?' David asked.

The major-general smiled. 'I can't say. There's still a fair bit to be sorted out. And then it's all down to the moon and tides.'

David listened to the distant rumblings. He thought of the blazing city. He knew that a lot of bombs would be falling on Whitechapel, and he wondered if Katherine would be all-right. The general didn't seem so concerned, his eyes thought-ful, faraway. He was doubtless thinking of the invasion, of the part he would play in it, of the fact that he could soon stretch himself in more exacting pursuits. The general didn't like paperwork; he preferred the sound of guns. He had not seen any action since the landings in Sicily, and he wanted to be back in his own world – the only world that he knew. David understood this much – he knew a soldier when he saw one – but what he couldn't accept was his father-in-law's insularity, his coldness, his assumed superiority, which extended even to Katherine.

Perhaps there were reasons: perhaps his age had simply hardened him. His wife had died when his daughter was two years old, and he had never remarried. Nor was he a ladies' man. His love of the Marines was all-embracing. And in that world of the most gross masculinity he had squandered all sentiment . . . Yet it went deeper than that. David thought it a shocking arrogance. At the major-general's centre, at the source of his being, there was nothing but the cold lust for power, for omnipotent authority. It sometimes frightened David, often made him squirm with shame. The general's nature was a harsh violation of all David believed in.

'Do you think Katherine will be alright?'

'Pardon?' the general said.

'I'm worried about Katherine in Whitechapel. They always bomb that a lot.'

The general sipped his Scotch and shrugged. 'Let's just hope so,' he said. 'There's nothing we can do anyhow. It's all a matter of luck.' He shuffled the papers on his desk, his grey eyes scanning over them. 'And you,' he said, looking at David. 'What do you think?'

David sipped his drink. 'About what?' he said.

'About the war,' the general said. 'About your own position

in it. You've never seemed comfortable in uniform – though your record is excellent.'

'You've seen my report?'

'Naturally. Why not?'

'I just wondered. It never entered my head that you might actually see it.'

'I see them all,' the general said. 'I check out every officer. You have the makings of a very fine soldier, but I still have my doubts ... I sometimes sense disapproval.'

David looked at the general's eyes, but didn't study them very long. They reflected a remote, professional interest that made him avert his gaze.

'You know well enough,' David said. 'I only enlisted because of the war. If there wasn't a war on at the moment, I wouldn't be a Marine.'

'That's true,' the general said. 'I'm well aware of that fact. That you don't want to be a professional soldier is perfectly natural. But that's not what bothers me. It's something more than that. Most men in the army are not there by choice, but that doesn't necessarily mean they're bad soldiers. That's not what I'm concerned with. What I'm concerned with is belief. A man doesn't have to believe in the army to believe in the war. And I don't think you do.'

'I'm not sure,' David said. 'I always contradict myself. On the one hand I believe that we're fighting a just war; on the other, I can't help but think that we're destroying our future.'

'Our future?' The general raised his eyebrows. 'I'm not sure what you mean by that.'

David had a sip of Scotch. He thought it might soothe his discomfort. He was embarrassed by his lack of conviction, his reluctance to show himself.

'I think the war is just,' he said. 'I find it hard to question that. We haven't really had too much of a choice: it's been a matter of self-defence. That's the positive side. It's where the contradictions start. I believe in the cause we're fighting for; how we do it revolts me.'

The distant rumbling continued. The guns rattled, the planes whined. He thought of Katherine in the darkness of Whitechapel: thought of fire and destruction. The general was staring at him, his grey eyes emotionless. David wondered how he could talk to the general of the things that made hearts beat.

'How we *do* it?' the general said.

'Yes,' David said. 'How we do it. What we do and what it means. I don't believe the end justifies the means; I don't want victory at any price.'

'Any price?'

'Yes. More than a thousand bombers over Cologne in one night. A hundred-thousand people left homeless in Dortmund. Fourteen hundred tons of bombs dropped on Kiel in a single raid. Half of Dusseldorf razed by fire, Hamburg turned into an inferno, the Abbey of Monte Cassino obliterated for all time . . . I wonder what will be left. We'll save ourselves and lose the world. We'll beat the Germans and hope to liberate a world that no longer exists.'

'The world will still exist,' the general said dryly. 'It will simply have changed its face a little.'

'I don't think it's a little. I think it's more than we can spare. We're destroying things that cannot be regained – and we're doing it on a monstrous scale.'

'Cities can be rebuilt,' the general said, 'and the dead can be replaced. The bombs won't stop women getting pregnant, and life will continue.'

'And what of Monte Cassino? What of what it represents? You can rebuild a city, but you can't remake its history; you can't obliterate the past and its culture and expect it to grow again. I remember something Churchill said. He was talking about the future. "It is my earnest hope," he said, "that we shall achieve the largest common measure of the integrated life of Europe that is possible without destroying the individual characteristics and traditions of its many races." That's what he said. I happen to think that he meant it. But how can we do it if we continue to destroy on this scale which is unparalleled in history? We can't get back the lost paintings. We can't remake the ancient relics. We can rebuild the Abbey of Monte Cassino, but not what was inside it. We're destroying European history. We're obliterating the past. The cities will be rebuilt and more children will be born, but they won't have a history to support them, they'll be starved of what matters. That's where the contradiction lies. In winning this war, we might lose all: we might find ourselves rebuilding a world in which nothing's worth having.'

The general smiled, raised his glass to his lips. He sipped his Scotch and then put the glass down and ran his finger around it.

'You're an idealist,' he said. 'Your heart bleeds on your sleeve. You see the world through rose-coloured glasses, but that world is a myth. All culture is transient. History constantly changes. Men hunger for what they're told they must have – and we can make that choice for them. What you say is romanticism. The reality is somewhat different. You see life through individuals when in fact you should be looking at numbers. Men live through other men. They only *think* they are unique. But in a world of increasing complexity, the individual is nothing. To survive, men don't need history: they need the myths that we give them. Men need to be ruled and the rulers are the ones who forge history. That history constantly changes. It is changed to suit the times. Men are numbers and they move to a pattern that is always set for them. The ruling classes dictate the choices. The choices offered serve only the state. The common man lives by the illusion that his history will support him, that he can choose his own course; but that history is a myth conceived and raised by his masters, and his freedom, expressed through his culture, is the illusion that binds him. We'll destroy the world, David. We'll destroy it and rebuild it. It won't be the world that you know, but the loss won't be noticeable.'

'And what about you?' David said. 'Are you one of the rulers?'

The general smiled. He obviously thought the taunt was childish. He ran his finger around the rim of his glass and then tapped the desk once.

'Not quite,' he said. 'I simply suffer less illusions. The ruler is always ruled, there's no top to the pyramid, but the man who knows his place can serve the state and thus serve himself best. Why do you think I like the army? It's a state unto itself. It's a pyramidal structure in which every man, each

66

cog, is utilized. The army is based on numbers. I see a sublime logic in it. It's a logic that offers me coherence, a mathematical progression. I suffer no contradictions. My past and future are mapped out. Short of premature death, I'll follow my course to its logical end.'

'And that's all there is to it?'

'All else is vanity. Vanity leads to self destruction. The destruction *you* speak of – the loss of history and culture – exists only in the mind and has no credence outside your dreams. Your idealism is fruitless.'

David couldn't accept it. He moved uneasily in his chair. With the drinks, because of tiredness, behind his fears for himself and Katherine, he felt himself unable to communicate any adequate defence. He heard the deep, distant rumbling, the chattering of the guns. In his mind he saw the aircraft, the sweating, frantic pilots, the searchlights dazzling their eyes, the flak bursting all around them, the black earth, flecked with fires and tracer bullets, spinning wildly beneath them. He saw the pounding Ack-Ack guns, the pointing, shouting crews, saw the moonlight washing over their wide eyes, off the grey, swaying barrage balloons. The walls would be exploding, the roofs caving in: he saw the sparks bursting upwards, the flames roaring around the debris, saw the dead and the wounded carried away, heard the cries from the rubble. Katherine was in it somewhere. She was a name, not a number. In the long history of man she was unique, individual, and no amount of political logic could change that fact. A louder rumbling echoed outside. The house shook imperceptibly. The general gazed up at the ceiling and then smiled and looked back at David.

'Alright,' David said, 'assuming I believe what I believe in: why does it worry you so much regarding the army?'

'Because you're undecided. Because indecision can be dangerous. Because an officer has no time for moral reasoning – he must act as he's bidden. Think of the possibilities, David. You're in an extraordinary situation. The war, by its very nature, presents a wealth of moral problems, and the officer who's undecided, who can't think purely in tactical terms, is likely to fail himself and his men. An officer can't always choose:

he often has to do what he despises. You talked about Monte Cassino, so let me elaborate ... Founded by Saint Benedict in the year 529, the original home of the Order, a symbol of the spread of learning throughout all of Europe, the Abbey, by your terms, is of invaluable spiritual value to man. Yet in 1944, as far as the warring armies are concerned, the Abbey is a military stronghold that commands the approaches to Rome and provides the strongest link of the Gustav Line ... Think about it, David. It is history against expediency. Think also of the individuals concerned ... On the night of January 18, when the first allied bombs fall on Monastery Hill, the Abbey is inhabited only by the Abbot, a priest, five monks, two or three sick peasant families, a deaf mute and General von Senger und Etterlin, commander of the 14th Panzer Corps. A professional soldier, the general is also a lay member of the Benedictine Order, a former Rhodes Scholar, an Oxford graduate, and though German, disapproving of the Nazis ... That such a man should be left commanding the very home of the Benedictine Order is one of war's singular ironies ... Put yourself in his position, David. What would you do? In order to save the Abbey you will have to surrender it; a refusal to surrender it will mean total, inevitable destruction. The general is a man of culture. Like yourself, he's an idealist. The agony of his decision must be great and yet he decides. He's a professional soldier. His first duty is to the army. He refuses to surrender the Abbey, and the allies destroy it. It takes four months to do this. The loss to the allies is incalculable. The general has performed his duty with the utmost fidelity, but the cost to his spirit must be terrible. Nearly a thousand tons of bombs are dropped on the Abbey; then two thousand guns complete the job. Four months later, in May, when the Poles finally take the hill itself, nothing is left of the Abbey but levelled ruins, a series of broken walls ... What would *you* have done, David?'

David didn't reply. The thought of it left him numb. He sat there while the silence of the room encouraged the question to tease him. The air-raid had ceased. The distant rumbling had disappeared. The general leant across his desk and looked at David, a smile on his thin lips.

68

'There is no morality in war,' he said. 'The moral man must compromise. He cannot abide by his principles when circumstances dictate otherwise. You are now a soldier, David. You have a duty to perform. You have the ability, but you might well succumb to sentimental revulsion. Should you do so, it would be disastrous. Your own men would pay the price. As an officer you cannot afford the luxury of self doubt and conscience. You must abide by the book.'

David finished off his drink. He put his glass on the general's desk. He stood up and went around the desk and peered through the window. He saw a mosaic of distant fires breaking up the night's darkness, clouds of black smoke obliterating the stars. He prayed that Katherine was all right.

'Perhaps you're right,' he said, letting go of the curtain and turning back into the room. 'My doubts disturb me as well.'

The general smiled, then stood up and stretched himself. 'No matter,' he said. 'We'll both know soon enough. In the meantime, you better get some rest. I'd suggest you sleep here.'

'What about Katherine?' David said.

'She's late,' the general said. 'That was an unusually long air-raid. She'll have quite a bit of work after that, and then she'll be quite exhausted. They're often at it half the night, and when they are, they don't come back till dawn. They often go for a drink at one of the unofficial clubs to settle their feminine nerves. Don't worry about it. Katherine can look after herself. She'll arrive here in the morning, looking pale and rather worn, and she'll sleep like a baby all day. They understand at the Ministry.'

A little worried, disappointed, he nevertheless had to accept it, and he let the general show him to the bedroom. He now felt extremely tired. His thoughts scattered and spun. He lay down in the darkness, between the cold sheets, and let the silence surround him and embalm him and cast him adrift. He started swimming through his mind, saw faces floating past, saw the fires illuminating the night, casting red light on ruins. Then he saw Katherine's face. Her dark hair coiled all around it. She floated towards him and then floated away, and he thought she was weeping. He tossed and turned in the bed.

He saw the ruins of Monte Cassino. They dominated a hill that was littered with shells and dead soldiers. A grey mist covered all. The mist filmed his cold skin. He had made his decision and now he couldn't face up to the cost. David groaned in his sleep. Katherine's face stared up from rubble. It was the rubble of Monte Cassino, of civilization. David tossed and turned. The bed warmed and drew him in. He wanted Katherine, her white naked body, but she drifted away from him. Once he opened his eyes. He saw the darkness of the room. He couldn't face it, so he closed his eyes again and surrendered to sleep. The dreams returned to assail him. They would not give him peace. He drifted out to where the past could sustain him and give him some hope.

'Katherine's dead,' someone said.

# CHAPTER FIVE

THE wall cracked and broke and split asunder and crashed down, making a calamatous din, sending sparks geysering upwards, filling the night air with a black, boiling dust and shaking the pavements. This was followed by an explosion. Glass shattered and bricks flew. The gas pipes shot out streams of flame that made the milling men ghostly.

Stryker skirted around the chaos. He heard a fire engine's wail. The men around him were shouting and staggering back from the flames, were running backwards and forwards with spades and pickaxes and sand buckets. The heat fanned Stryker's face. The noise was frantic, almost deafening. He cursed and turned along a dark sidestreet where the silence was soothing. Yet this silence was only local. The surrounding streets were a distant roar. He heard sirens and the clanging of bells and more muffled explosions. The whole city seemed on fire. A red glow filled the sky. The barrage balloons were floating in lava, reflecting destruction. Stryker cursed but felt exultant, felt a deep, rich excitement, felt the ribs of the whores against his boot, saw the corporal's bloody face. Then he came to a subway station. He saw civilians emerging. They were wrapped in drab clothes, and they blinked and looked around them, and clutched at their possessions and children and then wandered away. Stryker snorted at the sight of them, felt superior and immune. The excitement whipped his senses and filled him with the old, driving lust.

His shoulder bag was now empty. He had done his trading

during the raid. The contents had all gone to his two girls in Holloway, both of whom, fearful and thus grateful, had worked hard all that evening. The girls were very young; in fact they were both under age. Screwed by Stryker, then beaten, then completely terrified, they worked the streets between Holloway and Camden Town, picking up a few dollars. Stryker knew how to control them. He mixed brutality with generosity. He beat them up occasionally, then he plied them with cigarettes and Hershey bars. It was a cheap way to do it; at least as good as any other. He checked them out every weekend and they hadn't backfired yet. Stryker liked it that way.

He passed Lancaster Gate Station. People poured up from the subway. They clutched parcels and children, and some of them were laughing and shouting. Stryker pushed his way through them, was none too polite; they were Limeys so they didn't complain and he just kept on going. Kensington Gardens was to his left. He saw the trees outlined in darkness. Beyond the trees, at the far side of the park, the sky was a crimson sheet. Stryker felt his twanging nerves, felt the need for further action. He felt the knife between his gaiter and ankle, and the lust set his loins on fire. The whole city was bleeding. He heard explosions and distant rumblings. The night air smelt of smoke and conflagration, told the tale of disasters. Stryker loved it. The proximity of death was startling. It jolted him awake, made his mind blaze, set him free from his sluggish self.

Turning off the main road, Stryker went along a dark street and finally stopped at a peeling white door. Some steps led up to it; there were pillars at both sides; a sign announced it as the Allied Forces Club. Stryker grinned as he looked at it. It was now after closing time. He hammered his fist on the door and it opened and a grey-haired man stared at him. Stryker pulled out his card. 'Yeah,' he said, 'I'm a member.' The man grinned and motioned Stryker inside and closed the large door behind him.

The sudden light made Stryker blink. The bar was huge and very crowded. Nearly all of the clientele were in uniform; nearly all were quite drunk. Stryker blinked and looked around him. The cigarette smoke stung his eyes. He saw Americans and Canadians and Australians and Hungarians; the British and the French and the Poles. They were all shouting and laughing. A piano was pounding. A bunch of pilots around the piano had their arms about each other, swaying backwards and forth and bawling songs. Stryker liked it. He had been here before. He looked around at the women, most in uniform, some not, and he felt the old itch in his loins.

'A fucking whorehouse,' he murmured.

The bar was crowded and chaotic, a sweaty mingling of bodies, and Stryker had to force his way through for a drink. Buying a double Scotch, he pushed his way back out again, and stood there, surveying the activity. He felt light-headed and vibrant, almost incandescent. He was naked and nothing stood between him and all this phenomenon. Stryker drank his Scotch. His stinging eyes pierced the haze. The lights shone through the swirling blue smoke and washed over flushed faces.

Then Stryker saw the broad. She was standing alone near the exit. She was pale and very slim, wearing an expensive overcoat, and her dark hair, which surrounded the attractive, drawn face, had been showered in the powder from the debris.

Something cold slid through Stryker. It was the ice of his perceptions. It slid down and took hold of his vitals and then it released him. A sudden heat filled his loins. His mind swam up from the murk. The light washed across the girl and bathed her face in a startling radiance. Stryker's nerves settled down again.

The girl was drinking gin. She sipped slowly and thoughtfully. She was gazing around the room in a vague, distracted manner, and Stryker sensed that she wasn't at ease. It wasn't the bar. Stryker sensed that immediately. It was something outside, faraway: something private and personal. Then her gaze fixed on Stryker. Her eyes were brown and romantic. They reflected that idealism which could well become its own hapless victim.

Stryker sensed this immediately. His senses never let him down. He was suddenly overwhelmed by himself, by his intense inner logic. The brown eyes were staring at him. They wavered and turned away. Stryker stood there and just kept on staring and willed her to come to him.

This she didn't do. She didn't move from where she stood. Yet her eyes, as if obeying his will, slowly turned to his face again. He didn't smile at her, simply studied her face. His impulses raced through one another and then eventually merged. Now the girl looked away. Now Stryker felt very calm. He licked his lips and then he walked across the floor until he stood right in front of her ... She could look nowhere else.

'Staff-sergeant Stryker,' he said. 'Do you mind if I talk to you?'

The girl studied him vaguely, blinked, seemed far away, raised her glass to her lips and sipped her gin, held the glass in both hands.

'No,' she said. 'Not at all.'

Stryker liked her voice. It had a soft, sensual tone. The accent was classy, but she lacked the usual arrogance that went with it.

'I hope I'm not bothering you,' he said.

'No,' she said. 'You're not bothering me.'

'I'm on a weekend pass,' he said. 'It's my first weekend in London. I came in here and I didn't know anyone, then I saw you alone.'

'I've been here an hour,' she said. 'I came in with some other girls. They've just gone and I'm about to leave myself – when I finish this drink.'

'Let me get you another.'

'No thanks. I'd rather not.'

'I didn't mean anything by it.'

'I know. I'd just rather not.'

Stryker studied her carefully. She still seemed a bit vague. She was rolling the glass of gin between her hands, glancing up and then down again. He knew that something was troubling her. He had good instincts for that. She was troubled and that could make her vulnerable, which suited him fine.

'What's your name?' he said.

'Katherine. Katherine Strawhurst.'

'That sounds like a very English name.'

'Yes. I suppose it is.'

Katherine looked up at the American. He was tall and powerfully built. He had a roughly handsome, deeply tanned face with a thick shock of dark hair. He was obviously an experienced GI. There were battle ribbons on his tunic. His eyes, which were dark and unrevealing, held the faint glint of drink.

'I'm sorry,' she said. 'Your name ... I didn't quite catch your name.'

'Stryker,' he said. 'Just Stryker.'

'That's an odd name,' she said.

'It's an American name,' he said.

She laughed softly. 'Yes. An American name. I think that much was obvious.'

Stryker wanted to have her. She was the one he had to have. He could feel it in his loins, in his head, in his heightened reality. The noise of the room was all around him. The smoke swirled before her face. There was laughter, glasses rattled, the pianist pounded out a tune, voices bawled out some raucous war songs, a dozen languages clashed. Stryker stood close to the girl. It was both accident and design: the crowded room would not have left him much choice, but he wanted it this way. The girl glanced up and smiled. It was a quiet smile: remote. Stryker felt himself pouring around her and drawing her in.

'You've been out tonight,' he said. He spoke precisely and clearly. 'I can tell by the state of your hair. You've got powder all over it.'

'Powder?' she said. Her hand went up to her hair. She brushed her hair and then brought the hand down and studied it carefully. 'Yes,' she said. 'It's the powder from falling buildings. I was working tonight in Whitechapel. We were close to the worst of it.'

'Working?' Stryker said.

Katherine smiled. 'Not the pavements. I work part-time with the Women's Voluntary Service.'

'What's that?' Stryker said. 'I haven't heard of that before. And I see you're not wearing a uniform.'

His eyes frankly appraised her. She glanced briefly down

75

herself. She looked back up at Stryker and smiled, slightly mocking, if gentle.

'No,' she said. 'We don't wear uniforms. It's a voluntary organization to help out the homeless and so forth.'

'What's so forth?'

'You know.' Katherine shrugged. 'Portable laundries and kitchens, the distribution of clothing, the locating of missing relatives, sometimes breaking the good or bad news. That, or helping the doctors or nurses; or simply helping some family put their home back together again; or holding the hands of people who are trapped in the ruins; or getting down on your bloody knees and pulling them out.'

'Sounds rough.'

Katherine shrugged and glanced around her. 'Not particularly,' she said. 'It's almost routine by now. It's exhausting, but that can't be a bad thing when you can't sleep at nights.'

Stryker noticed the last remark. He wanted to ask her about it. Something told him that he better not do so, so he finished his drink instead. The girl was glancing around her: a vague, remote glance. She either had to look around or look at Stryker, and that made him feel confident.

'You're married,' Stryker said.

'Yes,' she said. 'You noticed the ring. Most men are quick at scouting out what they most need to know.'

Stryker grinned, a slow, charming grin. It was a grin that matched the tenor of his new voice and helped her relax. Katherine looked up at him. Her exhaustion had made her weak. She felt a little bit unreal, slightly dizzy, but she studied his face. It was a face that had been lived in. The features were strangely broken. The lips had a full, sensuous look at odds with the boxer's chin. He was obviously quite confident. It made her feel strangely comforted. She looked into his eyes and saw a darkness that she couldn't quite fathom. He put his glass to his lips. He watched her over the rim. There was an animal vitality in his stance, an almost physical aura. This made her feel uneasy. It also made him weirdly attractive. She suddenly realized that she might want him to touch her . . . and this made her ashamed of herself. He finished his drink, held the empty glass up high. He swung it to and fro and smiled at her and she nearly reached out to him.

'Another drink?' he said.

'No,' she said. 'I really shouldn't.'

'Why?'

'Because I'm tired, really tired, and it might do things to me.'

'Have another one,' he said. 'It might make you feel better. At its worst, it'll only help you to sleep. Have one on me.'

She smiled wearily and nodded. 'You win,' she said. 'I wouldn't like to offend an allied soldier. Gin and tonic. A single.'

Stryker got her a double, laced it lightly with the tonic, returned, gave it to her and watched her as she had the first sip. She closed her eyes and sighed, opened her eyes and glanced around her. She obviously hadn't noticed the difference, and she looked up and smiled.

'I feel better,' she said. 'I feel better already. I always knew I could depend on our allies when things got too rough.'

'Good,' Stryker said. 'I'm glad to be of service. I've met a lovely lady on my first night to London, and she even let me buy her a drink. I can write home about it.'

'And where's home, staff-sergeant?'

'New Jersey,' Stryker said. 'I'm a mechanic and I have my own business, but that's not really interesting.'

'Any family?'

'No. Not married, parents dead. I'm a regular GI and I pick up my friends where I find them.'

'And do you have many?'

'Friends?'

'Yes.'

'No. I usually get bored pretty quick, so I keep to myself a lot. I avoid complications.'

'But you told me you were all alone.'

'I didn't say I was lonely.'

'Then why did you want to talk to me?'

'You're not a man. You're a woman.'

Katherine felt herself blushing. She couldn't help but glance around her. The room was a roar of conversation that made

77

her feel dizzy. She looked back at the staff-sergeant. He was looking straight back at her. He towered above her and she felt his massive presence like a physical pressure.

She wondered why she hadn't left, felt a little ashamed. There was guilt in the thought that she had left David alone, and that now she didn't want to leave this bar. Perhaps it was the tiredness, perhaps the grief she felt. She remembered Whitechapel, the falling buildings, the climbing flames, the broken fingers clawing at the rubble, the cries of the wounded. She had worked hard tonight. It had been filthy, bloody work. She had found a whole family trapped by debris, the child without legs. Nothing made sense anymore. The violence left her in tatters. She sometimes felt that she couldn't take much more, that it would drive her insane. Then there was David. There was the nightmare of their marriage. There was the need that they felt for one another, the crippling lack of real passion. What happened to them in bed? Why did fear lock them in ice? Why did they both feel a shame that did not have to be? The questions never ceased to haunt her. She knew they haunted him as well. Like the blind they would reach for one another and find only a blank wall. She was tormented by this failure, wanted her body to find release, wanted someone with a touch devoid of fear to unravel her feelings.

Katherine froze with the shock of it. She glanced wildly around the room. She saw soldiers and sailors, generals and privates, WACS and whores all locked together. They were wreathed in a purple haze, sweating and gesticulating, laughing and singing and drinking as if they had no tomorrow. The world was at war. The children lay in the rubble. She dwelt within her skin, inside her mind, as if it didn't exist. The selfishness was gross, the shame something she deserved ... And yet her body, and the emotions it engendered, could not be denied.

She glanced up at the staff-sergeant. His smile was casual and confident. A world unto himself, self-assured and independent, he would take her without the inner conflict that froze David in anguish. What she thought about shamed her. It came from somewhere beyond her. This man's touch would be fearless; it would guide her ... And it might set her free.

78

Katherine finished her glass off. She did it with one gulp. She felt the strength in it hammering at her temples, felt her body dissolving. She held the glass up to the American. He grinned at her and took it. He wasn't arrogant, but he had a calm confidence that made her secure.

'Yes,' she said. '*I will* have another. And then I'll be off.'

Stryker went to the bar. He had to fight his way to it. He ordered the drinks and paid for them and went back to the girl. She took the glass from his hand. Her brown eyes were streaked with red. He saw beads of sweat shining on her forehead, beneath the dark hair.

'You look pretty,' he said.

'Do I?'

'Yes.'

'All girls look pretty to soldiers. It's our one contribution.'

The American smiled. 'Yeah, I suppose that's right. What I meant was, I find you attractive. You don't look like a housewife.'

'You mean, have I any children?'

'Yeah, that's what I mean.'

'No. I don't. Why do you ask?'

'I don't know. I just did.'

'Are you trying to make me, soldier?'

'Well, I don't intend to push. But I must admit, it did cross my mind. It's a natural instinct.'

'Ah,' she said. 'Natural instincts.'

'You can't make 'em or break 'em.'

She smiled at his deliberate drawling. It made him seem more of a rough-neck. He was grinning and the grin seemed self-mocking, like a shrug of the shoulders.

'Natural instincts,' she said. 'Only an American would talk about them. That's why you Americans think the English are all homosexual.'

This time he did shrug. 'Only the English men,' he said. 'Not that I really think they are. Just ninety percent of them.'

Katherine drank her gin and smiled. She found his impertinence refreshing. He obviously had his tongue in his cheek, and it made her feel casual.

'And the staff-sergeant,' she said. 'The staff-sergeant seems

79

rather cheeky. Is the staff-sergeant at home with his natural instincts? Or does he just feel he has to be?'

'I never thought about it,' he said. 'The question never entered my head. I'm a red-blooded, All-American boy, and I do what I have to do.'

'That sounds arrogant, staff-sergeant.'

'It's not meant to be. I'm no lady-killer, if that's what you mean. But I don't let it bother me.'

'I thought it bothered every man.'

'I didn't mean it that way. I didn't mean I'm immune to it. I mean that I accept it, that I accept the need as natural, and that I don't ever suffer any guilt when that need's satisfied.'

He knew he had her then. His every sense told him that. He saw it in the light in her eyes, between her unspoken words. Stryker knew it at that instant: he knew he would win. In her tiredness, in her need to talk to him, he saw her vulnerability. She was romantic and troubled. Her thoughts were here and faraway. She stayed with him because she thought of the trouble, because she wanted to flee from it. He didn't know what it was. He simply knew that it was real. It worked at her and it worked in his favour, setting her up. That's all he wanted. He didn't want to know the rest. He wanted the darkness and the moonlight above it and the white of her body.

She was drinking and looking at him, her gaze tentative and curious. She was smiling, but she wasn't as self-assured as her words tried to make out. Stryker moved closer to her. He didn't make it very obvious. He looked down at her and smiled, because he knew that her confidence must be his. The room roared all around them. The cigarette smoke swirled between them. They were close and the space between their bodies had a will of its own.

'No guilt,' she said. 'That's not a pleasure of the English. At least not of the English middle-classes. You should count yourself lucky.'

'I'm not lucky,' he said, giving her just what she needed, knowing exactly what she needed to hear and slipping it in. 'I don't see it that way.'

'And how *do* you see it?'

'I see it as normal,' he said. 'I see it as two people needing one thing and helping each other out. It doesn't have to be love, doesn't need to be for life. It's the body, and the body has its own needs – outside love and affection. People always confuse the two, don't know one from the other. If they know, they don't want to admit it, they think it's a crime. I hold no truck with that. It doesn't make any sense to me. I get pleasure from women, and if they get pleasure from me, then I don't see any reason for worrying. It's as normal as breakfast.'

Katherine laughed. She was amused by his choice of words. She was amused and she also felt release from something dormant and shadowed. She turned her head to the side, saw the packed, smokey room. The lights washed across a sea of flushed faces, shone on glasses and tables. She hardly knew where she was, didn't want to think about it. She didn't want to think of David or her father or the girls she had come here with. The tensions were too great. They had tortured her too long. Now a woman, she still felt like a child, as if her body imprisoned her. She had to find release, had to know where the failure lay, had to know if her body could express what it had hidden from David. So, Katherine laughed. The laughter hid what was escaping. She turned back to the American, to his calm, seductive confidence, and she put her head back and looked up at his dark, unrevealing eyes.

Who was he? What was he? How did he think? What did he feel? She didn't know, but she knew that he wanted her, and that his need was a casual thing. It was this knowledge that released her. It was his ease in her presence. She felt that she could unveil herself without causing him tremors. He would view it as natural, would scarcely think about it, would guide her and expect the response that would normally shame her.

Katherine's head started swimming. She understood what she would do. She felt dizzy and unreal and very vibrant, cast adrift from herself. She finished off her drink. The American took the glass from her. She blinked repeatedly and the American held her elbow and led her away.

'You need fresh air,' he said.

She didn't resist. She thought the idea very sound. The door opened and the cold air rushed in and then they stepped into darkness. Katherine looked up at the sky. The red glowing had disappeared. The bombed buildings had stopped their pained rumbling and her footsteps were echoing. The American still held her elbow. He was trying to keep her steady. She realized that she must be very drunk, but this thought didn't bother her. She knew what she would do, knew she had to do it now; had to know a man without fear or shame: a brief, self-assured lover. There was no sense of betrayal. No one ever need know. She would have this one night and discover if the fault was in herself. The American walked beside her. His boots rang on the pavement. He walked confidently towards Bayswater Road, and he held her quite close to him.

'Where are we going?' she said.

'To the park,' he replied. 'You're pretty drunk and you need some fresh air. You can sit down on a bench for a bit, until you feel better.'

'The park?' she said.

'Yes,' he said. 'The park.'

'Oh,' she said. 'Kensington Gardens. I suppose that's where you mean.'

He didn't reply. He didn't think it worth the bother. He was burning with the urgency of his need, and that's all he could think about. He saw the stars above, the pale orb of the moon; saw a few thin clouds crossing the moon and changing its face. The street was very quiet. His boots rang on the pavement. He felt the arm in his grip, sensed the blood coursing through it, and was filled with a bright incandescence, a voluptuous freedom. The girl stumbled at his side. He almost cursed, but checked himself. She leant against him and her body was warm, a soft, rhythmic pressure. He didn't say a word. There was nothing left to say. He wanted her, would have her this night, and then the dawn would be cleaner.

'We're at Bayswater Road,' she said.

Stryker didn't reply. He glanced up and down the road. The blackout was in force and the road, which was desolate, was dark. Stryker led the girl across it. Her head was lying on his shoulder. She had her arm around his waist and he felt that she might fall asleep. Then they reached the pavement. He saw the dark, outstretched gardens. The railings crossed his path and then stopped where a bomb had destroyed them. Stryker held the girl's arm. He walked her towards the bent railings. There was a gap where some railings had simply been blown out of existence. The girl stopped and looked at it. She then blinked and glanced around her. She seemed vague and her gestures were sluggish, as if she was sleep-walking. Stryker held onto her arm. She looked up at him and smiled. He led her carefully through the gap in the railings, then into the gardens.

Katherine felt she was dreaming. Her thoughts scattered and spun. She saw the darkness and the silhouetted trees, the shifting shadows of flower beds. The American held her by the arm. Her head was resting against his shoulder. She felt languorous and sleepy and unreal, not at all like her normal self. Of course she was drunk. She knew it and was glad. She felt free, liberated from herself, cast adrift from all petty cares. The trees whispered around her. The grass was soft beneath her feet. She thought of David and her heart went out to him with a sad, sentimental love. He was probably sleeping now. She hoped he was sleeping now. He had looked very tired when he came home, and that always had worried her. The stars were out tonight. They were distant and they glittered. She felt the hand of the American on her arm and she wanted his warmth.

It was strange when you thought about it. It was really very natural. She felt her body reaching out to be touched, to be exposed and thus sheltered. The clouds drifted across the moon. The moon shone down on her face. She turned around and placed her back against a tree and watched him leaning towards her.

His lips found her lips. She felt his tongue between her teeth. She closed her eyes and felt the weight of him against her, felt his hands on her hips. He was rocking her gently. She felt the long length of his thighs. She felt his tongue probing inside her mouth, felt his heat at her breasts. She was very conscious of him. She did not lose her awareness. She felt his fingers at her coat, at her blouse, and she couldn't ignore them. She released his probing tongue. She felt his weight against her loins. He no longer held her hips, but she rocked back and forth as he had shown her. The awareness was quite startling; the desire to use it more so. His confidence was filling her whole being and setting her free.

Katherine couldn't resist it: the feeling of freedom was too large, the sense of an imminent release overwhelmingly strong. Her flesh told her this truth; it overrode all other knowledge. He exposed it and he used it in the confidence of its natural destiny. Her blouse fell from her shoulders. Her skirt dropped to the ground. She felt the cold air all around her, felt his heat, felt his uniform's roughness. Nothing else really mattered. Her flooding loins were her source. She took his head in her hands and pulled him down till his lips found her breasts. The awareness never left her. It was more real than the real. Nothing given in the well of experience had equalled this moment. It was freedom beyond measure: immeasurable expectation. She wanted only the removal of her last vestiges of clothing, the aching void of her source to be filled before the world returned to her.

Katherine felt the man against her. She felt him slump towards the ground. She felt his hand brush her ankle, then she heard something snap, then he straightened, pressed against her once more, his body's heat burning through her. She opened her eyes. He was staring intently at her. Something frightened her, but she closed her eyes again and pulled his head down towards her. His tongue slid between her lips. She felt the beating of his heart. His heart was beating just above her right breast and he seemed to be crushing her. She wanted him to do it. Nothing else really mattered. She felt his left hand on her spine, felt him pull her in to him, felt the touch of something cold against her belly, pressing quite gently.

What was it? His belt buckle? No. Something sharp. It bit into her as his hand clamped on her mouth and stifled her scream.

The pain tore her apart. It obliterated all sense. She tried to scream, but his hand was on her mouth and she opened her eyes. She saw his fierce, intense stare. She saw the white of his teeth. She saw him jerking, and then the pain exploded beyond what she could bear. Nothing mattered anymore.

Nothing mattered but release. Her eyes went down and saw the glint of steel, cutting slowly across her. She couldn't believe it. The pain blocked off her terror. Her eyes rolled back and she saw the black sky, the glittering stars of the cosmos.

Stryker pushed her head away. He jerked the knife from her body. Katherine gasped and turned around and grabbed the tree; then she choked and collapsed. Stryker checked that she was dead. He cleaned the knife on the grass. He folded the knife and put it back behind his gaiter and then he walked from the park.

# PART TWO: JUNGLE

# CHAPTER SIX

STANDING at the railing of his attack transport, gazing out across the darkness, across the cold, choppy Channel, at the other boats and ships of the invasion convoy, David felt like a lost soul. Still shocked by Katherine's death, totally obsessed by its horrible nature, ashamed of the state in which her body had been found and more ashamed of his puritanical outrage, he was not quite himself. Something in him had been crushed. He sensed a numbing of his spirit. Trying desperately not to think of it, finding it impossible to forget, he felt the cold iron of the railings in his hands and gazed out at the convoy. It stretched out all around him. It rose slowly and sank down. Grey, dissolved in darkness, filling the air with a muffled throbbing, there were battleships and destroyers and cargo boats and landing craft, the minesweepers out front, the command ships behind them, the corvettes and gunboats and anti-submarine patrol craft spread out in a protective circle around them. David tried to feel part of them. He felt nothing but isolation. He held the railings as the wind of the sea whipped salt spray at his face. He was not alone. The whole deck was packed with men. Grotesque in the gloom, almost shapeless and too bulky, they were ladened down with weapons and entrenching tools and gas masks, with grenades and ammunition and explosives, with first-aid kits and rations. They looked like men from another world. They were smoking and softly talking. Aware of themselves as but part of the larger armada – that five thousand ships of an infinite variety, ten lanes wide, stretched across twenty miles – aware of this they were unusually reverent, speaking mostly in whispers. David didn't feel the same. He felt quite removed from it. Now trapped within himself, in that most hideous of memories, incarcerated in revulsion and disbelief, he passed his days in stunned privacy. The Atlantic Wall would soon be broken. The liberation of Europe was at hand. Swept up in the tide of history, borne along on momentuous events, he was no longer capable of comprehending it, unwilling to share it.

A midnight moon glided. The sky rumbled above him. He raised his eyes, as did the other waiting men, and looked up at the dark sky. The barrage balloons floated above them. The ropes trailed out from the ships. The sky was filled with drifting black clouds, above which the planes roared. David looked but saw nothing. The planes were hidden in darkness. They were heading towards France, carrying bombs and para-troopers, trailing gliders containing the Pathfinders, the first men to be blooded. They would parachute into darkness. The fleet could not give them protection. Their presence in the sky above the ships announced the start of the invasion.

Some of the men around David cheered. Others simply looked up in awe. The planes rumbled overhead for some time and then the silence returned. David couldn't connect to it. A different midnight still haunted him. She had died, she had been murdered in the grass with her skirt at her ankles. The very thought of it was stunning. The feeling of shock was overwhelming. Behind the horror of the murder itself was the thought of the circumstances. It had not been his Kather-ine. It must have been someone else. It was Katherine and she had died in the grass in a singular intimacy ... *No, sir, it wasn't rape. We found no signs of ... well ...* The police inspector had been more than discreet, in awe of taut major-generals ... *We found no sign of resistance either, sir. It would seem that she knew him ...* David couldn't believe it. His mind refused to recognize it. He accepted it and then he felt a guilt that was quite overpowering. Thus he watched the churning waves, saw the ships that would make history. He blinked and the convoy disappeared and the nightmare rushed in. It was all too unreal. It simply could not have happened.

It had happened and his mind refused to grasp it and he wanted to flee from it.

David looked below him. The sea swept past the ship. It was grey and the waves were white streaks that bubbled and hissed. The ship's engines throbbed. A mass of soldiers were all around him. He was jostled and he heard their mingling voices and the ringing of metal. The paratroopers would soon be dropping. They would land on the soil of France. They would fire the first shots in the battle for Europe, and many would not live to see the dawn. Yet this fleet would see the dawn. It would arrive out of grey mist. It would launch the greatest invasion in the history of man – and he, David Holmyard, would be part of it.

The romance of it eluded him. He felt no cause for cheering. He felt alone, cut off from this great drama, enclosed in his private hell.

The major-general had broken the news. He had shaken David awake. 'Katherine is dead,' were his first words. 'I think you'd best put your clothes on.' It had seemed like a dream. He still thought he was dreaming now. He remembered sitting up, wondering where Katherine was, and rubbing his eyes as his father-in-law spoke to him. 'Get dressed,' the major-general said. 'She's been murdered. The police are downstairs.' It was real enough after that. It had the reality of a nightmare: the police, the morgue, the hideous details, the burial, his own mother and father weeping at the graveside as the coffin was lowered. The sun had shone that day. He had expected it to rain. As if in mockery, the sun had shone upon him, supreme, inviolable. As for himself he could not cry. The pain had drained him of even that. Either that, or the curse of his upbringing had made even tears shameful. He drank a lot during those days. He drank a lot and did not weep. He simply travelled down into himself and resolved to remain there.

David stared out to sea. He saw the vast, silhouetted convoy. The barrage balloons floated above the ships, gently swaying and bobbing. Then he looked at the sea again. He could not believe what was out there. Packed with tanks and trucks and motor vehicles and guns, with two hundred thousand sailors and soldiers and marines, the massive fleet, the five thousand ships, was beyond comprehension. What sort of war was this? What on earth justified it? It seemed as senseless as the slaughter of Katherine in the gardens of Kensington. It was best not to think about it. Like her death, it mocked all reasoning. It was too vast for logical deduction, too deep to unravel. Yet he had to know its face. Repelled, he was fascinated. Curiosity could overcome confusion and put grief in a sheltered place. This war was a contradiction. All contradictions sprang from Man. When broken down, Man became men and complexities mutiplied. What caused the need for conflict? Why did violence solve all problems? If man's history had been written in blood there must be a reason. But was there? Would there ever be? Who could explain five thousand ships? What could explain two hundred thousand men on a voyage of destruction? There might never be an answer. Perhaps senselessness reigned. Katherine's death in the night, that most malignant contradiction, might be no more than the sum of man's reasoning, his sad limitations.

David walked from the railing. Men surrounded him on all sides. They were talking and vomiting and playing cards, writing letters to home. They were sprawled all over the decks, sitting precariously on the booms and davits; others were crushed together in the amphibious vehicles and assault boats, cursing each other and trying to sleep, tangled up in their webbing. David had to step gingerly over them. Their weapons were piled all around them. They were ordinary men and they talked in a blunt language, making jokes, trading insults and obscenities, wishing the night away. The army had made them anonymous; in this war they would be faceless. As the major-general had said, they would be numbers, dispensable digits. David shuddered at the thought. Such a number had killed Katherine. He had weakened her, seduced her, taken her into the gardens, and once there, out of what need, for some obscene satisfaction, he had forced a knife into her body and drained her of life. The killer was a number. He had no name, no face. He had disappeared leaving no more than the vaguest of clues. David glanced across the water.

He saw the silhouetted ships. They stretched back as far as the eye could see, and they went beyond that. They were British and American, Canadian and French. And most likely, somewhere in that vast fleet, was Katherine's killer.

'You look rather thoughtful, David.'

David blinked and turned his head. The sound of the voice had almost startled him. He relaxed when he saw the placid eyes of his friend, Robert Lovell. Robert was tall and languid. He was the captain of David's platoon. Unlike David, he had previously seen action with the Marines: first when the commandos had helped seize the Vietri Pass, then later on the bloody road to Naples.

'Did I startle you?' he said.

'Yes,' David said. 'Quite frankly, you did. That's a terrible confession for a Royal Marine officer to make.'

'Not so terrible,' Robert said. 'In fact it's commonplace tonight. Even officers in the Royal Marine commando are permitted some nervousness.'

'There's a lot of seasickness,' David said. 'That seems more prevalent than bad nerves. There's scarcely a spew bag left on the ship, which does seem ironic.'

Robert chuckled and glanced around him, ran his fingers through his dark hair. 'One can smell it at a very great distance,' he said. 'Most likely they even smell it in France. Now wouldn't *that* make things interesting?' The ship rolled and he bumped David. The deck vibrated beneath them. 'I'm not all that good a sailor myself,' he said. 'A yacht's much more my style.'

David didn't reply. The ship rolled and then groaned. There were rumblings from below, metallic echoes, the banging of pipes.

'What's happening down there?' he said.

'Nothing much,' Robert said. 'It's crowded and hot. The men are piled on one another; lots of scribbling going on – lots of letters, lots of postcards – and 2nd Lieutenant Stunell, who is not very happy, has been turned into the ship's official censor. The atmosphere is unusually Christian. A little fighting, a lot of sentiment. The conversation is unceasing: about home, about families; just occasionally, but not very often, about what happens tomorrow. The Chaplain is saying Mass. It was requested by a Jewish captain. The captain says that the Chaplain's God is his God, that all men are now brothers. I don't think that includes the Germans. No one's prayed for them yet. Apart from praying and talking and writing letters and trying to sleep, there's a large queue to the heads and portholes ... relief of the stomach or bladder; quite possibly both. I really couldn't recommend it. It's not quite the Savoy. In fact it makes one look forward to France in the hope of survival.'

'Any news from the Colonel?'

'Oh, yes. He's still alert. In fact he doesn't want his officers to fall asleep while the men are so restless. An excellent Marine. One might even say superlative. He wants us in the second forward hold at four o'clock sharp.'

'The briefing, I suppose.'

'Precisely.'

'Well, that's good. Strangely, though I don't feel heroic, I want to get started.'

Robert smiled gently. 'Yes,' he said. 'I know. A night like this is never easy to handle and goes on far too long. It's always the worst time. It affords too much time for thinking. And it's worse before the briefing because you don't know what you're doing, because you don't have the facts to play around with and keep you engaged.'

'At least it's started,' David said. 'The paratroopers must have landed. I don't envy them *or* the Pathfinders. Not out there. Not tonight.'

'No,' Robert said. 'It's not an enviable task. They're being dropped all over the country. They're cut off from one another. They have to work in the dark, they have no off-shore support, and Jerry's whole weight might be against them. I never did like the thought of that. Not being dropped in on a parachute. Not falling down through darkness, exposed, defenceless, never certain of where you might land or of what you might find there ... The Germans will be onto them all right – God help the poor beggars.'

'When do we go in?'

'I believe it's at dawn. At least we'll have daylight, and the

Fleet will be there to give us cover. It's more than those chaps have got.'

David glanced across the water. He saw the cruising ships, the darkness. He thought of the paratroopers falling into fields and swamps, into gardens and orchards, too bulky in their jumpsuits, overloaded with weapons, carrying mines and radar sets and lights and fluorescent panels, fighting off the dazed Germans, setting up the drop zones, each drop zone giving them away to more Germans who would come to destroy them. It couldn't be very pleasant. In the darkness it might be fearful. They were preparing the way for the invasion and the price would be high. How many gliders had landed by now? How many more had crashed? How many men were dead at this moment as he stood contemplating? David shuddered a little. The huge armada cruised around him. Awesome, majestic, with a strange, unreal beauty, it turned the cold Channel into a hybrid of shadow and light.

Katherine's killer was out there. He was on one of those stately ships. A liberator, a hero, justified by his existence, his secret demons undiscovered, his frightful passions disguised; all of this and he was also David's ally, both supporting the same cause. The irony was brutal. The very thought was overwhelming. The injustice of it, the sublime unshaken cruelty, was a mockery to reason. What was he like? What bleak compulsions motivated him? The questions had turned into an obsession, a fathomless hunger. How could life be so valueless? What sort of child grew up to kill? What perverse satisfaction was obtained by the thrill of the blade? Such compulsions were beyond David. They lived outside his experience. They violated his very nature, his belief in the inherent goodness of men. And Katherine. Why Katherine? What had made her go with him? Had she met him before? Had she known other men? Had David been betrayed or had the failure of their love driven her to it? These very questions gave him shame. They were so base, so self-serving. In his grief, behind the very real horror, he still thought of himself. He tried not to think about it. His grief and shame were contradictions. Yet like the knife that had twisted in her, it was twisting in him. His stomach churned. He felt the beating of his heart. Between his grief and his dread and his primitive sense of betrayal, he was torn and could not find his centre, could not unveil his true self. He had to know the killer, had to see that man's face. He had to look at the map of an experience that had led to this nightmare.

'Any news?' Robert said.

'Pardon?'

'About the murderer. I hope you don't mind me mentioning it. But I think you should talk about it.'

David shrugged. 'I don't mind,' he said. 'At least not from you. There's not much else I can do except talk about it. Yet it makes me feel futile.'

'Don't,' Robert said. 'It won't help you at all. It didn't have a thing to do with you. It was a hideous accident.'

'I'm not sure,' David said. 'I'm not sure that it ever is. She went with him and I'd like to know why. I think it was my fault.'

'That's ridiculous,' Robert said. 'You're just torturing yourself. You're trying to take the blame because you think that there has to be a reason. Well, there aren't always reasons.'

'Why?' David said. 'Why did he do it?'

'He's a killer,' Robert said. 'He's just a murderer, a psychotic. They're not all that uncommon, old chap, and that's something you should know.'

David didn't reply, simply shrugged and glanced around him. He saw the men on the decks, in the amphibious vehicles, in the landing craft, sitting along the booms, around the davits: an anonymous mass. They were laughing and cursing, writing letters and reading books. The ship ploughed through the water, chopping through the white foam, and the wind beat at their hair, tugged their uniforms, swept back towards England.

'Have you heard anything yet?' Robert said. 'About who he might be?'

'Not much,' David said. 'A little, but not much. She was last seen in the Allied Forces Club in Bayswater with an American, a GI, a staff-sergeant. Some of the regulars recognized her. Apparently she went there quite a bit. She usually went with some girls from the Women's Voluntary Service – though normally she always left with them. They say she was depressed that night. They left her on her last drink. She had told them she was going to go home as soon as she finished it. She didn't. This GI started talking to her. No one took too much notice, so they don't know what he looked like ... but they think he was a GI staff-sergeant who had been there before. They're not sure, but they think she left with him – or that they left close together.'

'Well,' Robert said, 'at least that's something.'

'Not much,' David said. 'Not much at all. There were a couple of hundred staff-sergeants on leave that weekend, and most of them are now with this fleet. They won't be easy to find. They'll soon be all over Europe. And we're fighting a war at the moment, which *does* make things difficult.'

Robert nodded his head, glanced casually around him. He turned back to David and took his shoulder and shook him a little.

'Come on,' he said. 'Let's go down below. The colonel will soon be starting his briefing and we don't want to miss it.'

They stepped over the lolling men, went through a green hatchway, and made their way down the steep, metal steps. A sudden blast of heat enveloped them. They smelt body sweat and urine. The engines roared and the long iron pipes rattled and the rivets protested. It was a dimly-lit hellhole. There was no place to sit. Bunks were piled to the ceiling, men seemed piled on one another, clothing hung from the pipes fixed to the walls, weapons covered the floor. The stench was atrocious, pinching the nostrils; it came from farting and urinating, from the sweat and the vomit, from the oil of the engines below. The men sat and sprawled everywhere. The companionways were packed. There were long queues to the heads, and more men were trying to vomit through portholes. Seasickness was prevalent; the men groaned as the ship rolled. They were pale, and in that weak, yellow lighting they seemed almost ghostly. David and Robert moved forward carefully, stepping between outstretched legs, went along an aisle between the many swaying canvas bunks, past the men trying to sleep or vomit or talk, came eventually to a metal-plated room at the end of the companionway.

'Home from home,' Robert said.

The room was filled with platoon officers. They were all squatting on the floor. The colonel was on his knees with an orders map spread out before him. The other officers surrounded him. The air was thick with cigarette smoke. The colonel's exec was standing just behind him, dishevelled and weary. David and Robert sat down. The colonel started to talk. He covered the overall plan for the invasion, then he came to their own task.

'This is it,' he said, pointing down at the map, tapping the paper with a pencil and glancing around him in a no-non-sense manner. 'It's a place called Port-en-Bessin. There's a harbour and a small town. It lies between the American and the British Canadian landings, and our job is to link up the two fronts. To take the town, we have to take the two hills above it. The town is well protected and those two hills are honeycombed with trenches. We have four-hundred and twenty men. We're going in in fourteen boats. We will land at Le Hamel and make our way to Port-en-Bessin from there. When we take the town and hills, which naturally we will, we will be relieved by the Americans and the Devonshires. You all have your specific tasks. I trust you will carry them out. Are there any further questions before we start?'

There were quite a few questions. There was obviously a certain nervousness. Some of the younger officers had never seen action before and were therefore simply seeking reassurance. The colonel seemed to understand this. He was light and off-handed. 'I don't know,' he would say, spreading out both his hands. 'Let's just wait and see what happens, shall we? We can't anticipate anything.' The meeting eventually broke up. It was close to five o'clock. The officers shook each other's hands, made a few nervous jokes, then scattered throughout the ship to collect their men.

'Oh, Holmyard,' the colonel said just as David was leaving. 'The major-general sends his regards. We've just received a message from the command ship, and it included his best wishes.'

David left the room with Robert. They made their way back through the hold. Already there was an increase in activity, as if the men had sixth sense. Then David realized what it was. The ship was no longer moving. They were finally lying off the coast of France, and the ship had dropped anchor.

'Not long now,' Robert said.

The hold was a lot noisier. The men were shouting and mixing together. They were dropping out of their bunks, untangling their equipment, adjusting their webbing and heading for the exits. Some of them looked nervous. A great many were simply seasick. Robert, who seemed a great deal taller than the majority of them, pushed his way through the mass of jostling bodies while David tried to stay close to him. The noise was now appalling. The men were shouting and pushing each other. Boots hammered on rivets, weapons rang against steel pipes, the canvas bunks creaked, and shoulder packs thumped into one another, like fists against punchbags. All these sounds echoed, reverberated, roared, while the men formed a heaving sea of khaki uniforms and helmets, their sweating faces washed into a common whiteness by the overhead lights.

David was confused. Like this mass, he was chaotic. His stomach tightened and he felt a strange excitement based on fear and relief. He was also thinking of the major-general. It was ridiculous to think of him at this time. The major-general was on the command ship, was doubtless engrossed, and would now, at the crossroads of history, find the world he belonged to. The major-general frightened David, was a distant, oblique threat. Even the sending of his good wishes was something that made David feel uneasy. He didn't know why. It was just something that bothered him. It had bothered him since the night he had talked to the major-general, the night he fell asleep and dreamed of Monte Cassino and awakened to the news of Katherine's death. The major-general had acted strangely, had been more outraged than stricken. David remembered his grey eyes, the lined granite of his face, his cold, harshly concentrated fury during the bleak days that followed. Like David, he hadn't cried; unlike David, he hadn't drank. Remote, unspeaking, radiating a throttled tension, he had organized the funeral, attended to all the relatives, and had then, after the burial, walked up to David with a fierce, unyielding light in his eyes. 'We will find him!' he had hissed to David, his fists clenched, his voice outraged. 'We will find him! He will not get away with it! I will see that he hangs!' David had been shocked, had almost recoiled. He had been stunned by the general's violence, by the force of his wrath, by the sight of his twitching, distorted features. Had the general felt the loss? David sensed that he had. Yet above and beyond this, much stronger than grief itself, the general had obviously felt outraged, in some strange way insulted.

Robert stopped at a crowded companionway. David fell in beside him. The Marines of their platoon were packed tightly together, looking bulky and inhuman in full field equipment, their weapons thrusting out in all directions and clattering together. Private 'Pip' Hunter, the platoon favourite, terribly young, was looking up at his friend Corporal Morgan and saying, 'Jesus, I'm scared, mate.' Morgan, another rifleman, tall and broad-shouldered, just shrugged and said, 'We'll give 'em hell, laddy.' Another corporal, Alf Brown, sharp-faced and aggressive, was checking his Sten gun and muttering, 'I'll do the cunts murder.' Someone snorted with mirth; there was cursing and giggling. 'Bugger this for a joke,' someone said. 'I haven't shit for two days.' A klaxon suddenly shrieked. It reverberated through the hold. It was the signal for the men to go on deck and line up for the boats. The klaxon shrieked in a demented fashion. A couple of the men twitched with shock. Sergeant Cowie, making a final quick inspection, patted more than one shoulder. 'Pull your backside in, boy. I want that buckle tightened. Put on that safety catch, Marine, before you blow someone's head off.' Private Tanner blushed and blinked. He put the safety catch on. The sergeant moved to another man as Tanner glanced all around him and murmured, 'Jesus, a real rookie trick.' The klaxon continued shrieking. It eventually tailed off into silence. The men stamped their feet, adjusted their chin-straps and held onto their weapons. Captain Lovell stepped forward. He had a beret on his head. He was tall, sophisticated, had a swagger stick under his right arm, and he glanced around the men with a humorous and friendly light in his green eyes.

'Alright, chaps,' he said. 'We're going up on the deck now.

I want you to stick together and get into our own boat as smoothly as possible. Try not to be too careless. It's a rather choppy sea. I don't want to lose any men before we even get started. That's all, chaps. No more speeches.'

The men moved towards the hatchways. The sides of the ship suddenly thundered. The ship rocked and immense bellowing sounds echoed wildly around them. More banging and clanging followed. The metal plates were being assaulted. The men glanced at one another and grinned, and moved out looking sheepish. The ship rocked and the noise continued. The ship's sides shrieked and trembled. David wondered what it was and then he looked across at Robert who was standing beneath a swinging light bulb. The bulb cast stark black shadows. The shadows darted across the men. Something smashed into the ship and then David realized that it was the sound of a landing craft being lowered. He blinked and looked around him. The noise threatened to deafen him. He shook his head and watched the men go through the hatchway, bent over, grotesque. There was the glint of steel steps. The steps swayed back and forth. Another landing craft smashed into the ship and the whole floor vibrated. The noise was appalling. Light and shadow fought each other. He saw Robert's green eyes shining out of a darkness, then the eyes moved away and disappeared.

In that instant David dissolved. He became part of the larger moment. He saw Robert and himself in the smokey rooms of Oxford; saw Katherine in a boat in the river with the sun in her eyes. A blinding anguish filled his being. The grief was greater than his life. He started shaking and he turned towards the wall and put his burning head to it. The metal was cold. It suddenly bellowed and vibrated. David thought of the major-general's need for vengeance, and he wanted no part of it. Let the killer fight his war. Let him disappear in smoke. Let the sound of the guns and the heat of destruction blot out what could never be regained. Katherine was dead. David shook with this very knowledge. He heard the clamour, felt the trembling of the ship, let the past fall away from him. Nothing mattered anymore. Nothing mattered but the moment. Each moment might now be the last, and that mattered a great deal. David took hold of a pipe. He was dissolving where he stood. He went down through himself and emerged to a thunder that tore the skies apart and rocked the whole ship. David couldn't believe it. It was too loud to be real. It was the naval bombardment and it thundered all around him, then it crushed him to nothing and picked him up and made him part of the war.

He climbed up to the deck.

# CHAPTER SEVEN

MONSTROUS, demoniac, thunder piled upon thunder, the massed guns of the invasion fleet belched flame and smoke, rocked the very ships on which they were mounted, whipped the grey sea up. The noise was beyond belief. It was a roar that filled the heavens. The men milling on the decks covered their ears and gritted their teeth. The guns pounded and recoiled. The huge barrels jerked back and forth. The smoke thickened and turned to black clouds that hung over the convoy. Their targets could not be seen. The beaches were nine miles away. Between the mother ships, in the surging grey sea, were the first of the smaller boats.

David gripped his Sten gun. The naval bombardment rocked the deck. He smelt smoke and cordite and oil, saw explosions of yellow flame. He fought through to his own men. The other soldiers were massed around him. Chains screeched in the davits, the windlasses rattled, and amphibious vehicles, held by the booms, swung out over steel helmets. David glanced through pallid faces, saw the sea's surging violence. Patrol boats cut white swathes through the assault craft and LSTs, their engines whining above the throb of the mother ships, still belching their flame and smoke.

The men were all around David, were overloaded and sluggish. The amphibious vehicles hung above them, swung uncertainly back and forth, finally hovered above the sea and were lowered, crashing into the hull. The men themselves were oblivious. They were deafened and confused. The loudspeakers blared out their directives and encouragement against the thunder of the naval bombardment and the roar of the boats. The men were clambering over the sides, were hanging from the scrambling nets. They were shouting and waving and crashing into each other; dropping and falling into the beaching craft that swung precariously beneath them.

The ships' guns continued pounding. The air was thunderous and smokey. David strained to see France, but saw only the pre-dawn's grey haze. He thought of that hidden land, of this monstrous bombardment, and wondered how anyone could survive this holocaust raining down on them. Then he looked across the sea. The ships stretched back to the horizon. Their ensigns snapped in the wind, the barrage balloons floated above them, the huge barrels of the guns belched smoke and flame, the small boats bobbed between them. It all seemed too much: both majestic and frightful. He saw the huge Rhino ferries and the smaller assault craft and the destroyers and the mine sweepers and the LSTs. They were all wreathed in smoke, were hazy and unreal. They rocked back and forth and the sea surged around them, and the roar of the bombardment was hellish, stunning the senses.

'Keep in line! Keep in line!' the loudspeakers blared. 'Away all boats! Good luck and God bless you! Keep in line! Away all boats!'

David reached his waiting men, his head reeling from the bombardment. The deck shuddered, rolled beneath him, swooped back up, and he reached for the railings. Captain Lovell was there, holding his swagger stick, leaning over the rail and looking down at the men in the nets. The sky roared and split asunder. Yellow flames flashed through the murk. David followed Robert's gaze and saw an LCT below, rising up and falling down in grey sludge, banging into the ship's hull. The men were hanging from the nets. They were weighed down with equipment. They were shouting and waving their arms and crashing into the landing craft. Then a man screamed. He was hanging down from the net. He had climbed down too low and now the rolling assault craft was crushing his legs against the steel hull. The man continued screaming. He kept clinging to the net. His head was thrown back and he was white-faced and his eyes were like marbles. The guns thundered and roared. Chains screeched and men bellowed. The assault craft rolled away and the man let go the net and fell down between the small boat and the ship. Another large wave rushed in. It washed over the assault craft. The man's head reappeared and the assault craft was picked up and smashed over the floating head and hit the ship. A few more men dropped into it. One sat up and shook himself. He spat blood and teeth onto the deck and leaned forward and vomited. The assault craft rolled and heaved. More men scrambled down the nets. The assault craft were banging against the ship and two more men were lost.

'The sea's rough!' Robert shouted. 'It's too bloody rough! And these men have got too much equipment! Some can hardly stand up straight!'

The guns continued thundering. It was like the end of the world. The bombardment was a clamour that went beyond mere sound and left the nerves hanging in shreds. David couldn't believe it. His senses couldn't take it in. He saw the boats being lowered, saw white faces and helmets, heard the shouting and banging and metallic screeching, felt the blast of the guns. The deck dipped and heaved beneath him, the smoke swirled around his eyes. He saw the grey mass of the sea and it was criss-crossed with white lines, the wakes from the ploughing, circling boats: the LSTs, the LCTs, the gunboats, the destroyers, the beaching craft and the mine-sweepers and the patrol boats. The ships rocked and the guns roared; yellow flame flashed through the murk. The transports tilted over and the nets hung in the air, and the men on the nets spun and shouted, kicking legs frantically. The assault craft bobbed beneath them, smashed into the ships' hull. The noise echoed and reverberated, drowned the screams of falling men, and the waves were a white-flecked grey sludge that swept over the decks.

Then another sound was heard. It was a deep, familiar rumbling. David looked up with the other waiting men at the dark, smokey sky. At first they saw nothing. They only heard the approaching rumble. Then the rumble became a roar and the roar became a thunder that formed an umbrella of sound above the ships' guns. The effect was startling. The whole sky seemed to shake. Then they saw a dark mass, and then the mass broke apart, became a thousand, two thousand, three thousand separate planes, flying over the massive fleet, almost wing tip to wing tip, four thousand, five thousand, six thousand, seven thousand, formation after formation, first the fighters and then the bombers, the Spitfires, the Thunderbolts, another thousand Mustangs, then the B-26s, fat bellied, filled with bombs, then the Fortresses and Liberators and Lancasters, making nine thousand planes. They flew one beside the other. Formation followed formation. They spread out above the fleet, above the five thousand ships, above the cruisers and destroyers and mine-sweepers and gun boats, above the men in the Rhinos and the LCTs and the beaching craft, above that two hundred thousand nameless faces that looked up in awe.

David held onto the rail, felt the shuddering of the ship. He saw the fleet that swept out to the misty horizon; saw the massed planes that filled the sky above and seemed to make the whole world shake. There were no words to describe it. It went beyond all human reasoning. Sight and sound had become one crazed dream that reduced him to impulse.

He looked at Robert Lovell. Robert's green eyes scanned the sky. Robert's green eyes reflected disbelief and a strange exultation. Then Robert looked below him, saw the LCT pull away, looked up and saw another LCT swinging out on a boom. He turned around to his men.

'That's us, chaps!' he shouted.

The men hardly heard him. They were looking at the sky. They were slapping each other's backs and some were waving their helmets and others were simply staring up in awe. David watched the landing craft. It swung out above his head. He saw its flat, metal bottom, its blunt nose, and then it was lowered. The ship suddenly tilted. The landing craft swung out. The ship righted itself and the landing craft shuddered and swung back and smashed into the railing. 'Hold it!' Robert shouted. 'Hold it there! We're going in now!' He was waving his hands frantically. The grey sea surged beyond him. The landing craft hung there, gently banging the railings, and the men, looking seasick and confused, started shuffling towards it.

'That's it,' Robert said, his voice crisp and authoritative, his swagger stick waving in the air, 'jump right in. Mind your ankles.' The men did as they were told: scrambled over the side. They were cursing and muttering under their breath, but they were helping each other. The massed aircraft roared overhead. The naval bombardment continued. The men muttered and groaned, but their voices were drowned out by the bedlam.

The landing craft swung to and fro. It hovered dangerously above the sea. In the sea, the mass of Rhinos and landing craft were heading out towards Normandy. David watched them. There seemed to be thousands of them. They were heading out in three directions, trailing white lines of foam, the armada of planes over their heads, the huge fleet all around them. The sea was very rough. The boats rose and then fell. They moved out while others circled the mother ships which were hazed in the dark smoke. That smoke pinched David's nostrils, swirled around his milling men. The guns roared and the barrels belched flame and the whole deck vibrated.

David tightened his webbing, held his Sten gun in one hand, felt sluggish from his mass of equipment, too heavy to climb. Yet climb he did. He did it almost automatically. He watched Private Tanner's backside swaying right before his eyes, then Tanner dropped down into the boat and David climbed on the railing. The fleet thundered all around him. He saw the mass of circling boats. He looked down between the railing and the side of the LCT, and he saw the grey sea rise and fall in a sickening fashion. Someone slapped him between the shoulders. He nearly fell overboard. He almost screamed, but instead he leapt forward towards that wall of pale faces. He heard the thunder of the guns, felt a fierce, tearing wind, saw a ribbon of sea, a steel wall, and then waiting hands grabbed him. At that moment he felt love: a love for the other men. He sat up and turned around and looked back and saw his friend Robert Lovell. Robert was still on the ship. He was the only member of the platoon left. He put his swagger stick under one arm, stood up on the railing, smiled down with an air of calm assurance and jumped into the landing craft.

'Lower away,' he said.

The planes were still flying overhead. The fleet's guns were still thundering. The chains rattled in the davits and the landing craft started sinking, moving down very slowly, swaying gently back and forth, the men crouched inside it looking forlorn, staring up at the rising hull. Then the transport keeled over. The landing craft swung away from it. It was swinging out high above the sea, and the wind whipped the huddled men. '*We're tipping over!*' someone shouted. '*Jesus Christ!*' someone cried. The boat swung out and hung there in the air, then swung back towards the ship. '*Watch your hands!*' Robert shouted.'*Hold on tight!*' Sergeant Cowie bawled. The landing craft hit the ship's hull with a fearful shrieking roar, then it jumped up and bounced and threw the men first left and then right. '*Fucking bastard!*' someone shouted. 'Hold your cocks!' someone added. '*Keep lowering!*' Robert shouted up at the ship. '*Stop standing there gawking!*' The chains rattled again. A porthole rose above them. They kept sinking and the hull moved away and then came back towards them. The men grabbed hold of each other, grabbed whatever they could find. The landing craft hit the ship and the men tumbled together and started cursing and disentangling themselves. Then suddenly they hit the water. There was a bizarre drumming sound. They were jolted and picked up and lowered down again; and then the icy grey water rushed over them and left them all drenched.

'*Cast off!*' Robert shouted. '*Let's go!*'

The engine roared into life. They moved away from the towering ship. David looked up, saw faces looking down, saw hands waving, heard cheering. Then he looked past the coxswain, saw the thousands of other boats. They were weaving in indefinable patterns between the ships and destroyers. The dawn light was grey. It was darkened by black smoke. The guns thundered all around him on the huge battleships, while the destroyers, like the Rhinos and landing craft, moved away towards France. Their own ship fell behind them. The sea rose and sank around them. It pounded the landing craft, made a harsh roaring sound, then rose up and poured in on the men, soaking them all. The men cursed and wiped their eyes, bailed the water out with their helmets. Some looked around them while others just sat there, seasick and despondent.

'These fucking boats,' Alf Brown said. 'I'd like to know who invented them. My fucking bath would float better than this.'

'Are we going in?' someone said.

'No,' someone else replied. 'We're just circling. We're gonna circle around the fleet all fucking day. Keep your hands on your spew bags.'

'We're going in,' Robert said. 'We're heading straight for Le Hamel. It will take a bit of time, but at least we won't be out here all that long.'

'Do you think it'll be heavily defended, Captain?'

'No. That's why we're landing there. Port-en-Bessin itself is very heavily defended, which is why we don't want to land there. We will beach at Le Hamel and go on a forced march from there.'

'I'm too sick,' Private Turner said. His face was thin and deathly white. 'I've been vomiting all night and I think I'm going to vomit again. It's this bleedin' seasickness.'

Alf Brown grinned maliciously. 'Fucking seasickness!' he exclaimed. 'You'll soon forget that when you land on that beach and get a fucking bullet in yer throat. *That'll* stop your seasickness!'

Private Turner went paler. 'That's enough,' Robert said. 'We'll have less of that nonsense, Corporal Brown. I want none of your scaremongering.'

The sharp-nosed cockney grinned. 'Right, sir,' he said. 'I think I got the message, Captain, sir.' He spat over the side.

The boat crashed through the waves, the waves poured over the sides, the boat rolled and water flooded around the men and rose up to their ankles. The men howled and groaned, started bailing the water out. The boat rose and fell sickeningly in the turbulent sea as David stood up and looked over the gunwale.

The massed guns of the fleet thundered. The planes continued to roar overhead. There was still no sign of land, but the thousands of other boats were cutting swathes of white foam through the grey sea. They were still surrounded by the immense fleet. The destroyers cruised on ahead of them. Far in front of the destroyers were the mine-sweepers, spread out in a huge V. The noise was incredible. Shouting voices rang back and forth. The guns thundered, the ships throbbed, the planes roared overhead; and the waves smashed against the metal boats and the men were all shouting. There was still no sign of land. A black smoke swirled through the mist. The patrol boats were whining between the ships and the landing craft, men blaring instructions through megaphones, their hair whipped by the wind.

Then two barges collided. One rose up and turned over. It rose slowly and gracefully, white and grey washing over it, and the men screamed and sailed through the air and started speckling the water. Helmets bobbed in the waves; pieces of equipment drifted past. The men rose up and waved desperate hands and then sank down again. It didn't seem real. They were being dragged down by their equipment. They were drowning right before David's eyes, and then they all disappeared. The guns continued their bombardment. The thousands of planes filled the sky. The mine-sweepers and destroyers and landing craft and gunboats continued their journey towards land as if nothing had happened.

'You see that?' Alf Brown said. 'They all drowned! These fucking bathtubs!'

David sat down again. He saw Robert looking at him. He huddled up and put his Sten gun between his legs and tried to keep himself steady. The boat made a swooping dive. The waves smashed all around it. They swept over the men and flooded over the deck, drowning boots and soaking weapons and clothes, making teeth chatter. The boat screeched in protest. The planes roared and the guns thundered. The mist began to give way to the pearly light of dawn, but the smoke from the guns filled the sky, blotting out the massed aircraft. David shivered with cold. He was soaked and turning icy. He glanced at the other men and they all seemed dejected, seasick or frozen or just weary, not at all like real warriors. As for himself, he felt seasick. He hadn't eaten since embarkation. His stomach churned, his head spun, and he felt hollow, drained of all energy. He didn't know how he could face it, didn't know how they could face it. The boat rose up and down, rocked left and then right, and the men, now attuned to this rhythm, groaned in despair. David looked beyond the coxswain. His back was outlined against the greyness. Within the greyness, far off in the distance, was a ribbon of darkness. David suddenly felt tense. He watched that dark line approaching. It was hazed in the mist and in a pall of black smoke, but he knew that he was looking at land, at the coast-line of France.

'There it is,' Robert said.

Some of the men stood up. Others couldn't be bothered moving. The boat rose and crashed down, the waves roared and slashed over them, and the sitting men cursed and grabbed their weapons and wiped salt from their eyes. The water splashed around their feet. It was green and very cold. A young corporal vomited, groaned aloud in despair, and murmured, 'God, just give me dry land. I don't *care* what happens then.' Alf Brown snorted and checked his Sten gun. It made a harsh, metallic snap. He stood up and wiped his lips with one hand and then gazed all around him. 'Fucking Jesus,' he said, 'what a scene. It's a right bleedin' circus.' David stood up behind him, saw the other boats all around them. The planes rumbling above were now lost in a dark haze, but the thunder of the bombardment was still deafening. David looked straight ahead. He saw the coastline materializing. It was covered in a pall of black smoke, and fires winked on and off. 'They're giving 'em hell,' someone said. 'There won't be anyone left to fight.' Sergeant Cowie, coughing lightly, said: 'Don't worry, lad. You'll get *your* fair share.' The boat dipped and rose up. Water roared in all around them. The men cursed and jumped back and sat down and started checking their weapons. David moved up beside Robert. They both studied the land ahead. It was emerging, taking shape, coming inexorably towards them, and the destroyers were turning parallel to it, taking firing positions.

'The beach should be secured when we get there,' Robert said. 'I only hope to God that it is.'

Far ahead, between the mine-sweepers, the sea suddenly exploded in innumerable columns of grey sludge. Then they heard the actual blasts: they made a muffled bass roaring. The columns continued to mushroom between the mine-sweepers, soared slowly, hypnotically towards the sky and dissolved to white spray. The mine-sweepers moved left and right. They were between the destroyers and the land. They were heading for the beaches and the landing craft were following them, weaving in mysterious patterns, the sea bursting up over them. More mines were exploding. The spiralling columns multiplied. The water soared up and outwards and curved back to the sea as white spray. Then the destroyers started firing: their big guns belched flame and smoke. The thunderclaps came one after the other in rapid succession. David saw the explosions: they were yellow and red; they flared up and died away in the dark hills coming closer, first a dozen, then dozens, then hundreds, one after the other.

The sea roared around David. The sky screeched and thundered. The boat rocked up and down, and smashed through the churning sea, and the other boats were leaping all around it, wreathed in drifting black smoke. David looked at the approaching hills. He saw the outlines of small towns. They were dark and flames flickered up from them, and more shells were exploding. The whole coastline seemed on fire. The fire rained down from the sky. It came from the battleships, from the cruising destroyers, from the massive armada of fighter planes and bombers that was now filling the skies beyond the hills. The spectacle was stupendous. The whole world was flame and smoke. In that din, in that blazing holocaust, there could be no tomorrow.

David couldn't believe it. It was beyond his comprehension. He held his Sten gun in one hand, gripped the gunwale with the other, and stared straight ahead in a trance, his eyes filled with the flame and smoke.

'We're going in,' Robert said. 'That's Le Hamel. We're going in now.'

He turned to the men, told them to check their equipment. Sea-sick, confused, already tired beyond belief, they did as they were told and then crouched down and looked at each other. Some started cracking jokes. At least one man was praying. Another vomited and wiped it from his tunic and blushed with embarrassment. David looked beyond the cox-swain. The land was now very close. He saw hills of brown and green, a small town, a cavalcade of destruction. The earth heaved and spit fire. The fires turned to boiling smoke. The explosions rumbled and roared beyond the thunder of the guns, geysered up in jagged fingers of red and yellow, spitting brown earth and sand. And now the destroyers were all around him. They towered above the landing craft. They were moving east and west, and then they fell far behind as the landing craft raced towards the beach. The beach was a boiling hell, its air thick with sand and smoke; it rushed towards them and the other growling boats – and then the whole sea exploded.

David jerked his head around, felt the blast of the explosions, heard the roaring as the water boiled up and cascaded above him. The boat rocked and shuddered. The men tumbled against each other. David gripped a metal rail and glanced around and saw the grey, churning sea. At first he thought they were alone. He heard the chilling whine of shells. The sea exploded all around him and then he saw the other boats, thirteen of them scattered here and there, between the geysering water. The whole commando was isolated. The fourteen boats were heading for Le Hamel. The whining shells and the roaring, soaring water told him something was wrong. He gripped the rail tightly. The sea exploded between the boats. The deck beneath him rose up with a harsh drumming sound and he plunged to the left and hit Robert. The noise was catastrophic, it ricocheted around his head. His head hit Robert's pistol and he felt a sharp pain and then Robert grabbed his shoulders and pulled him upright. He glanced around him. The sea exploded between the boats. The boats were weaving between the huge, roaring geysers, leaping up, crashing down again.

'Damn it!' Robert shouted. 'The beach hasn't been cleared! That's a German battery firing from Longues! They'll cut us to pieces!'

The shells kept raining down. The sea roared and exploded. The water mushroomed in huge green-white columns and rained down on their heads. David clung to the rail. The deck rolled and dipped beneath him. The sea roared and swept across the whole boat and almost tore him away. He gripped the rail tighter, blinked his eyes, heard the shouting, looked back into the hull and saw the men tumbling together, a tangle of arms and legs, their helmets floating in water, their rifle barrels rattling and clanging as they righted themselves. Then David looked at Robert. Robert was kneeling by Private Fowles. The private's portable radio was crackling and someone was talking. The sea exploded near the boat, roared and soared above their heads. The boat was picked up and almost turned over, but then it crashed down again. Someone screamed out with pain. The men rolled about and cursed. The sea close to them settled, but more violent explosions tore the sea between the other landing craft. David put his head down. The deck heaved and groaned beneath him. Robert turned from the crackling radio, climbed sluggishly to his feet, and then bawled into the right ear of the coxswain.

'Swing east!' Robert bawled. 'We'll have to try somewhere else! The colonel wants us to drift to the east until we find somewhere safer! Turn now! *Turn it round!*'

The coxswain did as he was told: he followed the other thirteen boats. They headed out of the line of fire of the battery in Longues, following the smokey, blazing coastline, moving slowly, drawing closer each minute. The exploding sea fell behind them. The naval bombardment thundered above them. The whole of the coastline, from Le Havre to Cherbourg, resembled one fantastic inferno. They drifted about a mile. It took a very long time. The sky above was filled with planes, the destroyers cruised back and forth, and the guns of the distant naval fleet formed a thunderous concerto. Front and rear were more boats: they were heading in for different beaches. They seemed small and faraway, weaving left and then right, and between them, in the sea, was a holocaust of mushrooming explosions. The Germans hadn't been eliminated. Their inland batteries were retaliating. Now blasted by the fleet, bombed and strafed by the planes, they continued to bombard the invasion forces with murderous shell fire.

For the moment, the commando was safe. The men had time to look around them. They saw the other boats in the distance, churning forward, bouncing roughly, rising up in slow motion on heaving mountains of sea before spinning and tipping their men out and crashing back down again. Then the men looked at the land. It was now very close. They saw a cove behind a barrier of steel pylons and concrete cones, and the other boats were heading in towards it, getting ready to beach.

'Prepare to disembark!' Robert shouted. *'We're going in now!'*

The men took their positions. The beach rushed out to meet them. The sea was calm and the boat ploughed through the waves with a rhythmic vibration. David stood beside Robert, held his Sten gun in his right hand, felt nothing but a feverish curiosity, an intense need for dry land. The boats raced towards the beach. There were forested hills above it. Steel pylons and concrete cones and hedgehogs littered the water.

Then the very air exploded. It roared and filled with fire. There was a wall of shooting flames to the left and the noise was appalling. A fierce heat swept over David. He saw the nightmare to his left. He saw a boat rising roaring, in a jagged, yellow furnace, burning bodies and parts of bodies spinning above a water sprout, their screams daggering through the noise of the explosion as they dropped down again. The boat crashed bottom up. It screeched and twisted on the steel below. The water hammered and roared all around it, then more shells exploded. David saw that blazing pyre, heard the screams of the burning men. He saw arms waving from the water, heads bobbing, helmets floating, and then more shells fell down amongst them and the whole sea went mad.

The explosions were everywhere. The sea soared up between the boats. Another boat ground across a buried mine and was hurled on its side. The men poured out of the hull. The boat crashed down upon them; crushed some of them while others bobbed up from the turbulent water. More explosions rained down. The boiling fountains soared upwards. The men still in the sea were wriggling out of their webbing or crying for help as their packs dragged them down. A boat smashed through some pylons. The pylons screeched and started buckling. The boat climbed up the bent steel, roared furiously in midair, then slowly toppled over and crashed down on the now collapsed pylon. Its ramp fell open. The men jumped into the sea. It came up to their waists and they started wading for the shore and then the water all around them started spitting.

David heard the machine-gun fire; it was high-pitched and savage. The sea spat around the men and the men threw up their arms and started screaming and sinking beneath the waves. David grabbed hold of the gunwale, felt helpless and unreal. He looked at Robert and Robert was shouting, then it all went to pieces.

David thought he heard the shell. It was a screech that filled his head. It screeched down and spread out above his head and exploded around him. He felt himself picked up. He spun around and saw the sea, saw a jumble of helmets and berets and faces, then crashed into the heaving, howling deck and rolled onto his back. The roaring filled his ears. A tunnel of water engulfed him. It smashed his head back to the deck and tore the gun from his hand and left him floundering and choking up sea-weed. He shook his head and blinked his eyes, heard the roaring and shouting, got to his hands and knees and looked around him as the boat started spinning. The beach turned away from him. He saw an open stretch of sea. He saw Robert kneeling down beside the coxswain whose head was all bloody. David didn't know what was happening. His head was ringing and he felt sick. The coxswain had slid down the bulwark and his face was split open. David saw the bone beneath, the thick blood pouring out. He retched and then climbed to his feet and men tumbled around him.

The boat was still spinning, drifting parallel to the beach. David saw the other boats, and at least four were smoking while some were grinding onto the beach. It all seemed unreal. The beach was spitting and exploding. The men were being cut to pieces by machine-guns as they waded for shore.

Then Robert stood up. He looked despairingly at David. He stepped forward as the sea soared up behind him with a fierce, screaming roar. Robert plunged towards David. The front of the boat climbed towards the sky. Robert crashed into David and they both tumbled backwards and fell into the men piled up behind them. David's head hit something hard. The blow almost knocked him senseless. He blinked and found a boot in his face, arms and legs wrapped around him. Then the deck was spinning over, screeching against a greater roar. David saw the grey sky, watched it spinning around him, closed his eyes as the sea rushed towards him, plunged down through cold darkness.

He thought he was drowning. It was dark and had no bottom. He assumed that he was still plunging downward, but then he suddenly resurfaced. A vivid light filled his eyes. The air rushed into his lungs. He choked and coughed water and breathed deeply and then glanced all around him. He saw a pair of wide eyes. Hands were splashing before them. He tried to reach out but his pack dragged him down and he grabbed at the straps. His fingers felt numb. The water closed all about him. The sea exploded and spun him around and he shot to the surface. He gasped for air again, heard a cataclysmic roar, was picked up on a wave and swept forwards as he groped at his harness. Another face floated past. The mouth formed a desperate O. The man screamed out for help and then sank and David's boot kicked his sinking head. David's fingers found a buckle. He tugged wildly and thoughtlessly. He started sinking and then the pack slipped away and he kicked to the surface. The vivid light washed over him. The sea exploded all around him. He saw a body spinning up through the air, arms outstretched as if crucified. Then he swallowed more water, spat it out and kicked his legs. He heard the whine of the machine-guns, saw the sea spitting water, saw blood bubbling from a floating beret and started swimming towards shore.

He was fifty yards out. Other men floundered around him. They were shouting and swimming and trying to help each other as the grey, convulsed sea heaved on all sides, sprayed by shells and machine-gun fire. David just kept swimming. He was now near the pylons. He saw two sappers high up on a large concrete cone, kneeling over, bodies framed by the dark hills. They were fixing an explosive charge. The concrete suddenly spat lines of dust. The sappers threw up their arms and started dancing and splashed into the water. Then the charge went off: the obstacle exploded with a fearsome roar. Steel rods and pieces of concrete and clouds of dust filled the air where the cone had been.

David kept swimming. He fought against the force of the blast. He saw the smoke clear away and then a squat landing craft rattled over the remains of the obstacle and headed on towards the beach. The beach still seemed far away. It was exploding and spitting sand. A group of men were congregating beyond the shell fire, at the base of the hills. David wished he were there with them. His lungs seemed to be on fire. He reached a pylon and hauled himself up and just lay there, exposed. Bullets whined above his head. A man clutched his head and sank. Another landing craft crashed onto the beach, its ramp down, the men pouring out. David clung to the pylon, heard the roaring and whining. He knew that death was all around him, but it didn't really seem all that important.

Eventually he looked up. The sea was suddenly quite calm. The Germans had stopped firing and he heard the sea breeze, and the sand swirled across the nearby beach where the survivors were resting. David slid into the water. It came up to his chest. He forced himself forward, past a still smouldering landing boat, past the silent, drifting corpses, past the helmets and berets that floated upside down in the gentle green waves of the Channel. He finally reached the beach. It was pock-marked with black holes. The men squatted on their haunches or lay flat on their backs or simply stood there and stared all around them. David flopped down on his belly and closed his eyes, too weary for words.

# CHAPTER EIGHT

OF the fourteen landing craft that had headed for the beach, four had been destroyed, nine were damaged and beached, and only one had managed to return to the mother ship. Sixty men had already been killed or seriously wounded, and the rest of them, scattered over at least a mile of beach, were exhausted and in very low spirits. Only half had arms and equipment, others had no boots, and some had actually swum ashore minus trousers. Nevertheless, during the three hours that it took the colonel to collect his scattered men, the beach itself was a hive of activity. With their ramps down, the nine damaged landing craft could now unload their mass of equipment and supplies: Bren gun carriers, 'flail' tanks, bazookas, mortar guns, ration boxes and boxes of ammunition, reels of wire and thick rope. While the 'flail' tanks rumbled off the beach and up the road, their chains lashing the ground before them, detonating all mines, and clearing the way along the route the men world take, the men themselves helped to unload the LCTs, sort and check the equipment, and tally up the full extent of their losses. These were considerable. They were close to catastrophic. Fifty percent of the ammunition and most of the rations had been lost; four tanks had gone down with the sunken LCTs; and, most important, all the radios had been smashed and they were left with only the local field telephones. Effectively this meant that they no longer had communication with the American and British forces on either flank; more brutally, it meant they couldn't call for help.

After sending his more reliable NCOs along the beach to collect his scattered men, and after ensuring that the medics were taking care of the wounded, the colonel, now soaked, his face covered in wet sand, called his officers together for a briefing. He told them that they were drastically short of equipment and ammunition, that they no longer had contact with their American and British link-up forces, and that they had no choice but to head on for their target.

'We're about fifteen miles from Port-en-Bessin,' he said quietly. 'We will go on a forced march from here, engaging the enemy where we can, and collecting any weapons we need once we've sent them all packing. We will go through Les Roquettes, here, and La Rosière, here, and then we'll take Port-en-Bessin from the rear, as was originally planned. I don't think it will be easy, but I do think it will be better than sitting on our backsides on this beach. We'll move out in two hours. We can't wait longer than that. Meanwhile get Private Fowles, who's a genius with radios, to check out every radio, salvage every working part, and then put the bloody pieces together until we've got something working. *We must make that contact!*'

David felt it was impossible. He was too exhausted for optimism. Relieved that Robert was still alive, that most of his platoon was still in shape, he nevertheless felt totally deflated, almost tired beyond measure. He didn't want to fight this war. He wanted to lie down and sleep. He wanted to forget the landing craft, the hellish noise of the gunfire, the bodies and limbs floating in the water, his rising sense of sheer helplessness.

He left the briefing with Robert. They went down to the water's edge. Private Fowles was there and they gave him the good news, and then they looked out at the fleet. It seemed very far away, was wreathed in black smoke. The planes were flying to and fro, the ships' guns were still thundering, and the Rhinos and gunboats and landing craft and barrage balloons were swarming in across the Bay of the Seine. By now the din was palatable. It was even beginning to sound natural. It came from the sea, from the sky and from inland, a constant screeching and thundering, an ever-present distant rumbling, the sound of bombs and bullets and collapsing buildings: an extraordinary millennium. David wanted to be rid of it, wanted to lie down and sleep. He wanted to swim out to the fleet, huddle up in a bunk, and awaken in the summer air of England. It all seemed far away now.

'How do you feel?' Robert said.

'I feel awful,' David said.

'You're not alone,' Robert said. 'We all do. It was a terrible start.'

'And what about Port-en-Bessin?'

'What about it?'

'Do you think we'll reach it?'

'We have to,' Robert said. 'We just have to. We have to link the two fronts up.'

There was a sudden loud explosion. The sea soared up around some pylons. The pylons buckled and spun lazily through the air and fell back to the sea. David didn't even flinch. He gazed obliquely to his left. He saw some demolition engineers swarming over the adjoining obstructions, carrying cables and packs of explosives, framed by the morning light.

'The men are tired,' David said. 'They're close to total exhaustion. They've lost most of their weapons and equipment; there's not enough to go around.'

'We'll get the weapons,' Robert said. 'We'll have to take them off the Germans. We'll give what we've got to our very best men, and we will use those men to tackle the Germans. We'll build up as we go along.'

'That doesn't sound simple.'

'No,' Robert said. 'It's not simple. It will cost a lot of sweat and a lot of men, but that's what we will do. Now let's get organized.'

They walked across the beach to the base of a hill, where their men were now gathered. The men were wet, covered in sand, seemingly quite exhausted, but were beginning to get their spirits back. Surrounded by equipment, they were checking the remaining weapons and dividing them up amongst themselves. Two of the privates, who had come in without trousers, were trying on the spares of their mates, blushing as they did so, grinning rather sheepishly, and suffering a great deal of ribaldry. Private Fowles had already picked out the most likely radio from the smashed sets scattered around him, and was busy taking parts from the others.

'Can you do it?' Robert said.

'I don't know, sir,' Fowles replied. 'I think so, but it's a matter of trial and error, and that could take a long time. When do we leave, sir?'

'In an hour,' Robert said.

Fowles rolled his eyes. 'No way, sir,' he said. 'At least not unless I really strike it lucky. I'll just have to try all these parts, and I can't do that marching. I'll just take them all with me.'

'A fucking circus,' Alf Brown said. He was checking his beloved Sten gun. 'We waltz in like a bunch of fairies, they shove their dicks down our throats, and they don't even have to show their faces. We deserved what we got.'

Robert looked at him with distaste. 'We didn't deserve what we got,' he said. 'We got what we didn't expect, and that's something quite different.'

'Yes, sir,' Corporal Brown said, grinning up at his platoon leader. 'I hear you loud and clear, captain, sir. I stand reprimanded.'

'I want to see them,' Private Morgan said. Morgan had fought at the Vietri Pass. 'I want to see those fucking Kraut bastards. I want to make them all pay.'

Robert, obviously relieved that the men were beginning to hate the enemy again, gently took Sergeant Cowie by the elbow and led him away. Once out of earshot of the men, he asked the sergeant how he thought the men would hold. The sergeant said that they were all very tired, that they were despondent about their losses, but that they were growing more bitter about the Germans and this could be a good thing. He felt that the sooner they engaged the enemy the better; that a victory, no matter how small, would put them back in the right mood. Robert thanked him, told him to organize as quickly as possible, then walked across to the beach dressing station with David.

Private Turner lay on his back on the sand, his brown eyes clouded with pain, blinking and licking his lips, glancing vaguely around him. His left leg had been split open from the thigh to the ankle and was now held together, temporarily, by large safety pins. There was blood all over his tunic. His right arm had been crushed. He was sweating and his whole body twitched, as if out of control. He looked terribly young.

Robert knelt beside him, stroked the private's feverish brow. 'How are you?' he said gently. 'Are you comfortable? Do you feel any pain?'

The young man's lips shivered. His brown eyes rolled around. They stared at Robert, but they didn't really see him, then they rolled away again.

'Mam?' he said. 'Here, mam. The jam. Oh, Patsy. Dear Patsy . . .'

His voice trailed into silence. His eyes closed and he started mumbling. Robert sighed and stood up and looked at David, and then they walked back to the men.

After an hour, they were organized. The whole commando was on the beach. They milled about in their separate platoons and got ready to march. The demolition men had finished. The tanks had moved on ahead. The men moved out in long, irregular columns, kicking up clouds of sand. David stayed close to Robert. He now had another Sten gun. He was lighter than he had been on the boat, and he felt strangely naked. They marched up a dirt track. The forest closed in around them. They could hear the flail tanks up ahead, their chains lashing the ground. No mines went off. The trees blotted out the sun. David held his gun tightly, felt tired and disconnected, and tried to keep himself from falling asleep. His thoughts scattered and spun; his throat was dry and he felt ill. He knew that action was imminent, that it could not be avoided, and yet he felt nothing other than great fatigue. He had never been so tired before: it made him numb and unreal. He looked at the snaking column, at the long lines of men, and he wondered how they managed to stay awake, if they felt any fear.

He closed his eyes and his thoughts collided. The rooms of Oxford, the flat in London. He saw Katherine and Robert and himself in a pub by the river. Brown eyes, flowing hair. Where was she? Was she dead? Katherine gone and the major-general somewhere else, supervising the landings. No pain in the thought. The brown eyes, the flowing hair. The coffin lowered and his own parents weeping while the general quivered. The general, the major-general. Grey eyes and great rage. No sign of rape and he will hang and he's somewhere out here. Who was he? Where was he? Was he with the link-up forces? An American, a GI, a staff-sergeant, probably not far away. Not that it mattered. Not that it meant anything. The forest rustling and the sound of marching feet and the draining exhaustion. All that death on the boats. The terrible noise, the shocking violence. Far away now, a thing of the past, and not ever quite real. You couldn't feel grief here. It was not the place for mourning. It was quiet and your feet kicked up leaves and you couldn't think straight.

He didn't know what was happening. The men were spreading out all around him. They were shouting and some-one mentioned the Jerry guns and they kept spreading out. The whole column was breaking up. The men were advancing in long lines. They were weaving through the trees in scattered groups and David saw Robert's back. Robert was waving his right arm, holding up his swagger stick. He had a Sten gun in his left hand and he was running and the whole platoon followed him. Their feet kicked up the leaves. Sunlight flashed on and off them. They were weaving left and right through the trees, over three hundred men. '– fucking bastards that shot us!' Corporal Brown? Private Morgan? '– Oh, God! The safety catch! Jesus Christ . . .' Who was that? Someone nearby. Hard to tell in the gloom. Sunlight flashing on and off, across his eyes, across their backs, a pack jumping, a man stumbling and running on, someone suddenly shrieking.

'*Mortar*!'

The forest ahead exploded. A whole series of explosions. One, two, three, then an abrupt, hellish din and the trees blown apart. The men around David fell. He followed them down and looked ahead. The earth shuddered and noise piled upon noise as he saw the explosions. It was quite a bit ahead. The men were scattered in all directions. They were waving their hands and shouting and falling down beneath a deluge of foliage. The grass waved before his eyes. The earth shuddered beneath his body. Explosions tore the ground ahead, hurling earth and trees upwards, causing men to spin around and fall down and writhe about and scream loudly.'– fucking bastards!' Corporal Brown. 'Keep down!' That was Robert? He looked up and saw Robert holding a field phone, a hand over his left ear. More explosions. The sound of rifles. The savage roar of a machine-gun. Robert shouting, 'Stay down! They're going in! They're making contact right now!' Who was making contact? What was happening and where? He looked ahead and saw sunlight flashing off the running men, saw the mortar shells exploding between them, saw them spinning and falling. It went on for a long time. Lumps of trees flew through the air. 'What the fuck?' Corporal Brown. 'Let's go get 'em! What the fuck's going on?' More explosions ahead. A constant demoniac noise. He looked ahead and saw shadows in motion in a rainfall of foliage. They were obviously being slaughtered. The shells exploded, the machine guns roared. Earth shot upwards and a tree disintegrated, its branches whipping through other trees. You take pride in your guilt. Gin and tonic, no ice. I'm sorry, but I can't call it off; we run mobile laundries. He looked straight ahead. The ground shook, the air roared. The men out front had disappeared and the gunfire was further away. More explosions in the forest. The trees tearing and crashing. A long silence then one last explosion, leaves drifting to earth.

'Alright! Let's move out!'

David climbed to his feet, brushed the earth from his battle-jacket. All around him, in the gloom, in the striations of sunlight, the other men were standing up and doing the same. 'Fucking great,' Corporal Brown said. 'The first engagement and we miss it. I just wanna see a Jerry face. That's all I ask.' He was holding his Sten gun, his cockney face outraged, glaring at Robert as Robert went to the telephone and asked permission to advance. The permission was granted. They moved forward again. They heard gunfire up ahead, spasmodic, finally tapering off. They moved carefully through the gloom. Beams of sunlight flashed over them. They came to where the mortar shells had fallen and the wounded were lying. The ground was littered with shell holes. The upturned trees were charred. The medics knelt down among the wounded men with hypodermics and bandages. The men shuddered and groaned softly. Some were burnt black and blistered. A man carefully took his hand from his throat and watched the blood splashing out. Then they passed the wounded men, went up a steep incline. A few more shots rang out above their heads, and they heard lots of shouting. They moved slowly between the trees, watched for land mines and booby traps. They reached the top and the sunlight washed over a grey German bunker. There were dead all around it.

David tried to take it in. It was revolting; obscene. The men had used grenades on the bunker and the roof had collapsed. The dead lay in the rubble. They were bloody and torn. Their arms were outflung and their clothes were in tatters and the white dust of the debris covered charred skin. He saw a torso minus limbs, the tripe of someone's belly. A German lay with a dead Marine across him, a knife in his throat. The German guns had been destroyed, were split and badly bent; someone had put grenades down the barrels and blown them apart. David had to avert his eyes. He felt ill, yet strangely calm. Only now did he realize that he had seen dead men before – in the water, on the beach – and that it was something he was already adjusting to. He felt a little surprised.

The surviving men were jubilant. They were slapping each other's backs, cracking jokes as they wandered between the dead and picked up various weapons. The weapons were passed around. The men collected ammunition. They loaded up and reformed into platoons and moved forward again.

David fell in beside Robert. The men formed up behind them. The whole commando filed down the other side of the hill and found themselves on a winding country road. The morning sun shone down upon it. The breeze was cool, but growing warmer. Around them was a checkerboard of fields and thick woods and streams. The road was sunk between high banks. That made it potentially dangerous. If they were attacked from the land or by air, there would be no escape. The colonel ordered them off the road, made them climb the right-hand bank. The men climbed up the bank, scrambled through the dusty hedgerows, and swarmed into the grassy field at the other side.

The field was long and broad. It was surrounded by trees and bushes. At the far end was another bank, surmounted by hedgerows, running from one side of the field to the other. The men spread out and marched towards it. They had their weapons at the ready. The tanks rumbled on ahead, flattening the tall grass, their chains lashing the earth.

There was a sudden vicious roar. Two lines of dust curved through the men. Some of them jerked and fell down, while the others shouted and raced on ahead. 'Crossfire!' Robert howled. David looked at him blankly. 'They've got machine guns at both ends of the field behind that bloody hedgerow!' Robert suddenly started running. Corporal Brown raced ahead of him. The men out front were running through the murderous fire, heading straight for the hedgerows. More of them fell down. The machine-guns kept roaring. Bullets lashed through the grass in long lines of spitting dirt, the lines darting back and forth and then crossing and racing back out again. David ran with his men, saw the other men fanning out. They were running at the crouch, weaving crazily from left to right, shouting loudly and firing from the hip at the unseen machine-gun nests. Then the mortars opened up. The ground roared and exploded. Men were hurled up and outward, weapons flying from their hands, limbs akimbo and flailing about and smashing back to the earth. A mass of earth showered over David. He blinked his eyes and kept running. His lungs were on fire, he saw the mass of men before him, and the ground roared and soared up all around him. He didn't think to raise his gun. He held it down by his side. He saw Private 'Pip' Hunter glancing at him with large glistening brown eyes. Then the earth boiled all around him. The breath was sucked from his burning lungs. He heard a scream and he thought it was himself, and he seemed to be spinning. His whole body crashed into something. He saw light and swirling darkness, reached out and grabbed hold of the earth and spat dirt from his mouth. Something tugged at his shoulder. He was jerked and pulled around. He opened his eyes and saw Pip looking down, his brown eyes large and frightened. Pip's mouth opened and closed. '– all right, sir?' A shriek. The ground exploded and roared up behind his head and he fell upon David. David gasped and closed his eyes. The earth showered down on his face. The explosion reverberated and passed away and was replaced by the other harsh sounds. The machine-guns. The rifles. The men shouting and the explosions. The pressure left him and he got to his knees and saw Pip's trembling smile. '– I thought you were –' Blinking repeatedly. Shaking his head from side to side. Glancing around at the mass of running men, the boiling earth, the winking guns. David stood up very slowly, feeling dizzy and bruised. He wiped dirt from his face and smiled at Pip, and then Pip started running. David followed him, gasping, his lungs burning, feeling nothing but the urge to keep moving and avoid the explosions. They roared and boiled all around him. The men were jerking and falling down. He saw a line of dirt racing towards him and whipping on past. The hedgerow was coming closer. He saw a tank climbing up the bank, saw figures in field grey jumping back and then scattering before it. A bunch of men were behind the tank, were crouched low and firing. The back of the tank rocked up and down, seemed to hang in the air, then it roared and crashed down on the other side. The men swarmed up the bank. They poured down the other side. The explosions suddenly stopped and there was the sound of rifle fire and he heard a lot of shouting and screaming. David just kept on running. He didn't know what else to do. He saw Private Tanner standing just ahead, blinking bewildered eyes. '*Keep going!*' David screamed. He hardly knew he was doing it. He punched Tanner between the shoulders, and the private jerked and then raced ahead. They reached the bank at the same time, clambered over the dusty hedgerow, stumbled down the other side and heard the cheering of the men to their left. They both froze with the shock of it.

The tank had crashed down on the German mortar crew. Both the gun and the men were crushed. David saw a flattened mass of blood and bone, but it left him unmoved. He was gasping for breath, felt dizzy and a little sick. His head was spinning and he felt quite confused, divorced from himself. The men were examining the German dead, stripping them of weapons and ammunition. They were all dead but one, and that one was trying to crawl away. David watched him, fascinated.

It was too hideous to be real. The man's legs had been crushed, there was a huge hole in his back, and he was lying flat out on his belly and pulling himself forward. Then Corporal Brown stood over him. He looked down at the man and grinned. He aimed his gun at the back of the man's head and then pressed the trigger. The man's head disappeared.

'*Brown!*'

It was young Pip. His gentle eyes were inflamed. He dropped his rifle and dived at the corporal, his two hands outstretched. Brown laughed and stepped aside, grabbed Pip by the collar, held the boy at bay while he kicked and swung with both fists. Corporal Brown was laughing. He started to shake Pip to and fro. The boy swung with his fists and started sobbing, and then Brown let him go.

'You bastard!' Pip sobbed. 'You rotten bastard!' He turned away and sat down.

Corporal Brown laughed, wiped his lips with one hand, glanced around him with a broad, mirthless grin.

'Fucking kids,' he said. 'You wouldn't credit it. Whose side is he on?'

Robert stepped forward, his face pale and drawn, walked up to the grinning cockney and glared at him, his whole body shaking.

'No more!' he hissed. 'You understand me, Brown? If I ever see you do that again I'll have you sent down.'

The corporal spat on the ground. 'Excuse me, sir,' he said. 'It's just that I thought it was a war and that's what we'd been trained for. I'm a little confused, sir.'

'We kill when we have to,' Robert hissed. 'We don't make a pig of ourselves.'

The corporal grinned at him. Robert turned and walked away. He went along the bank towards the other machine-gun nest, his swagger stick under his right arm, his Sten gun in his left hand. David sat down on the grass, put his arms around his knees. Pip Hunter was sitting just beside him, wiping his eyes dry.

'Sorry, sir,' he said to David, his eyes red, his face pale. 'I just couldn't stand to see him do that. There was no need for that.'

David smiled at him. He couldn't think of what to say. In fact, he could hardly think at all; he felt numb and unreal. The confusion. Corporal Tanner. His fist thumping Tanner's back. His own voice, that strangely feminine wail, urging Tanner to run. Could that be called leadership? Was that how you fought a war? Was it nothing but exhaustion and confusion, this developing numbness? He tried to think about it. He saw the cockney, Corporal Brown. The corporal had his Sten gun above his head and was performing a jig. Some of the men were giggling. Some were looking disgusted. The corporal kicked up the dirt around the dead and then tripped on a gun barrel. He fell on his backside, stretched out as if sleeping, placed his hands behind his head and closed his eyes, a dreamy smile on his face. Pip Hunter was looking at him. The boy's face was drained and shocked. Still almost a child, he had nevertheless stopped to help David. Now David thought about it. It had all been quite confusing. He had run as the other men had run, without motive or thought. No, it wasn't leadership: it was instinct or accident; he had travelled very far along a tunnel of narrowing imperatives. The ship now seemed like a dream, like something from another time. He felt that he had been here for years, in the noise and the chaos. It was something to think about. It was something he couldn't grasp. He felt older than he had ever felt before ... and impossibly tired.

'Up and out! Up and out!'

David couldn't believe it, didn't think they would demand it. Exhausted, confused, a little ashamed and strangely proud, he saw the men around him climbing to their feet, offering jokes and loud groans. He looked at the dead. A fine dust fell upon them. They looked like a bunch of charred rags, and their silence was total. David climbed to his feet. He felt the aching of his bones. He remembered being picked up and shaken in that awesome explosion. How strange it had been. How miraculous it now seemed. Picked up and smashed down to the earth and now marching ahead. He had been close to death. That fact gave him his touch of pride. He had not yet fired his gun or faced up to a live German, but he had come through his baptism of fire and that was at least something.

The men marched across the next field. The morning sun still shone upon them. The tall grass brushed their legs and formed a shimmering sea all around them. Planes rumbled to the east and west. They heard the sound of distant conflict. Obviously, far away, on both flanks, the invasion was progressing. The men continued marching. The wounded lay across the tanks. The tanks moved out ahead with their chains lashing down in search of mines. No mines went off. The field stretched out before them. They moved around a farmhouse that had been hit by a stray bomb and was now a heap of rubble and broken beams. They saw some bodies in the ruins. A young girl lay in the mud. She had dark hair and her eyes had rolled back and her left breast was missing.

'Liberation,' Robert said, walking side by side with David. 'We've come to liberate the French people and this is what happens. Simple farmers. My God . . .'

David didn't reply. He tried not to look around him. They passed the farm and the wind brushed his face and he suddenly felt lost. A strange anguish shook him. He thought of the girl in the mud. He wanted to run back and pull the girl's dress down and cover her up. Then he thought of Katherine. It all suddenly came back to him. He had a vision of her sliding to the ground with the blood draining out of her. The image was shocking; it shook him leaf and bough. He felt lost, disconnected from himself, as he glanced all around him. He saw the swaying yellow grass, the bright haze of the sky. There was a hill and the men were swarming up it and David was with them. He saw this David as a separate entity, as but one of three hundred men. The men were climbing the hill, swarming down the other side . . . then he heard the harsh chatter of the guns and he knew it would start again.

Only now did he feel the fear, sweeping over him, scalding him. It was mixed up with the twin image of Katherine and the farm girl, with the sudden, startling memory of himself in the water, his boot kicking the head of the man beneath him, helping to drown him. David knew fear on the instant. It was a fierce new experience. He had known fear before, but never with this vicious, gnawing vividness. The guns chattered beyond the hill. He heard shouts and a muffled roar.

Mortar, he thought, with his fresh, soldier's instinct; they're using mortars at the bottom of that hill: that must be the first town. His stomach heaved, his throat tightened. He ran surrounded by other men. He scrambled up to the top of the hill and started weaving between trees. There was a brief loss of sunlight. The leaves rustled around his feet. He saw Pip Hunter trip and fall down and quickly jump up again. Pip glanced nervously around him. Amazingly, he seemed embarrassed. He saw David and he blushed and then smiled and started running again. The men ahead were all shouting, weaving in and out of shadows. A loud roar and the ground nearby erupted and blew a whole tree apart. Private Tanner slapped himself, cried out and fell down, rolled around on the ground and then sat up and shook his head dazedly. David just rushed on past him. He sensed that Tanner was all right. He heard the shooting from the drop not far away and then he plunged into sunlight.

'Mortar! *Get down!*'

The noise rushed down upon him, spread around him and enveloped him. He threw himself to the grass and then the roar shook him senseless and he found himself sliding downhill. He was rolling, turning over, swallowing pebbles and dirt, reaching desperately to get a firm hold on the shifting, pulsating earth. Then he stopped, almost retched, shook his head and glanced around him. Feet pummelled the grass, the boots kicking up earth, and then something smashed into his head and he fell back again. Boot, he thought dazedly; someone kicked me with their boot. He sat up and shook his head and looked down and saw a man's bloody body. The man was obviously dead. He was lying across Private Morgan. Private Morgan was struggling to get up, bawling, 'Get this cunt off me!' David slithered down the hill, heard a chattering machine-gun. Beyond Private Morgan's head, not far below, he saw the walls of grey buildings. He grabbed hold of the dead man. He saw Morgan's flushed face. Morgan pushed at the dead man as David pulled, and the corpse rolled away. '— fucking stupid! Couldn't move —' The earth erupted close by. They heard the roar and they covered their heads as it rained down upon them. Then Morgan was up and running. He ran and slithered down the hill. The men ahead of him were racing for the town, braving gunfire and mortar shells. David also did this, plunged through fear and out again, slithered downhill as the bullets whipped around him and some other men fell. He reached the bottom, saw Robert and Corporal Brown. The battered cockney was squatting on the ground with his gun in his lap. Private Tanner was also there. He had blood on his forehead. '– fucking branch!' he was shouting at Private Morgan. '– tree blew up and it hit me!' The ground roared and boiled nearby. A grey smoke swirled around them. When it cleared they were face down on the ground, rising slowly, uncertainly. Private Morgan spat dirt. Coporal Brown cursed in anger. Private Tanner sat back against a tree with his eyes wild and blind. 'I'm hit,' he said quietly. He looked down and fell sideways. He rolled onto his back and his stomach slopped over his thighs. He choked once and then died. Another screech split the air. The ground exploded and dirt rained down upon them and made them start running.

David didn't know where to look. He felt the burning of his lungs. He saw houses and walls of grey stone and some hedgerows and gardens. The men were pouring through the village. They were firing as they ran. They were darting in and out of dark doorways, guns spitting, arms arching. Then grenades were exploding. An upper window blew out. A shapeless body flew out with the glass and thumped down on the road. David stopped at a low wall. He was not far from the houses. Sergeant Cowie was kneeling down on the ground, waving the men on. '– snipers! Watch the windows!' The men raced all around him. The sergeant stood up and started to run and the earth roared beside him. David slid behind the wall. Earth and stones showered down upon him. The roar subsided and he jumped to his feet and ran up to the sergeant. Cowie was on his hands and knees. He was shaking his head from side to side. '– bloody mortars!' he said, and spat a tooth out. '– *got to get rid of them!*' David helped him to his feet. He heard the roar of a jeep. He looked up and saw the jeep racing towards him with some men in the back. They were dressed in German uniforms. They were firing sub-machine-guns. The wall behind him exploded and he jerked his gun up and then he heard a louder roar at his side. The jeep went into a skid, screeched around in clouds of dust. A man threw his hands up and toppled out and then the whole jeep turned over. Someone screamed and a man went spinning. The jeep crashed down upon him. It bounced up and then smashed into a wall and rocked wildly from side to side. David glanced to his left. Corporal Brown just kept firing. He was firing and he sprayed the rocking jeep and then it burst into flames. There was an awful, anguished scream. A trapped man flapped his arms. He was blazing and his scream was demented and then it suddenly stopped. Corporal Brown raced ahead. David followed him automatically. He almost stopped when he saw three civilians crouched low in a doorway. It was a woman and two children. The woman wore a black scarf. She had her arms around the children, and the boy and girl were covering their ears. Sergeant Cowie raced up to David. '— thanks,' he said. 'Bloody near thing.' David blinked and then ran across the road and saw some men kneeling down. '— up above!' A finger jabbed. '*That fucking cunt in that window!*' David looked and saw a bobbing silhouette and then a dull winking light. The gun's chatter was vicious. The wall near his head spat dirt. He jerked back and saw Pip Hunter's eyes, large and brown, almost luminous. Pip was pointing across the road. He wanted David to look across. David looked and saw the black hole of a door beneath the sniper's high window. '— *Captain Lovell!*' Pip was shouting. '— *gone in there to get him!*' David glanced up at the shadow in the window, heard the gun's vicious chatter. Robert, he thought: he's gone in there; he shouldn't have done that. Then the window exploded. Glass and wood showered on the road. There was a silence and then a Sten gun shrieked, then silence again. David looked up at the window. He saw a shadow waving arms. '— got the fucker!' '— good man!' '— Let's get going!' They jumped up and started running. They were crouched low and weaving. They heard shots from the other end of the street, but nothing came their way. David felt his lungs burning. He crashed into a wall. He held his gun up and looked inside the house and then Robert came out. Robert stood in the doorway, glanced up and down the street. There was still the sound of gunfire, but in general the fight had been won. No prisoners were being taken. The desultory firing told that tale. The Marines were jumping in and out of doorways, putting an end to it.

David got to his feet. He felt exhausted beyond measure. The air was filled with smoke, occasional shots still rang out, and the scattered houses were pockmarked with bullets and great gaping holes. Then David saw the civilians. They were emerging slowly from the ruins. They seemed shabby and were covered in dust and their faces were strained. An old man advanced on David. He was wearing braces and a black beret. He was toothless and white-haired and gaunt, and he kissed David's cheek.

'God bless you, my son,' he said.

# CHAPTER NINE

THE three early morning battles were merely the prelude to a whole series of large and small skirmishes The three-hundred plus commando, their ranks gradually diminishing, were spread out across the fields, walked through orchards, crossed rivers, were met by isolated pockets of resistance and some larger grouped forces. The fights were bloody and exhausting. They gained weapons, but lost men. They were fired on from the hedgerows, had to charge pillbox entrenchments, and were frequently faced with routing the Germans from the farms and small villages. It was an arduous fifteen miles. The Germans materialized and vapourized. They came with rifles and machine-guns, with mortars and tanks, with grenades and bayonets and knives. The commandos were well spread out. The fights were usually localized: first a group on the left flank would engage in a skirmish, then a group on the right would take their turn; now the men out in the front would find themselves in a crossfire, then the men in the middle would be mortared. It was bloody and confusing, made all planning obsolete: a battle on the left flank might rage for thirty minutes before the men on the right flank got to it. In this sense there were no rules: some men hadn't yet fired their rifles. They would hear the noise and see the battle raging without being involved in it.

To David it was a dream. It was a tempest without end. He saw the smoke, smelt the cordite, felt the jarring explosions, and ran forward until he was stopped or until the battle itself was done. He was in the thick of the action, saw the dead and the dying, fell down and stood up and ran on – but it made little sense to him. He saw the Germans at a distance, rarely met them face to face, would see them as vague, field-grey figures, darting backwards and forwards. They threw up their arms, spun around and fell down; they were flung into the air on clouds of black, boiling earth and they tumbled back down like rag dolls. Sometimes David fired his Sten gun. He aimed at the distant figures. The gun would roar in his ear and pummel his right arm, but he never knew if he had hit someone or not. It was all too confusing. It was a series of fragmented images . . . Pip Hunter in a doorway, kneeling over, retching violently, glancing up and then blushing with embarrassment and grabbing his rifle and running. A sudden swirl of dust, the roar of a collapsing wall, a pair of hands waving desperately through the murk, a French civilian's taut face . . . It was exhausting and shocking. It stripped him down to the bone. He felt excitement and then he felt a fear that made the images brighter . . . The ground erupting ahead. Corporal Brown rolling cursing. Robert firing his Sten gun from the hip, the smoke swirling around him. Then Brown running crouched low, shouting crazily and firing, suddenly standing by a pillbox, dark against the white concrete, bending down, a grenade through the black slit, jumping sideways, exploding. The awesome, destructive roar. The boiling clouds of steel and powder. Brown rolling down the slope and then running back up and standing over the ruins and firing his Sten gun, shouting, *'Take that, you fuckers!'* It didn't seem real, was beyond comprehension; there was no time to stop and think about it, no way of forgetting it. Just another small village. The deadly gardens and hedgerows. The walls exploding and the bodies tumbling out and the screams of the dying men. He saw civilians in the streets. They were crouched low and running. They were wandering back and forth in a daze while their homes disappeared. A dead horse in a paddock. An old woman in the rubble. A young Frenchman with an FFI armband and beret executing three SS men with a pistol . . . David saw it and turned away, tried not to see too much, moved forward through the smoke and the noise, fired his gun.

watched men falling. He didn't know if he had hit them. It could have been anyone. He stuck close to his men as they moved across the fields around the farms, through the small, deadly villages, against a wall of resistance. He didn't quite comprehend it, didn't think it was himself. He heard the noise as he choked in swirling dust and rolled through chaos and screamed.

A man raced from a barn. He was a blur against the trees. The barn exploded behind him, roared and collapsed, and the man flung up his arms and staggered sideways and shrieked and fell down. He was obviously a German soldier. He was kicking his legs and howling. Corporal Brown swung his arm and the grenade sailed through the air, then the earth around the man boiled and roared and the man disappeared. They all ran towards the barn. David saw its dark interior. Men were clawing at the wreckage and groaning as flames crackled over them. Some grenades were thrown in. David fell to the ground. The grenades went off, one, two, three, four, and the noise was appalling. A machine-gun roared and stopped. The flames flickered over silence. David stood up and ran around the barn with the rest of his men.

He felt exhausted and numb. It went on and it never stopped. They crossed fields, took the farms and small villages, and it wasn't yet noon. His sense of time was destroyed. He existed only in the present. He lived for moments of dread and relief, for each stunning reprieve. He tried not to see the Germans, never saw a live face, only saw them as figures in the distance: puppets dancing in fire and smoke. The noise hammered all thought from him. The constant movement made him dizzy. He saw the dead and they were covered in dirt and did not look quite human.

They finally arrived at their objective. They were in the neighbourhood of the port. Before the town was a large wooded hill filled with German shock troops. It was now just after noon. The men were totally exhausted. They had fought so many battles, some large and some small, that they no longer knew where they were, perhaps cared even less. They sprawled around a wide field. A gutted farmhouse was nearby. A patrol was deployed to check it out and returned with the all clear.

The men stretched out and rested. They looked haggard and filthy. The wounded were laid out around the tanks and bren-gun carriers and jeeps. The wooded hill loomed above them. It seemed dark and mysterious. Beyond it lay the town of Port-en-Bessin, their ultimate objective.

The colonel called his officers together. The men huddled beneath a tree. The tree cast a large shadow, offered coolness, an invitation to sleep. The officers looked as if they needed it, seemed shrunken and weary. They smoked cigarettes and listened to the colonel, who was bright-eyed but drawn.

The colonel told them that they were completely cut off, that the radios were still not working, and that he had sent some patrols to make contact with the Americans who were to supply the artillery support for the attack. In the meantime, he added, the men should be allowed to just rest.

The officers nodded, yawned sleepily and rubbed their eyes, then scattered to await news of the artillery support.

It was just after noon.

David walked away with Robert. They both sat beside a tank. They drank some water and then Robert lit a cigarette and inhaled with real pleasure. He put his head back, closed his eyes and sighed deeply. David thought of him entering that village house, and a shiver slid through him. He would not have done it himself. Of that he was quite certain. He wondered if he could *ever* do that, but it seemed inconceivable. There were men and there were soldiers. David obviously was the former. No longer offered a choice, he would do what he had to . . . but beyond that he didn't dare think about. They would now attack the town. It seemed impossible that they could do so. Decimated, cut off, exhausted almost beyond measure, it was ridiculous to think that they might now take that hill, take the heavily defended town beyond it, then take the two hills beyond the town without due rest and care. No one could expect it; no man could be expected to do it. It was farcical, a bizarre, cruel joke, and David wanted no part of it.

'Well,' Robert said, 'we finally made it. It was a rough fifteen miles.'

David didn't reply. He didn't know what they had made. They had made it to this hill, but this was only the beginning, and he couldn't feel grateful for that. In fact, it didn't bear thinking about.

'Are you all right?' Robert asked.

'Yes,' David said, 'I'm all right. I'm just so tired I can't even think straight. I don't think I can move.'

Robert smiled but kept his eyes closed. He was smoking his cigarette. His Sten gun lay on the ground between his feet, a reminder of things to come.

'You've been blooded,' he said. 'You've had your baptism of fire. And I must say, you came through it rather well. I hope you feel proud of yourself.'

'Rather well?' David said. 'I came through it rather well? I don't know what you mean by that remark. I hardly did anything.'

'You led your men,' Robert said.

'I wouldn't quite define it that way.' David played with the oats around his legs. 'I can't remember leading anyone.'

'You never do,' Robert said. 'You never remember it very clearly. But that doesn't mean you haven't done your job... and in your case, you have.'

David glanced around him. The whole field was filled with men. They were lying in the grass, sitting under the trees, leaning against bren-gun carriers and tanks, some sleeping, some smoking. David wondered who they were. He wondered how they had come this far. They did not seem the kind who could do what they had done and would soon have to do all over again. Yet they had swarmed and fought around him. He had felt their shifting mass. They had ran through swirling smoke into gunfire, some killing, some dying. These men were just like him, had also moved as in a dream; once ordinary, now touched by death and horror, they had subtly changed. He felt this change in himself, felt the awe and the wonder. He had come through a murderous terrain, and as yet he was untouched. Yes, he had done his job. In some strange way he had done it. He had been through that dark place and emerged, and was not finished yet.

'What did I do?' he asked of Robert. 'What precisely was my job? I fired my gun and I advanced with the other men, but I didn't lead anyone.'

'You're wrong,' Robert said. 'You were an officer and you were present. You didn't turn back and you didn't fall apart – and that's all that matters. You'll do the rest when you have to.'

David wondered about that. He wondered how he could ever do it. He wondered how he would ever know what to do and how to then do it. His training hadn't prepared him for this. No training could possibly do so. It was chaos – and survival meant luck, no more and no less. He didn't think he would do anything, didn't even want to try. He would simply stick close to his men and hope for the best.

'What about Port-en-Bessin?' he said. 'Do you think we'll manage to capture it?'

'We have to,' Robert said. 'We have to link the two fronts up. It's not a question of will we or won't we; we quite simply have to.'

David smiled. 'You're a good Marine,' he said. 'Your devotion to duty is quite extraordinary. I wish I could share it.'

'Don't you?'

'No.'

'You're just tired,' Robert said. 'You're exhausted and you've lost track of things, but you'll fight when you have to.'

'Perhaps,' David said. 'But that's no guarantee of success.'

'I must admit,' Robert said, stubbing out his cigarette, 'that we aren't in the best of situations. Naturally it would have been easier if things had worked out as originally planned. We didn't anticipate those guns. We didn't plan to land a mile east. We didn't plan to have a fifteen-mile forced march through the country and arrive at our objective with depleted forces. Now we're totally cut off. The damned radios still aren't working. If the Americans don't give us that support, I don't know what we'll do.'

The Americans couldn't give support. The patrols returned with this news. The Americans had also had a very difficult landing, and were currently still pinned down on the beaches. There would be no artillery support.

The officers groaned at the news. The colonel bit his lower lip. He turned around and glanced up the wooded slopes and he didn't seem happy. He turned back to his men.

'We can't do it,' he said. 'There's no point in even considering it. That hill is literally swarming with troops and we have to reduce them. *We must have a radio!*'

Private Fowles was working at it. He was surrounded by bits and pieces. He had a radio that he thought had looked hopeful, but now he was sweating. Private Fowles had thick glasses. The sun flashed on and off them. He said he thought he could do it if they gave him more time, so David patted him on the shoulder and left him to it and went back to see Robert.

'I don't know,' David said. 'He's working at it. It's all up to him now.'

The men lolled in the field. The sun shone down upon them. They slept or played cards or smoked cigarettes, and some even wrote letters. Occasionally the ground shuddered. They heard far-off, muffled rumblings. The noise came from both flanks and they saw the glint of aircraft in the distance. The war was still going on. The allied armies were advancing inland. The men cursed and started wandering back and forth and stretching themselves. Some glanced up at the hill: it seemed ominous and challenging. The men wandered back and forth or simply rested, waiting for something ... Time passed very slowly. The afternoon sun was cooler ... Private Fowles suddenly let out a shriek and the men all looked at him.

The radio was working.

The colonel immediately got in contact with the Navy and asked for gunfire support, to be followed by low flying attacks. The Navy confirmed and the surrounding men cheered, then prepared for the assault on the hill. Some of them plugged their ears; others nervously checked their weapons. The NCOs raced to and fro and regrouped their platoons. Finally, an hour later, when the bombardment was about to start, the men were massed around the base of the hill, kneeling down at the ready.

David sat beside Robert. Their men were kneeling behind him. They looked up at the thickly wooded hill, at its long, shifting shadows. A breeze murmured through the trees. They saw the fall of brown leaves. The hill was dark and exceedingly quiet, as if devoid of all life. In that sense it was deceptive. The hill was heavily fortified. It was swarming with tough,

seasoned troops who would offer no mercy. David shivered.
His throat was dry and he felt sweaty. The men around him
were fixing bayonets, and that made him feel sick. He didn't
want to see the Germans, didn't want to see their faces: he
wanted to view them as distant, faceless shadows and pretend
they weren't real men. The bayonets clicked into place. The
sound made David twitch. He held his Sten gun and looked up
at the hill as the shadows raced over it. The hill was frightening.
It held the fear of the unknown. It was dark and its silence was
watchful: a strange, brooding force. Looking at it, David
shivered. He felt cold and distraught. He was shaking and he
tried to conceal it from the men all around him. The men were
muttering to one another, were softly cursing and swopping
jokes. They were massed around the base of the hill, and they
were all looking up it.

The sky suddenly shrieked. There was a booming in the
distance. The shriek turned into a roar and then the shells were
exploding, a holocaust of fire and boiling smoke, tearing the
trees apart. The ground beneath the men trembled. The hill
above boiled and roared. The trees cracked and split apart and
flew upwards on huge waves of yellow flame. Then the trees
crashed down again. Leaves and branches flew through the air.
The trees mangled together and tore each other to shreds and
collapsed back to the earth in clouds of dust. The whole hill
seemed to shake. Fires were breaking out all over it. The flames
flickered and soared up and spat in swirling smoke and bright
sparks. They heard the booming in the distance. The shells
shrieked and whistled down. The explosions thundered and
tore the trees apart and filled the air with black boiling smoke.
Then they saw shadowy forms. The shadows were small and
faraway. They were racing to and fro and waving arms, and the
flames soared about them. More explosions shook the hill.
Tree trunks spun in the sky. They plunged through the
boiling smoke and crashed down on the small, shifting shadows.
A shadow turned into a torch. The torch rolled down the hill.
It passed through a cloud of smoke and reappeared and
crashed into a tree. The bombardment went on and on. The
trees flew up and then collided. They hit the ground in clouds
of dust and then bounced up, and rolled and slid down the

hill. More shadows burst into flames. The flames rolled down the hill. The smoke boiled up and covered the whole hill and blotted everything out. The watching men started coughing, blinked their eyes and covered their ears, looked up and saw the dark swirling smoke, the flickering flames. The bombardment went on and on. The ground shook and the noise was deafening. The hill erupted and the trees flew through the air, trailing black smoke and fire. The destruction was enormous. It seemed that nothing could survive it. The explosions stopped and a silence descended and the smoke hazed the hill.

'Jesus Christ,' someone said.

The planes came almost immediately. They filled the air with a low rumbling. They flew in from the sea, first the bombers, then the fighters, one formation, then two and then three, swooping over the hill. Again there was the noise. Again the hill burned and boiled. Again the trees were torn up and sent flying through the air and crashed back to the earth in clouds of dust. The dust billowed up with the smoke. The smoke spread out and swirled. It swirled around the explosions, around the spitting, crackling flames, formed a tapestry of dark grey and yellow, tinged with orange and purple. The bombs fell in neat lines, fell slowly and obliquely. They dropped in amongst the trees and the ground roared and erupted, and the trees were torn apart by the blasts. Then the fighter planes came in. They screeched down and up again. White light flashed all around them as their guns strafed the seething mass below. Then the German guns retaliated. Tracers spat through the sky. Flak burst amongst the planes in black clouds, and a plane started blazing. It turned and then twisted, went into a steep spin. Smoke trailed out behind it, the flames flickered around it, then it disappeared behind the roaring hill and they heard the explosion. The other planes continued strafing. They screeched up and down again. Their guns roared and poured a murderous stream of fire into the smoke and the flames.

The waiting men were silent, were stunned by the spectacle. It was difficult to comprehend that some Germans still lived, that the fire and the smoke and the explosions had not killed them all. The planes were now beyond the hill. They were attacking the town itself. They climbed up and disappeared behind the hill and then they climbed up again. The waiting men could hear the noise. It was muffled and faraway. It was an accelerating thunder that shook the ground on which they were kneeling. The sky beyond the hill darkened, was filled with a crimson smoke. The tracers criss-crossed between the diving planes; the clouds of flak multiplied. It went on a long time. The hill itself was settling down. The clouds of smoke were drifting backwards and forwards, over charred trees and flickering flames. Finally there was silence. The planes flew back towards the sea. There was a roar from the men around David, and he hurled himself forward.

The base of the hill seemed far away. It had seemed close before. The ground rose just a little, and the smoke swirled around him and blinded him. He heard the shouting men about him. He couldn't understand a word. Their packs jumped up and down as they ran, and their weapons were rattling. David ran behind Robert. He saw Robert's swagger stick. It was strapped to his belt and it was bouncing up and down as he ran. Robert was holding his Sten gun. Corporal Brown was close behind him. The smoke was swirling down from the hill and made the running men hazy. David felt his legs moving, felt the pounding of his heart; his throat was dry and the smoke stung his eyes and he felt a bright fear. The ground was rising more steeply now. It crumbled and slid beneath his feet. He saw a tree and he darted around it and the earth loomed before him. He was finally on the hill. He registered the thought automatically. He was breathless and his lungs were on fire, and then he heard Robert shouting.

The ground erupted behind him. He heard shouting and screaming. A blast of hot air pushed him forward as dirt rained upon him. He gasped and kept going. There were more explosions all around him. The men ran and clambered up between the trees, dark and shapeless in swirling smoke. Another explosion nearby. David slammed into a tree. He felt stunned and he wiped blood from his nose and saw a mass of dark figures. They were weaving between the trees, all crouched low and shouting: more explosions and the sheets of yellow flame in the murk with trees toppling. Men jerked up and fell back, wrapped themselves around the trees, rolled down the hill, knocking the legs from beneath other men. David shook his head and ran. The hill was steep and he was slow. Another roar and the earth boiled around him and slammed him back down. He clawed at some foliage, spat dirt from his mouth. Someone grabbed him by the collar and jerked and he was back on his feet. Still blind, he stumbled forward, saw the ground rise up ahead, heard the firing of rifles and Sten guns, saw flames spitting through darkness. The men were vague in the smoke. They were jumping behind trees. A vicious roar and dirt jumped from the earth in long, ragged lines. A man flung his arms up. Another shrieked and spun around. Another tumbled down the hill towards David and rolled right on past him. Bullets whipped above his head, made a vicious, hissing sound. A shell exploded at the base of a tree, and the tree toppled over. It crashed down on some men. The men screamed and were buried. David saw an arm flapping beneath the trunk as he skirted around it. '*Medic! Where's the medic?*' The earth boiled up and roared. David clung to a tree and let the blast pass away, and then he hurled himself forward again, hardly conscious of doing so.

The men were shouting all around him, were kneeling down and firing, and David looked up and saw some hazy figures, crouched low, racing left and right. The men around David fired: their guns seemed to roar in unison. Some of the men ahead flung their arms up, spun around, tumbled down. David dropped to his knees, heard the roar of a machine-gun. Branches flew apart and fell on his head as he raised his Sten gun. '– *fucking machine-gun nest!*' Corporal Brown? Private Morgan? He glanced up and saw Brown stepping forward, his right arm curving over. The rifles continued firing. David stared up the hill. The hand grenade exploded, tore a bush from its roots, and two shadows jumped up and fell back as the roar filled his ears. Leaves and twigs whipped around him. Corporal Brown raced up the hill. David found himself rushing towards the bushes which quivered dementedly. He stopped and gasped for breath. A cloud of dust fell back to earth. The machine-gun had been blown onto its side and the barrel was bent. David blinked and almost choked. He saw a face like a pomegranate; beneath the strips of shredded flesh and bloody pus he saw the dull glint of bone. The earth roared up behind him. A body tumbled against him. He fell forward and jumped up again and saw Pip Hunter's eyes. The eyes were dark and luminous. He saw a smile and they were gone. He climbed out of the trench and clambered upwards and threw himself down. *'Grenade!'* Someone nearby. The blast curled itself around him. He felt the light deluge of earth, and looked up and a man was there. The man was standing just above him, eyes bright beneath his helmet, broad and pale-faced and very calm as he looked right at David. David jerked his Sten gun up. The man was firing from the hip. David fumbled for the trigger and the man spun around before he found it. A rifle cracked in his ear. Private Morgan muttered something. '– fucking cunt!' and then David was running, jumping over the dead man. He crashed into Pip Hunter. They almost bounced off one another. Pip fell down and got back on one knee and stared up at a bayonet. David saw the thrusting German. The Sten gun roared in his hands. The German shook and staggered back and then very slowly slid down a tree. David didn't see him fall, didn't know that he had killed him. He saw Pip jumping up, heard him shout, felt the thrashing of bushes. A man rushed straight at David. David saw the bayonet. He stumbled back as Pip swung with his rifle at the man's weaving head. David heard the dull thud. The man grunted and jerked sideways, rolled into a bush as the rifle flew out of Pip's hands. Pip staggered forward slightly, found his balance and stooped down. The German rolled around and reached for a grenade as David squeezed on the trigger. The gun bucked in his hands. It made a fearsome, shocking din. The earth around the German exploded and spat leaves and twigs. The German quivered spasmodically, shook violently and thrashed the ground; his body arched and he slapped his own face and then David stopped firing. The German didn't move. Numerous small holes pumped blood. David looked at him as Pip grabbed his arm and started pulling him uphill. '– *thanks, sir! Didn't notice!*' Pip released him and ran. He wove between the hazy trees. David lost him in the dark swirling smoke, heard a roar, fell through silence.

He opened his eyes again, shook his head and looked uphill. Leaves were raining down over his head and sharp twigs stung his face. Pip was kneeling beside him. He was firing his rifle. Sergeant Cowie was waving his right arm and shouting at Robert. '— *to the left! Behind that clump of trees! Dug in behind there!*' A tree was burning close to Robert. The flames flickered beyond his head. He looked up and turned around and waved to David. '— *and you, Corporal Brown!*' David and Brown ran forward. The cockney was grinning crazily. Robert waved his left hand and the cockney nodded. '—*machine-gun! Grenade!*' Bullets lashed the nearby branches; the roar of the machine-gun was deafening. Robert slapped David's back and he got up and ran beside Brown. They ran left and then right. The bullets hissed and whipped about them. Corporal Brown broke to the right and David ran to the left of the roaring trees. He couldn't see the Germans. He saw the barrel spitting fire. He knelt down and aimed his gun at the bushes and the gun roared and bucked. The leaves around the tree danced. The gun started turning towards him. He couldn't move and then he saw Corporal Brown coming in from the other side. Brown ran and swung his arm. David saw the grenade spinning. It disappeared behind the trees and exploded with a shattering roar. David jumped up and ran. He raced Brown to the dugout. He ran up the raised bank and started firing before he stood on the rim. The bullets lashed the foliage. He heard a scream and looked down. A man was struggling beneath some bloody corpses, his mouth open, eyes wide. He looked despairingly at David. He screamed within a cloud of smoke. Corporal Brown stood on the rim and fired his gun, and the man's scream was silenced. David ran around the hole, saw some men leaping across it. A German rose from the bushes straight ahead, a Mauser gun in his hands. Someone shot him; the gun dropped and he jack-knifed, flopped forward as David raced past him, his own Sten gun roaring. Corporal Morgan was just ahead. He had turned back and was weaving. He staggered out of the swirling smoke, fell against a tree trunk, held his hand out to touch David's face and murmured, 'Jesus, it hurts.' His hand touched David's cheek. He suddenly coughed and spit blood. He slid down David's body and rolled over and his chest was a mass of blood. David knelt down and checked. Corporal Morgan was dead. David stood up and ran through the trees and then burst into sunlight.

# CHAPTER TEN

THE town stretched out below him. It was burning and smoking. The narrow streets were filled with rubble, houses blazed and collapsed, and dark figures scurried through the swirling smoke. David choked and gasped for breath, hardly knew where he was, saw a sunken flak ship in the harbour, heard the roaring of guns. Bullets stitched the earth around him. He ran forward and almost fell. He slammed into Corporal Brown and the corporal stumbled forward and cursed. The sudden sunlight was fierce. It made David's eyes sting. He glanced down the slope that led to the town and saw that it was swarming with men. The Germans were retreating into the streets. The Marines were advancing against heavy fire. Some mortar batteries from the town were bombarding the slope, the explosions decimating the forward platoons. The earth roared and rained down. Shapeless figures spun through the air. Bullets made the dirt spit and jump up in oblique, darting lines.

David suddenly ran forward. He knelt down beside Robert. Glancing back, he saw the smouldering forest, heard more shouting and shooting. '– *half still on the hill!*' Robert bawled. '*We're going straight for the town!*' David rubbed at his eyes, felt immeasurably tired. He was aching all over and he felt a little faint and light-headed. A sudden roar of soaring earth. A blast of hot air slapped at him. He crouched low and put his hands across his head and felt the dirt rain upon him. Then he blinked and looked up, saw Robert lifting one hand. The hand swayed in the air, seemed to hang there forever, then dropped and sent them all running forward.

The earth bellowed and shook, exploded, surged upwards: a shapeless mass somersaulted through the smoke and crashed down and lay still. David gasped and shook his head, felt the burning of his lungs. The noise hammered at his ears and tugged his clothes, and he felt himself falling. The ground blew up in his face, a tunnel of earth swirled around him: he saw sky and then the dark swinging earth and he crashed down again. He didn't let go of his Sten gun, started rolling down the hill. He crashed into another man who was struggling to get up, and they both tumbled down the hill together. The earth shuddered and roared; they choked in clouds of swirling dirt. The other man fell away and David slithered to a halt and reached out and put his hand in something wet. He blinked and looked up. A man lay face-down before him. His back was split open from the neck to the hip, and David's hand was groping inside that large wound. David retched immediately, vomited and rolled away, wiped his hand on some grass and stood up and saw men all around him. They were racing through the smoke, aiming downhill as they ran, and David gasped at fresh air and then turned and followed them down.

'*Lieutenant! Over here!*'

He heard Sergeant Cowie's voice, saw his hand wave through the murk, turned around and slithered down the last few feet while bullets whipped all about him. He crashed into the huddled group. They were sheltering behind a bren-gun carrier. Up above, an unknown private fired the gun, swinging wildly from left to right. Robert stood up and looked, quickly dropped back again. Bullets whipped all around them and ricocheted off the bren-gun carrier. '*They've broken through!*' Robert shouted. '*They're going in! We better go now!*' The ground exploded nearby. A shower of earth swept across them. The bren-gun was roaring above their heads and then it suddenly stopped. They heard the private sobbing. '– *Oh my God! Jesus Christ!*' The barrel made a ringing sound as it dropped down, as Robert jumped up. The private was sobbing wildly. His whole tunic was soaked with blood. He looked about eighteen years old, and he held his own body. '*Get him down!*' Robert shouted. '*Let's get the hell out of here! Get him down!*' Sergeant Cowie clambered up. He got in beside the private. He held him under the arms and started lifting him out and the private threw his head back and screamed. Sergeant Cowie froze immediately. '*— you're tearing me apart!*' The private threw his head back and screamed again while the earth boiled behind him. Sergeant Cowie dropped down. Earth and stones rained on the private. The private fell back, then Cowie reappeared and started pushing him over. The private screamed again. '*— you're killing me! Jesus Christ!*' Cowie stopped and Robert hammered the carrier with the stock of his Sten gun. 'Get him down!' Robert bawled. '*We've no time! Just get that man down from there!*' Cowie grabbed hold of the private. The private screamed and lashed out. '*You bastard! You're tearing me apart! Oh my God, you're killing me!*' Cowie forced him over the side. Some other men pulled him down. The private kicked and then fell on the ground and stared wildly around him. He was bloody and sweat-stained, his eyes wide, body shivering. He reached over and took hold of Robert and hissed, 'Please, sir, just shoot me!' Robert knelt down beside him, stroked the boy's fevered brow. 'Here,' he said. 'Morphine. Take this. The medics are coming.' The boy swallowed the pills. His head fell back on the ground. He stared around him and then he screamed, '*Kill me! For Christ's sake, it hurts!*' The men all looked away. Only Corporal Brown kept looking. Robert stood up and looked at Sergeant Cowie and shouted, '*Let's go!*' The bren-gun carrier suddenly roared. Its tracks mangled the soil. It lurched forward and the men fell in behind it and followed it down.

David stuck close to his men. The bren-gun carrier was protecting him. He glanced obliquely to the left and saw a street running down to the harbour. The street was littered with bodies. The dead and wounded lay in the rubble. Marines were jumping in and out of doorways, and grenades were exploding. The bren-gun carrier rumbled on. David stayed close behind it. He heard the vicious hiss of bullets all around him, heard the roar of the mortar shells. Then Sergeant Cowie shouted. He was up on the bren-gun carrier. '*— mortar crew! And a bloody machine-gun! Blocking the street!*' The bren-gun carrier stopped. The bren-gun suddenly roared. A mortar shell exploded just ahead, then the answering fire came. Bullets ricocheted off the carrier. '– *bloody hell!*' Sergeant Cowie. The bren gun stopped firing, then it started again, then it stopped and Sergeant Cowie started shouting. '– *the machine-gun! Got it! They're scattering! Go for them now!*' The men suddenly broke apart. David passed the bren-gun carrier, saw the sides of two houses and a street and a mountain of rubble. The Germans were clambering over the rubble. They were firing as they retreated. A three-man mortar team was blocking the street and attempting to cover them. David raised his Sten gun, started firing as he ran. The men around him were all doing the same and two Germans flopped over. Then the mortar went off. The third German shrieked and fell. There was a roar behind David and he knew the bren-gun carrier had been hit. He didn't stop to look around. Sergeant Cowie, he thought. Corporal Brown raced ahead and riddled the bodies around the quivering mortar gun. He then kicked the gun over. The other men swarmed around him. A fusilade of shots came from the street and a few men fell down. David dropped and rolled away, rolled into a brick wall, slithered onto his belly and saw Pip Hunter hugging the far wall. Pip was running crouched over. The wall exploded above his head. He disappeared inside a doorway, then his hand reappeared. The grenade sailed through the air, fell beyond the piled rubble. Some Germans jumped up and started running, and then the blast caught them. It was an explosion of white dust. It hurled the Germans in all directions. Their bodies thumped back on the mountain of rubble and slid down and were still.

David jumped up and ran. He raced toward the piled rubble. He heard the crunch of glass and stones beneath his feet and then a German materialized. He had jumped from a doorway, was four feet away. David fired without breaking his stride and the German fell back. His head hit the door frame. The gun dropped from his hands. He looked in amazement at David and then he started to fall. David fired another burst. The German quivered like an epileptic. He went down and David saw a flash of red and then he reached the piled rubble.

Corporal Brown was halfway up it, his arm swinging above his head. Bullets ricocheted off the broken stones and the dust kicked around him. There was a deep, resounding roar. A man screamed, someone bawled. David heard the voices shouting in German as he climbed to the top. Bullets whistled past his head. He fell flat on his belly. He was choking in the dust and he coughed and then blinked and looked down. Corporal Brown was standing there. A wounded German was shouting. Corporal Brown was spraying the street from left to right and more Germans were falling. The rubble suddenly erupted. Corporal Brown disappeared. The smoke cleared and Corporal Brown was in a doorway, beside young Pip Hunter. Pip was pointing along the street. David looked and saw a tank. It was lumbering directly towards him and its barrel was dropping. David lay there, hypnotized. A hideous roar came from beside him. He looked up and sergeant Cowie was there, holding the bren gun. The sergeant shook as the bren gun roared, started spraying the advancing tank. The tank fired and the shell screeched above them, exploded beyond them. Then Pip was running forward. He ran straight for the tank. A group of soldiers were massed behind the tank, and Corporal Brown fired at them. The soldiers ran around the tank. Pip fell down on the ground. Sergeant Cowie and Corporal Brown fired at once in a murderous cross-fire. The Germans started to scatter, ran to both sides of the street. The tank lowered its gun while Cowie and Brown sprayed the fleeing soldiers. The soldiers spun around and fell. One man crawled, another writhed. Bullets spat around the sergeant and he grunted and fell to his knees. He dropped the gun. Pip jumped up and ran. David reached up to pull the sergeant down, but he just started jerking. '– *over here!*' David's shriek. The bullets spitting around the sergeant. The sergeant twitching and jerking and falling back as Pip jumped on the tank. David reached out for the sergeant. The dirt jumped up around him. Holes appeared in his tunic and blood squirted out and splashed on the rubble. '*Sergeant Cowie!*' Screaming wildly. The sergeant huddled up and twitching: the dirt jumping around him and more holes in his clothes, the blood spurting. David looked and saw Pip. Pip was jumping off the tank. A muffled roar and the tank shook and stopped as Pip rolled on the ground. More bullets stitched the sergeant. The sergeant was unrecognizable. Corporal Brown was standing out in the street, spraying calmly from left to right. A man climbed from the tank. He was screaming and wriggling. He was on fire and he beat at his own body and fell back inside. Another explosion from the tank. Yellow flames shot up around it. Pip crouched down behind it with his arm swinging over his head. The firing Germans exploded. They fell about in clouds of dust. The ground around Sergeant Cowie stopped spitting, and then David crawled up to him.

Sergeant Cowie was still alive. His mouth opened and he gasped. His whole chin had disappeared and his body was one mass of blood. David looked along the street. The remaining Germans were disappearing. They were escaping around the corners at the end of the street, but more Marines were already moving in on both sides. Sergeant Cowie's mouth hung open. There was no jaw to support it. His eyes were closed and his breathing was harsh, and then it stopped and he died.

David picked up his Sten gun, slid slowly down the rubble, saw Pip and Brown hugging the wall as they moved up the street. David ran up beside them. He patted Pip on the shoulder. The boy looked at him with glistening brown eyes, then smiled shyly and walked on.

The street was littered with dead men. The wounded cried up from the dirt. More Marines were pouring down the street behind them, searching the houses. Shots continued to ring out. Grenades went off inside the houses. A Marine standing at a shattered upstairs window heaved out a dead German. Corporal Brown spat on the ground. He kicked a corpse at his feet. ''Ello, Fritz,' he said. 'How's yer doin'? You sprechen sie English?' He laughed and walked on. Pip's brown eyes went left and right. They all came to the end of the street and saw the bomb-shattered harbour. All the houses were in ruins. A German flak ship had been sunk. The civilians were emerging tentatively from the ruins, glancing warily around them. Some were more alive than others. They kissed the weary Marines. Corporal Brown patted the rump of a girl who looked at him with large eyes. 'What's my prize, luv?' he said.

The girl gazed around in awe. The air was filled with smoke, the whole town was in ruins, and more Marines were pouring into the harbour. They were lighting cigarettes, dangling their legs over the water. Some were looking out at the distant fleet, but it didn't seem real to them. More shots rang out. The mopping-up was continuing. The men pouring into the harbour were filthy, and desperately weary.

David sat down to rest. Corporal Brown sprawled out beside him. Pip leant against a wall with his eyes closed, licking his parched lips. David also closed his eyes. His head started to spin. He plunged down through a sickening chaos, a dark tunnel of fear. He opened his eyes again, felt the strength draining out of him; he started shaking and he wanted to sleep, but he didn't dare do that. It had all been too much. His body couldn't take much more. He was drained out, hollow, an empty shell, and he felt close to nausea. Then Robert walked towards him. The afternoon sun shone around him. He stopped and gazed thoughtfully at David, and he seemed very old.

'Get up,' he said. 'We have to take the hills. We're regrouping right now.'

David couldn't believe it. It went beyond the bounds of reason. He put his head in his hands and closed his eyes and the world started spinning. He looked back up at Robert. Robert nodded and smiled gently. Corporal Brown rubbed his eyes and stood up and kicked lightly at Pip. David felt a great despair. It filled him up and consumed him. He watched Pip getting wearily to his feet and gazing dazedly around him. Pip also rubbed his eyes, seemed remote and a little shaky. He glanced around at the other milling men as they groaned and stood up. David looked beyond the town. He saw the two hills rising steeply. They were littered with pillboxes and trenches and a mass of shellholes.

David didn't want to go up there. He didn't think he could do it. The very concept was beyond his comprehension, and yet he stood up. Robert patted him on the shoulder. Robert's green eyes were clouded. He seemed gaunt, the mere ghost of himself, and he offered a weary smile. David picked up his Sten gun, went to join his remaining men. They followed the column marching through the town, towards the two soaring hills.

Their boots crunched on the rubble. They climbed up and down again. The houses on both sides of the street were still smouldering and crumbling. Walls rumbled and collapsed. Sparks shot up into the air. The smoke drifted from shattered windows and broken walls and drifted up to the sky. Shots were still ringing out. A holding action was in progress. He saw a group of Germans marching under guard, their hands on their heads. The prisoners were gaunt and weary. Some civilians spat at them. The Germans stood aside to let the column pass, and David tried not to look at them. Instead, he surveyed the hills. They rose one beside the other. The sun shone down upon them and he saw the white glint of pill-boxes.

David closed his eyes briefly. His head started to spin. He felt sick and he opened his eyes again and saw the men fanning out. They were heading for the left-hand hill, were swarming up the lower slopes. They started running and the German guns fired and it started again.

David fell down and crawled, stood up and ran on, weaved through the roaring earth and the swirling smoke as if divorced from himself. The hill was dry and barren, littered with shell-holes; it shuddered and bellowed and whipped around him and made his head reel. He crouched low and kept running. It was a steep, arduous climb. A gun roared and stitched the dirt around his feet and he threw himself sideways. '— *machine-gun!*' He saw Robert. Robert waved a hand wildly. A group of men broke away and charged uphill, firing their rifles. One was racing out ahead. He was tugging at a grenade. David saw the low wall of a bunker, a black slit spitting fire. The man shuddered and staggered back. The grenade fell from his hand. '*Look out!*' and the other men started scattering as the grenade rolled towards them. Too late. An explosion. The men danced in clouds of earth. Their arms waved and they fell and rolled back down, their bodies twitching spasmodically. Robert slapped David's shoulder. They both jumped up and ran. The machine-gun in the black slit swung towards them and started to roar. '— *to the left! A grenade!*' David turned left and ran. He saw a line of dirt arcing towards him and he tugged at his belt. He crashed into a bush. The ground erupted around him. He was deafened and the dirt rained upon him as he crawled up the slope. The sun cut through the murk. He saw the white wall of the bunker. The barrel of the machine-gun was poking out and spraying the men below. David held his grenade. The roar of the machine-gun was demoniac. He wondered where Robert was, then he saw him at the far side of the bunker. David felt a great fear. He was close to para-lysed. Robert pointed at that dark roaring slit and David jumped up and ran. He hugged the wall of the bunker. The gun poked out and roared. He pulled the pin and put his hand near the barrel and dropped the grenade in. The machine-gun stopped roaring. He heard shouting in German. He pressed his back to the wall and it shuddered and he heard the explosion. Smoke drifted through the slit. There was screaming from within. Robert ran up to the slit and poked his gun in and squeezed the trigger. The gun made his body shake. It made an inane, shocking roar. He jumped back and there was silence from within and he waved the men on.

David followed him around the bunker. Bullets whipped past their heads. Up ahead was a German slit trench, and David saw their dark helmets. A German suddenly stood up. David sprayed the general area. The German twitched and jack-knifed and flopped forward as another one jumped up. David saw the grenade. It was spinning slowly through the air. David dived to the side and hit the ground and the blast swept above him. The dirt rained down on his back. He spit it out of his mouth. He glanced up and saw Marines racing past him, pouring into the slit trench. David jumped to his feet. He saw some Germans and Marines struggling. They were hanging over the rim of the trench and punching each other. A knife glittered in the air: a Marine screamed and died. A line of bullets stitched the rim of the hole and a German danced backwards. The men were fighting with bayonets, were shouting and screaming. A mortar shell fell and the earth roared and whipped all around them.

David ran forward, held his gun at the ready. He felt alert to his own brimming fear, incandescent with panic. Then it all changed. His men poured back down the hill. They were falling about and dying in great numbers, and the noise was insane. Someone crashed into David. He fell back and slithered down. He looked up and saw Pip's large brown eyes, his mouth open and shouting. '– *crossfire! Sheer murder! From that other hill, sir!*' A sudden blast and Pip floated away and the gunfire rushed in. '*David!*' It was Robert. He was crouched low and waving. '– *back down! We have to retreat! – the other hill! Get those guns!*' The ground erupted around Robert. He was flung back down the hill. The dust swirled all about him as he thrashed at the earth and rolled over and jumped back to his feet. David followed him down, saw the other swarming men. Lines of bullets were stitching the earth and the men were all falling. David jumped over bodies, saw blood and white bone. He tripped on a leg and fell over and rolled down to the bottom.

They tried taking the second hill. They tried it once and then twice. The sun sank as the body count grew and the hills turned to smoke and fire. David thought it was insane. He felt his own spirit breaking. He was shattered by the noise and the violence, and the fear took a hold of him. He tried to control it. He blessed the sanctuary of chaos. He loaded and fired and reloaded and advanced and retreated. The second hill was heavily fortified. It was seemingly invincible. It had to be taken before the first one could be held, but already the price was too high. The earth roared and soared upwards. Shapeless shadows somersaulted. Broken bodies and dismembered limbs littered shellholes and trenches. David couldn't ignore it. The fear made him embrace it. He now fought with the lust to see it end: no more and no less. The hill boiled and roared. The German pillboxes spat fire. The bullets stitched the ground in long jagged lines that chopped over the huddled men and tore through them. The sun sank even lower. The Marines were badly decimated. They slithered back down the slope, between explosions, under gunfire, and eventually regrouped at the bottom, exhausted, despairing.

A haunting silence reigned. The hill above was a field of dead. It was a nightmare of shellholes and bodies, and a pall of smoke covered it. The sun was now going down. The darkness crept across the hill. The men rested while the colonel and his officers engaged in discussion.

The hill had to be taken. There was no question about it. They had to take it in order to link up the two fronts and seal off the whole invasion area. They couldn't take it from the front: it was too heavily fortified. They had to find a way up and then come down from the rear, clearing the Germans out as they descended.

Now Robert spoke up, his voice soft, somewhat shaky; he had led both of the assaults on the second hill and was showing the strain. Speaking to the colonel, he said that during the attacks he had noticed a small zig-zag path leading to the top. He wanted to collect every available man, lead them up that path, and make one last effort to take the hill. The colonel would remain behind with a smaller defensive force; and if Robert was successful they would then be able to box the Germans in. The Colonel agreed to this.

It was dark when they left. It was their first night in France. They climbed up the path circling the hill and no one tried stopping them. The sky was clear; the stars glittered above. They spread out and started moving down the hill, a mass of crouched, bulky shadows. The silence was chilling; it gave life to David's fear: every rattle of a bayonet, every cracking of a twig, made him twitch. He strained to see through the darkness. His own breathing was too loud. He saw a line of shadowy men on either side, but they gave him no comfort. Pip Hunter was to his right. Corporal Brown was to his left. Robert moved out ahead, crouching over, his swagger stick jumping. Then Robert waved one hand. The men fanned out across the hill. Two mortar teams set up their guns, one left and one right. David led his men forward, his heart pounding, his throat dry, stopped just behind Robert, kneeling down, and gazed into the darkness. He saw a series of pillboxes. They were stretched out below him. In the trenches linking up the pillboxes was a dark mass of soldiers.

David didn't want to do it. The darkness nurtured his terror. He saw the men fanning out on either side, creeping down towards the pillboxes. They finally stopped and were still. They blocked off the whole summit. They curved around to both sides of the pillboxes, forming a semicircle. Then Robert raised his hand. He looked at both mortar crews. The men nodded and Robert dropped his hand and the still night went mad.

A pillbox exploded. The second shell fell too short. The men crouching down near the pillboxes hurled grenades at the trenches. The whole area exploded. One explosion followed another. The exploding grenades lit up the night, illuminating the spinning men. Then the Marines started firing. Their massed guns roared and rattled. They jumped up and started running down the hill, threw grenades as they went. White fires flared up and died. Clouds of dust swept over the trenches. The Germans didn't seem to know what was happening, and they fired down the hill. The Marines kept swarming down. The mortar guns fired ahead of them. The pillboxes were blind at the rear, and another exploded. The Marines swarmed down the hill. They were hurling grenades and shooting. They moved quickly and the semicircle tightened and throttled the Germans.

David swallowed his own bile, let the fear push him forward. He saw Germans silhouetted in flashes of white light, racing backwards and forwards, flinging their arms out and falling down. A machine-gun roared beside him. A stream of fire spat from its barrel. It disappeared as David raced down the slope, crouching over his Sten gun. He heard shouting and screaming, saw the shadows at the trenches: the Marines were firing down at the Germans and shuddering and falling. The earth roared up nearby. The blast knocked David sideways. He rolled away and struggled up to his feet and was pushed on ahead. The men were racing all around him. He was pummelled and pulled. Some explosions illuminated their faces in a ghastly white light. Then he stumbled through darkness, started choking in smoke, rushed through it and came to a bunker and a trench filled with fighting men. He saw the glint of knives and bayonets, heard screams and loud oaths. A Marine ran from the front of the bunker and the bunker exploded. Dust and debris filled the air. David crouched down by the wall. A German started clambering out of the trench and he looked straight at David. David shot him; he fired a short burst. The German threw up his arms and fell back with his mouth hanging open. Then David jumped up, raced past the seething trench, followed a group of men down the hill, saw Pip Hunter and Corporal Brown. Pip was hurling a grenade. Corporal Brown was firing his Sten gun. David joined them, stood close beside Pip, started firing downhill. The Germans scattered and spun. A grenade roared and died. '– *let's go!*' David heard his own voice as he raced down the hill. More Germans materialized. They sprang up from the dark earth. There were pinpoints of light and their guns roared and David fell down. Bullets ricocheted around him. The noise rang in his ears. He found a grenade and pulled the pin, and rolled over and threw it. The explosion was instantaneous, died away and left a scream. Someone raced ahead and fired his gun once and the scream was cut off. David jumped to his feet. A hand fell on his shoulder. '– *almost down!*' It was Robert. The ground exploded nearby. '– *they're retreating! – soon have them boxed in! – near the bottom right now!*' The ground roared and heaved around them. David's lungs were on fire. He was picked up and crushed by a huge fist and fell back to earth. He retched and almost choked, spat the dirt from his mouth, found his gun and then saw Robert's grin as he jumped up and ran. The hill was steeper now. Detonations lit the night. He felt the force of the blasts, and the clouds of dirt swirled and hissed around him.

'– *keep going! We're almost –*'

David saw a German helmet. He fired without thinking. Another dark shape raced up on his right and he turned and his gun roared. Too late. Something hit him. He saw stars, then the ground. A boot kicked him and a bayonet glinted, flew away as the dark shape fell. Pip thrust down with his rifle. The dark shape merely grunted. Pip's bayonet protruded from its back, and then it was withdrawn. David got to his feet, felt the blast of the explosion: white light and a sudden searing heat and he rolled to the side.

Pip screaming and pinioned. The German thrusting down hard. Pip's eyes large and brown, almost luminous, his scream quite demented. David groped for his Sten gun. '– *No! No! No!*' Oh God, Pip! No gun and David rose to his feet as Pip grabbed at the bayonet. The German jerked the bayonet out.

Pip shrieked and David jumped. He hit the German and they rolled on the ground and David started to choke him. The German gasped and kicked beneath him. His two eyes were huge orbs; they were frightened and David smashed down with his fist and the eyes disappeared. David started to sob. He banged the German's head up and down. His hands were wet and he knew it was blood, but he just couldn't stop. Another explosion did it for him. He blacked out and recovered. He saw Pip's severed fingers on his chest, the bloody stumps of his hands. Pip's brown eyes were open. There was more blood on his chest. David sobbed and found his gun and stood up and ran on down the hill.

The night roared and spat fire. Silvery explosions tore the darkness. The smoke swirled all around him, around the men on either side, blew away to reveal a pillbox, Robert pressed to the wall. The earth roared and subsided. A sub-machine-gun was roaring. Robert ran around the front of the bunker and returned as a human torch. '– *Aaaaaaahhhhhhheeeeeee!*' Not Robert. A black rag in the flames. Falling down and rolling over and shrieking and shuddering hideously. Not Robert; couldn't be. The roaring fire of the flamethrower. Someone else screaming horribly and blazing and popping and dying.

David sobbing and running forward. Corporal Brown by the bunker. Standing legs apart throwing a grenade, then the Sten gun's sharp roar. An explosion: dust swirling; the flames dwindling to darkness. Brown stepping out and firing his gun and stepping back and then shouting. '– *got the cunt! Fucking bastard!*' His mouth opening and closing, looking into David's eyes and reloading and hugging the wall. Then another explosion: swirling dust and flying stones, the burning friend now a smouldering rag on the rim of a trench. The snap of a Sten gun: David's brief, anguished sob. The sudden roar of a machine-gun and a wall exploding right behind Brown ... Brown falling. David with him. The gun changing direction. David looking down and seeing the bottom, the colonel's men rushing up. Germans running left and right: boxed in, in a crossfire. Silhouettes: earth exploding and subsiding, shapeless forms crawling, shrieking.

Corporal Brown suddenly ran. He fired his gun from the hip. David followed and the gun bucked in his hands and he knew it was over. The corporal shuddered and staggered. He dropped his gun and hit a bunker. The wall exploded all around him and he wriggled and flapped, and then slid down the wall and fell sideways.

David started crawling towards him. He couldn't remember having fallen. Both legs were on fire and he was bleeding, but that didn't mean much. He crawled across the torn earth. He heard the cheers of the Marines. He kept crawling towards the bunker and he reached out and touched Corporal Brown's face. The corporal didn't move. The vicious cockney was dead. David sobbed and rolled onto his back and looked up at the stars.

He had survived his first day.

# PART THREE: WILDERNESS

# CHAPTER ELEVEN

THE small town lay just outside Paris, and by the time Stryker got to it there wasn't really all that much left of it. Kantaylis drove the truck slowly through the ruined streets, his eyes blinking repeatedly behind his thick spectacles, taking in the piles of rubble, the shattered brick walls, the charred beams and the shellholes all around him. The air was still dusty. The dust permeated everything. The August sky was grey, filled with dark, drifting clouds, a hazy light falling over the ruins and the still, ghostly silence.

'A fucking graveyard,' Stryker said. 'Only the rats are still living. You wanna come back to France for a vacation, you won't find much left of it.'

Kantaylis was driving the truck. His helmet bobbed on his head. Stryker was sitting casually in the seat beside him, a BAR in his lap.

'I don't like it,' Kantaylis said. 'It's too quiet, staff-sergeant. There oughta be some people around here. I don't want no snipers.'

Stryker grinned. 'Fuck the snipers,' he said. 'There's a cellar full of wine somewhere here, and I mean to get hold of it.'

'Right,' Kantaylis said. 'That's a real sweet idea. I just wanna be around to sample some. I don't want my balls shot off.'

'You ain't got no balls,' Stryker said. 'That's why you stick with me. You wanna keep the skin on your back, you stay dumb and obedient.'

Kantaylis didn't reply. He just grinned in his dopey fashion. He adjusted the glasses on his nose and looked around him and he still couldn't credit it. The devastation was total. The whole town had been obliterated. He had seen a lot of towns like this on the push up from Cherbourg, but he still hadn't managed to take it in.

'You remember St. Lo?' he said.

'Yeah,' Stryker said. 'I remember. There wasn't a fucking building left standing. We sure had some fun there.'

Stryker wasn't really interested. He wanted to find the hotel. He was hoping the cellar wouldn't be buried in a great mass of rubble. He stroked his gun and glanced around him. The broken walls were grey and black. The rubble climbed up on both sides of the truck and buried windows and doorways. There weren't many doors left. There were no windows at all. Smashed furniture and charred wooden beams had been hurled up and scattered. The town was like a graveyard; it was covered in white dust. The dust drifted along on a light breeze, whispered through the strange silence.

'There won't be snipers,' Stryker said. 'There won't be anything at all. There'll just be a couple of greasy Frogs with their heads in their hands. We won't have no trouble, kid.'

Kantaylis wasn't that certain. He didn't like this desolation. He had known this silence many times before, and it could be deceptive. He turned the truck around a corner, saw some people along the street; they were digging laboriously at some rubble, their backs bent and their heads bowed. Kantaylis looked at Stryker. The staff-sergeant nodded slightly. Kantaylis drove up and pulled in and stopped, and the people looked up.

'English?' Stryker said. 'You speak English?'

A man stepped from the group. He had a beret on his head. He was old and white-whiskered and shabby, looking up without smiling.

'Yes,' he said, 'I do. Americans?'

'Yeah,' Stryker said. 'We're Americans.'

A woman stepped forward. She wore a dusty black dress.

She had a scarf around her head and she was fat and her eyes were demented.

'My son,' she said, 'is buried down there ... And the Americans killed him!'

'You speak English as well,' Stryker said.

'Liberation!' the woman snapped, and spat at the truck. 'You come bombing the women and children, and it's called liberation. You are worse than the Boche!'

She turned back to the rubble, clawed at it with her hands; she was weeping and she cried out in French, a fierce drawn-out litany. The old man took off his beret, bowed his head and looked up again. The other people were still gathered around him, studying the truck.

'I am sorry,' the old man said. 'These are bad times for us all. The Americans came over. They bombed us. Now nothing is left.'

'Yeah,' Stryker said. 'I know what you mean. But you want liberating, you got to pay. When did the troops come through?'

The old man shrugged. 'Three, four days ago. There was very great resistance by the Boche, and that made it all worse.' He raised his hands and glanced around him. 'You see what has happened.' He looked back at Stryker and smiled sadly. 'In gaining freedom, we lost all.'

Stryker was impatient. 'Yeah,' he said. 'A real tragedy. You got any idea where the hotel is? We want the hotel.'

'The Hotel Domfront?'

'That sounds like it,' Stryker said.

'Down there,' the old man said, pointing along the street. 'Around the corner. There is some of it still standing. But why the hotel, monsieur?'

Stryker grinned. He spat some chewing gum on the ground. It landed near the old man's booted feet, making him step back.

'We're gonna liberate it,' Stryker said.

Kantaylis gunned the motor. The wheels churned up clouds of dirt. The men and women jumped back towards the rubble as the truck roared away. Stryker laughed and Kantaylis grinned. The skeletal ruins swept past them. They saw more

French people digging at the rubble, glancing up as the truck passed. Then Kantaylis slowed down. The truck bounced over a mound of stones. Kantaylis pulled the wheel down and the truck turned to the right, and they saw a large group further on, milling about in the road.

'Frogs,' Stryker said.

'A lot of noise there,' Kantaylis said.

'That looks like the hotel they're in front of. What the fuck are they up to?'

Kantaylis drove towards the people, slowed down as he approached them. There were about twenty people forming a rough circle, all shouting and waving. Stryker picked up his BAR. Some people looked up at the truck. Kantaylis braked and the truck came to a halt with the engine still running.

'Prepare to run,' Stryker said.

Kantaylis kept it ticking over. The BAR rested on Stryker's lap. A couple of men broke away from the shouting crowd and walked up to the truck. One of the men had a leg missing; he hopped over on crutches. The other wore an FFI armband and carried a pistol. This one looked up at Stryker. He had a dark, intense face. He waved the pistol in a welcoming gesture and glanced at Kantaylis.

'Americans?' he said, looking back at Stryker.

'Yeah,' Stryker said. 'We're Americans.'

'Good,' the man said. 'I am glad to see you. We must have some order here.'

Stryker glanced at the shouting crowd. They formed a heaving, waving circle. The circle moved in and back out again, as if trying to reach something. Then a fist swung up and down. Stryker saw kicking feet. A cloud of dust was swirling around the shifting mass as someone cried out in French.

'What's going on?' Stryker said.

'Collaborators,' the man said. 'Please! You must hurry! These people are going to kill them. They were hiding in the cellar of the hotel and now the people want blood. Collaborators and *prostiteurs*.'

Stryker glanced at Kantaylis. The private grinned and blinked his eyes. Stryker jumped out of the truck and Kantaylis followed, an M.1 in his hands.

'You're in the FFI,' Stryker said. 'Don't *you* want to kill them?'

The man's dark eyes blazed at Stryker. 'I am not an assassin!' he snapped. 'These people must be given a trial. They are not always guilty.'

Stryker pushed through the mob. They made allowances for his uniform. They were mostly peasants who worked the surrounding fields, and they respected authority. Stryker knew this and used it: he bawled in an authoritative voice. The jostling people at the front let him pass and the FFI man followed him. Kantaylis remained behind the group, had his M.1 at the ready. Stryker's BAR was pointing at the sky and the peasants respected it.

'Tell them to shut up,' Stryker said.

The FFI man nodded, rattled off a burst in French. The mob moved back a little and Stryker looked down at the battered collaborators. Four men and two women. They were all covered in dust. All six had been badly beaten, and the two women now had shaved heads. They were tear-streaked and pitiful. Stryker thought they looked grotesque. He hardly saw the battered men, but the women on their knees made him burn. He was fascinated by the shaven heads. It made their eyes seem very large. It made them look more exposed than total nudity could ever have done.

They looked up at Stryker. One of the girls started to plead. Someone stepped forward and slapped her on the face and she put her head down again.

'*Biche*!' someone hissed.

'Boche whores!' a woman shrieked.

'God have mercy,' one of the kneeling girls whispered. 'I am innocent. I swear it!'

Stryker burned with revulsion. He wanted to touch their shaved skulls. They were adolescents, pale-faced and fearful, and he wanted to have them. Stryker felt his growing need. He saw the moon and the stars. He saw the men and they, too, were on their knees, heads bowed and defeated. They all looked like civil servants. The girls had once been quite pretty. Stryker thought of all the girls between here and St. Lo, the available, ragged victims of chance, the spoils of the victor.

He had taken them in the ruins. He had worked his will on them: in the night, beneath the moon and the stars, on the rough, broken rubble. Stryker burned with the recollection, saw a trail of destruction. He looked around him at the breathless, angry mob and he tried to control himself.

'A fair trial,' the FFI man said. 'They must have a trial.'

Stryker glanced at him. A woman suddenly rushed forward. She had a club in her hand, she shrieked something in French, and then she swung at one of the men on the ground. '*Batard!*' There was a thud. The man shrieked and fell back. Someone kicked at his head and the woman thumped him again, then Stryker stepped forward and grabbed her and threw her aside. The man on the ground sat up. He covered his face with his hands. He was sobbing and he rocked back and forth and someone spat on his head. The other victims didn't move. They kept their eyes on the ground. The girls' dresses were torn, and one of them covered her breasts with her hands. Stryker looked at the gasping French woman. She was gaunt and outraged. She held the club in her hand and glared at him, trembling all over.

'Sitting in the cellar with the wine!' she hissed. 'Filling their bellies!'

Stryker looked thoughtfully at her. 'The wine?' he said softly.

'Yes, monsieur, the wine! The wine of Monsieur Graumont who was killed by the Boche. It was done in his own hotel. He was tortured and then shot. From this very street we heard his terrible screaming, and then he was shot. And this filth – ' she pointed at the collaborators – 'this filth entertained them!'

' – *no choice!*' One of the girls had raised her shaved head to scream it. '*I had no* – '

A man stepped forward and slapped her. Her head jerked and she gasped. She put her hands to her mouth and stifled a sob and looked down again. She had small, dirt-stained breasts.

'*Biche!*' the man hissed.

'That's enough,' Stryker said. He turned to the FFI man beside him. 'And what do *you* think?'

The FFI man shrugged. 'I do not know,' he said. 'These four

172

men, certainly: they are all collaborators; they are informers and they worked with the Boche during the whole occupation. Many died because of them. Many were tortured or deported ... As for the girls.' He shrugged again. 'It is difficult to say. They lived in the hotel with the Germans, but they may not have volunteered. The Germans, monsieur, were not gentlemen when it came to the ladies.'

Stryker wanted the girls. He wanted the wine in the cellar. He wanted to still the urge deep within him, to throttle his tension. He thought of the girls in the hotel, of the Germans crawling over them: if they had been innocent before, they certainly would not be innocent now. This war was flesh and blood. The whole of France was a whorehouse. Stryker wanted to have them down in the cellar, to greet them with fresh truths. Both the girls were on their knees, their shaved heads turned down. They seemed frail and their bodies were shaking, and Stryker liked that.

'They're pretty young,' Stryker said.

'Yes, monsieur, they are young.' The FFI man glanced casually at the girls and then back at Stryker. 'I think they should have their say.'

'Kill them!' someone shouted.

'Shut up!' Stryker snapped. 'And the men,' he said, turning to the FFI man. 'What about them?'

The Frenchman looked at the kneeling men. They were being prodded and spat at. Their dark suits were in tatters, they were covered in dust, and their faces were bloody and bruised. They all had their heads bowed, didn't speak, were breathing harshly, had the air of men who knew that they were finished, that only death would release them.

'They are collaborators,' the Frenchman said. 'There is little doubt about it. But it's not a question of innocence or guilt; it is a question of law and order. You are an American, monsieur. You represent law and order. You cannot permit these men to be shot down like dogs in the street.'

'Why not?' Stryker grinned. 'You've just said they're guilty. If you try them, they're gonna be shot anyway – so why not right now?'

The Frenchman seemed shocked. He stepped back a little.

He looked at Stryker as if he couldn't quite believe that an American would say this.

'You cannot mean this!' he said. 'You are an American! Americans don't do such things!'

'I'm doing nothing,' Stryker said. 'These *people* are going to do it. These people are demanding satisfaction and I think they should have it. It's their town; it's not mine.'

'I will not permit – !'

'Let *me*,' said another man, stepping out of the crowd, smiling grimly at Stryker and waving a German Luger before him. 'It is only right, monsieur. It is justice. We must have satisfaction.' He stopped in front of Stryker, quite deliberately cocked the Luger. 'The people will not be content until these swines are dead.'

Stryker looked up at the hotel. The front wall had been blown away. It was late afternoon and dark shadows fell over the piled rubble. The hotel's entrance was almost buried. The whole lobby had been gutted. Charred beams were hanging down from the ceiling, over more piles of rubble. The rubble had poured through the front door. The actual door itself was buried. The rubble fell from the remains of the wall and ran down to the shouting mob.

'Anyone else in there?' Stryker said.

'No,' the Frenchman said. 'There were others, but they escaped through the back door before we could get them.'

'The back door?' Stryker said.

'Yes, monsieur, the back door. It leads onto the road out of town, and they had a car parked there.' He looked at Stryker, glanced around him at the crowd. When he looked at the man with the Luger, his lips twitched disgustedly. 'You must not permit this,' he said to Stryker. 'Guilty or not, you must not allow it. We must have law and order in this town. You must set an example.'

Stryker studied the pushing mob. The men wore berets and shabby suits. The women were dressed in aprons and faded dresses, and had scarves on their heads. They were all demanding satisfaction, waving fists and shouting loudly, spitting at the people on the ground, at their bowed, trembling heads.

174

One of the girls shuddered violently, covered her breasts with her hands. A man looked up with terrified eyes, licked his lips, dropped his head again. A cloud's shadow passed over them. The dust blew lazily around them. Stryker looked at the girls and felt the urge to place his hands on their shaved skulls.

'I want the girls,' Stryker said. 'I want to take them back for questioning. They lived with the Germans, so they must have heard a lot of idle talk. Army Intelligence will want them.'

The FFI man stiffened. 'I will not permit – ' he began.

'Excellent!' said the man with the Luger. 'I find that most acceptable. Give the Americans the girls. Let the Americans interrogate them. Let the Americans make full use of the whores while we deal with the men.'

'*Mercy! For God's sake . . . !*' It was one of the kneeling men. He had looked up and his eyes were wild with panic and his two hands were shaking. The man with the Luger walked up to him, swung the Luger at his head. There was a terrible cracking sound and the kneeling man fell on his side. Blood poured from his forehead; one of his hands twitched in the dirt. Someone else walked up and kicked him in the ribs, and he gasped and then groaned.

The FFI man raised his pistol. 'I will not permit – ' he said. The stock of Stryker's BAR suddenly smashed into his elbow and he let his pistol drop to the ground. His eyes bulged in amazement. The two girls stared at Stryker. Beneath the shaved heads their eyes shone with a desperate hope. Stryker motioned with his BAR. 'Stand up,' he said curtly. The girls jumped up and raced to his side while the kneeling men came to life. They started to wave their hands and plead. Stryker backed off through the crowd. He saw dust swirling up as feet kicked at the men, as hands reached out and tore at their hair and they started to shriek. The crowd surged around Stryker. The girls clung to his arms. Their eyes blinked and they licked at their lips and were dazed with relief. The crowd devoured the kneeling men. They were kicking and clawing. They were shouting and hissing as Stryker broke free and urged the girls towards the waiting truck.

Kantaylis had jumped back in. He was revving the engine. The girls climbed up and sat beside Kantaylis and then Stryker climbed in. They didn't have much room, were crushed tightly together. They looked down at the dust-covered crowd, saw fists rising and falling. Some of the people had clubs. Some were wielding huge stones. The men buried in the middle were screaming and shouting dementedly. Then a shot rang out. Kantaylis started reversing the truck. Another shot rang out as he found the first gear and abruptly roared off along the street.

'Turn right,' Stryker said.

'The next turning?'

'That's it.'

Kantaylis turned right at the corner, then Stryker ordered him to turn right again. Kantaylis did as he was told. He glanced once at the girls. His eyes blinked behind the glasses as he grinned and then licked at his lips. The sun was now going down. The gaunt ruins cast dark shadows. The truck ground over a low mound of rubble and then bounced down again. Stryker looked for the back of the hotel; when he saw it, they pulled in. Kantaylis turned off the engine and looked around and grinned at the girls.

'Get out,' Stryker said.

Stryker hopped out his side. Kantaylis got out the other. The ray of hope in the girls' eyes started fading and they glanced at each other. They didn't get out of the truck, simply stared all around them. They finally looked at the back door of the hotel, and all hope disappeared.

Kantaylis grinned at them. He had seen bald girls before. There had been quite a few during the advance through shattered France; and these two, like the ones he had sampled with Stryker, were possessed of a terrible resignation. They huddled close to one another. One lightly touched the other's wrist. Glancing down at Kantaylis's dopey grin, they both smiled with despair.

'I like the one with the brown eyes,' Kantaylis said. 'I think she's real cute.'

Stryker took him by the elbow and led him away a little. He looked up and down the street, saw the drifting dust, the shadows, the broken walls and charred, splintered beams, the skeletal ruins. It appealed to Stryker. This desolation was his shelter. He would do it in the darkness of the cellar and their fear would enhance his life.

'You like being with me, kid?'

'Yeah, Stryker, of course I do.'

'You think you could get along without me, kid?'

'Well, no, Stryker, I guess not.'

'You've had a good time, kid?'

'Yeah, Stryker, it's been great. I never did nothin' before you. I mean I never did *nothin*'.'

'That's right, kid,' Stryker said, 'you've been through a lot lately. You've been through a few battles – St. Lo, Argentan – and you've come through it all without a scratch because ole Stryker was with you.'

'That's right, staff,' Kantaylis said, licking his lips and blinking. 'I can't deny that for a minute. It sure has been something.'

'You've learnt a few things, right? You did a few things you never dreamed you'd do ... Now isn't that right, kid?'

'Right, Stryker.'

'You wanna keep it that way, kid?'

'Yeah, Stryker, you know that.'

'Okay, kid, so you'll do what you're told. No matter what. You will do it.'

'Well, Stryker, I ...'

'No arguments, kid. You're either with me or against me. You ain't innocent, Kantaylis – not any more – and a few words here and there could slip out. You know what I mean, kid? A few tales could be told. Now I don't want that to happen to you, kid, so you gotta stick with me. Stay dumb and obedient, kid.'

Kantaylis blinked. He offered Stryker a nervous smile. He looked up at Stryker, who was tall, and then he looked down again.

'Sure, staff-sergeant,' he said. 'I get the message. You don't have to worry.'

Stryker patted him on the shoulder. 'That's a good boy,' he said. 'Now I'm gonna take these two whores inside. I want some time to myself, kid.'

'Right, staff-sergeant. Sure ... I understand.'

'Okay, kid, you stay by the truck. Keep your eyes on the street.'

Stryker went back to the truck, waved his BAR at the two girls. 'Okay,' he said, 'shake your fucking asses. Get out of the truck.' The girls looked at the BAR, glanced nervously at one another. They climbed out of the truck and the one with the torn dress was covering her bare breasts with her hands. Stryker motioned towards the hotel. The girls meekly walked towards it. They were dishevelled and they kept their heads down, resigned to their fate. The whole country was a whore-house; these two girls knew the score. They had no choice but to walk ahead of Stryker, his gun at their backs. They entered the hotel. It was dark and devastated. Splintered beams were lying across one another, over huge piles of rubble. The silence was eerie. It made their footsteps echo. The girls hesitated and then walked ahead when Stryker prodded their spines.

'The cellar,' Stryker said. 'I want the cellar. Where the fuck is it hidden?'

The girls didn't dare speak. One of them raised a hand and pointed. Stryker prodded them both with the gun and they walked to the lift. The shaft was filled with debris. He saw the mangled lift below. There was a stairway to the side and the girls looked at Stryker and he nodded. They went down the stairs. The stairs were narrow and dark. Their footsteps echoed when they got to the bottom and walked into the cellar.

It was large; almost cavernous. The cold air was numbing. Stryker saw the crates of wine and there were more than enough to fill the truck. Stryker grinned. The girls turned around to face him. They seemed terribly young, very frail, and were aware of their own fear. The darkness washed over them. They had large, glowing eyes. They were thin and had been merci-lessly battered, and he liked that as well. Stryker motioned to the floor. The girls lay down on their backs. They both closed their eyes and opened their legs and Stryker's shadow fell over them.

Stryker went to work. He did it quickly and methodically. He tied their hands and their ankles, then he went and got some rags and he gagged the girls to keep them from screaming. Then it all fell away from him: their eyes hypnotized him; they were glazed and they glowed in the darkness with that ultimate disbelief. Stryker flew out of himself. His burning need found release. He was filled with a fierce incandescence, a voluptuous freedom. His breathing was harsh. There was sweat on his brow. He saw the agony and the limitless horror in the whites of their eyes. The whole world was a whorehouse. It was blood, sweat and tears. It was a catacomb of conquest and submission, a well without bottom. Stryker sank down into it, saw the darkness on either side, saw the dead men on the beaches, the bloated animals in the fields, saw the dispossessed struggling along the roads while the bombs dropped amongst them. How many towns had died? How much blood had been spilt? Stryker saw the corpses strewn amongst the rubble: men, women and children ... He went down into it. The white eyes drew him in. He was choking, gasping for breath, and yet he just couldn't stop. It got worse every time. There were no limits to invention: each hunger appeased just gave rise to a larger hunger, to the need to go out beyond himself through a tunnel of nightmare. Stryker saw the rolling eyes, saw the bound, writhing bodies. He saw the countless refugees, the hungry children, the weeping women, and he saw the dark mosaic of blood that was left on the rubble. It got worse every time. The push through France had taught him that. Across the fields, through the villages, along the choked, dusty roads, he had learnt that the killing was not enough to wash him clean of the filth. It was the stench of the slaughterhouse. It was the noise and the heat. It was everything that made the world pestilent and drove him relentlessly ... Stryker gasped and found release. It was a temporary peace. He saw the whites of their eyes rolling upward through darkness and silence. He finally controlled himself. He wiped his hands on some rags. He got his breath back and picked up his gun and then walked from the cellar.

'Hey, Kantaylis!' he said. His voice was soft and strangely hollow. Kantaylis turned around and saw him in the doorway, standing still in the darkness. 'Hey, Kantaylis!' he said again. Kantaylis blinked and licked his lips. 'I'm finished,' Stryker said in that strange way. 'I left you Miss Brown-Eyes.'

Kantaylis entered the hotel. Stryker followed him in.

Stryker led him to the steps of the basement and Kantaylis went down. Stryker stood there and grinned. He felt possessed, demoniac. He felt magically aware of himself and in total control. The footsteps echoed down below. He heard a sudden, hollow gasp. Kantaylis started rushing back up the stairs, gasping and choking. Stryker held up the BAR. He waited for Kantaylis to appear. Kantaylis burst out of the darkness and bent forward and threw up on the floor. Then he leaned against a wall. He was white-faced and shaking. He looked at Stryker with horrified eyes, and he was sweating all over.

'Oh my God, staff-sergeant! Jesus Christ! Oh my God, what the . . .'

Stryker aimed the gun at him. Kantaylis froze immediately. He seemed to shrink against the wall and he looked at Stryker's BAR and his young eyes had the glazed hue of marbles. Stryker held the BAR on him. Kantaylis tried to control his gagging. In the darkness, in that all-pervasive silence, he felt limitless dread.

'You're an accessory,' Stryker said. 'You understand what I'm saying, kid? You're an accessory and that means you got no choice: you'll do what I say.'

Kantaylis stayed against the wall. His head was spinning and he felt sick. Behind the sickness was a paralysing fear that would now never leave him. He looked up at Stryker. The staff-sergeant's eyes were gleaming. The staff-sergeant was dark and monolithic, blocking off all escape.

'Yes, Stryker,' Kantaylis whispered, his voice shaking. 'Anything you say, Stryker.'

Stryker made him go back down there. Kantaylis didn't want to do it. He was willing to do anything but that, but Stryker made him go down. Stryker guarded the truck. Kantaylis carried the wine crates up. He had to make a lot of trips to the cellar and it took him a long time. Stryker just stood there smiling. He cradled the BAR in his arms. He watched Kantaylis growing breathless and sweaty, saw him retching and sobbing. Then eventually it was done. The truck was packed tight with wine. Stryker made Kantaylis get behind the wheel and drive them away.

The town was dark and silent. The dust whispered across

the ruins. They saw the four dead men lying in the street, their limbs outstretched and broken. There was a full moon in the sky. It shone down upon the debris. The truck drove away into the night and went back towards Paris.

# CHAPTER TWELVE

THE POW camp was stretched across a sodden plain just outside Paris, a mass of tents and men that stretched back to the horizon, beneath dark clouds and a deluge of rain. Stryker cursed, turned the collar of his greatcoat up, and walked through the mud, along the barbed wire of the compound, looking in at the shabby, dejected Germans who milled aimlessly between the tents. There were more than ten thousand of them. The camp was growing every day. The prisoners were brought in in trucks, dumped into the compound, and were soon lost in those thousands of other faces, those defeated and haunted eyes. Now the rain poured down upon them. The thunder rolled overhead. Stryker cursed again and went to the gate and went inside the guard's hut.

'Fucking filthy weather,' Stryker said. 'You're fucking lucky you're inside.'

Sergeant Lelchuk was in a chair. His booted feet were on a boiler. He had close-cropped dark hair, his face was flabby and pock-marked, and his huge belly flopped over his belt. He looked up lazily at Stryker, his grin knowing and sardonic, then put down his copy of *Life* and picked up his cigar.

'You got a pretty foul mouth for a staff-sergeant,' he said. 'And I'm just an innocent sergeant from Mechanicsburg. I'm shocked, staff. I really am.'

Stryker snorted. 'Go beat yourself,' he said. 'You sit here on your ass reading books while we get our balls shot off.'

'I got a hernia,' Lelchuk said. 'That's a terrible thing to have.

It's worse than being shot at by the Krauts. You oughta sympathize, staff.'

Stryker shook his greatcoat down, warmed his hands on the glowing stove. The hut was filled with the smoke of Lelchuk's cigar, and it made Stryker cough.

'I'll be moving two truckloads of those fuckers out tonight,' Stryker said. 'I'll be here at midnight.'

'You mean I'm losing some more of my prisoners, staff?'

'That's right, Lelchuk. I'm doing you another favour. I think of you working your ass off, so I lighten your load.'

'You got an authority for this move, staff-sergeant?'

'Yeah, Lelchuk, I got the authority. I *always* got the authority.'

Stryker threw a brown envelope on the sergeant's lap. Lelchuk sighed, dropped his feet to the floor, and carefully opened the envelope. It contained an authentic looking document and a thick wad of ten-dollar bills. Lelchuk counted the money slowly, wetting his finger like a bank clerk. Satisfied, he stuffed it into his tunic pocket and pinned the order to the wall.

'I don't know how you do it,' he said. 'You sure must have some elbow.'

'Don't ask,' Stryker said. 'You won't be told no lies. Just see Colonel Jodl at eleven o'clock sharp and he'll organize the men he's taking with him. Now let me into the compound.'

Lelchuk shivered and put his coat on. He took some large keys off the wall. He opened the door of the hut, a blast of cold air swept in, and he shivered again and led Stryker out.

The gate stretched across a dirt track. A bren-gun carrier stood beside it. A dripping private was sitting behind the gun, surveying the compound. He looked down without interest. Lelchuk opened the gate. Stryker walked into the compound and the gate closed behind him and he saw the mass of prisoners in the gloom. They were milling about aimlessly. They were oblivious to the rain. The tents seemed to stretch away to the horizon and were criss-crossed by muddy roads.

Stryker turned his collar up, pushed his way through the prisoners. They were thin and unshaven and begrimed, and their eyes had no lustre. They took little notice of Stryker; he

was just another passing figure. He walked along to an unusually large tent and bent low and stepped inside.

'Hello, colonel,' Stryker said. 'Keeping warm?'

Colonel Jodl was squatting down on a canvas sheet. He was
surrounded by other officers. Their tunics were undone, they
looked distinctly untidy, and a small kerosene lamp cast a
flickering yellow light on their faces. The colonel looked up
at Stryker. His face registered cool distaste. He glanced briefly
at the other kneeling men, and then he looked back at Stryker.

'Yes, staff-sergeant,' he said, 'we're trying to stay warm.'
He stared steadily at Stryker. His eyes were dark and intelligent. 'I would remind you,' he said, speaking softly, in perfect
English, 'that an NCO is supposed to salute an officer – even
a prisoner-of-war.'

Stryker snorted. 'Oh, yeah?' he said. 'I must try to remember that, Fritz. I'll kiss your ass when I'm doing it.'

The colonel's expression didn't change. He kept his eyes
on Stryker's face. He didn't move from his position, and he
held his hands out to the kerosene lamp.

'Is it tonight?' the colonel said.

'It's tonight,' Stryker said.

'Good,' the colonel said. 'I'm delighted. At least you're
efficient.'

Stryker just grinned. 'Midnight,' he said. 'Sergeant Lelchuk
will be here at eleven to check that you're ready. I want you
all here together. The trucks will be here at midnight. I have
a warrant that says you're being moved on to the camp at
Dreux – but you'll be dropped off on the outskirts of Melun
and then it's all up to you. There'll be no transport after that.
That's not part of the deal. You can go the fuck wherever
you want, but you'll go it alone.'

'We'll be going to Germany,' the colonel said.

'Good for you,' Stryker said. 'I'm told there's not much of
it left. Given that, you might even find it civilized.'

'You do realize, staff-sergeant, that when we rejoin our
army, we will be a very valuable addition to their defences ..
You do realize that, staff-sergeant?'

'I'm not interested, Fritz,' Stryker said. 'I just don't give a
fuck.'

'And you found the wine, staff-sergeant?'

'Yeah, I found the wine.'

'You have the name of the man who will buy it?'

'I have the name. Deal complete.'

The colonel smiled bleakly. There was mockery in his dark eyes. He had fought against the Americans at Avranches, and might now be able to fight them again. He did not appear grateful.

'You have the wine,' he said to Stryker. 'You have your black-marketeer. You also have considerable money in your wallet. You may now leave my tent.'

'Adios, Fritz,' Stryker said. 'I might see you around. And I hope to hell you don't come too close. I just might lose my temper.'

Stryker left the tent. He walked back across the compound. The thunder rolled and the rain was pouring down, drenching the milling men. Fucking Krauts, Stryker thought. They can't smell their own shit. We oughta string them all up by their feet and cut their balls off. He pushed a few prisoners aside. They just blinked and let him pass. He wiped the rain from his face and reached the gate and bawled out to Lelchuk. The door of the guard's hut opened. A bright light poured through the gloom. Lelchuk ran across, buttoning up his coat, and opened the gate.

'Goddam rain!' he shouted.

'Midnight,' Stryker said. 'Just make sure those fuckers are ready. I don't want no accidents.'

Lelchuk nodded and closed the gate. Stryker walked off through the mud. The mud was almost up to his ankles and it made him more angry. That fucking German, he thought. That supercilious shit. I should have let him rot there in the compound; you can't do them a good turn. He kicked the mud and walked on. The barracks loomed just ahead. They had belonged to the Germans and he wondered if the colonel had ever used them. He really felt angry. That Kraut bastard had been mocking him. If we hadn't made a deal I'd have kicked the cunt's teeth down his throat. Stryker was really boiling. He wanted to break loose and explode. He couldn't stand this goddamned rain, and the mud was like the slime in the slaughterhouse. He finally reached the barracks. He went up the wooden steps. A GI was standing furtively beside the door and now he stepped up to Stryker.

'Are you Stryker?' he said.

'*Staff-sergeant*,' Stryker said.

'Oh,' the private said. 'I'm sorry, staff-sergeant. I wanted to speak to you.'

'I'm wet,' Stryker said.

'Terrible weather,' the private said.

'Yeah,' Stryker said with some impatience. 'What the fuck do you want?'

'I need some penicillin.'

'Oh?' Stryker said.

'Yeah, staff, I need some penicillin. I heard you might help me.'

'You got the pox, kid?'

'I didn't say that.'

'If you need penicillin go to sick quarters.'

'I can't do that, staff-sergeant.'

Stryker grinned tightly. A dumb fucking kid. Probably married with two in the cradle and a wife who was cherry. They were all the same: a bunch of suckers in the whorehouse. Too shy to wear a rubber or wash. Should've been drowned at birth.

'You got the pox,' Stryker said.

'Yes, staff, I got the pox.'

'And you don't want the Big P on your back. You don't want the pox compound.'

The private hung his head, flushed and humiliated. He had hoped it was going to be easier, but he'd heard about Stryker.

'That's right, staff,' he said. 'I'm married, you see. We just got married a year before I was shipped. And I've got me a kid.'

'You fucking filth,' Stryker said. 'You fucking kids are all the same. They oughta castrate the whole lot of ya – send you home with some tits.'

The private didn't reply. He kept his eyes on the floor. He was drenched and he shuffled his feet, just hoping for clemency.

'You got the money?' Stryker said.

'Yes, staff, I've got the money.'

'You'll need a whole course,' Stryker said. 'How much have you got?'

'A hundred dollars,' the kid said.

'I want three-hundred,' Stryker said.

'I don't have that kind of money, staff. And I've no way of getting it.'

'I'll lend it to you,' Stryker said. 'You'll have a month to pay me back. It'll cost you fifty percent on the top, but there's no other way.'

'I can't get it in that time.'

'You'll have to get it,' Stryker said. 'Flog your ass to the officer corps. You can get it. You have to.'

'What if I'm shipped out before that?'

'Then I'll want it back immediately.'

'And what if I can't get it immediately?'

'I'll chop your nose off, kid. I'll carve up your face. You know that, kid. You must have heard the stories. Now that's the deal. Do you want it?'

The kid wanted the deal. He had to have his penicillin. Stryker told him he would be in touch tomorrow, then the kid walked away. Stryker watched him go, stood there boiling with rage. A fucking whorehouse, he thought. The world's a whorehouse; they oughta scorch the earth clean. He opened the door of the barracks, slammed it viciously behind him. The sound made a lot of heads jerk around, but they looked away quickly. The light washed over Stryker; it made his eyes sting. He glanced along the two lines of bunks and felt the need for some action.

'A fucking whorehouse,' Stryker said. 'This place is filthy. A bunch of pigs in their trough.'

Nobody answered. A nervous silence reigned. Even the new men had been here long enough to know exactly what Stryker meant.

'You all had a good day, boys?' Stryker's hands were on his hips. 'You all dragged your sweet asses through the mud? You sure do look exhausted.'

Nobody answered. They were reading and writing letters. They were engrossed in these tasks to the point where it didn't make sense. The sight of them amused Stryker. The whole bunch was scared shitless. They were all hoping that Stryker wouldn't see them, that the next man would suffer. Only Kline was unmoved; that motherfucker was playing cards. His lean face was totally expressionless as he dealt out the deck.

'Hi, Kantaylis,' Stryker said. 'How you keeping, kid? You seem a bit quiet.'

Kantaylis was on his bed. He was pretending to read a comic. He looked up at Stryker, blinking rapidly, his thick glasses flashing.

'Yes, staff-sergeant,' he said. 'I'm okay. I'm just a bit tired.'

Stryker snorted. He knew what the kid meant. The kid now had a nightmare of his own to keep him awake at night.

'You wanna wrestle with me, kid? You wanna roll on the floor? You look like you could do with the exercise. How about it, Kantaylis?'

Kantaylis started to get nervous. He had always been Stryker's boy. He was dumb and Stryker always protected him ... Now he wondered about that.

'Relax, kid,' Stryker said. 'It's your night off. Go back to your comics.'

Stryker grinned and looked around him. They were all avoiding his gaze. He saw Corporal Bliss sitting on his bed, quietly smoking a cigarette. Stryker didn't like Bliss, couldn't stand that fucking Jew: that fucking Jew, with his blond hair and blue eyes, was protected by Kline. Stryker couldn't understand it. He knew it wasn't homosexual. Kline just didn't like to see Stryker beating up on the boy. You just couldn't figure it. Who could like the greasy yid? This fucking war was being fought for the Jews – and that yid, he survived ... Kline thought him a good soldier. He probably had a point there. If you thought back on the long haul through France, you had to give the Jew credit. He had come through it all right, had earned his goddamned stripes. But that didn't make the fucking kid special; he was just a survivor ... Stryker burned to think about it. He thought of the men who had died. Real Americans had fallen in the mud while the yid just walked through it.

'Hey, Bliss!' Stryker shouted. 'How you keeping? Long time no touch!'

Bliss turned his head slowly, brushed his blond hair from his forehead, gazed along the room without smiling, picked at his lower lip.

'I'm fine, staff-sergeant,' he said. 'I'm doing just fine.'

'Good,' Stryker said. 'I'm glad to hear it. I knew Kline'd look after you.'

Kline looked up from his cards. His lean face was expressionless. Stryker grinned and walked along between the bunks and stopped at the table. The cards were all over the table. There were a lot of beer bottles. Cassavetes wasn't here because the fat slob was dead, his tripe slopping over the rubble in a street in St. Lo. Yet Kline was still here. Kline wasn't that dumb. In fact, Kline was getting so fucking smart he might have to be dealt with. Stryker felt the urge; it was growing stronger every week: he had liked Kline in the past, but now Kline was getting under his skin. Stryker didn't forget anything. He liked to store up old grudges. He wanted total control of the barracks, but Kline kept on blocking him. Kline protected the Jew boy, often put Stryker down. He did it quietly, with no trace of superiority, but it didn't rub easy ... Kline had to be dealt with.

'Hey, Kline,' Stryker said, 'get off your ass. Let's have us a mix.'

'No thanks,' Kline said, looking flatly at Stryker. 'I'm playing a pretty good hand. I don't need no distraction.'

Stryker grinned. 'Good hand, my ass. I ain't never seen you win that fucking game. You just ain't got the instincts.'

'Thanks, Stryker. You're a real friend in need. I'll bear it in mind.'

'You got a beer, Kline?'

'I've just finished mine. But I sure have one hell of a thirst, so if you're buying, I'm taking.'

'That's right, Kline: if I'm buying, you're taking. But the day I have to buy a fucking beer I'll suck my own cock. What about your little buddy, Bliss? Has *he* got a beer?'

'I don't know, Stryker. Why donja ask him?'

Stryker looked across at Bliss. The blond kid was still smoking. He was looking straight at the table, at Stryker, and he didn't seem frightened.

'Hey, Bliss,' Stryker said. 'You got a beer?'

'No, Stryker, I don't.'

Stryker knew the kid was lying. He wanted to pick him up and smash him. One time he would have done it, but now he would have Kline to contend with. Stryker didn't want that yet. He wanted to do the job right. He wanted to see Kline go down for all time, his knowledge obliterated.

It was that goddam Captain Mann; he should have minded his own business. He had heard about a few of Stryker's more modest activities and had said he was going to report it. Stryker hadn't wanted that – it would have meant the Stockade – and he had known that Captain Mann was going to order an investigation as soon as they had taken St. Lo ... Captain Mann never got that far. He died in the battle of St. Lo. He was found with a bullet in his back, as if shot when retreating ... Kline had been there at the time. It had been smokey and confused. There was a lot of action going on at once; a lot of noise and confusion. Kline never said anything. He had never mentioned it since then. But Stryker sensed that Kline knew what had happened and would talk if he had to ... That's why Kline was uppity. That's why he often blocked Stryker. That's why Stryker couldn't beat up on the Jew and encourage Kline's anger.

'No beer, kid, eh?'

'Sorry, Stryker, no beer.'

'I believe you, kid. I really believe you. I just hope you're not lying.'

A beer can cracked open. Stryker turned back to the table. Kline had picked a can up off the floor and was wiping his lips. Stryker looked at him. Kline didn't bother smiling. He had another drink, wiped his lips and put the can on the table.

'The last one,' he said softly. 'Didn't even know I had it. Just looked down and there the fucker was. Tastes real good right now.'

Stryker started to boil. He forced it down with some effort. He unwrapped a stick of Wrigley's and popped the gum into his mouth, grinning casually at Kline.

'You motherfucker,' he said.

'I should be so lucky,' Kline said.

'You would if you could,' Stryker said. 'I don't doubt that a minute.'

Kline had a slug of beer. He put a card on the table. Another GI slapped his hand on the table and said: 'Fuck it! That's me out!' He pushed his chair back and stood up. Another man stepped towards it. Stryker gave him a glance and he stopped and started flushing all over. Stryker grinned and gave a nod. The man sat down, relieved. The game continued while Stryker just stood there, chewing his gum.

Stryker didn't like cards. He didn't like any games. It pissed him off to sit down and do nothing except pass the time away. All these yo-yos were zombies. They had no imagination. Even Kline, when you really thought about it, did nothing but hang around.

'That's a good hand there, Kline.'

'Shut your fucking mouth, Stryker.'

Stryker grinned and kept chewing his gum. 'I'm just trying to be helpful,' he said.

Kline looked up at him. His dark eyes revealed nothing. He dropped a card lightly on the table, but he didn't look down. He spoke softly to Stryker.

'You remember Boletti, Stryker?'

'Yeah, Kline, I remember. The poor motherfucker went to the Stockade for peddling rations.'

'That's the one, Stryker. I thought you'd remember him. He was peddling rations and the MPs warned him off – but for some reason he just wouldn't stop, and he got the Stockade.'

'Yeah,' Stryker said. 'He was dumb. He deserved what he got.'

'I don't know,' Kline said softly. 'He was a pretty good GI. He was really pretty popular in the company: he did a few favours.'

'A few favours,' Stryker said. 'You mean he licked ass. And he got what he fucking deserved: six months in the Stockade.'

'Pretty strange,' Kline said softly. 'Boletti just wasn't the type. A bit dumb, but a heart of pure gold, and as straight as they come. As I remember, Boletti was frightened. The MPs warned him off. But Boletti, he just kept on doing it; he was too scared to stop ... What frightened him, Stryker? That's the mystery. Who was making him do it?'

Stryker chewed his gum, kept the grin on his face. His eyes narrowed as he looked down at Kline, but he didn't say anything.

'Thing is,' Kline said softly, 'that it didn't end there; that when Boletti was sent down he went down to a pretty rough time. You know what the Stockade's like. It's pretty rough at its best. They work you over with clubs and bare knuckles if you don't stay in line ... Now I was talking with some guys. They said Boletti wasn't that type. They say he was the sort of meek guy that shouldn't have got into trouble. But he got into trouble. At least the screws picked him out. Seems that this particular sergeant had an interest in Boletti; kept taking him down to a cell and beating the shit out of him. These guys thought it was pretty strange. They said there was no reason for it. They said Boletti lost an awful lot of weight and that his kidneys are ruined. These guys couldn't figure it. It just didn't make sense. Then the word got around that there was someone behind it, that someone on the outside had put the word on this sergeant and told him to stomp on Boletti. They didn't know who it was. Or if they knew, they weren't saying. But the word was that the guy who was encouraging the treatment was an NCO in Boletti's own company ... Now I don't think that's nice.'

Stryker's jaws worked on his gum. He had his hands on his hips. Kline had a drink of beer and wiped his lips and put the can down again. The rain drummed on the roof.

'Boletti's coming back,' Kline said. 'In fact, he's due in right now. I just thought I'd let you know, Stryker, 'cause I don't want no trouble.'

'Trouble?' Stryker said. 'What sort of trouble? I think Boletti's a sweet guy.'

'Good,' Kline said. 'I'm delighted. Let's keep it that way.'

Stryker turned and walked away. He felt the anger coursing through him, felt the violence and revulsion and rage, that obscure need for vengeance. He wanted to smash Kline, wanted to take him apart; he didn't want to have to hang around here and be hit by Kline's flak. Who the fuck did he think he was? Did he think he could get away with it? The smart-ass had an ace up his sleeve and was beginning to use it ... Stryker burned with the need. He walked back down the barracks. His hands were opening and closing by his sides, and he wanted to use them ... Tear the place apart, break Kline down bone by bone, stomp the bones into the mud of the compound and bury them deep ... The bunks passed on either side. The bright light stung Stryker's eyes. He saw Kantaylis sitting up very straight, looking at him with dumb eyes ... Stryker had to do something. He just couldn't sit back and take it. He had to have a drink and think it out, so he turned to Kantaylis.

'Hey, Kantaylis,' he said, his voice thick. 'Let's go for a beer.'

Kantaylis jumped up immediately. His face was beaming with relief. The light flashed off his glasses as his feet hit the floor and he stood up.

'Right, staff!' he said. 'Great idea! Just give me a second!'

Someone murmured and someone laughed. Stryker looked back at the table. Two of the players were laughing at Kline – and Kline was gazing at Stryker. Stryker saw Kline's lazy grin. It made his rage burn even brighter. He wanted to walk back along the barracks and kick Kline's fucking teeth in.

'Something funny?' Stryker said.

'Not at all,' Kline replied. 'Just delighted that you're taking your buddy. You're protecting him well.'

The men around the table laughed. Stryker's grip was being loosened. Pretty soon he wouldn't have a thing to say: he'd be licking Kline's boots. Stryker burned with this knowledge. It made him want to destroy the world. He wanted to start with Kline, work his way around the table, and then take the whole barracks apart and raze the camp to the ground. Stryker looked at Kantaylis. The kid was buttoning his overcoat. Stryker grabbed him and threw him at the door and said, 'Fuck them! Let's go!' The kid stumbled through the door. An icy wind blew the rain in. Stryker walked out and slammed the door behind him and glanced over the compound.

The thousands of tents were now in darkness. Ten thousand shadows moved between them. Stryker wanted to get his hands on a flamethrower and charge in amongst them. The thunder rolled above. A silvery deluge swept the steps. Stryker cursed and pushed Kantaylis ahead, their boots squelching in mud. He felt the wind on his face. The surrounding barracks were blacked-out. He thought of London, of its dark, shielding streets, of white eyes in the park. Stryker burned with the need. Kantaylis stumbled ahead of him. Stryker looked up and saw the machine-guns towering over the barbed wire. The wind howled around the buildings. It beat harshly at Stryker's face. Kantaylis walked up some steps and opened a door and a bright light shone out.

Stryker followed him inside, let the door slam behind him. The bar consisted of some planks over barrels, was noisy and smokey. Stryker asked for some money. Kantaylis gladly gave it to him. Stryker bought two halfs of Scotch and walked back out and sat down on the steps.

The icy rain lashed over him. The moaning wind whipped all around him. Kantaylis sat down beside him and said, 'Jesus! We're not drinking out *here*!' Stryker didn't reply. He had the bottle to his lips. He drank deeply, then passed it to Kantaylis and said, 'Drink! I said *drink*!' Kantaylis did as he was told. He had to keep up with Stryker. He drank and passed the bottle back to Stryker, as the night howled about them.

'They're all against us,' Stryker said. 'Those fucking mothers all hate us. They hate me, but they hate you even more, so you better watch out, kid.' Stryker drank some more Scotch. He passed the bottle to Kantaylis. The kid shivered with the cold and wiped the rain from his face and drank deeply. 'Yeah,' he said, 'you're right. They don't like me anymore. They don't like me 'cause I stick close to you, but I don't mind that, staff.' He passed the bottle to his mentor. Stryker drank an awful lot. His profile was silhouetted against a deluge of silvery rain. 'I'm glad you understand,' he said. 'I'm glad you know what the score is. That Kline, he's trying to take over, and they're all on his side.' He had another drink. He passed the bottle to Kantaylis. The kid was now glowing with pride and he drank like a man. 'We've got to stop them,' he said to Stryker. 'They're gonna get out of hand. As it is, I can't get any peace unless you're in the barracks.' He passed the bottle to Stryker. The staff-sergeant drank deeply. He wiped the rim of the bottle with one hand and passed it back to Kantaylis. 'Fuck the lot of them,' he said. 'I'm gonna sort that lot out. I'm gonna sort out that Kline and then I'm gonna make the others feel the heat.' Kantaylis had a good drink. He forgot the rain and the wind. He glanced across at the compound and it tilted and then righted itself. 'You're a good kid,' Stryker said. 'You have a sense of what's right and wrong. You stick with ole Stryker and none of those fuckers will touch you. You and me, kid, we'll beat them.'

Kantaylis had another drink. The bottle was nearly empty. He passed it to Stryker and shivered as the wind swept the rain across. 'I'll get Kline,' Stryker said. 'But first I want to get Boletti. I want to take that motherfucker apart – him and the Jew boy.' Stryker finished off the bottle. He looked at it disgustedly. He threw it in the mud and smashed it under his boot, then he opened the second bottle and drank and passed it over to Kantaylis. 'That Corporal Bliss,' Kantaylis said. 'I don't trust that guy, staff. I don't trust him 'cause I know he don't like you. That's all I need, staff.' Stryker patted the kid's knee. He put his hand out for the bottle. The kid, who hadn't managed to have a drink, passed it back without comment. 'That's right,' Stryker said. 'You got good instincts, kid. I've never trusted that fucking Jew since I met him ... Too smooth for my liking.' Kantaylis nodded his head thoughtfully. Stryker had another drink. He didn't pass the bottle back to Kantaylis, and the kid didn't ask for it. 'I'm gonna get them,' Stryker said. 'I'll get the whole fucking bunch of them. And then I'm gonna cut out of here. You and me, kid. Together.' Stryker had another drink. He eventually finished the whole bottle. He threw it in the mud and stood up and then kicked it to pieces.

'Let's go back to the barracks,' he said.

They stumbled off through the mud. The thunder rumbled overhead. The wind howled and the rain continued pouring, soaking them both. Kantaylis swayed and almost fell. Stryker pulled him to his feet. The kid blinked and wiped the rain from his glasses and stepped forward and slipped again. His arms waved and he shrieked. The mud splashed up as he fell. It splashed up over Stryker, and he cursed and stared down at Kantaylis. The kid was rolling about there. He was mumbling and moaning. The whites of his eyes shone through the mud and the night's swirling darkness. Stryker laughed and kicked the kid. Kantaylis grunted and rolled away. He was covered in mud and he made a squelching sound when he moved. Stryker laughed and staggered on. He saw the barbed wire of the compound. He thought of the German colonel and his men who were now getting ready. The very thought of it amused Stryker. Let them fight their fucking war. Let the war itself raze the whole earth and leave it clean as a whistle. Stryker laughed and kicked the mud. He kicked again and again. His humour left him and he felt the old violence, that obscure need for vengeance. Kantaylis stumbled up beside him. Stryker pushed the kid away. He cursed and climbed the steps to the barracks and kicked the door open.

*'Fuck you all!'* Stryker bawled.

The bright light assailed him. He saw the heads jerk around. He walked up to the first bunk and tipped it over and threw it down on its occupant. The man shrieked and hit the floor. The bed was lying on top of him. The next man started jumping from his bunk, but Stryker got in there first. He grabbed the man by one arm, swung him round and let him go. The man shot across the room and crashed into a cupboard and the cupboard fell across another bed. Men were scattering and bawling. Another bed was kicked over. Stryker cursed and worked his way down the room while the men hugged the walls. Then Stryker suddenly stopped. He stopped in front of the card table. The chairs were all empty, but the table was covered in bottles and cards. Stryker picked it up and threw it. It crashed into the end wall, hit the floor with a thud, and rolled about between the smashed, clattering bottles.

Stryker turned to find Kline. There was no sign of the sergeant. Stryker saw Corporal Bliss on his bed and he clenched both his fists. Then Stryker froze. He saw Boletti in the corner. The fat corporal was now very thin and his dark face was frightened.

'Boletti!' Stryker said.

'Hello, Stryker,' Boletti said.

'So you're back,' Stryker said. 'Back at last. I'd like to settle an old score.'

Boletti licked at his lips. He backed nervously against the wall. He glanced desperately at the men all around him, then he stared right at Stryker. The staff-sergeant walked towards him. Boletti shrank within himself. He pressed his back to the wall and looked at Stryker, his eyes large and pleading.

'*Please*, Stryker,' he said. 'I've been through enough already. I went down for six months and kept my mouth shut. *Please*, Stryker! No more!'

'But you're back,' Stryker said. He was smiling and walking forward. 'You're back and I wanna give you a welcome. Come on! Shake my hand.'

Stryker stopped in front of Boletti. He held out his huge hand. Boletti licked his lips and stared down at the hand, but he didn't dare touch it.

'*Please*, Stryker!' he said. 'Let me go, leave me be. It's my kidneys, staff-sergeant. For God's sakes! I just couldn't stand it!'

Stryker punched him in the stomach. Boletti shrieked and doubled over. Stryker took him by the hair and pulled his head up and then started slapping him. Boletti's head jerked left and right. His face smacked against the wall. His hands flapped about loosely and Stryker punched him again, and he shrieked and doubled up and Stryker kneed him. Then Stryker went to town, worked savagely and methodically: Boletti's body became a rag doll, bouncing backwards and forwards. He finally crashed into a wall, slid slowly to the floor; there was blood on his face and he was holding his belly and blubbering. Stryker moved in to kick him. A chair smashed against Stryker's spine. He whirled around and saw Corporal Bliss panting, staring at him with wild eyes.

'No more!' the Jew hissed. 'You understand, Stryker? *No more!*'

Stryker simply exploded. He hardly knew what he was doing. He grabbed Bliss and smashed him into a wall and kept punching and kicking. Bliss never made a sound. His hands waved ineffectually. His body rocked and his head became a blur, a white mask streaked with red. Then Bliss grunted and collapsed. He slid slowly down the wall. His head rolled on his shoulders and he sighed through bloody lips and fell sideways. Stryker stepped back and gasped. He was quivering with tension. He stepped forward and kicked Bliss in the ribs and then he walked from the barracks.

Not much later, feeling calm and alert, he led the Germans to freedom.

# CHAPTER THIRTEEN

MADAME BOULLARD, sitting on the couch in the middle of the large, rococo-styled room, her grey hair piled on her head, her heavy body draped in black, looked up and smiled politely as Stryker entered. The room was bathed in muted crimson. The girls moved lethargically amongst the soldiers. The soldiers sat along the bar and reclined in deep armchairs, had their arms around the girls on the sofas, hands stroking their powdered thighs. Stryker stood near the cloakroom, chewed his gum and glanced around him. A girl giggled, a soldier laughed, glasses tinkled and chairs squeaked; and on the two flights of stairs that led to the rooms, couples wandered up and down and felt each other. A fucking whorehouse, Stryker thought; a typical example of French culture. He looked back at Madame Boullard, at her flabby, rouged cheeks, and saw that she was sitting between two girls, both wearing loose dressing gowns. The girls were pretty and very young, about fifteen years of age; they were the most expensive girls in the house, and Stryker had a share in them. He stepped into the room. Madame Boullard rose to greet him. She smiled politely, but her grey eyes were cool and devoid of illusions.

'Bonjour, m'sieu,' she said softly. 'It is so nice to see you again.'

'Oh, yeah,' Stryker said. 'I'm sure it is. Let's go to the bar.'

'You would like a drink, m'sieu?'

'That's right. I'd like a drink. I can't stand this fucking hot-house. A double Scotch would do fine.'

'Your manner of speech pains me, m'sieu ... So intelligent ... So crude.'

'That's me, baby: crude and uncultured. Now let's go to the bar.'

Madame Boullard walked ahead of Stryker, her hands clasped against her belly, her dress rustling and trailing on the carpet which was faded and worn. The chairs along the bar were full. The GIs leaned on their elbows. They smoked Chesterfields and drank double measures and stared into the mirror. The mirror ran the length of the bar. It reflected the room behind them. The eyes of the GIs moved back and forth, perusing the action. Stryker slouched against the counter. Madame Boullard went behind it. She poured Stryker a double Scotch and set it down on the counter before him. Stryker studied the glass.

'A good Scotch,' he said.

'You should know, m'sieu,' she said.

'Difficult to come by,' Stryker said. 'That's why it's so costly.'

'It is costly, m'sieu.' She shrugged her shoulders and sighed. 'But in times of war one must expect it. I remain philosophical.'

'You need more?' Stryker asked her.

'I always need more, m'sieu. The Americans are no different from the Germans: they like to drink and relax.'

Stryker grinned. 'You fat cow,' he said. 'You don't give a fuck who holds Paris – just as long as they pay.'

His obscenity pained her. Her eyes fluttered with disdain. She raised her chubby hands and waved them gently, indicating the crowded room.

'But what can I do, m'sieu? I merely supply a certain need. What is a poor woman to do but bow down to the fates? Could I have refused the Germans entrance? Could I now refuse the Americans? And finally, when the Americans have gone, I will welcome the French back.'

'You're a patriot,' Stryker said.

'I am a working woman, m'sieu. I serve whoever walks through my door, no matter the uniform.'

'Pretty neat,' Stryker said.

He glanced across the room. The ladies wandered back and forth. Their fingers trailed over the heads of the soldiers, stroking gently, invitingly. Stryker felt a quiet revulsion. He thought of what went on in here; Paris conquered and Paris liberated were one and the same. The city's windows were shuttered. Bodies writhed on the beds. The parting of the flesh to greet flesh was the soldier's reward. All heroes were the same: they had to smell the sweating crotch. They would tear off their medals to expose themselves, vain and pathetic. It disgusted Stryker; it enthralled him and sickened him. He wanted to take a whore and slit her open, see the pus dripping out. Someone laughed and someone giggled. He heard the rattling of glasses. A drunken GI was being helped up the stairs by a slim, dark-haired whore. Stryker saw her ass-cheeks; they strained against a silk skirt. He wanted to slip it in there, between her thighs, feel the trembling release. Stryker needed it more and more. He had to soothe his own revulsion. He had to find that fierce and ultimate satisfaction which forever eluded him.

'Another whisky, m'sieu?'

'Yeah,' Stryker said. 'That's great. Another double and make it on the rocks. It's hot as hell in here.'

Madame Boullard poured the drink. She slid the glass across to Stryker. He had a sip and put the glass down on the counter and stared at the Madam. Her fat fingers were intertwined. Her hands rested against her belly. She looked like every Frenchman's grandmother, but her grey eyes were jaded.

'You have the penicillin, m'sieu?'

'It's in your office,' Stryker said.

'You went into my office, m'sieu? That is really most rude.'

Stryker grinned. 'I never had any manners. I'm just a working man and I like to do things my own way. Don't complain, lady. Just take it while you can. You got girls here and some of them get sick and they need to be cured. I should get an award.'

Madame Boullard smiled a little. A GI called out for some drinks. She went along to the end of the counter to serve him, then came back to Stryker.

'How're my girls doing?' Stryker said.

'They are doing very well, m'sieu. They do not do as much as the rest, but they *do* make more money. Young girls are very popular. The Americans like them nubile. I am careful who I let them go with, which means they stay clean.'

'But they're paying?'

'They are paying.'

'That's a low rental you got.'

'Not so low. I have certain overheads, m'sieu. I feed them and clothe them and look after their health; and this building, m'sieu, is expensive to light and keep warm. You do not have such expenses. You do not have any trouble. It is I who must deal with the *gendarme* and the Military Police.'

'You pay them?' Stryker said.

'We have an understanding, m'sieu. They either come here for a girl or for francs; either way they are satisfied.'

'A filthy business,' Stryker said.

'You should know, Monsieur Stryker. The wounded soldier is not the only victim in a war of this kind.'

Stryker knew about the victims. He specialized in the breed. He had found them in the ruins, in the small, shattered towns, in the dust-enshrouded columns of refugees that the planes liked to strafe. The victims had haunted eyes, were very young and very old, had the dust of the debris in their throats and on their torn, shabby clothes. The victims always stood in ruins. They shuffled along in faceless crowds. They looked up at the troops rolling past in trucks, raised their hands just like beggars. The victims were in their thousands. They were scattered across Europe. They were young and they were old, and the former suffered more than the latter. The old lay down and died, the young simply had to live: they surrendered their flesh and their spirit to the victors who chose them. The bright-eyed boy pimps. The dull-eyed child whores. The francs converted into food and salvation when their legs had been outstretched. Stryker knew it and had used it. He had favoured the moon and stars. In the night, in the graveyard of the ruins, he had found a brief peace. Now Stryker burned with the knowledge. His own revulsion was relentless. He had finally reached that stage where the flesh in itself was not enough ... he had to go far beyond that.

'I'll soon be leaving,' he said. 'You better order while you can. I've got plenty of stock and I wanna convert it into francs. You can have a reduction.'

'Where are you going, m'sieu?'

'I'm going to Germany,' Stryker said. 'I've developed a real interest in that country. More so since it's been pulverized.'

Madame Boullard smiled. 'I didn't know you disliked the Boche.'

'I don't like *anyone*,' Stryker said. 'I love the ruins of France.'

Madame Boullard stopped smiling. She unfolded her chubby hands. She studied her fingers for a moment, and then patted her grey hair.

'Penicillin?' she said.

'You name it, you got it.'

'I believe Americans are dying because of a shortage.'

'I *have* heard that rumour.'

'I need spirits,' Madame Boullard said. 'I need any kind you can get. Whisky and bourbon and cognac. I need gin for the British.'

'Ah, yes,' Stryker said. 'The fucking British.'

'You can supply this, m'sieu?'

'I can supply it,' Stryker said.

'And cigarettes, of course. I need as many as you can carry.'

'And you'll pay on delivery?' Stryker said.

'But naturally, m'sieu.'

Stryker grinned. 'Okay,' he said. 'I'll bring you all I can get. I'll deliver by truck tomorrow lunchtime and we'll settle the deal.'

'Do you think that's wise, m'sieu?'

'What?'

'Delivering in daylight.'

'Yes. It's much worse at night: the patrols are out then. Don't worry. I'll be here at lunchtime. I won't be wearing my uniform, and the goods will be in a civilian truck.'

'And how will you get it out of camp, m'sieu?'

'In an ambulance,' Stryker said. 'I bring it out in an ambulance. I park the ambulance in a farm just outside Paris, then I transfer the goods to the truck and drive up to your front door. Not an eyebrow will be raised, Madame Boullard. Let go of your knickers.'

Her lips twitched with distaste. She examined her fingernails. She dabbed lightly at one eyebrow with her finger and then studied Stryker.

'I will not see you after that?'

'No,' Stryker said, 'you won't see me. You pay me this month's rental on the girls and then you can keep them. No more Stryker. They're yours.'

'That is very kind, m'sieu.'

'Consider it a bonus.'

'Perhaps you would like a girl now. It's the least I can do.'

Stryker grinned. 'No thanks,' he said. 'Too many cocks have been in that cunt and I don't want no part of it.'

She refused to be drawn by him. Her distaste was quickly smothered. She put her elbows on the counter, placed her chin in her hands, and studied him with cold, perceptive eyes.

'That is something I have noticed, m'sieu. In your business it is quite unusual. You have never taken one of your own girls . . . nor any of the others. That strikes me as odd, m'sieu.'

'Not odd,' someone else said. 'Not odd at all. Ole Stryker, he's got his own little playmate. Now isn't that right, Stryker?'

Stryker turned his head slowly. Kline was leaning against the bar. He was gazing at Stryker and his lean face was totally expressionless.

'Hello, Kline,' Stryker said, straightening up, speaking carefully. 'What brings you out of the barracks? Trying to lose your virginity?'

Kline didn't smile. 'I got bored,' he said. 'I got bored kicking the shit out of Kantaylis – for Boletti and Bliss.'

'Oh, yeah,' Stryker said, 'that little incident. I don't know what came over me.'

'I know what came over you. My absence came over you. The minute I walked out the door you went on a rampage. I told you about that, Stryker. I said I didn't want that. I told you not to cause any trouble, but I don't think you listened.'

Stryker couldn't believe his ears: no one had talked to him

204

like this before. The motherfucker was actually reprimanding him – almost giving him orders. Stryker started to burn. He had to control his mounting rage. He glanced around him and saw that they weren't alone, that some men had moved in on them. They were GIs from Stryker's company. They weren't looking, but they were listening. They sensed that this would be a confrontation and they wanted to witness it. This thought burned him even more. He wanted to smash Kline there and then. He wanted to do it, but he knew it would be foolish, a mere halfway house. No, he wanted Kline cold, wanted to finish him completely. He had plans and those plans would have to wait until the time was just right. Stryker looked back at Kline. Kline was staring straight at him. The fucker was leaning casually against the bar, and his face was expressionless.

'You said you didn't want that?'

'That's what I said, Stryker.'

'And just who the fuck do you think you are, Kline, to tell *me* what to do?'

'Are you pulling rank, staff-sergeant?'

'No, I ain't pulling rank. I'm just saying that I don't take fucking orders from a cunt like yourself.'

Madame Boullard looked nervous. She glanced casually to the side. Two large Frenchmen wearing suits and pullovers stepped up to the bar. They didn't say anything, just stood there and watched. They were standing behind Kline, and Stryker grinned and put some gum in his mouth.

'They're not orders,' Kline said. 'I'm just telling you to lay off. I didn't mind it at first, but now it's all getting a bit out of hand. You're going crazy, Stryker. You don't know when to stop. The odd brawl was bad enough, but now you're just a goddamned ape on the loose. I've been watching you since London. Something happened to you over there. Something really got through to you, Stryker, and it must have been rough. You changed after that. You were bad, but you got worse. Then I watched you during the whole push to Paris, and you just went bananas. You're out of control, Stryker. You're not acceptable anymore. It's your business when it doesn't touch me, but now you're getting too close. You're disturbing me, Stryker. You're beginning to make me lose sleep. You come

205

into my barracks and you wreck the fucking place and you knock the shit out of my friends. I don't like that, Stryker.'

Stryker chewed his gum. He looked thoughtfully at Kline. Kline's face was no longer expressionless: it was flushed with quiet rage.

'*Your* barracks?' Stryker said.

'Yes,' Kline said, '*my* barracks. I live there and that makes them mine and I don't want you wrecking them. My barracks and my men. They come under my command. I take orders from you, but that doesn't mean I have to take your shit. It's all over, Stryker. I'm telling you to lay off. You give an official order and I'll make sure it's obeyed – but you don't have any power beyond that and I want you to know it. They're my men, Stryker. I won't let you abuse them. You try and pull another crazy stunt and I'll have you degutted.'

Stryker had to control himself. He sensed the watching eyes waiting. He was burning with a violent rage, but he had to control it.

'How'll you do that, Kline? I'd like to know. Is it just you and me?'

'No, it ain't just you and me. I wouldn't give you that satisfaction. It's not me who'll degut you – it's the Army. I'll just give them the means.'

'I don't follow you, Kline.'

'I think you follow me, Stryker. I think you know that I know a few things that could get you sent down. Who was frightening Boletti, Stryker? What really happened to Captain Mann? How can prisoners keep escaping from the compound night after night? You follow me, Stryker. You wouldn't just get the Stockade. You'd get the fucking book in your face and you wouldn't come out. I'll do it, Stryker. If I have to, I'll do it. So from now on you keep your fucking nose clean and don't aggravate me.'

Stryker found it hard to grin. It was difficult, but he managed it. He chewed his gum and turned his face away from Kline and stared straight at the mirror.

'I'll think about it,' he said.

The two Frenchmen watched them. Kline kept his eyes on Stryker. Stryker stood there and stared at the mirror, then at

Madame Boullard's eyes. No one said a word. Stryker didn't make a move. Kline finally turned away and walked out without once looking back. They all heard the door slam. Madame Boullard heaved a sigh. The two Frenchmen moved back into the gloom and the watching men disappeared. Stryker just stood there. He saw his own dark reflection. He felt the rage boiling up and exploding and stripping his senses.

'Tomorrow,' he said to Madame Boullard. 'I'll see you tomorrow.'

He left the bar and walked out. The streets of Paris were dark. He walked along towards the Porte Saint Denis, muttering under his breath. He hardly knew he was doing it, was only conscious of his rage. He wanted to find Kline and smash him flat, make him swallow his arrogance. Kline had humiliated him. He was stripping Stryker of his authority. He was kicking Stryker's legs from beneath him and grinding his face in the mud. Stryker cursed and walked on. He turned into the boulevard. He saw the stacked chairs of the closed sidewalk cafés, the dark shuttered windows. He had to get rid of Kline. He couldn't let that fucker live. That sonofabitch knew far too much and was willing to use it. Stryker stewed in his rage. He wanted to take the world apart. He felt the knife between his gaiter and boot, and he wanted to use it ... Strip the flesh off the bone, see life's substance and meaning, smell the rot and let it all ooze away and vapourize into clean air ... Stryker cursed and then trembled. A few army trucks passed by. He saw American and French soldiers on patrol at the end of the road. Fuck the French and their city. Fuck the Americans for guarding it. Stryker turned left and passed some stacked tables and knocked on a wooden door.

He had to wait a long time. He cursed under his breath again. The wind blowing along the boulevard was cold and aggravated his bad mood. The Frogs were always slow. They were more slow when frightened. The man inside would definitely be frightened and was probably checking him.

Stryker hammered on the door again. He heard hesitant footsteps. 'It's Stryker!' he said in a loud voice. 'Open the door!' The bolt was finally withdrawn. The door opened a little. A pair of frightened eyes looked at Stryker and then he was waved in. Stryker pushed the man aside. He walked into the dark hall. The door was closed behind him and bolted, then the frightened man looked at him. The man was small and pot-bellied, his black hair greased down; he had the face of an overgrown child and was in his mid-forties. Stryker gave the man a glance of contempt and his lower lip trembled.

'I am sorry,' he said softly. 'One never knows. One cannot be too careful.'

Stryker wasn't interested. He simply stared at the frightened man. The man shrugged in an apologetic manner and then mumbled, 'This way, please.' Stryker followed him up the stairs. They were narrow and very dark, smelling of dust and decay, a faint hint of urine. Stryker felt disgusted. He thought of the man's unwashed body. He thought of his days hiding in here, peering out through the window. They finally reached the top of the stairs. A light shone from a bedroom. The man stepped aside and Stryker walked in and saw the woman on the bed. She was wearing a grey skirt and blouse, had no shoes on her feet; was attractive in a blowsy sort of way, her blonde hair uncombed. Stryker grinned at her. He saw the shadows beneath her eyes. She did not return his smile and Stryker sat down on the room's only chair. He looked up at the Frenchman. He was standing nervously in the doorway. He stared bleakly at Stryker and then sat beside the blonde on the bed. The blonde's tired eyes were cold.

'How you been keeping?' Stryker said. 'You don't look so well.'

He had said it to the blonde. Her blue eyes stared into his. He saw nothing but a weary contempt, then she stared at the floor.

'Okay?' Stryker said.

The Frenchman shrugged forlornly. 'As good as can be expected,' he said. 'But that isn't too good.'

Stryker grinned. He knew what the Frenchman meant. The Frenchman was a collaborator, the whore beside him was a German, and both of them were currently being sought by the National Council of Resistance. The blonde was the Frenchman's mistress, had helped him in his work. His work had involved spying on all the other Frogs and helping to make up the deportation lists. He had lived well for a time. He had fucked his blonde whore. They had lived in an apartment above the Rue de la Paix, but now they were hiding out in this empty café. The Resistance were all over Paris. They were searching for collaborators. Those that were found were either delivered to the courts of justice or summarily executed in the streets. The Frenchman was frightened and had good reason to be: he had to get out of France before de Gaulle was properly organized and the blade of retribution fell upon him.

'You look tired,' Stryker said. 'You obviously haven't been sleeping well. You shoulda let me know about that – I'd've brought you some cognac.'

The blonde's blue eyes looked at him. They were cold and contemptuous. Stryker grinned and she looked down at the hands intertwined in her lap.

'Please,' the Frenchman said, speaking softly and reasonably. 'We have no time for your strange brand of humour. Did you bring the passports?'

'*One* passport,' Stryker said. He looked deliberately at the blonde. 'One passport. That's all I could get. You can take it or leave it.'

The blonde stared straight at him. Her hands twisted in her lap. The Frenchman licked his lips and glanced at her, then he turned back to Stryker.

'But Monsieur,' he said, 'I do not understand.'

'It's simple,' Stryker said. 'You asked for two and I got one. It's made out to a certain Monsieur Graumont. You can take it or leave it.'

The Frenchman licked his lips, wiped some sweat from his forehead. He glanced desperately at the blonde, but she had her gaze fixed upon Stryker. She didn't move. Her hands had stopped their formless twitching. She simply stared with a luminous hatred that transcended all fear.

'I don't believe you,' she said.

'One passport,' Stryker said.

'I don't believe you could only get one. I refuse to accept this.'

Her blue eyes blazed at Stryker. Her face was pale and very

thin. She had small pointed breasts and they trembled beneath the thin blouse. Stryker looked at her, grinned tightly, maliciously. He looked at the Frenchman and saw that he was blinking and sweating. A feeling of power engulfed Stryker, soothed his recent humiliation; he felt the knife between his gaiter and boot, and he wanted to touch it. He saw the Frenchman's dark eyes. They were filling up with panic, were flitting left and right between Stryker and the blonde on the bed. Stryker looked at the blonde. Her blue eyes held cold fury. Her hands lay very still in her lap and her legs were curled under her.

'I don't believe you,' she repeated.

'This is monstrous,' the Frenchman said.

Stryker grinned and pulled the passport from his pocket and waved it before him.

'One passport,' Stryker said. 'Take it or leave it. The choice is all yours.'

The Frenchman licked his lips. His face was pale with fear and shame. He raised his hands and let them drop back to his sides and then he glanced at the blonde. Her blue eyes turned towards him. They were hard and asked for nothing. The Frenchman wiped the sweat from his forehead and looked back at Stryker.

'You expect me to leave her?' he said. 'But I can't! It is monstrous!'

His eyes flitted back and forth, saw contempt on both sides, settled on the floor and remained there as he held out his hand.

Stryker looked at the blonde. The whore was trying to stare him down. Her blue eyes knew the truth when they saw it, and they saw it right now. Stryker studied her breasts, saw the curve to her legs. His gaze roamed from her feet to her throat and then fixed on her eyes again. The eyes were filled with knowledge; in that knowledge there was hatred. The hand of the Frenchman was outstretched ... and then he looked up.

'I want paid,' Stryker said.

'You *have* been paid,' the Frenchman said.

'The price has gone up,' Stryker said. 'I want her. Right this minute.'

The Frenchman's eyes widened. He glanced quickly at the blonde. She didn't move, so he looked back at Stryker, mouth open, eyes desperate.

'You can't mean this!' he said.

Stryker grinned and dangled the passport. He swung it to and fro before the Frenchman, but he stared at the blonde.

'Take it,' Stryker said. 'Take it now and get out. Get out and leave me here with your whore. That's the price. It's your choice.'

The Frenchman started to sob. He covered his face with his hands. His body shook as he wept, and Stryker grinned and looked across at the blonde. She didn't look at the Frenchman. She looked directly at Stryker. Her eyes were luminous above the dark shadows, suffused with cold fury. Her breasts trembled beneath the blouse. Her hands didn't move at all. There was silence between them as they listened to the Frenchman's choked sobbing.

'Take it,' Stryker said. 'Fuck off out of here.'

The Frenchman stopped sobbing, glanced up with red eyes. His face was drained of colour, and he sweated and shook uncontrollably. Stryker swung the passport gently. The Frenchman suddenly snatched it. He then stood up and rushed for the door, but stopped there to glance back.

'God forgive me,' he said.

A wracked sob broke his lips. He left the room and rushed downstairs. The door slammed and then he was gone, leaving silence behind him.

Stryker looked at the blonde. She was still staring at him. She was sitting up straight on the bed with her legs curled beneath her.

Stryker felt her contempt. It charged his blood with excitement. He looked at her eyes, at their venomous blue depths, and he felt himself drawn to her hatred, dissolving around her. She didn't move. She had her hands in her lap. He saw her body spreadeagled beneath him, felt the whorls of her flesh. Stryker shivered with revulsion, felt the lust and the outrage. His own hatred boiled up and overran him and swept him away. Stryker reached down to his gaiter. He gripped the knife and held it up. The blade snapped out and flashed in the

211

light before the widening blue eyes. He placed the knife on one knee. The blue eyes fell upon it. They turned around and looked directly at Stryker and at last he saw fear.

'Take your clothes off,' he said.

# CHAPTER FOURTEEN

THE truck rumbled awkwardly along the winding dirt track that cut through the French countryside, passing desolate, shattered towns, the remains of tanks and half tracks, the barren fields containing dead cows and shell-holes and broken gliders, the peasants who stood beneath grey skies, watching the aircraft. The aircraft filled the whole sky. They were heading towards the Rhine. Stryker glanced up and wished he was with them, on the move once again, travelling deep into Germany where the Reich was in chaos and the spoils of the victors would be plentiful.

'Christ,' he said, 'just look at them mothers. They won't leave a thing standing.'

The other men looked up. They were in the back of the truck. The truck rocked and they were thrown against each other, their helmets askew. Boletti crashed into Bliss, mumbled an apology and sat up straight. Both Boletti and Bliss had very badly bruised faces, and they both moved uncomfortably in their seats. Boletti fingered his chin strap. His anxious eyes surveyed the sky. The planes rumbled above the grey, sludge-like clouds in massive formations.

'I hope they don't,' he said. 'I don't *want* a thing left standing. If we go there, I don't want to see anything, I just want to walk through it.'

Stryker stared at him. He felt a brimming distaste. The little wop was scared shitless and he didn't even bother trying hide it. He was sweating quite a bit. He kept fidgeting with his webbing. He had never seen action before and he wasn't cut out for it. They were all the same, the wops. They had nerves like wet spaghetti. They couldn't fight a war to save their lives; hardly knew what a rifle was. Stryker stared at Boletti, saw the sweating dark skin. The little wop was glancing nervously around him, looking for friends.

'Hey, Boletti,' Stryker said. 'What's the matter? You got diarrhoea?'

Boletti stared at him. 'What's that, staff-sergeant?'

'Diarrhoea,' Stryker said. 'I thought you mighta crapped your pants. You're sure moving your ass around a lot. You nervous or something?'

'Yeah,' Boletti said frankly. 'I'm nervous as hell. I never fired at anyone before. And I never been shot at.'

Bliss looked at him and smiled. It must have taken him some effort. His lower lip was split and the chin of his handsome face was swollen.

'Don't worry about it,' he said. 'The nervousness is natural. It doesn't matter a damn if you're nervous. We all know what it feels like.'

'Speak for yourself,' Stryker said. 'Don't put words in my fucking mouth. You chickens get nervous, okay, but don't speak for me.'

Bliss didn't reply, simply stared right at Stryker. There was no fear in his eyes and his broken lips formed a small smile. It made Stryker burn. He knew the fucking yid was mocking him. He had heard about the run-in with Kline, and it had given him confidence. Stryker spat out of the truck. The dust boiled up from the ground. He saw a bloated cow lying in the fields, its belly split open. Stryker wanted to fix them all. He wanted to wipe those fuckers out. He didn't want to have to take this aggravation any more than he had to. A small farmhouse whipped by: a black, gutted shell; there was a tent in the garden beside it, and some people were kneeling there. They glanced up at the passing truck. They had pale, haunted faces. The sky above them was a grey desolation broken up by the aircraft.

'Fucking Frogs,' Stryker said. 'A bunch of fucking baboons. We have to come to France to save their necks and they don't even wave at us.' He spat out of the truck again, saw some gliders in a field: they had buckled and split down the middle and disgorged their contents. 'Dead Americans,' Stryker said. 'This country's full of dead Americans. We rot in the fields and the Frogs try to use us for manure. Fuck the whole lot of them.'

He looked around at the men. Their eyes were dark beneath the helmets. They were being jolted by the truck and the barrels of their rifles clanged together. Boletti and Bliss sat side by side. Stone and Yurick sat opposite them. The only one who had seen action before was that fucking Bliss.

'I'm choking to death,' Yurick said. 'This goddamned dust is gonna kill me. I got asthma and I tried to tell them that, but they just wouldn't listen.'

He grinned nervously at Stryker. The dust was swirling through the truck. Already the five of them were filthy and very dry-throated.

'Asthma,' Yurick said. 'I can hardly breathe the air of Florida. So they send me to France and I almost suffocate on the roads. They just don't give a damn.'

Private Stone jerked at his webbing, wiped sweat from his nose, grinned from a thin, pimpled face and bent forward and sneezed.

'S'cuse me,' he said.

'Fucking asthma,' Stryker said. 'You'll worry about more than your asthma if this town isn't empty.'

Private Yurick grinned nervously, fingered his chin-strap. He put his right hand to his mouth and coughed lightly, blinking through the thick dust.

'What's a holding action?' he said. 'I don't know. I never did this before.'

'It's probably nothing,' Stryker said. He looked at Yurick's bent nose. 'The town fell about four weeks ago, but now they think they got snipers.'

'Snipers?' Stone said.

'Yeah, snipers,' Stryker said. 'You get these fucking fanatics and they hide in the cellars, then they come up when the town has been cleared and they start popping off. They kill the fucking Frogs. It's their only good point. They harass the

fucking Frogs, but then we have to go in and sort them out.
I don't know why we bother.'

Yurick looked disturbed. He glanced at Bliss and Boletti.
Private Stone simply sat there and grinned, a dumb look on
his face.

'Jesus,' Yurick said. 'Jesus Christ. And *we* have to do that?'

'That's right,' Stryker said. He was grinning at Private
Yurick. 'We go in and we clear out the snipers and then we go
home.'

'There's only five of us,' Stone said.

'That's all we need,' Stryker said. 'There's never more than
a couple of snipers, so we don't need an army. These towns
are dead, for fuck's sake. They're filled with old men and
women. The Germans only need a couple of men to keep us
occupied. It's a waste of fucking time. They only kill the
fucking Frogs. But the army thinks they have to be cleared
and that's all there is to it.'

'What if there's more?' Yurick said.

'What d'ya mean?' Stryker said.

'What if there's more than two or three? What do we do
*then*?'

'Reinforcements,' Bliss said. 'We call in for reinforcements.
We just stay there and wait till they come. That's all there is
to it.'

Stryker took out a stick of Wrigley's, popped it into his
mouth, started chewing and looked hard at Bliss, at his handsome blond features. He doesn't look like a Jew, he thought.
He looks like a real American. That Yurick, *he* looks like a Jew;
you can tell by the nose.

'Don't get caught,' Stryker said. 'Don't let them fucking
Germans catch you. They get one look at your circumcised
prick and they'll lop off your balls.'

'I'm not Jewish,' Yurick said. 'I've been circumcised already.
And I won't let no goddam German catch me. They won't
see me for dust.'

Bliss didn't say a word. He just stared straight at Stryker.
His blue eyes were clear and very calm, with just a slight hint
of mockery. Stryker wanted to smash him, wanted to see the
bastard crawl, wanted to wipe the mockery out of his eyes and

216

replace it with fear. Stryker itched with the urge. He felt a quiet, controlled ferocity. He thought of what Kline had said and it made the itch turn into cold rage. You went bananas, Kline had said. You're just an ape on the loose. Stryker thought about that and clenched his fists and watched the brown fields glide past. That Kline was a smart fucker. He knew how to twist the screws. He was twisting them and causing Stryker pain, disturbing his balance. Kline would soon be taking over. Him and Bliss knew too much. Kline had obviously told Bliss what he knew, and that made them both dangerous. Stryker glanced all around him. He felt a strange claustrophobia. He looked out of the rumbling truck and saw some ruins, jagged fingers of granite. A fine dust blew around them. The fields beyond were desolate. They were brown and they were littered with the wreckage of tanks and half tracks. Then there was Boletti. That little fucker must hate him. He had six months in the Stockade to remind him of what Stryker had done. Stryker shivered at the thought. You just couldn't trust anyone. He chewed his gum and looked back into the truck, at the men in the swirling dust.

'Hey, Boletti,' he said, 'don't look so sad. You'll soon be in action.'

Boletti's eyes rolled towards him. They were dark and very wary. Boletti fingered the strap of his helmet and licked his dry lips, tried a trembling smile.

'I'm saying my prayers,' he said quietly. 'I hope to hell they're not there.'

'You're hoping they're not there,' Stryker said with disgust. 'I don't know what the fuck you're doing here. You're no soljer, Boletti.'

'That's right,' Boletti said. 'I'm no soldier. I'm a civilian and I don't want to fight. I just want to go home.'

'Jesus,' Stryker said.

'You've got the right idea,' Bliss said. 'I agree with you totally. I can't wait to get out of this uniform and put on some real clothes. Just fly me away from here.'

Boletti smiled gratefully at him. Stryker snorted in disgust. He spat his chewing gum out at the dust behind the truck, saw charred trees and dead animals and debris, heard the planes high above. He looked at Bliss and thought of Kline. He was glad Kline wasn't here. That fucker was back in the compound, guarding the Germans. Stryker thought of Kline and burned. He remembered what Kline had said. The rage shook him and made him clench his fists and look out at the land again. The fields were littered with wreckage, the passing villages were in ruins; the wind blew the dust around the empty houses and the charred, twisted trees. Stryker felt claustrophobic. He had not felt that before. It swooped down and made him feel suffocated and then it released him.

'This goddamned dust,' Yurick said. 'I can't breathe. Just let me outa this truck.'

'I don't mind,' Stone said smiling. 'I'll sit here till the war ends. I'd rather sit here and choke in the dust than see a German up close.'

'You haven't got asthma,' Yurick said.

'I get constipated,' Stone said.

'Shut your mouths, the fucking pair of you,' Stryker said. 'Just keep your mouths shut.'

They stayed silent after that. The truck rumbled along the road. Bliss put his head back and closed his eyes and held on to his rifle. The fields unfurled behind them. The truck churned the dust up. Yurick picked at his nose and then coughed and adjusted his helmet. Another village passed by: there were black crones in the ruins; ragged people were queuing up for rations while the dust swirled around them. Stryker chewed some more gum. Boletti whistled and then went quiet. The truck roared and bounced over a mound of rubble and then started to slow down. Stryker saw the shattered houses, the rubble and the dust. The truck stopped and Kantaylis, who was in the driver's seat, turned around and put one finger on his glasses and gave them a dopey grin.

'This is it, staff,' he said loudly. 'Do I stay here or drive on?'

Stryker chewed his gum thoughtfully, held his BAR at the ready. He leaned out of the truck and saw a group of men coming towards him. They all looked like Frenchmen. The dust swirled around them. They came up to the back of the truck and looked up at Stryker.

'The Americans?' one of them said.

'That's right,' Stryker said. 'We were told you were having trouble with some snipers. You put in a complaint.'

The spokesman smiled gently. His coat flapped about his belly. He had a ruddy face and thinning grey hair and his hands waved before him.

'Hardly a complaint, Monsieur,' he said. 'Merely a routine notification. We think there are two of them. They keep moving about. A few people have been shot. So we called.'

'They move about?' Stryker said.

'They move about,' the man said. 'But this morning they shot two more people. We think we know where they are.'

'Great,' Stryker said. 'And where's that?'

The man pointed along the street. Stryker leaned out and looked. He saw two rows of gaunt, blackened ruins, the whole street strewn with rubble.

'Down there,' the man said. 'In that building at the corner. As you can see, it is miraculously untouched. They are hiding in there.'

'Any Frogs down there?' Stryker said.

'Pardon?' the Frenchman said.

'Any Frenchmen. Any women or children. I don't want any accidents.'

'No,' the man said. 'I have cleared this whole area. We have lost too many people already. You may go unmolested.'

Stryker spat his gum out. It landed at the Frenchman's feet. The Frenchman stepped back and Stryker grinned and then jumped from the truck.

'Okay,' he said. 'All out!'

Bliss and Boletti jumped down. Yurick and Stone were quick to follow. Kantaylis climbed down from the driver's cabin, carrying an M.1. He walked up to Stryker, pushed his glasses back up his nose. He looked at Bliss and then gave a dopey grin and placed himself close to Stryker. Stryker looked at Stone and Yurick. He wanted to draw the German gunfire. You normally used replacements for that, but Stryker had other ideas.

'We're gonna spread out,' he said. 'We're gonna cover the whole street. I wanna get into that building so I'll stay on this side with Kantaylis.' He looked at Stone and Yurick. 'You two

219

take the opposite side. Just stick close to the wall and advance until you're facing the building.'

'Then they'll see us,' Stone said.

'Keep indoors,' Stryker said.

'And what about us?' Boletti said. 'What do we do?'

He looked at Bliss and then at Stryker. His dark eyes were very nervous. Bliss simply looked at Stryker and offered him a slight, knowing smile.

'You don't have to tell me,' he said. 'You want us out in the street.'

Stryker grinned. 'You know the drill,' he said.

'What does that mean?' Boletti said, looking sideways at Bliss.

'It means we draw their fire,' Bliss said. 'It means we're out in the open. It means our back-up consists of two inexperienced men and that Stryker and Kantaylis are well covered.'

Boletti blinked his large eyes, wiped sweat from his forehead. He glanced along the debris-strewn street and it seemed almost naked.

'What's your bitch?' Stryker said. 'It's fucking standard procedure. Someone's gotta stay on this side, someone's gotta stay on that side, and someone's gotta draw the German fire. I don't know what your bitch is.'

'I'm not bitching,' Bliss said. 'I haven't said a damned word. I simply explained the procedure to Boletti. That's all I did, staff.'

'Wait a minute,' Boletti said. He glanced desperately around him. He saw the Frenchmen and he flushed and turned away and looked directly at Stryker. 'Do we have to go down the middle of the street? I mean, is that really necessary?'

'Yes,' Stryker said. 'It's really necessary.'

Boletti fingered his shirt collar. He glanced at Yurick and Stone. Stone was smiling and Yurick was looking puzzled, wondering what all the talk was for. Boletti stared at them, licked his lips and looked around him, glanced along the desolate, exposed street and then turned back to Stryker.

'Why us?' he said.

'Why not?' Stryker said. '*Someone* has to do the fucking job, so why not you and Bliss?'

'You're more experienced,' Boletti said.

'That's why I'm taking this side,' Stryker said. 'I gotta hug this wall and get under that building, and then get inside the motherfucker when I see where the snipers are.'

'Okay,' Boletti said. 'I get your point. But why me and Bliss?' He glanced desperately around him, looked at Yurick and Stone. They looked back and Boletti turned away and wiped sweat from his forehead. 'You know what I mean,' he said. 'That's a job for the replacements. Last men in always take the dirty jobs. That's what normally happens.'

Stone and Yurick looked at him. Yurick's mouth was hanging open. Boletti kicked his feet nervously at the ground and watched the dust rising up. He did not look at the replacements. He looked up once at Bliss. The corporal stood there and looked right at Stryker, his eyes strangely mocking.

'That's correct,' Bliss said quietly. 'That's the normal procedure, staff. You have a dirty job, you use the replacements. It's always been done that way.'

Stryker grinned at him. Bliss didn't look away. Boletti shuffled his feet in the dust and avoided all eyes.

'I buy that,' Stone said. 'That's what I always heard. Last men in always take the dirty jobs. It's a pretty fair rule.'

'Fair?' Yurick said. 'What the hell do you mean, *fair*. We walk down that road and we're dead. Is that what you call *fair*?'

'Sure,' Stone said smiling. 'Someone has to take the shit. These guys have been through it all before. So why them and not us?'

'You're fucking crazy,' Yurick said.

'That's the rule,' Boletti said. He looked briefly at Yurick and then dropped his eyes back to the ground.

'Fuck the rule,' Stryker said. 'I'm in charge of this outfit. I want Bliss and Boletti in the street, and that's all there is to it.'

He looked directly at Bliss. The corporal shrugged and smiled a little. 'You're the boss,' he said. 'You give the orders. I'm just waiting to start.'

'Okay,' Stryker said. He pointed at Yurick and Stone. 'Go on over there,' he said. 'Keep inside as much as possible. Keep your eyes on that building, on the fucking upstairs windows, and if anything moves don't ask questions, just take aim and fire. Don't take any chances. If nothing happens just move forward. When you get to the end house, the one facing the snipers' building, get inside and cover those upstairs windows. I'll be under those windows. Boletti and Bliss'll be in the street. The minute you see anything move, start firing your rifles. Don't try to be marksmen. Just aim for the fucking windows. You just gotta keep the snipers' heads down while Bliss and Boletti get off the street. Then I'll go inside. You'll keep the snipers distracted. You keep firing until you're told to stop, and that's all there is to it.'

Stone nodded and smiled broadly. He obviously thought it was exciting. Yurick scratched at his forehead and stared in an accusing manner at Boletti. Boletti gazed along the street. He looked desperately at Bliss. Bliss was pulling the bolt of his rifle and surveying the street.

'Let's go,' Stryker said.

Stone and Yurick crossed the road. They reached the first broken building. Stone looked inside the door and waved to Yurick and they both disappeared. They reappeared four doors along: there were obviously holes in the walls. They inched past a few more doors and then disappeared inside again. Bliss moved out with Boletti. They moved slowly along the street. They were completely exposed and Bliss kept looking up to both sides. The Frenchmen nodded at each other. They murmured their appreciation. Stryker waved at Kantaylis and they both hugged the wall near the Frenchmen. They crouched low as they went, jumped in and out of doorways; they found holes in the adjoining walls of the bombed houses and they just walked right through them. Stryker looked at Stone and Yurick. They disappeared and reappeared. Stone was always in the lead and Yurick kept looking nervously about him. Yurick was dumb. He rarely looked at the upper windows. He kept looking at Bliss and Boletti in the middle of the road. Bliss was slightly ahead. He was scanning both sides of the street. Boletti was walking slowly behind him, too frightened to look up. The Frenchmen murmured their approval. They watched the soldiers at work. They watched the staff-sergeant nearing the building, moving slowly and carefully. The staff-sergeant was crouched low. He was creeping up to the door. The two privates, at the end of the street, were slipping into the house. The Frenchmen nodded judiciously. They watched the men in the middle of the road. They were corporals and the one out ahead was looking up to his right.

The two shots rang out at once. The wall exploded above Stryker. Boletti yelped and staggered back and dropped his rifle and looked around in amazement. Bliss was rolling away from him. A dark doorway swallowed Stryker. Boletti murmured 'Jesus Christ!' and then dropped to his knees and fell over. Bliss rolled onto his belly. His rifle was slanted up the rubble. It was firing, and Bliss was cursing softly and working the bolt. The dirt spurted up around him. A second shot just missed Kantaylis. Kantaylis was crouched low near the door that had swallowed up Stryker. ' – *the other side!*' Bliss was shouting. '*Above Yurick and Stone!*' He saw the faces of the privates at the window, eyes wide with amazement. The wall exploded near Kantaylis. He yelped and darted forward. He saw Stryker and he fell through the door and his glasses fell off.

Bliss still lay behind the rubble. It was too low for protection. Something tore through his leg and then he heard the shot and knew he was hit. '*Stryker!*' he yelled furiously. '*Goddammit, where are you?*' Stryker stood in the doorway and grinned and let the sniper find Bliss. 'Jesus, Stryker,' Kantaylis said. He was wiping dirt from his glasses. 'Shut your mouth,' Stryker said. 'Shut your eyes. Just don't fucking see it.' Stryker looked up at the window. He saw the sniper's head and shoulders. He heard the shot and saw Bliss twitch and yelp and roll away from his rifle. Bliss looked up at the sky. '*Godammit, Stryker!*' he screamed. His chest exploded and the shot reverberated and the sky whirled about him.

Kantaylis put on his glasses. He glanced across at Stone and Yurick. Yurick's face was at the window and Stone was leaning out of the door. Another shot hit Bliss. His body jumped and his arms flapped. Stone aimed up the face of the building and fired off a wild shot. Then Stryker stepped forward. He had seen that Bliss was dead. He brought the BAR up to his waist and started firing and his whole body shook. The wall around the

223

window exploded. Dirt and plaster rained down on Stone. He jumped back and disappeared through the doorway and Stryker kept firing. '*Kantaylis!*' Stryker shouted. 'What?' Kantaylis said. '*Get the fuck over there!*' Stryker shouted. '*I'll keep the cunts down!*' The BAR roared in his arms. Kantaylis blinked with disbelief. 'Over there?' he said. 'You mean across the street? Jesus Christ, Stryker, no.' Stryker cursed and stopped firing. He whirled around and grabbed Kantaylis. The BAR clattered to the floor as Stryker threw the dazed Kantaylis at the window. Kantaylis hit the wall violently. His helmet bounced on the rubble. Stryker grabbed him by the collar and pulled him up as another shot rang out. A part of the window frame flew off. '*They're firing back!*' Kantaylis yelped. Stryker picked up the rifle and shoved it at Kantaylis and said, 'Here, you stupid fucker, keep me covered.' Another shot rang out. The bullet hit the wall behind them. Kantaylis pressed the glasses down on his nose and took aim and then fired. His shoulder jerked back. The sound reverberated around the room. He pulled the bolt and fired off another shot as Stryker hurled himself forward.

Kantaylis saw Stryker running. He saw the BAR in his hands. Stryker darted left and right and kept going and Kantaylis kept firing. The dirt kicked around Stryker. He heard the shots ringing out. He saw Stone and Yurick looking through the window, their eyes wide with amazement. Fucking rookies, he thought. He saw the doorway rushing at him. The dirt kicked up around him and he hurled himself forward and crashed into the edge of the doorframe and spun around and fell through.

'Staff-sergeant!' Stone exclaimed.

'Jesus Christ,' Yurick murmured.

'*What the fuck do you think you're doing?*' Stryker yelled. '*You fucking pair should be upstairs!*'

Stryker clambered to his feet. He was still holding the BAR. He pushed Yurick aside and tramped over the rubble and saw the stairs buried in the shadows. 'I didn't realize – ' Stone began. ' – thought you meant – ' Yurick said. '*Now those fuckers'll be expecting us!*' Stryker bawled. '*I oughta make you go first!*' Stone flushed with confusion. Yurick looked out at

Bliss. Stryker pulled a grenade from his belt and rushed straight up the stairs. They were narrow and very steep. They led up to a landing. Beside the landing was a huge, jagged hole that looked over the street. Stryker looked high above him. He heard the clattering of boots. He crouched down with his back near the hole and then he swung the BAR up.

The footsteps stopped on the top landing. He heard them whispering in German. He held the BAR in one arm with the stock pressing into his right thigh. The Germans whispered again. Their footsteps edged towards the stairs. Stryker looked up and saw a broken bannister directly above him. That was the top landing. That's where the Germans were. They were deciding whether or not they should come down and then they shadowed the stairs. Stryker held the BAR up. He had the grenade in his left hand. The shadows advanced down the stairs and Stryker pulled at the pin with his teeth. Then he heard footsteps below. He heard Stone whisper, 'Quiet!' Stryker cursed and dropped the grenade down the stairwell and squeezed on the trigger. The BAR made an awesome roar. The wall and bannister flew apart. The grenade below went off as a German hit the stairs and bounced down in a tangle of arms and legs. The exploding grenade reverberated. Stryker kept firing the BAR. A scream lashed through the explosion and it sounded like Stone and then the second German stumbled down the stairs, clutching his body. Stryker didn't stop firing. 'Oh, my God!' Yurick yelped. Up above the German shuddered and danced and fell back and jerked rhythmically. 'Jesus Christ!' Yurick yelped. 'Jesus Christ! Oh my God! I'm all bloody!' Stryker finally stopped firing. He rushed straight up the stairs. He checked that the two Germans were dead and then he moved further up. The other rooms were all empty. Stryker went back down the stairs. He found Stone near the bottom, his head pointing down the stairs, his upper chest and face a mass of blood, the flesh torn from his throat. Stryker stepped over him. He found Yurick in the rubble. He was covered in Stone's blood, but otherwise he hadn't been touched.

'You were lucky,' Stryker said.

'*What*?' Yurick said.

'You were lucky you didn't get it too.'

'*What*?' Yurick said.

Stryker pushed him outside. The street's grey light fell around them. The Frenchmen were walking along the street, chattering excitedly. Stryker walked across to Bliss. The corporal was spreadeagled on the ground. His helmet had come off and his blond hair was shivering in the breeze. He had been hit five times. There was blood all over his clothes. His face was very pale and his blue eyes looked up at the grey sky. The Frenchmen stood around Boletti. They were looking down and pointing. Stryker knelt down and checked that he was dead, and then he stood up. He saw Kantaylis walking towards him. His eyes were wide behind the glasses. He was holding his rifle and smiling with mild, dopey pride. Kantaylis stood beside the Frenchmen. Yurick wandered up and joined him. They all stood there with the dust blowing around them, looking down at the dead men.

'Day's work done,' Stryker said.

# CHAPTER FIFTEEN

STRYKER woke early and heard the rain drumming on the roof. He cursed softly and looked around him. The other men were still sleeping. They were tossing and turning on their bunks and he thought of the sweaty sheets. A bunch of pigs, he thought. Bags of shit and warm piss. You dig as deep as you can go and you get nothing back but the stench. He looked up at the roof. Thick wooden beams criss-crossed the ceiling. He looked at the far wall and saw the large swastika that no one had bothered to pull down. A German barracks, Stryker thought. What the fuck were Germans like? You killed them but you didn't learn anything except that they bled. The beams above were in shadow. The rain drummed on the roof. Stryker thought of the ten thousand Germans sleeping under the tents. They were nothing but meat. They were flesh on normal bone. The scourge of Europe had proved itself as nothing against Stryker's will. Stryker thought this and grinned. He thought of Bliss and Boletti. Two thirds of his problem had been solved, but now there was Kline. Kline was not sleeping now. He was out guarding the Germans. He was standing in the rain in the grey light of dawn and he would soon be coming in to see Stryker.

The rain drummed on the roof. It made a low, metallic sound. It was falling on the corrugated iron and pouring down past the windows. Stryker didn't like the rain; it always did something to him. He would rather have the moon and the stars, the white eyes in the clear night. Now he twisted on the bed, reached out for some Wrigley's; it was better than tooth-paste and Stryker was concerned for his teeth. He unwrapped a stick, slid the gum between his lips, lay back and looked up at the roof and thought of what he must do.

Stryker wanted to go to Germany. He suddenly wanted to get out. He had picked at the lean meat of France and his hunger was not appeased. Stryker had to have more, had to reap the whirlwind, had to take all he could before the old days reclaimed him and crushed him. He didn't want the stockyards, didn't want that anonymity. He wanted to be what he had become, and to stay that way always. Stryker wanted power. He wanted his kingdom on earth. He wanted wealth and the limitless horizons of strength based on terror. He never thought to define it; he simply let it consume him. He lay on his bunk and chewed gum and he knew he must have it.

The rain drummed on the roof. Stryker cursed and sat up. He rubbed lightly at the stubble on his chin and it made a slight rasping sound. He shuddered and shook his head. There was phlegm in his throat. He felt the fullness of his bladder and he thought he could smell his own sweat. The flesh on the white bone. The blood and the stench. You dug deep and you got nothing back but life's steaming corruption. Skin sliding on skin. The jolting spasm and the flood. The sweat and the slime and the friction: it was sometimes called love. Stryker couldn't believe it. He didn't want to experience it. Let the animals rut in the shit-pile and leave him in peace. Stryker needed more than that: he needed freedom and space. He had to go out beyond what was given at no matter what cost.

The rain drummed on the roof. He felt it hammering at his mind. He had never liked the rain and now he wanted to stand up and scream. Wake all the fuckers up. Let them know who he was. He looked at them as they tossed on the bunks, many snoring or groaning. A bunch of fucking pigs. Sweating flesh on stained sheets. A lot of numbers that dotted the maps in the battle for Europe. Stryker wasn't impressed. He knew a hero when he saw one. A hero was a dumb prick like Stone, a slimy Jew like that Bliss.

Stryker got out of bed. His bare feet touched the cold floor.

He thought of Bliss and Boletti in the street, the dust blowing around them. That's the way it always went. You learnt your lessons too late. He had taught both the fuckers a lesson, but they couldn't appreciate it. Stryker shivered with the cold, heard the sleeping men snoring, put on his pants and socks and boots, and then picked up a towel. The rain was drumming on the roof; it was pouring down the windows. Stryker wrapped a bar of soap in the towel and then walked down the barracks. He stopped by Kantaylis. The kid was mumbling and tossing. Stryker leaned over and shook his bony shoulder and his eyes started blinking.

'Wha, wha?' he mumbled.

'Waken up,' Stryker whispered.

'What?'

'Waken up, for fuck's sake! We got a long day ahead of us.'

Kantaylis blinked and looked around him. His eyes seemed strange without the glasses. He yawned and scratched his chin and licked his lips and then stared up at Stryker.

'Stryker!' he said. 'What's the matter?'

'Nothing,' Stryker said. 'I just want you to get up. We're leaving this fucking dump tonight, and I want to get organized.'

'Leaving?' Kantaylis said.

'That's right. Are you fucking deaf? I said we're leaving and I want you out of bed in two minutes flat.'

Kantaylis looked a bit bewildered. He rubbed his eyes and licked his lips. Stryker patted him on the cheek and stood up and walked along to the wash room. The cold water stung his face. It slapped him awake. There wasn't a fucking shower in the place, and Stryker didn't like that. He took all his clothes off. He scooped the water up in his hands. It was icy and he threw it all around him and used a stiff scrubbing brush. He was meticulous about his testicles. He dreaded the clap. When he was finished, he dried himself carefully and powdered his private parts. Then Stryker relieved himself. He dried his penis with some tissues. He applied some more powder to his penis and backside, then he started getting into his clothes. He put on a jock-strap. He put it on very carefully. He wanted to protect what he had found was no longer of use to him. Stryker thought of the ruins of Europe, thought of

229

terror and blood, thought of the dark park in London, of that first blinding ecstasy. Stryker didn't need penetration: it no longer released him. He wanted something beyond what was given, and the blade was his key. Stryker buttoned up his shirt. He tightened the belt around his waist. He cleaned his teeth with a brush and cold water, dabbed cologne on his neck. He didn't like to smell himself. His general revulsion was increasing. He only wanted the stench of truth revealed, the slow stripping of flesh and bone. He put his tie on. He was meticulous about the knot. When this was finished, he combed his dark hair and looked deep in the mirror.

Stryker saw himself. He saw the fathomless eyes. He saw the dark swirling depths of a world beyond his own comprehension. A sudden claustrophobia seized him. He felt a sharp, fleeting panic. It passed away and he knew that he was free to walk into his kingdom.

Kantaylis entered the washroom. He was skinny and bone-white. He ran his fingers through his disarrayed hair and blinked out of blind eyes. There was a towel over his shoulder. A bar of soap was in his hand. He was wearing a vest and shorts, and he shivered and looked blankly at Stryker.

'What's happening?' Kantaylis said.

'Morning, kid,' Stryker said.

'What's happening? What do you mean, we're leaving? Are we being shipped out?'

'No,' Stryker said. 'We're not being shipped out. We're just gonna get the fuck out of here and head straight for Germany.'

'I don't understand, Stryker.'

'You don't have to understand, Kantaylis. You just have to do what you're fucking told. So get ready to leave.'

'Jesus, Stryker, that's desertion.'

'Fuck desertion. We're going.'

'Jesus, Stryker, they'll catch us. Swear to God. We just won't get away with it.'

'Yes we will,' Stryker said. 'We're not running the other way. We're heading for the front, we're just following the army, and they never stop men going that way.'

'I don't understand.'

'You're too dumb to understand. We're going in an ambulance and we're following the troops and the MPs will just wave us through. We won't have no trouble.'

'Why Germany?' Kantaylis said. 'I don't wanna go there. There's fighting all over that place and I don't want no part of it.'

'I don't care what you want, Kantaylis. I just don't give a fuck. You're in deep and I won't let you out, so you better accept it. I need a driver, Kantaylis. That's about all you're good for. Besides which, I think you need educating and I'll do that deed for you.'

'We'll be court-martialed,' Kantaylis said.

'They'll have to find us first,' Stryker said. 'And they're not gonna find us, 'cause we're gonna disappear into Germany and never be seen again.'

'Disappear?' Kantaylis said.

'You got ears,' Stryker said. 'Now wash your fucking face and get dressed. I wanna get organized.'

Stryker waited for Kantaylis, watched the kid getting washed. Kantaylis simply splashed water on his face and then vigorously dried himself. He did not wash his neck. He left his body untouched. He had blond hairs running down his skinny legs, and his skin seemed transparent. He didn't wash his legs or arms. He didn't remove his underpants. Stryker shivered with revulsion and wondered how the kid lived with himself. Kantaylis finished quickly. He put his shirt and tie on. He finished dressing, combed his hair and cleaned his teeth, then he turned to face Stryker.

'I don't want to,' he said.

'You're gonna have to,' Stryker said.

'I'm scared,' Kantaylis said. 'I'm really scared. We just can't get away with this.'

'Shit,' Stryker said.

'It's the Stockade,' Kantaylis said.

'You'll get the Stockade anyway, Kantaylis, when they find what we've done.'

'I didn't do it, Stryker.'

'You were an accessory, Kantaylis. And you've done quite a few things since then. You're involved with me, kid.'

'They'd probably never find out.'

'I'd make sure they found out.'

'Jesus, Stryker, just let me go.'

'No, kid. You're all mine.'

Kantaylis blinked his large eyes. His face was drained of all colour. He was thinking of the pleasures he had had, and of the price he must now pay. His hands shook a little. His shoulders started to slump. He picked up his towel and soap and looked deep in the mirror.

'Okay,' he said. 'Let's go.'

They left the barracks shortly after. Kline was still on guard duty. The men were still lying on their bunks, but the rain had stopped pouring. Stryker smiled as he left. He was thinking about ole Kline. He knew that he couldn't avoid Kline, but this wasn't the time. Stryker looked across the compound, saw the barbed wire and the tents. The ground was all muddy and the German prisoners wandered about in it. The sky above was grey. The black clouds drifted lazily. Kantaylis walked beside Stryker with his head down, kicking the mud up. The kid was alright. He was recovering from his shock. Another day, another dollar, another whore in the ruins, and he'd soon forget he ever had a conscience. Stryker patted him on the shoulder. The kid gave him a bleak smile. Stryker grinned and walked into the sick bay and went into an office. The walls were bare wood; there was a desk and some chairs. Corporal Poulin was stretched out on a couch, his hands clasping his belly. Stryker shook him awake. The corporal waved his hands wildly in the air, jerked upright and stared at him.

'Jesus Christ,' he said thickly. 'What time is it?'

'Five o'clock,' Stryker said. 'In the morning.'

'Jesus Christ, I've only had two hours sleep. My head feels like a punchbag.'

'You drink too much,' Stryker said.

'Yeah, I drink too much.'

'I'm in a hurry,' Stryker said. 'Where's the ambulance? Is it ready to roll?'

'Yeah, it's ready,' Poulin said. 'It's round the back of the sick bay. Now give me that requisition order. I don't want my balls fried.'

Stryker gave him the requisition order. The corporal studied it carefully. He finally leaned over and put it on his desk and grinned slyly at Stryker.

'It's authentic,' he said. 'I don't know how the fuck you do it. You oughta get a medal for initiative. You sure are some mover.'

'Has it been filled up?' Stryker said.

'Yeah, Stryker, it's been filled up. I don't wanna know what's inside it. Rhinehart and Horwitz filled it up about three hours ago. I just kept my eyes closed.'

'You've got your requisition order.'

'Yeah, I got that. You sure seem to know what you're doing. I just hope you stay lucky.'

The corporal lay back on the couch. Stryker walked out with Kantaylis. They walked around to the back of the sick bay and came to the ambulance. Stryker opened the front door, took the keys out of the ignition, then went to the back of the ambulance and opened it up. Kantaylis couldn't resist looking, saw crates of gin and Scotch, saw hundreds of packs of cigarettes and smaller boxes of penicillin. Stryker counted them all. He nodded his head with satisfaction. He then closed the doors and told Kantaylis to get in the driver's seat.

They left the camp as dawn was breaking. A pearly light filled the sky. Kantaylis wasn't too familiar with the ambulance, but he soon got the hang of it. Stryker told him to head for Paris. Kantaylis did as he was told. He no longer had a choice and he knew it, so he kept his mouth closed. Stryker studied the passing fields, saw the charred, gutted buildings; the small villages drifted past on either side, half destroyed and still sleeping. Other army trucks passed by. There were bren-gun carriers and half-tracks. Armed soldiers patrolled some of the towns, looking wet and quite weary. Kantaylis drove at normal speed. He didn't want to be stopped. They were in fact stopped a few times, but Stryker just flashed his forged pass. At such times Kantaylis sweated. He was stunned by Stryker's confidence. Stryker liked to swop jokes with the MPs before moving on. Then they reached a small farm. Stryker made Kantaylis pull in. He had to stop in the muddy ground behind the house and then he had to get out. A swarthy Frenchman emerged. He had a conversation with Stryker. The Frenchman took some money off Stryker and nodded his head. Stryker opened the doors of the ambulance. There was an old van parked beside it. He told Kantaylis to unload the ambulance and put the stuff in the van. Kantaylis did as he was told. He was sweating when he finished. He saw Stryker emerging from the farmhouse, wearing civilian clothes. He told Kantaylis to go and change. Kantaylis went into the farmhouse. The swarthy Frenchman gave him some clothes and he took off his uniform. Kantaylis emerged as a peasant. The beret made him incongruous. Stryker made him get into the van and drive back to the road. They soon reached the streets of Paris. A hazy sun shone on the rooftops. Stryker made Kantaylis stop behind the Porte Saint Denis, in a very narrow cobblestoned street that was now wide awake. Kantaylis put on the hand brake. He saw some people having lunch. He realized that he hadn't had breakfast and he felt very hungry. Stryker got out of the van. He knocked loudly on a wooden door. It opened and an old woman stood there, dressed in black, her hair grey.

'Monsieur Stryker!' she said. 'A surprise! I had thought you weren't coming.'

'You thought wrong,' Stryker said. 'I just got held up. I had to do a sniper patrol and it took the whole day up.'

'Is it safe to unload?'

'It's safe,' Stryker said. 'It's safe if you don't stand there yapping until the MPs come.'

The old woman smiled bleakly. She held the door open wide. She disappeared inside and Stryker made Kantaylis unload the van. Kantaylis did as he was told. He carried the stuff inside the house. He left it in the hallway while Stryker disappeared inside a room. Kantaylis unloaded the van. It seemed to take a long time. He was sweating and his muscles were aching, but he finally finished. He knocked on the room door. Stryker stuck his head around. He grinned at Kantaylis, waved an enormous wad of francs, turned back to say farewell to the lady and then left the room. He smacked Kantaylis on the shoulder. They climbed back into the van. They drove through the streets of Paris, headed back through the countryside, and then pulled in once more before the farmhouse. They both changed back into their uniforms. They returned to the ambulance. Kantaylis drove onto the road, headed back towards camp, and by late afternoon they were parked once more outside the sick bay.

They both got out of the ambulance. It was getting dark already. Kantaylis stamped his cold feet on the ground and looked up at the sky. It wasn't going to rain. The clouds were drifting away. Kantaylis looked back at Stryker and saw him wrapping the francs in brown paper. The finished package was thick. Stryker leaned into the ambulance. He put the money beneath his seat, closed both doors and locked them, then nodded and started walking towards the barracks.

Kantaylis followed him. He didn't know what else to do. His feet kicked up the mud and he felt very hungry and weak.

'I wanna eat,' he said to Stryker.

'Not yet,' Stryker said. 'We'll eat when we get on the road, and not before then.'

'It's almost evening,' Kantaylis said. 'I haven't had a thing all day. I'm starving. I just want to eat. It won't take me long.'

'No,' Stryker said. 'I'm not interested in your fucking belly. We'll eat when we get on the fucking road. Now shut your damned mouth.'

He walked into the barracks. Kantaylis followed him in. The lights were on and the men sprawled on their bunks, looking sleepy and bored. Stryker looked around for Kline. Kline wasn't in the room. Stryker walked to his bed in the corner and started filling his kit bag. Kantaylis just watched him. Kantaylis didn't dare pack his. He still couldn't believe they were going, didn't know what to take. Stryker packed up methodically. A few men watched him casually. They obviously thought he was going on leave, but they didn't dare ask him. Stryker filled the bag with watches, added jewellery and scent, packed it tight with a lot of brown parcels filled with dollars and francs. Then Stryker was finished. He tightened the rope on the kit bag. He stood up as the door opened wide and Kline entered the barracks.

Kline walked straight down the room. He was wearing worn fatigues. He looked tired but his lean face was filled with a terrible rage. He stopped in front of Stryker. His dark eyes were blazing. Stryker noticed that his hands were by his sides and that his fists were not clenched.

'What happened?' he said.

'What're you talking about?' Stryker said.

'I'm talking about Boletti and Bliss. Now what the fuck happened?'

'What the fuck do you *think* happened? It was a sniper patrol. They bought it and that's all there is to it. It's a common occurrence.'

'Yurick says they were the middlemen.'

'That's right. They were the middlemen.'

'They shouldn't have been the fucking middlemen. The replacements get that shit.'

'Not with me,' Stryker said. 'I don't play it that way. I figure the replacements haven't got the experience to see what the fuck's going on, so I keep them away from it.'

'You're giving me shit, Stryker.'

'I don't see it that way. I'm just saying that if you send an inexperienced man down the street, you might as well shoot him in the head. He's in the middle of the road. He's too slow to take action. Meanwhile your good men are trapped beneath the target and they can't even get a shot off. That doesn't make sense to me.'

'Your good men go up the stairs.'

'I never thought about that.'

'You thought about it, Stryker. You've done it a million times. And you know as well as I do that the replacements are the ones who take the chances. That's how it's laid down, Stryker.'

'Not with me,' Stryker said. 'I lay it down my own way. I do the job and I make the fucking rules and you don't have a goddamned say in it.'

'Fuck you,' Kline said. 'I won't let you get away with it. Yurick says that the back-up fire was late – and that that was you, Stryker.'

'Fuck Yurick,' Stryker said. 'That cunt's just a replacement. He didn't know what the fuck was going on. He was pissing his pants.'

'He said you were slow, Stryker. He said Bliss lay there a

236

long time. He said you didn't even start to fire until Bliss had been killed.'

'So what?' Stryker said. 'You just can't win 'em all. I got off as fast as I could – but that was too late for Bliss.'

'You're lying,' Kline said. 'I don't believe a word of that. We all know how fast you are, Stryker, and there's no one to touch you. It was deliberate, you cunt. You held off till Bliss was dead. You sent him and Boletti down that street because you wanted them dead.'

'Okay,' Stryker said, 'that's your story. Now go beat yourself.'

Kline's dark eyes were blazing. He was quivering with rage. He clenched his fists and opened them again, his whole body twitching. Stryker stood there and watched him. Stryker wondered if he would move. He saw the whites of Kline's eyes, the dark pupils, the fury behind them. Stryker wanted him to do it, wanted to resolve it in public; he wanted Kline on the floor beneath his boot, and he wanted to crush him. Then Kline stopped his quivering. His fury turned to cold loathing. He stepped back and he looked right at Stryker and his eyes had no mercy.

'Fuck you,' he said. 'You wanna fight, I won't fight. You wanna draw blood, you won't draw it – I won't give you that pleasure. You've gone as far as you can go. I'll stop you dead where you stand. I'll have your fucking head in a basket, and you won't get it back. I'm gonna put in a report, Stryker. I'm gonna make a full report: I mean Bliss and Boletti and Captain Mann and all the rest of the shit. You won't have a leg to stand on. It's fucking murder as well as graft. Your number's up, Stryker, and I'm calling it. I'll report you tonight.'

Stryker looked at Kline's eyes, saw the loathing and the rage. He knew that Kline was not talking for effect, that he meant what he said. The fucker would tell on him. He would lay it all out. Stryker knew it as he stood there looking at him, at his dark, blazing eyes.

'Tonight,' Kline said softly. 'I'll do it tonight. I'm gonna have a wash and then I'm gonna put in my report. They'll fucking bury you, Stryker.'

He turned and walked away, started taking off his clothes.

The other men in the barracks had been listening and they now turned their heads aside. Stryker smiled at Kantaylis, a tight, murderous smile. He went back to his bed and sat down and looked over at Kline. Kline took off his clothes, wrapped a towel around himself, grabbed some soap and then walked from the room.

Stryker picked up his kit bag. He walked out of the barracks. He didn't look back at the men and the door slammed behind him. He stood on the steps outside. The door opened and closed. Kantaylis came up beside him and blinked, and looked frightened and lost.

'Jesus Christ,' Kantaylis said.

'That fucking cunt,' Stryker said.

'What the hell are we gonna do, Stryker?'

'We'll fix him for good.'

Darkness had fallen. The camp was muddy and cold. The thousands of tents in the compound stretched back to the black sky and merged with it. Stryker looked all around him. Most of the men were indoors. Stryker burned and then was blinded by his rage as he walked down the steps. Kantaylis followed him. He didn't know what else to do. He watched Stryker put his kit bag in the ambulance and then withdraw an explosive charge. 'Jesus Christ,' Kantaylis said. 'Shut your mouth,' Stryker said. Kantaylis blinked and Stryker pushed him ahead, his fist brooking no argument. Kantaylis stumbled through the mud, saw the guns on the watchtowers. He was whipped by a fierce, blinding terror that offered no exit. ' – no, Stryker!' he hissed. Stryker grabbed him by the throat. 'We will do it!' Stryker hissed, his eyes wild. 'That's all there is to it!' Kantaylis started to sob. Stryker pushed him on ahead. He stumbled and fell against the wooden barracks, and Stryker pushed him again. Kantaylis couldn't stop sobbing. The terror filled his whole being. He saw the darkness and the mud at his feet, and he knew he was trapped. Stryker pushed him along the wall. They turned the corner at the end. They stopped at the wall that formed the back of the washroom, and Kantaylis saw the piled gasoline cans. He couldn't stop sobbing. He was shaking all over. He looked at Stryker, saw Stryker's eyes gleaming as he dropped to his hands and knees. Stryker didn' mind the mud. He hardly knew the mud was there. He crawled forward on his hands and his knees beneath the floor of the barracks. He stopped just beneath the washroom, fixed the charge to a wooden strut; he set the timing for three minutes and then he crawled back out again. Stryker stood up. Kantaylis just stood there sobbing. Stryker looked at the piled gasoline cans and then grinned at Kantaylis. ' – *Stryker, no!*' Kantaylis sobbed. 'Shut your face,' Stryker said. He grabbed Kantaylis by the collar of his coat and dragged him away. Kantaylis sobbed and almost vomited. He couldn't believe this was happening. He looked up and saw the barracks above him, all the windows blacked out. Kantaylis stopped and just stared. Stryker pushed him forward roughly. Kantaylis staggered through the mud and kept sobbing and trying to control himself. He suddenly came to the ambulance. Stryker made him climb in. Kantaylis sat behind the wheel and Stryker sat down beside him and closed the door. Kantaylis blinked and looked ahead. He could see the barracks from here. Stryker told him to turn on the engine, and Kantaylis obeyed. The ambulance hummed quietly. Kantaylis suddenly stopped sobbing. He looked straight ahead with red eyes and then he broke down again.

There was a roar and a flash. The end of the barracks exploded. The roof shrieked as the corrugated iron started buckling, and the wooden walls splintered and blew apart as the yellow flames soared up. Then the gasoline cans went off. They made a demoniac noise. The gasoline geysered up to the sky in sheets of roaring white flames. Kantaylis covered his ears. He couldn't stand that awful noise. He saw the sheets of flame soaring and falling and leaping over the barracks. The flames ate at the walls. A wall rumbled and collapsed. A shower of sparks exploded over the flames and filled the dark sky with crimson. Kantaylis just stared at it. He couldn't believe that it was happening. The burning gasoline soared up and fell down and then swallowed the barracks.

Stryker didn't say a word. He watched the flames with bright eyes. The other ambulances in the sick bay started roaring into action, all heading for that murderous inferno. Kantaylis wanted to get moving. He was sobbing with shame and terror. Stryker grabbed him by the wrist and almost crushed it and Kantaylis stopped sobbing. The pain filled his whole arm. He wanted to weep but he was frightened. He then looked at the mad eyes of Stryker and he knew he was lost.

Stryker just sat there staring. He watched that hellish inferno. He watched the stretchers coming out, the victims wriggling and screaming, and he felt incandescent with triumph. The burning men filled the ambulances. The ambulances raced towards the main gate. They were heading for a hospital with an operating theatre, and that hospital was thirty miles away.

Stryker made Kantaylis follow them. The guards just waved them through. They left the camp and drove along the dark road and the night fell about them. Kantaylis tried to control himself. He vapourized and lost himself. He was lost and now Stryker would guide him, and that's all that mattered. Stryker told him where to go. He felt the ambulance vibrating beneath him. The dark fields rose and fell on either side as they headed for Germany.

# PART FOUR: OASIS

# CHAPTER SIXTEEN

HIS dreams were of death, of Port-en-Bessin, of the smoke and the blood and the ruin, of the murderous chaos. David saw the charnel-house, went winging over the smouldering hills, heard the roaring of the guns, the screaming men, relived everything brilliantly. He tossed and turned in his sleep, felt the throbbing of his leg wound, was pulled briefly to the surface and sank down again, murmuring words he could not recall. Where was he? Who was he? His leg burned and then healed. He slept and awakened and then fell asleep again and saw the ruins of battered Caen beyond the windows, the hospital's grey walls.

David's dreams were of death, of the war's blinding crucible, of all he had learnt and been forced to cast aside when Katherine died and the war made him forget her. Now, he remembered, saw her spiralling in silence, let the passing of the weeks bring back his strength, force him out from oblivion. David lay in the hospital, saw the dead wheeled in and out, thought often of Port-en-Bessin and his own hazy part in it, dwelt frequently on the days before that, before Katherine was murdered.

The days had passed into weeks. One month led into another. Beyond the walls of the hospital, above the awesome ruins of Caen, he heard the growling of tanks and half-tracks, the high rumbling of planes. His leg was mending and the war continued. The allies poured through France and Belgium.

The guns roared beyond earshot, the men died in the mud, and strange places like Arnhem and Nijmegen and s'Hertogen-bosch were being added to the dialectic of death.

David slept and awakened, felt reluctance, slept again, tossed and turned on the hospital bed, heard men groaning around him. His dreams were of carnage, of the night's murderous yield, of the hills above the town of Port-en-Bessin, of the gardens of Kensington. The dead were wheeled in and out, the wounded cried in delirium, and David saw the torn limbs, the drained faces, the gaping wounds on the rustling sheets. This was war's final truth, its only worthy revelation: it was what lay behind the beating drums and the waving of flags. David saw it and was changed, felt his innocence fall away, felt himself opening out with a hunger that destroyed old illusions.

He lay back on his bed, let the days pass into weeks, traced the meanings of his dreams through the labyrinths, scratched the truth from his waking hours. He felt the healing of his wound, the gradual return of health and sanity, and he sat up and opened his eyes and saw the world in a new light. The war had torn him from Katherine, had released him from his pain, and then, through the blood and the ruin, it had given him fresh resolve.

'A bullet in the thigh,' the nurse said. 'You'll limp a bit, but you'll live.'

'Good,' David said. 'That sounds excellent. I'm glad I'm in one piece.'

'For you the war's over,' the nurse said. 'You should count yourself lucky.'

'No,' David said. 'It's not over. For me it's just start-ing.'

He lay back against the pillows, saw the glint in her green eyes, felt the heat of a long forgotten need, dissolved into him-self again. He slept and awakened, felt the pinch of the needle, saw the green eyes materialize and disappear, drifted down to the labyrinths. He saw the flames in the forest, the smoke swirling around shadows, an arm curving through the air, almost graceful, the still night exploding. The whole of France was in ruins. He saw the landscapes of a nightmare. He saw white dust on the black face of the ruins, saw a sullen grey sky. Katherine's killer was out there. He filled the light and the shadow. He filled David's dreams, slyly haunted his waking hours, set a spark to the inchoate rage that crept out from the dying fear. David lay in the hospital, watched the days pass into weeks, and observed, as he listened to the rumbling guns, his own bleak transformation.

'You look better,' the nurse said.

'Good. I feel better.'

'You don't talk much.'

'No. I don't talk much. There's not much to say.'

He couldn't say what he felt. He couldn't even describe it. The days passed into weeks, the stench of blood became routine, and the allies marched through the streets of Caen while David lay there and brooded. He thought often of Katherine, of her death and his pain, of the loss of that pain in the hell of Port-en-Bessin, of this new man who lay in the hospital, dreaming of vengeance. Yes, he had changed. He could feel it and see it. He was no longer young, felt no fear, no confusion, and dwelt only on what a man learnt of his nature when he lay with the mud in his face. The wounded cried out in their sleep. The nurses rushed back and forth. There was weeping and the murmur of conversation, a pained, hopeful banter. David ignored it all. He merely viewed it as a distraction. The planes roared overhead, the troops marched past the windows, and David lay there and kept to himself and let it fill him with fresh resolve.

'We've taken Brussels,' the nurse said.

'Good,' he said. 'I'm delighted.'

'You don't *sound* delighted,' she said.

'I feel tired. What's the time?'

The hypodermic's silvery gleam, the shifting green of her eyes, the dropping down and drifting into silence, into forests of changing forms. He saw flames, swirling smoke, an arm curving through the air, Corporal Brown, Sergeant Cowie, Pip Hunter's wide eyes, the still night exploding around them, Robert blazing and shrieking. It was more than he could bear.

245

He groaned aloud and turned over. His white fingers found the sheets, turned to claws, found the mud, kept on digging. Deeper down it was darker. Katherine walked beneath the moon. Moonlight glided on the water, on the grass, on the trees of the park. He cried out and watched Katherine, her pale flesh, her brown eyes, walking slowly, side by side with her killer, that faceless American. David looked at her eyes. He saw the dread and accusation. 'You believe in logic and reason,' she said, 'but that doesn't help us.' What price his logic? What price his bloody reason? He cried out and saw the moon through the trees, the killer's swift, gleaming blade. David sobbed and gripped the sheets. Katherine lay crushed in the mud. He saw the killer, saw his shadow disappearing, then he cried out again.

'All right,' the nurse said. 'You're awake now. Settle down. Take a deep breath.'

Her eyes shone in the darkness. She was wiping his fevered brow. The coolness of her palm was quite pleasant, gliding over his face. David licked his dry lips, felt the beating of his heart. There were no more troops moving through Caen, and the night's silence gripped him. He looked up at the nurse. Her blonde hair was pinned back. She was smiling and he saw in her green eyes a slight trace of mockery.

'A bad dream?' she said.

'Yes,' he said. 'A bad dream.'

'They'll get better when you get really well. We'll have to give you a rubber sheet.'

She chuckled and turned away. He felt flushed and confused. He saw her buttocks, the swaying of her hips, as she walked through the door. Then she was gone. Light shone in from the corridor. He thought of her remark and then blushed and lay back on the pillows.

It was easier when awake. He could wipe his own brow then. He could lie back and let the cold hatred keep him sane through the long days. He watched the pale-faced walking wounded, saw the men writhe on their beds, heard the murmurings of the padres and priests, the dying whispering gratitude. The ruins of Caen were beyond the windows. A fine dust covered all. He heard the ringing of pickaxes, the sliding of rubble, heard the wailing of women and children as more dead were uncovered.

David lay there and changed, watched his own transformation; he felt something inside wrench and break and then finally leave him. Closing his eyes, he saw Katherine, her outstretched naked body. Her thighs were parted and her legs were upraised and he hovered between them. Within love there was lust. His own lust had led to fear. With his intellect, with his cowardly abstractions, he had gelded himself. Katherine whimpered beneath him. Her hands fluttered and cajoled. And romantic, idealistic, puritanical, he was secretly shocked. Now he saw her swollen breasts, saw her dampened pubic hair, saw the parting of her thighs, the white flesh, the buried shaft of his penis. Had he really felt revulsion? Had he viewed it as obscene? Had he seen it, with intellectual distaste, as a necessary vice? David saw Katherine's body. With eyes closed he surveyed her. 'It's all right!' Katherine hissed. '*It's all right!*' And then she sank back and disappeared. David suffered his failure. He watched her torn, confused flight. He saw her footsteps leading into the moonlight in that garden in Kensington. What price his logic? What price his bloody reason? He knew the price when he saw the killer's blade flashing under the moonlight. David saw it and was numbed. He no longer felt the pain. He felt guilt, and he felt a cold hatred for that dark, faceless man.

'What's happening?' David said.

'I didn't know you cared,' the nurse said.

'I'm interested,' David said. 'I like your voice. Now tell me what's happening.'

'We've captured Belgium and Luxemburg,' she said. 'We're closing in on the Rhine.'

She was checking David's pulse, glancing at him and smiling. He felt the stirring of a long forgotten need and it made his face burn. David shifted uncomfortably, felt the fingers stroke his wrist. He looked up and saw the nurse's cool smile, the green eyes slightly mocking. She was tall and rather thin. He thought she was in her late twenties. There was a dry, amused carnality to her features, a casual permissiveness. She stroked David's wrist, was staring at him and smiling. She chuckled and then she walked from the ward, her hips swaying invitingly.

David lay back and burned. His sudden erection had startled him. He slid his hand beneath the sheets and touched himself and then withdrew it and smiled. The ward around him was busy. The nurses rushed back and forth. The patients shouted jokes and read books and groaned loudly and whimpered. David saw the limbs in traction, the bloody stumps of the tourniquets, the plasma dripping methodically through the tubes, the writhing heaps on the stretchers. He closed his eyes to it. He felt sensual and ruthless. He no longer felt locked within himself, intimidated by lust.

'You're improving,' the nurse said.

'It still hurts,' David said.

'Badly?'

'It keeps me awake.'

'That's a good sign,' she said.

David tried to find sleep. He let the darkness embrace him. The sliding rubble, the ringing of pickaxes, all receded to silence. Katherine's body beneath him, spreadeagled, agitated, beads of sweat and dark hair on her face, her eyes closed, features strained. David pushed deep inside her. There was no shame, no fear. She enfolded him, a sublime velvet glove, drew him in, slid around him. David almost groaned aloud. He opened his eyes and glanced about him. He saw the broken limbs, the scorched flesh, the hideous wounds, the crisp, busy nurses. It was growing dark outside. He saw the jagged ruins of Caen. *We dropped 8,000 tons of bombs on Caen and now nothing is standing*. David felt guilt and rage. He knew what had killed Katherine. She had walked with her own murderer in the gardens of Kensington to try to find what David had denied her. Now he saw it all clearly. There was no point in denying it. He felt guilt and that cold, ruthless rage that had given him new life.

'You're not smiling,' the nurse said.

'Should I?' David said.

248

'You have a sweet face,' the nurse said. 'I'm sure it must have smiled once.'

'A long time ago.'

'And so grim now,' she said.

'I'm older now. I feel it in my bones. I don't see much to smile at.'

'Smile at me,' she said.

'I feel tired. Let me sleep.'

'Rubbish. You know you can't sleep. You're always saying you can't sleep.'

'I want to sleep now.'

'Go ahead. Have bad dreams.'

'That's not a nice thing for a nurse to say.'

'That's better. You're smiling.'

The days passed more slowly, stretched out, lingered on, and David finally clambered out of his bed and placed his feet on the cold floor. He discovered that he could walk. It was a heartening revelation. Like an old man he leant on his walking stick, exploring the corridors. There were worse wards elsewhere. Throats rattled, limbs flailed. The doors of the operating theatre hypnotized him, ejecting God's wrath. David choked back his bile. He saw the white sheets stained with blood, saw the suction machines trying to rescue men who might choke on their own spit. No one stopped his explorations. His stick rang on the tiled floors. He saw a room filled with bins and the bins were piled with amputated limbs. Here a foot, there a hand; here intestines, there a scalp; in the sink, in the shadows near the back, a mess of blood, bone and spleen. David slowly backed away. He saw the silent, smouldering hills. He saw his friend Robert Lovell as a blazing rag screaming dementedly. David choked back his bile. He kept his weight on the walking stick. He kept walking and his joints started loosening and behaving as normal.

The hospital was immense. The wards were jampacked and noisy. The ambulances came from the front, disgorged their bloody contents and then drove more men back towards the Rhine. David looked out at Caen. The ruins stretched to a grey sky. He saw the shell of the church of S. Pierre, the tower rising from rubble. Civilization had died here. It was dying all over Europe. *We'll destroy the world*, the general had said. *We'll destroy it and rebuild it.* David wondered about that. He wondered how they could possibly do it. *It won't be the world that you know, but the loss won't be noticeable.* Perhaps the general was right. Perhaps it didn't make any difference. *Cities can be rebuilt and the dead can be replaced. The bombs won't stop women getting pregnant, and life will continue.* The general knew his facts. He had the cynic's flair for numbers. His numbers had no history nor future; their one role was expediency. Yet was Katherine but a number? Could Katherine's death be reduced to that? David wondered if the general's dry logic could be used to breach this truth. Katherine wasn't a number. The dead of Caen were not numbers. The living were the embodiment of History; the dead summed up Man's tragedy.

David felt hot and cold. He felt guilt and fierce rage. He now knew that the blood on his hands had been caused by neglect. Who had sent Katherine away? Who had driven her to such need? It was he, it was his fear of reality, that had robbed her of every hope. Katherine had looked elsewhere. Wanting life, she had gone to death. And like the dead of this smouldering Caen she was more than a number.

'You're walking well,' the nurse said.

'I *feel* well,' David said.

'I notice you don't have your cane.'

'I'm no longer an old man.'

David wanted to live. He saw her searching green eyes. He saw a woman almost thirty years old, looking older, lips carnal. David knew what he wanted. There was no romance to it. He wanted to bury himself in her flesh, to reaffirm his own manhood. The very thought made him smile. Such an ambition was ridiculous. At his age it was more than belated; it was close to pathetic. Yet he now knew what he wanted. He now knew he had to have it. He would never again have to face up to the shame of his cowardice.

'Your pulse is fine,' the nurse said.

'It should be racing,' David said.

'I better fetch that rubber sheet,' she said.

'You can fetch something else.'

Her eyes flashed, her lips smiled. Her scratching fingers released his wrist. On her thin frame her breasts seemed enormous, the white tunic stretched tight. David returned her smile, felt a tingling of excitement. He was lying on top of the sheets, turned towards her long thighs. The nurse looked down and smiled, bit lightly at her tongue. He had awakened in delirium, in pain, to see her featured in fantasies. She was lethargically sexual. Her angular body beckoned to him. He remembered the nights waking to pain, seeing light from her office. Men had entered and departed. Soft chuckling, muttered oaths. She had been on the night-shift at that time and it hadn't seemed real. Now David wondered about it. He sensed a challenge in her smile. He thought of Katherine and he knew she was dead and now he wanted the future.

'And what can I fetch?' she said.

'I thought you might have known,' he said.

'You used to never talk much,' she said. 'Now it seems you're impertinent.'

'Am I?'

'Yes.'

'In times of war, manners change.'

'And what should I fetch you, first-lieutenant?'

'You're the nurse,' David said.

She chuckled and flounced away. David lay back and smiled. He felt coldly amused, almost unreal, divorced from his old self. It was easy, after all: there simply had to be a motive. A man had to lose himself in something larger than his private concerns. Katherine had known that. *You need a focus for your life . . . and it will have to come out of yourself, not out of your reading . . .* No doubt she had been right. She had known him for what he was. And he had used his idealism as a shield against the adult's realities. Katherine had paid for it. He in turn had paid through her. The toe of the star-gazer is often stubbed, and he had suffered accordingly. No more, he now thought. There would be no more of that. The innocence of the child could be destructive to the growth of the man. David had learnt his lesson. He had learnt it with Katherine's death. And in the hellish dream of Port-en-Bessin he had fully accepted it. Now he wanted no idealism, wanted no coward's self-deceptions. He only wanted to expose himself to the truth at no matter the cost.

Katherine's murderer had known the truth. He had gained her trust and then killed her. In so doing he had accidentally robbed David of his self-wounding innocence. There was a debt to be paid, a score to be settled. If David needed a cause larger than himself, he had found it in this. He would find Katherine's killer. He would dig deep for the truth. It was a motive, a focus for his life, and it burned the fear out of him.

'I used to see you,' David said.

'That sounds interesting,' the nurse said.

'It was when I first arrived, when I was bad, when the pain woke me up at nights.'

'Poor boy,' the nurse said.

'You were beautiful,' David said. 'I used to think I was dead, and then I'd waken up and see you down there.'

'That sounds interesting,' the nurse said.

'There were a lot of men,' David said.

'Yes,' she said, 'there *were* a lot of men.'

'Why not me?' David said.

The nurse didn't come that night. He had sensed that she wouldn't come. He saw her standing in the doorway looking at him, bright light all around her. Then she disappeared. He fell back and cursed softly. He reached down with one hand and touched himself, now pulsating, engorged. His eyes closed over silence. The grey ward dissolved around him. He touched himself and felt a child's simple pleasure, undiluted by guilt. He heard silence, saw darkness, drifted down through Katherine's eyes, saw the hill above the town of Port-en-Bessin, the explosions, the dying men. Corporal Brown was there. He dropped his gun and hit a bunker. The wall exploded all around him and he wriggled and flapped, and then slid down the wall and fell sideways. David started crawling towards him. He crawled across the torn earth. He kept crawling towards the bunker and he reached out and touched Corporal Brown's face. The corporal didn't move. David sobbed and rolled away. He looked up at the stars and blacked out and awakened to Katherine. Her hair fell around her face.

252

Her dark eyes gazed down upon him. She was weeping as she gently stroked his forehead, in the gloom, in a hellish din. They were inside an ambulance. David couldn't sit up. He glanced down and saw blood on his thighs, splashed over his belly. David screamed. The ambulance roared and then shuddered. He heard Katherine's sobs dying in the void and then he saw a dark ward.

'Where am I?'

'You're all right.'

'Am I hurt?'

'You're all right.'

'What's happening?'

'We've given you an injection. You're all right. Go to sleep now . . .'

The ward was quiet at nights. Sometimes troops moved past the windows. He heard the aircraft in the dark sky above, heading towards Germany. One dream within the other: the past within the present. He slept and usually awakened at nights, to the ward's weeping silence. The dying and the damned. Missing limbs, mangled faces. Throats rattled and lips blubbered prayers, spitting bile and black blood. The days and nights merged. He hardly knew when he was awake. In the nights, in that whimpering silence, there was light from her window.

David studied the light. It was at the end of the ward. It poured out from the ward nurse's office, boring down through the darkness. It didn't seem real. He saw the nurse dressed in white. Her back was turned to him and her tunic fell off her bared shoulders. David heard a throaty chuckle, a man's muffled oath. He felt the throbbing of his leg and he dropped back and slept and awakened. The days and nights merged. The sky droned, the streets rumbled. There was pain and it made him awaken when the ward was in darkness. He kept seeing the beam of light, heard the movement within the office, saw a breast, the smooth curve of a shoulder, a flash of blonde hair. David dreamed of that throaty chuckle. He reached down and touched himself. He saw brown eyes and green eyes, dark hair and blonde hair, saw Katherine and the nurse all at once, saw the flames in the forest. Pip Hunter's severed fingers. The blazing torch that was Robert. There were dreams within dreams and now David awakened to see the green eyes gazing down, one soft hand on his forehead.

'You seem excited,' she whispered.

'Yes,' he said. 'I think I am.'

'You were touching yourself.'

'All children do.'

'Poor boy. What's the answer?'

Her hand slid beneath the sheets. It wandered over his body. She was smiling and her green eyes were gleaming in that sad, silent darkness. David just lay there. He felt the tapestry of her fingers. They were warm and they traced a line across him and down to his belly. David didn't close his eyes. He looked up and saw her lips. They were wet from the travels of her tongue, curving back in a teasing smile. David felt his heart beating. He saw the rise of her breasts. Her hand was sliding over his stomach, fingers outspread and searching. There was no guilt in this; there was no hesitation. Her fingers shivered through his pubic hair, fell upon his stiff penis. David closed his eyes. He travelled down through himself. He reached the source of himself, felt her fingers, the slow sliding of willing skin. David thought of Port-en-Bessin. Her fingers moved up and down him. He thought of Katherine and of how he had forgotten when the forest exploded. There had to be acceptance. The body must have its dominion. The gentle pumping of the nurse's warm hand was more real than the deepest thought. David responded to it. He forced himself up through his flesh. He felt the shaft of his penis in her hand, and it offered the truth. He stopped thinking of Katherine. He stopped thinking of the dead. He dissolved and was absorbed by her fingers and it gave him release.

David went with the spasm. He let it whip his senses bare. His body shuddered and then he gasped lightly and looked up at her green eyes. She was withdrawing her hand. She wiped it dry and then cleaned him. She straightened out the sheets and then smiled and leaned over and kissed him. David felt radiant. He was burning with freedom. She licked his forehead lightly with her tongue and then chuckled and left.

She didn't come the next day. She didn't appear the following night. David reached down and tentatively touched himself, then he cursed and lay back. The sleeping came easily. There were no dreams to remember. He awakened at dawn and got up and walked out to her office. She wasn't there. Another nurse sat at the desk. She glanced up as David smiled and walked away, exploring the hospital.

The corridors never slept. The trolleys lined the bleak walls. There was blood and the stench of piss and vomit, the white sheen of the dead. Nurses rushed back and forth. Doors opened and closed. The surgeons wandered about looking haggard, their smocks soaked in tripe. David walked to the entrance. He looked out over Caen. The broken walls rose from the rubble, the charred beams framed by grey sky. David gazed at the destruction. It stretched as far as the eye could see. He thought of Robert, of Corporal Brown, of Pip Hunter, of Sergeant Cowie, of all the men who had come here to die and fertilize the torn earth. Katherine's killer had come here also. Was he dead or still alive? David looked out across the devastation and determined to find him.

The nurse returned that night. He heard her moving about the office. She was there a long time and then she came out and entered the ward. There was whimpering and groaning. The fruits of war filled the silence. David watched the nurse walking up and down, checking pulses and charts. She didn't look at him. He knew the slight was deliberate. She moved quietly back and forth, her tall body at ease, a lethargic sensuality still obvious through the moon-fractured darkness. David cursed and sat up. She couldn't help but look at him. Her green eyes were mocking as she smiled, before she turned and walked out. David cursed and lay back. He felt hurt and humiliated. He looked at the light in her office, saw her wandering back and forth. David suddenly stopped hurting, felt a swift, total calm, swung his legs off the bed and stood up and padded along the quiet ward. He didn't know who might be watching. He didn't really give a damn. There was only one thing left to do, and he knew he would do it. He stepped into her office. The bright light assailed his eyes. He blinked and

255

saw her standing against the wall, her smile strangely challenging.

'What do you want?' she said softly.

'I want you,' David said.

# CHAPTER SEVENTEEN

HE wanted her and he took her. He had her over the office desk. The act was quick and violent and reckless, the light blazing above them. Her green eyes, her wet lips, the stiff, engorged nipples, a faint smile as her head rolled to the side, her teeth biting her tongue. She seemed wanton, amused; she finally closed her eyes and gripped him. He held her legs behind the knees and pushed them back and thrust himself deeper into her. It was intensely unreal. It had the vibrancy of a dream. She was groaning and this sound mixed with the anguish of the men in the ward. David knew it was reckless. He knew that someone might walk in. The very thought of this filled him with excitement and a raw, driving urgency. He saw her breasts, her heaving belly, saw the rumpled clothes around her. Glancing down he saw the shaft of his penis, moving in and out rhythmically. It was a simple animal act. The body would have its own dominion. He pushed her legs further back and she cried out and clutched at his shoulders. The light blazed down upon them. Her naked buttocks slapped the desk. David slid his hands under her spine, pulled her close, felt her writhing. The other men cried in their sleep. A plane droned, a jeep roared. She looked up and he saw the green eyes, very bright, almost blind. It was more than he could bear. It made him want her all the more. He remembered all the nights he had awakened to that amused, throaty chuckling. She was wanton, unashamed. He knew this when she threshed beneath him. She did not dwell on false dreams or sentiment, but understood her own needs. David drove into her. She swore and then groaned. She had closed her eyes again and her face was lying sideways on the desk. David saw her naked shoulders, the sweat on her breasts, the blonde hair that coiled across her cheeks and was trapped by her teeth. She swore and held him tight. Her thighs gripped him and guided him. He wondered at his own easy skill, at his fierce, guiltless pleasure. The light assailed his eyes. He felt intensely unreal. He saw the shaft of his penis, hard and glistening, moving in and out rhythmically. The nurse cursed again. She was a body, not a name. She was wanton and she took from his flesh only what she required. David saw her writhing form. It filled the room and enveloped him. She was cursing and then she gasped loudly and shuddered and gripped him. David came at that moment. The spasms shook him and released him. He collapsed across her body and just lay there, his feet on the floor.

He left the office shortly after. He couldn't remember what he had said. He returned the next night and reached for her, feeling no need for small talk. She smiled as he undressed her, slid her hand between his legs, chuckled softly and then started groaning when he burned up inside her. His surrender was total. The addiction was complete. He had an alcoholic's thirst for the lessons of her well tutored flesh. Thereafter it was enslavement. The days died, the nights inflamed him. He was shocked by the extent of her knowledge, delighted to share it. In her body he found release. He saw his hidden self revealed. All the old fears, all the crippling inhibitions, fell before his new confidence.

The other patients cried in pain, the stench of death filled the ward, the doctors fought against blood and smashed bone while David crawled from his old self. Her green eyes drew him in, her knowing lips drained him of need, and he searched for intimations of peace in the vice of her thighs. What she gave him was renewal. What he felt was excitement. On her desk, in the bright light, in the night's stunning silence, in the sweat and the heat of their affair he was finding his strength.

'Why me?' she once said.

'You're available,' David said.

'Ah!' she said. 'The light from the window! You saw me at nights.'

'Yes,' David said.

'Poor boy,' she said. 'You must have felt terribly deprived. I hope you feel better now.'

'And you?'

'I feel good. It always makes me feel good. I don't feel any better than before, but that isn't an insult.'

They moved out of the office. They began to meet elsewhere. In the gutted shell of Caen it wasn't easy, but she always arranged it. David had her in a truck. He had her standing against some ruins. He was excited by this touch of the sordid, and he knew this amused her. It was so unlike himself. His own indifference was a shock. She would chuckle as she hitched up her skirt, the planes droning above them. David did what she wanted. He gladly practised the unthinkable. On his knees, on his back, in the rubble beneath the moon, he would feel his senses coming alive and giving him fresh resolve. She mocked his aspirations, surrendered, mocked again, took her fill and then combed her blonde hair, softly hissing obscenities. He was startled, intrigued, couldn't believe she was so casual; like a whore she could dissolve into rapture, re-emerge as a blank wall. David wanted to get to know her. He wanted her to give more than her flesh. He wanted to know about all the men who came and went – and then he knew he was jealous.

'There's a war on,' she said.

'Is that the reason?' David said.

'I don't know. I suppose it might be. Does it make any difference?'

'Yes,' David said.

'Poor boy,' she said. 'So young, so pretty, so sensitive. I think you need love.'

'You're a whore.'

'I don't charge.'

'I don't know why you don't.'

'Jealous?'

'Curious.'

'Same thing. What's the point in this talk?'

She chuckled and pulled him down. He heard the bombers overhead. They were flying towards the Rhine, towards Germany, and he wanted to follow them. Her lips found his lips, her hands trailed down his spine, her thighs parted to receive him, to hold him, to keep him enslaved. He forgot the shifting ruins, was deaf to the droning sky; while the first bombs were falling on the Reich he was shedding his old skin. He relished what was revealed, took a pride in what was learnt. As she bit him, as her fingers probed and stroked, he touched the secrets of history. The flesh opened and closed. The revealed night held its wonders. This woman, this body without a name, was at one with the constant earth.

'Why?' David said.

'I just want it,' she said.

'Wanting it's one thing,' David said. 'But why so many men?'

'Why not?' she said. 'There's a war on, after all. They come and they don't stay very long, and they never return.'

'That's it?'

'That's it. Why? Does it shock you? What's the difference if it's one man or twenty? It's the same thing each night.'

'That's perverse,' David said.

'You poor boy,' she said. 'How on earth can you do what you do when you find me so sinful?'

'That's not quite the point.'

'It never is for the man. The man sneers when the woman doesn't oblige; he then spits when she does.'

'That isn't always true.'

'Isn't it? Isn't it really? Yet you call me a whore. You seem shocked by my affaires. You tell me I'm perverse, but you don't include yourself in that judgement. Why me? Why not you?'

They only met to make love, only touched in the night, never saw one another in daylight, never spoke just as friends. David found it exciting. He knew she wanted it that way. He knew it, but he didn't know why and the reasons intrigued him. The lack of history was exciting. The unreality drew him in. The transient nature of the whole situation made it much more intense. Yet he had to know the answers, had to make her submit; he had to have her absolute surrender or nothing at all.

'What's your name?' he said.

'I thought you knew that,' she said.

'Sister Lawrence,' he said. 'That's not enough.'

'Why?'

'It just isn't.'

'You're getting intimate,' she said.

'That's a joke,' he said.

'No,' she said. 'It isn't. I don't mind this ... but don't get involved.'

'I *am* involved.'

'Sex. Let's make that the limit. You'll soon be gone just like the others. The war's still going on.'

'Does that explain the other men?'

'It explains a certain amount.'

'Florence Nightingale.'

'Don't be sarcastic. My name's Rachel. All right?'

'No,' he said. 'I'm hungry. I have to know more. Married? Any children? Born where and when? And how can a nice girl like you teach me such wondrous tricks?'

'Jesus,' she said softly, 'you're a bastard ... and you seemed such a nice boy.'

'Married?'

'No more.'

'Separated?'

'He's dead.'

'The war?'

'Yes, but don't worry: he's a man I don't miss.'

'Children?'

'No.'

'Ah! All those men!'

'Poor boy. All this childish psychology. I just happen to like it.'

Her green eyes, her blonde hair, her thin, jaded face were now streams of light filling his dreams and replacing the horrors. Yet he still thought of Katherine, of how she had died, of the man who had put the knife to her and then disappeared. David felt that he was growing. He sensed a fresh acceptance. He was certain that the child in him had died, that his fears had been conquered. He used Rachel as a matrix. Within her he had shaped himself. Between the past and the future was her body, that sublime resting place.

Nevertheless, it hadn't ended. For him the war would go on. The major-general, writing letters from the war zones, never let him forget this. *We must find him, David. I believe he is still alive. This madman, whoever he is, must be found and then punished.* The letters effected David profoundly. They came with depressing regularity. They came from where the guns were still firing, from where death held dominion. David knew it couldn't end. The major-general wouldn't let it end. He also knew, when he cared to think about it, that the general was right. David had to know the killer, had to know that man's face, had to go in pursuit of the truth at no matter the cost. *It's important*, the general wrote. *We must make amends for it. We must find this beast and bring him to justice. He must not go unpunished.* The letters disturbed David, threw him back upon his guilt, raised a challenge that could not be ignored lest the old fears return. David couldn't ignore the killer. He had to know Katherine's seducer. He had to know if the man was still alive, but he wasn't quite ready yet. Her green eyes, her blonde hair, the practised touch of her fingers: he had to drink deeper of Rachel, to make her his own. It was a primitive need. It was the road to affirmation. Conquer her and he could conquer himself and face whatever the future brought.

'Do you still see them?' David asked.

'Who? The other men?'

'Yes,' David said, 'the other men. You knew who I meant.'

'Why? Is it important?'

'Yes.'

'You poor boy. Don't tell me you're jealous already. I don't think I could stand that.'

'I thought you cared for me.'

'And is that what you need?'

'Maybe.'

'Dear God, you're a child. Please don't complicate matters.'

'We're like animals.'

'So?'

'I don't think that's enough.'

'Pleasure and satisfaction are enough. And that's what we're both after.'

'No,' David said. 'I don't think that's all we need. I don't think you're as cynical as that. We all need something more.'

'Love?'

'Maybe that. Maybe just some affection. I don't think we can do what we do without some kind of feeling.'

'Put it down to masturbation. You touch me, I touch you. It's a simple biological urge – with love or without it.'

'Do you like me?'

'You're sweet.'

'And the others?'

'What about them?'

'Is it better when you actually like them? Or do you just close your eyes?'

'You sound angry.'

'I'm just curious.'

'That's a lie.'

'As you wish.'

'Yes,' she said. 'It's better when I like them – but the difference is minimal.'

'And with me?'

'God, your *vanity!*'

'I'm sorry. I have to know.'

'You're a child. You simply need reassurance. But I like it with you.'

'I gathered that,' he said. 'I want to know *how much* you like it. I don't want to be a name in your notebook. I can't settle for that.'

'Love,' she said again.

'Not necessarily,' he replied.

'Poor boy. You need love. I can tell. Lay your head on my breasts.'

263

Her mockery was constant, unmalicious, slightly teasing, making her seem older than she was, slightly soiled, more alluring. David couldn't resist it: he had to crush her condescension, had to understand the weakness that gave her strength, the fears that her humour suppressed. He had to do this for himself. Though childish, it was necessary. He had to build up a meaningful relationship to make concrete his growing pride. This motivation was obscure. He never chose to analyse it. He merely saw the green eyes, the gentle mockery of her smile, and in the wilds of his changing emotions she was mixed up with Katherine. There was a debt to be paid, a lurking guilt to be erased, and he sensed that the conquest of Rachel would mitigate his past failures. He thought of Katherine and felt ashamed; her memory reminded him of neglect. And if the fear of his own body had robbed her of life, he would not suffer such a sin again. The flesh and the mind were one; without instinct, reason died. David looked at Rachel's smile, at her knowing, jaded face, and he felt that he could now brave the world without fear or illusions.

'You're hiding something,' he said.

'I'm hiding nothing,' she said. 'God, you're so young, so naive. Your conversation's exhausting.'

'How many men a week?'

'I don't know. I've lost count. I don't even remember all their names. They just came and then went.'

'All patients?'

'Mostly patients.'

'You felt pity?'

'I felt randy.'

'When did this start? When you were young?'

'Dear God, you're exhausting.'

She sighed and shook her head. Her smile was tender and amused. They were lying on the bed in her room, both of them naked.

'There's no mystery,' she said. 'The mystery's all in your head. You refuse to accept that I can do it for the pleasure it gives me. All right, I was married. The marriage was a disaster. We were both very young and inexperienced, and it just didn't work. Eventually it turned sour. He started accusing me of being frigid. There was no thought in his head that it was him, that I had to be guided. In the end we fought a lot. We probably hated each other. He started beating me up when he was drunk, and I finally left him. Are there enough clichés there? The truth always seems clichéd. Anyway, he soon left for France and he died at Dunkirk. By that time I was on my own. I was having various affaires. I was learning that sex could give me pleasure, and I didn't feel shame. I didn't want to marry again. I didn't want to be owned. I was drawn to men who wanted my body, but who didn't want me. It's as simple as that. It's elementary, dear Watson. There's no need to get worked up about it as if I'm a special case.'

David felt that he was drowning. He reached out and touched her body. *We were both very young and inexperienced, and it just didn't work.* He kissed her breasts and her belly. She sighed and pushed him down. He surrendered to the damp warmth of her thighs, felt her melting around him. The truth was commonplace. Her life reflected his own. *There was no thought in his head that it was him, that I had to be guided.* David put his tongue in Rachel. He drank deeply and was cleansed. She cried out and he felt a great warmth that absolved him from sin. The past could be forgiven. The future could be faced. Now released from his ignorance, now unshackled from his past, he could skirt around the trap of his own frailty and look to the future. He drank deeply of Rachel, let her living flesh anoint him. Her thighs parted and he entered her body and felt briefly at peace.

'You're so desperate,' she said. 'I'd like to know why you're so desperate. It's not sex with you – it's something else. What was this girl like?'

'What girl?'

'Dear God. Do you think you can lie? I can see it in your eyes, I can feel it. You whole body announces it.'

'Woman's intuition?'

'Don't be facile. I want to know. You asked me about my past, now I ask you. You're the one who's obsessed with it.'

'Obsessed?'

'Obsessed. And you know what it means. Now tell me about the girl. I want to know. I love to hear about failure.'

265

David told her about Katherine. He told her over a period of days. She was intrigued and it drew her closer to him, made her reach out to touch him. They started meeting in daylight. They drank *calvados* and talked at length. The planes droned overhead, more troops poured through the streets, and as the dust from the black ruins choked the air David laid himself naked. Rachel understood failure, knew all about shame: like himself, she had bled in the night before learning her lesson. David told her about Katherine. He did not avoid the death. The planes droned overhead, the troops kicked up the dust, and Rachel reached out and touched David's face, without mockery, with tenderness.

'Poor boy,' she said. 'And now you have to find the murderer. Do you think that's going to do any good? Just accept it. It's over.'

'It's not over,' David said. 'I can't pretend it didn't happen. I can't sit back and let things take their course. I owe Katherine some effort.'

'You owe Katherine or yourself? Is it a debt or is it vengeance? You can't repay Katherine anymore; you can just vent your hatred.'

'It's not hatred.'

'It is.'

'If it is, it's justifiable.'

'True, but it won't do any good; it will just eat you up.'

'Let it,' David said. 'I need something beyond myself. It's more important than hatred or revenge. It's a moral commitment.'

'That's sad,' she said.

'There are worse things,' David said. 'We can't always get what we want; we can't be what we'd like to be.'

'And what do you want?'

'I want you,' David said. 'I want you and I know you want me, but you won't let it happen.'

'It's a luxury we can't afford.'

'Why?'

'There's a war on.'

'Do you love me?'

'I don't know. I try not to think about it. During war, you can't trust your own emotions. You might not have a future.'

'God,' he said, 'you're exhausting.'

David studied the ruins of Caen. It had been conquered two months ago. He saw the charred, broken beams, the smashed remains of good furniture, the black, skeletal walls reaching skyward, the planes in the grey clouds. The whole city had been flattened. The desolation was total. In the church of S. Etienne he saw the refugees queuing for soup. It was a war of liberation, the liberated slept in rubble, and children cried while their mothers searched for food, while the old people grumbled. There were very few young men. The cripples were plentiful. The planes droned overhead, the troops marched past the debris, and the dust spiralled up and drifted down and made Caen like a graveyard. David felt a healthy rage, a certain shame and disgust: his education, his halcyon youth, had not prepared him for this. Yet he had to accept it, had to come to terms with it: if the old world had died a new world was in the making; it would rise from the blood and destruction and find its own measure. David was part of it, was flesh and blood within it. Like Europe, he had lost his old self and must now don a new skin. The innocent child had died. The grown man was in the making. He saw all of this in Caen, in Rachel's eyes, and in his own aching need.

Rachel also was part of it. Her teasing presence was all pervasive. Out of nightmares and fevers, out of weakness and pain, she had come as a life-affirming gift. David studied the dreadful ruins, heard the silence, saw the shadows, often thought of Rachel standing in the rubble, her white thighs exposed. In a sense she belonged here. Her promiscuity matched the times. In this world of daily slaughter all relationships were transient; and Rachel, who took what she could grab, had simply faced this harsh truth. This was no time for commitment: there was no time for love. She offered warmth and the solace of her body, but she withheld the future. David suddenly saw it. He recognized what she had taught him. He understood that the war must separate them and that life must go on.

'You'll soon be leaving,' she said.

'Yes,' he said, 'I know. Our good doctor's getting ready to discharge me and send me to Germany.'

'We haven't got that yet.'

'We will any day now.'

'And then?'

'The general won't let me fight; he'll put me into Intelligence.'

'Katherine's murderer?'

'Yes.'

'And you still want that?'

'Yes.'

'It won't do you any good. Understand that. You won't learn a thing.'

'I've got to do it,' he said.

'That's why you can't hold me,' she said. 'That's why I'll take my men where I find them ... they all leave in the end.'

'It's important.'

'It always is. The reasons don't really matter. In the end all that matters is that they're gone and that their need has gone with them.'

She still saw the other men, often disappeared with them, would return with a small smile on her lips, her green eyes enigmatic. She mocked him, teased him, deliberately kept him at a distance, offered only her body, promised nothing beyond that, and thus forced him to accept that it must end, that he could make no claims on her. David accepted it. In a sense it was preordained. The war was still going on, the major-general continued writing, and somewhere out there, moving forward with the Americans, was the man that David now had to find. Who was he? Where was he? Was he in fact still alive? The questions haunted David, rarely stayed long from his thoughts, made him burn with a strange grief and rage, an indefinable hunger. Rachel was right: there could be no true commitment. Beyond his need for her, his possible love, was this greater obsession.

'I'll tell you a secret,' Rachel said.

'What's that?' David said.

'The medical staff are being mobilized. We're moving up to the front.'

'When?'

'At the weekend.'

'And how long have you known this?'

'The orders came through a few weeks back. I thought you should know.'

'Most considerate,' David said.

'You're angry,' Rachel said.

'Why didn't you tell me before?'

'I didn't want a sad scene.'

She was smiling at him. He felt hurt and humiliated. He turned away and gazed out the window, saw the stark ruins of Caen.

'You're a bitch,' he said.

'Poor boy,' she said. 'You're hurt. I can see it in your eyes. You have such naked eyes.'

'Is that a compliment?'

'Yes.'

'And now it's goodbye.'

'Not necessarily,' she said. 'Why not come with us?'

David looked at her. Her smile was slightly mocking. Her blonde hair fell around her thin face, the green, enigmatic eyes.

'Why not?' she said. 'You have to go to the front anyway. You wouldn't be questioned travelling with us. You could go where you want then.'

'Do you *want* me to come?'

'I wouldn't put it that strongly. But you *are* such a sweet boy after all ... you might do me some good.'

'I thought you wanted nothing steady.'

'I still don't,' she said. 'You can come, but I must have my freedom. Don't try to possess me.'

David couldn't understand it. Her green eyes told him nothing. There was tenderness in her smile, but there was also some mockery, an amusement at his obvious confusion. How could he ever know her? When would she speak the truth? She would undress and take him to her body, but her mockery protected her. Protection from what? From commitment? Responsibility? In her need for the many men, for constant sex, he sensed a taut, buried dread. David wanted to share it with her, wanted to share himself with her; he was certain that his love could protect them and bring them both peace.

He saw her eyes, her mocking smile, saw the ruins of Caen beyond her. Above the ruins was the grey sky that stretched across the rubble of Europe. David had found an oasis here, had found his strength in her body. He now thought of how far he had travelled to come to this resting place. The dead were everywhere; they littered the fields and the hills. He thought of Robert and young Pip, of Corporal Brown and Sergeant Cowie, of all those who had travelled here to die and leave him standing alone. A cold wind blew through Caen. The dust moaned around the ruins. There were more troops pouring through the shattered streets, being driven towards Germany. David saw them through the window. They moved past Rachel's head. Her weathered face, now framed by the window, was a map of the changing times.

What had she taught him? How much had she given him? She had taught him to accept his own body; she had given him confidence. All this and more. Probably more than he had realized. She had helped him to live, had removed guilt and fear, had led him to his own suppressed violence, to the nature of conflict. David had wanted vengeance. He had found strength in hatred. *It will do you no good*, she had said. *It will just eat you up*. He now knew that she was right. He knew that violence begat violence. He knew that Katherine had died, that she was gone, that retribution was pointless.

Yet he still wanted the killer. He felt a blinding curiosity. He kept his hatred at bay, but the mystery of the murder hypnotized him. Katherine's killer was in this war. In a sense he represented it. The violence in Man was not often based on logic, and the blood that was shed sprang from weakness. What was that weakness? What made men destroy? David had to find the killer, had to know the face of death, had to touch it without feeling hatred or destructive outrage.

He now sensed that Rachel knew this, had always known it, was moved by it; and as he looked at her green eyes, at the black ruins beyond her, he knew that he would have to make that journey and explore his own boundaries.

'All right,' David said, 'I'll go with you.'

'Poor boy,' she said.

# CHAPTER EIGHTEEN

'WAR is like love,' Kanin said, 'it always finds a way.' One hand fell on Rachel's knee, the other swept around the room. 'Bertolt Brecht,' he said. 'A man of some wisdom.' They were in the lobby of the Hotel de Ville, and it was crowded and noisy. 'I give you the spoils of war,' Kanin continued in a sonorous manner. 'Brussels in December in 1944 – a city making love to the victors, releasing its buried oats.' He drank his cognac and smacked his lips, put the glass back on the table, winked at David and pressed Rachel's knee, the smoke swirling around him.

'You're drunk,' Rachel said.

'I'm *always* drunk,' Kanin said.

'Yes,' Rachel said. 'I've noticed that. You're a very bad influence.'

Kanin laughed and snapped his fingers, glanced around for a waiter. He still had his right hand on Rachel's knee, making David feel angry. He tried to avoid Rachel's eyes. They were bloodshot and furtive. He wondered how much more she could take, how much more she could punish him.

'More cognac!' Kanin shouted.

'We've had enough,' David said.

'*You've* had enough,' Kanin said. 'For me the war's just beginning.'

David felt a mild revulsion. He watched Kanin order the drinks. The journalist was flushed, his dark hair streaked with grey, wiping beads of sweat from his face as he spoke to the waiter. They had picked him up in Evreux. He had simply thumbed a ride. He had stayed with them in Mantes, in Paris, in Rheims, had charmed Rachel by the time they crossed the border, was still with them in Brussels. David wanted to lose him. He wanted to forget the whole journey. Thinking back on their travels, on the widespread ruin and misery, on Rachel's metamorphosis (or, more likely, her return to form), he felt only a fathomless confusion, the hint of despair. Kanin finished giving his order. He waved the waiter away. The waiter, a Walloon, nodded curtly and returned to the bar.

'Why not?' Kanin said. 'It's our last night in Brussels. I think another drink is in order, since tomorrow the guns will fire.'

He gave a lascivious chuckle, pressed Rachel's knee again, and turned to survey the crowded lobby. David followed his gaze, saw the smoke, the milling bodies: the Americans, the Canadians, the British, the liberated civilians. The noise was atrocious: a band played, people sang; the floor shook beneath dancing feet; there was shouting and laughter. Through grey smoke the green eyes, looking at him, slipping sideways, the smile, the trace of mockery, flickering over her lips, now chapped by the cold Belgium winds, casual humour more forced. David watched the returning waiter. He carried the drinks on a tray. The tray swung around the head of a Canadian 1st Army sergeant, was lowered parallel to Rachel's face, the glasses neatly set down. Kanin quickly paid the waiter. He was careless about his change. He blew a kiss at Rachel, grinned broadly, picked up his fresh cognac.

'To victory!' he said.

They all drank to victory. The band played another tune. A British 2nd Army corporal, standing close by their table, threw his head back and whooped like an Indian, poured some beer down his shirt front. Kanin watched him and grinned. Rachel giggled and shook her head. Kanin reached out for her knee, but she caught David's glance and nervously moved her knee to the side. David was surprised. Such discretion was foreign to her. He thought of the journey up from Caen and tried to beat down his growing rage.

'Louvain,' Kanin said. 'I've never heard of the place. Is anything happening in Louvain? I want something to write about.'

'It's in northern Belgium,' Rachel said. 'It's west of the River Meuse. I don't think much is happening there. I think it's just a regrouping area.'

'Jesus,' Kanin said. 'That's all I fucking need. Any day now I'll get me a message: a Dear John from New York.'

'Your time will come,' David said. 'Montgomery's 21st has cleared the whole west bank of the Maas to provide a defensive flank on the right of the Canadian 1st. The British 2nd Army is now lined up along the Maas as far south as Maeseyck and is joining with the U.S. 9th in the Geilenkirchen area to prepare for the assault across the Rhine. That crossing is due to be made any day now, and we're going to Louvain to catch up with the 21st and follow the troops into Germany. If it's casualties you're after, you'll get them . . . I hope your editor's satisfied.'

Though patently unfair, David couldn't resist the sarcasm. Now flushing, a bit embarrassed, he picked up his drink, let the cognac burn its way down his throat, knew damned well why he'd said it. Rachel was staring at him. She opened her mouth to say something. Instead she picked her glass up, had a drink, put the glass down again. Kanin seemed to be oblivious. He was either deaf or very drunk. He raised a hand and waved above the crowds at some friend by the bar. David glanced at Rachel. She did not return his stare. Kanin smiled, put his elbows on the table, his chin in his hands.

'I was on Utah Beach,' he said. 'I covered the battle for the Falaise Gap. Before that I was in Africa and Sicily. I think my editor's satisfied.'

David felt his cheeks burning. He glanced briefly at Rachel. He thought of her in Paris, of her mocking, throaty chuckle, of the men she had picked up on the journey through France before Kanin stepped into the picture. Of course she had warned him, had made her position clear; she had agreed to let him come on one condition – and now it was choking him. From Caen to Lisieux: the dusty roads, the smashed towns, the dead cattle bloated in the fields filled with shellholes and debris, the scorched trees, the silence. Where was the doctor now? The obsessed, deranged doctor. 'The stench of death haunts me,' he had said. 'Take off your clothes, dear.' They had drank a lot that night. They had been travelling for days. Was it drink or the crippling exhaustion or just Rachel's malice? No matter: it had happened. David had watched them disappearing. He got drunk and crawled into a truck, observed the wild streaming sky. Next day they moved again. The convoy drove towards Bernay. The doctor, in a jeep, went the other way: 'No more for me, thanks.' Leaving David and Rachel. The long hospital convoy. More dust on the roads, desolation, despair everywhere. David had to control himself. Her mocking smile was no help. That night, on a stretcher in an ambulance, he took it out on her body. 'No claims.' And he agreed. As he travelled down her flesh. Orgasm, forgiveness, repentance, then more roads, more shattered towns . . .'

'Sorry,' he said to Kanin. 'I didn't mean it that way.'

'Not at all, kid,' Kanin said. 'I just want you to know.'

Kanin drank his cognac. His glass rang on the table. A cloud of smoke wreathed his flushed face, his sharp hazel eyes. He winked again at Rachel, lascivious, knowing, one hand reaching out to her knee, David watching her strained smile. He wanted to kill Kanin. It was a very personal desire. It had nothing to do with logic or reason; it was mindless possessiveness. From Lisieux to Bernay. From Bernay to Evreux. The wounded captain from the French 2nd Armoured Division, one arm missing, his brown eyes intense, still remembering Paris. 'We were the first to reach there. General Leclerc was our Commander. I lost my arm in the Boulevard Montparnasse. I hope you don't mind, *chérie*.' Rachel didn't mind, her smile mocking David's grief, the captain's one hand in her hand, disappearing in darkness. Then dawn, the long day, the next night in a truck, David locked in her body, the white flesh concealing, taking out his new anger on her belly, on her breasts, on her trembling spine. 'I warned you.' You bitch. 'You can't claim me.' You whore. Then orgasm, forgiveness, repentance, then more roads, more shattered towns. Was there ever an end to it? Could he ever explain it? 'I told you,' she said. 'You can't hold me. You must learn to live with this.' He tried to learn:

nothing. His heart breaking: broken. Then days without pity in Evreux, the tents sagging in muddy fields. The trucks rolled down from Belgium. They brought the wounded from Arnhem. David saw her, the green eyes, the blonde hair, her smock drenched in fresh blood. Despair: waving hands. '*Oh my God, it's too much!*' Stumbling into the tent from the surgeons, too tired, too removed. He didn't touch her that night. He didn't think it was wise. Next morning he awakened to find her gone, her bed hardly slept in. What price his logic? It was primitive possessiveness. Returning, looking sleepless and haggard, she had managed a trembling smile. 'A sweet boy,' she said. 'Nerves all shot to hell. How could I refuse those huge eyes? I can't help it; I'm weak that way.' David slapped her face. A mistake: she slapped him back. He grabbed her and shook her and they fought and then fell on the camp bed. He took it out on her body. His rage gave him vitality. 'You're so good when you're angry,' she crooned. 'We should do this more often.' And after that: disgust. A mild revulsion with himself. Wondering just what it was she wanted from him, why she wanted to punish him.

Kanin was talking. His cigarette smoke wreathed his face. He said: 'Yesterday I interviewed a member of the Armée Blanche, an eighteen year old Flemish kid. I was asking him about life under the Nazis, and he wasn't impressed. He said that between 1940 and August this year about 7,500 Belgians were shot, 10,000 were put into concentration camps, and 500,000 were deported. Other quaint forms of suppression used were special summary court martials, mass executions, terrifying increase in the powers of the Gestapo and SS, the application of numerous medieval, and effective, tortures, and the usual thorough extermination of the Jews. Naturally, like a good 300,000 fellow *réfractaires*, the interviewee spent most of his youth in hiding, emerging only to perform acts of sabotage on railways, canals and power cables, including, would you believe, the sinking of two German torpedo boats in Antwerp harbour. As stated: this hero is a piddling eighteen years old. Both his parents are dead, were in fact shot right in front of him, and at the moment, in cahoots with the *Front de L'Indépendance*, he is searching out, and executing, various unwanted collaborators, including members of the Flemish Nationalist Movement, the Walloon Nazi Movement and the Flemish Collaborationist Community. The war may be over for some, but for others it goes on ... And I should point out to you, since you're both looking so bored, that that Walloon who served the drinks looks like a Nazi.'

They looked automatically at the waiter. He was halfway across the lobby. The tray above his head, nodding curtly, working quickly, he was weaving in and out between the tables, through the dark, smokey chaos.

'Report him,' David said.

'A moral decision quite beyond me.' Kanin reached out to pat Rachel's knee. 'They shoot the innocent as well,' he said.

He glanced briefly around the room. The cigarette smoke covered all. All the tables were crowded, men and women jostled between them, and the floor was too packed for proper dancing. How many nationalities? How much fear now being forgotten? David listened to the noise: people bawling, the band discordant; the amused shrieks of women, glasses breaking, soldiers thumping the tables. It was unreal, heartbreaking; in fact rather like New Year's Eve: the quixotic, rather desperate affirmation that life must continue. Kanin waved at another friend; like all journalists, he kept in touch. He turned back to the table and grinned at Rachel, his sharp eyes suggestive.

'Liberation,' he said. 'Celebrations amongst the ruins. The skeletons dance on the tombstones, not knowing they're finished.'

'That's morbid,' Rachel said.

'And inaccurate,' David said. 'We've liberated most of western Europe. It will soon be all over.'

'I'll believe it when it happens.' Kanin lit a cigarette. 'I don't think the Krauts are finished yet.' Puffing smoke. 'They won't give in.'

'It's not finished,' David said. 'I think that's true enough. But it can't really go on much longer. They can't hold out for too long.'

Kanin grinned. 'Remember Paris?' he said. 'The war wasn't finished there either. I think Paris was dying.'

David flushed and glanced at Rachel. He knew just what Kanin meant. Kanin didn't give a damn about Paris beyond what it had offered him. David drank some more cognac. His throat burned, his head swam. Rachel didn't talk much anymore, but that fact was no great help. What had happened on the road to Paris? What had merited such punishment? Head swimming, David sank down through the noise, the jostling mob all around him. The sodden field outside Evreux: grey sky, the tents flapping. The trucks rolled down from Belgium, from the other packed hospitals, disgorged their bloody contents onto canvas, returned to the distant guns. Days without pity, tortured nights without end, rotting limbs being hacked off and thrown into bins, scorched flesh being peeled off the bone, the bone cracking and crumbling. Was there ever an end to it? Who on earth could explain it? Other than pain, what could possibly matter to the paratroopers stretched out on the beds? It may have been too much. At the least, too much for Rachel. David thought of the convoy, of the trucks and the dust, of the doctors, the nurses, the ambulances – all dwarfed by the stark ruins. Then the camp outside Evreux, the bloody climax to their travels: the writhing wounded, the dead piling up, the nurses sobbing and sweating. They were a long way from the front. This was where the dying came. Beyond hope, numbed to all but their pain, the men cried out and died. Was that what changed Rachel? Did that turn the final screw? With her smock drenched in blood, her eyes wild, she crept out of his tent. 'A sweet boy.' When returning. 'Nerves all shot to hell.' And then slapping one another, falling down to the bed, the act of love as vengeance, as release from self-loathing ... after which nothing could be the same.

They moved out a week later. Dust and further desolation. In the main street of Evreux, beneath the skeletal walls, the journalist with his thumb in the air, saying, 'Hi! My name's Kanin.' Then through Mantes to Paris. Rachel's eyes, Kanin's grin. Kanin kissing her breast, saying 'One for the troops,' Rachel giggling and rubbing his neck, her green eyes mocking David. After that, a great void. Her skin cold to David's touch.

Why? 'You're a dreamer,' she said. 'For God's sake, don't involve me!' What logic could resolve it? What reason could ease the hurt? 'I *like* Kanin! He doesn't *cling* to me! He'll just come and then go!' God forbid the thought of Paris. The romantic city. An air of jubilation in all the streets, slyly mocking his misery. Rachel's eyes, Kanin's grin. The lights reflecting from the Seine. Along the boulevards the jeeps and the trucks, the FFI hunting traitors. David wandered around Paris: sidewalk cafés, ancient bridges, the leaves tumbling from the trees, Les Halles, Montmartre, the Esplanade des Invalides, soldiers pouring up and down the Champs-Elysées, their eyes sensual, agog. David drank it all in, walking bleakly, alone, likewise tempted by the shopgirls (breasts pert, hips coquettish), by the whores along the Boulevard Clichy, by the crowded *charcuteries*. He tried to forget Rachel; failing that, he tried perspective: men were still being shot in the streets, snipers hid in the rooftops. Would it ever really end? How many collaborators were marked for death? While the beatings and executions continued his own pain should be negligible. Yet logic hangs itself; before emotion it bows down. The sounds of mass at St. Sulpice, the giggling girls in Saint-Germain, the smell of *bouillabaisse* from the restaurants – all reduced him to misery. David suffered and bled, poured the salt on his own wounds, let Rachel grind the salt deeper in, let the pain turn to rage. He would have no part of her; let her rut with her journalist. And then Rachel would return, a brief night, a stolen hour, hair dishevelled, her eyes streaked with crimson, her body enslaving him. 'You can't love me,' she said. 'I won't let you do that. This war ... Oh my God, this filthy war. I don't think I can take it.' How could he argue? What resistance was left? Like a beggar he would take his stolen flesh, endure hunger tomorrow.

'Let's dance,' Kanin said.

'No thanks,' Rachel said. 'I think I'm too drunk to stand up. I just want more cognac.'

Kanin ordered more drinks. The noisy crowd was undiminished. Above the roar of the crowd, from outside, the sound of planes heading east.

'The Americans,' David said. 'They're bombing Germany again. I wouldn't like to be there tonight. I think London was bad enough.'

'Don't weep,' Kanin said. 'They're getting what they deserve. The quicker that country is flattened, the better for all of us.'

'You believe that?'

'I believe it.'

'David doesn't,' Rachel said. 'Our young David wants to fight his Goliath with no more than a slingshot.'

'He's romantic,' Kanin said. 'He believes in the future. Like the whole world in 1919, he thinks this is the last one.'

'And you don't?' David said.

'No, I don't,' Kanin said. 'When this is over we'll have Russia to contend with. There's never a last one.'

The waiter brought the drinks. He put them neatly on the table. David paid him, didn't bother to check his change, cast a quick look at Rachel. He was shocked by her appearance. Her sunken cheeks told of exhaustion. Beneath the blonde hair, dishevelled, her green eyes were crimson, her smile devoid of mockery, afraid, her tongue licking her lips. She met his gaze briefly. Sipping cognac, she turned away. Her shoulders were slumped in fatigue, her sensuality likewise. Kanin leaned across the table, whispered something in her ear. She smiled bleakly and then Kanin laughed, pressed her knee once or twice.

'What's the joke?' David said.

'A little secret,' Kanin said. 'A dirty little secret between us, very private and intimate.'

'Not about me, I hope.'

'No, David,' Rachel said. 'Why on earth should we joke about you? I'm surprised you're so sensitive.'

'I wouldn't impose,' David said.

'You're not imposing,' Rachel said.

'If you want me to leave – '

'Jesus, kid, what the hell has you worried?'

Kanin sounded quite genuine; was genuine, no doubt: he didn't know about David and Rachel, had never been told. Now he studied David closely, slightly frowning, a little

280

puzzled, one rough hand curved around his glass of cognac, the other resting on Rachel's knee. David was shocked. He suddenly realized that Kanin liked him. He glanced down at the hand on Rachel's knee, stifled anger, looked up again.

'I'm sorry,' he said. 'I'm just bitching. I want to get moving.'

'You want to leave here?' Kanin said. 'You want to leave this fun and frolics? Jesus, kid, go get yourself a girl; there's no shortage in this place.'

'I meant Brussels,' David said.

'A fine city,' Kanin said. 'It's only been liberated three months and it's already debauched.'

'We leave at dawn,' Rachel said. 'I think that's early enough for me. I don't want to sleep until we leave. I don't want to sleep *ever*.'

'You need sleep,' David said.

'We *all* need sleep,' Kanin said.

'Fine!' Rachel snapped. 'So we'll sleep! When this bloody war's over!'

They both looked at her, surprised. She had closed her eyes, was trembling. She opened her eyes again and stared at them, from one to the other. Her eyes came to rest on David, rarely blinked, kept on staring, thin fingers curved around the glass of cognac, tapping it rhythmically. Something cold slid through David. He didn't know what was happening. Her green eyes, red with drink, were like glass, reflecting something like madness ...

From Paris to Rheims. The great cathedral untouched. David looked into her eyes and remembered, saw the dust on the battered roads. What had happened to Rachel? What had finally broken loose? The throaty chuckle reduced to tense giggling, her green eyes started clouding. The convoy moving forward, the 2nd Army wreathed in dust, Rachel sitting on the edge of a truck, surveying shellholes and ruins. 'Don't touch me! Oh my God! Jesus Christ, just look at that!' The green eyes, a jade wildness, filled with dazed disbelief, sweeping over desolation and death, sliding back to his face. 'Jesus! Oh my God! Get me Kanin; I need a drink.' Kanin grinning, wiping dust from his face, reaching out with his flask. 'Okay, kid?'

David nodded. He watched Rachel drink the Scotch. He looked out at the flat fields, the smoke, the troops marching behind them. *Why?* 'I don't want you. I don't want any children. I want nothing that has to be returned. I don't want love in this place.' He couldn't understand it. She was cracking and he sensed it. He turned his eyes away from desolation, from the dust of defeat. What price his logic? He felt nothing but grief. While the convoy rolled on, crossed the border, roared through Douai, while the bombs fell and the blood flowed far away, he felt only his private grief. He saw Rachel close by Kanin, saw Kanin embrace her. They drank Scotch and her green eyes flickered wildly, her hands blocking the noise out. The trucks rumbled and roared. The tanks thundered around them. Above, in a sky turning black, the planes flew towards the Rhine. From Douai they came to Brussels. The gutted Palais de Justice. Rachel's eyes reflecting greyness from the Porte de Namur, watching tanks growling past the Royal Palace, holding Kanin's broad shoulder. *What children?* 'My God! I meant *you* – don't you see? I didn't mean the children we might have. I meant the child I want *rid* of!' David had to turn away. He saw the lights of the hospital. He turned back and saw the blood on her smock, her hands plunged into water. 'It never comes off,' she said. 'It looks like it, but it doesn't. I scrub them for hours, but it stays there. I can smell it. I feel it.' David turned away again. He stumbled into the night. He found Kanin in the Hotel de Ville, drinking Scotch in that noisy room. 'She can't last,' Kanin said. 'The skin's peeling from her brain. I do what I can, but it's useless: she wants sex for oblivion.' Then he and David drank. The Scotch brought the dawn close. After that they drank often together, keeping Rachel between them. David suffered bleak confusion, loving Rachel, fearing Kanin, feeling shame because he couldn't break away, let alone bring her back.

He forgot Katherine then. He forgot where he was going. Rachel's eyes, their gradual loss of strength and lustre, froze him into the present. Katherine's death was in the past. The major-general was in the future. Slyly linking past to future was the killer, that oblique, faceless shadow. The killer was in the present, a manifestation of the Now, both inside and outside himself, dominating the landscape. The killer's shadow was the war, the desolation, the destruction; David saw the horror filming Rachel's eyes which knew that slaughter was senseless. What mattered but the loss? No analysis could find the reason; past and future became mere abstractions in the heat of the present. In this sense he forgot Katherine. He saw her killer over all. The rage he felt was at the war, at the generalized destruction, at the more intimate, highly personal loss of each divine individual ... in truth, he meant Rachel.

'Stop staring,' Rachel said.

David blinked and glanced at Kanin. The present was very bright and too noisy, crowds writhing through blue smoke.

'I'm sorry,' David said. His eyes swept around the lobby. The smoke swooped and then swirled, coiled around the bobbing heads, exploded when mouths opened to shriek, coiled and flowed, wreathed the revelry.

'Damn you,' Rachel said. 'Your sad eyes, your sensitivity. Why the hell do you have to sit there and stare? Have you never been fucked, child?'

The wild green eyes, the pale face, the dishevelled blonde hair, the glass tapping up and down on the table ... David couldn't help staring. He was oblivious to the taunt. He saw Kanin leaning forward. Kanin took her wrist and said, 'Hey, that's enough. The kid didn't deserve that.' Rachel jerked her head away. David thought she was sobbing. He was drunk and he couldn't be sure, but he felt a great sympathy.

It rushed over him, overwhelmed him. Kanin's hand was on her wrist. David suddenly felt great love for them both, a fierce need to protect them. Rachel sniffed and wiped her eyes. She was shivering; seemed broken. David thought of the blood in the tents, the long journey to madness. 'Jesus Christ,' Kanin said. He was stroking Rachel's head. Rachel sniffed and put her head on his shoulder, fingers scratching the table. David felt overwhelmed. The rage was draining right out of him. He saw her hands plunged in the water, the blood floating around her arms, the blonde hair tumbling down around her eyes, the eyes blinking dementedly. 'You poor girl,' Kanin said. He wiped sweat from her forehead. David felt incandescent with warmth, felt a need to envelop them. Looking up, he saw the lobby, heard the noise, saw the people. The band played while the heads bobbed through blue smoke: life's brief affirmation ... David lost himself then. He touched the world beyond himself. He looked at Kanin as he stroked Rachel's head, and felt pity and wonder.

Nothing seemed real after that. The band stopped, the crowd roared. The band started up again, the crowd roared, the heads bobbed through the swirling smoke. David saw the man approaching. He was instantly recognizable. Taut-faced, a weary doctor from the convoy, he emerged from the roaring crowd. Kanin waved, the man nodded. He walked up to their table. He was sweating and he seemed agitated, shoulders slumped, looking down.

'Thank God I've found you,' he said. 'The lid's blown off the pan. The Krauts have launched a counter-offensive in the Ardennes, and we've got to get moving.'

David and Kanin looked at him. They both thought it was a joke. They glanced briefly at one another, at the doctor, then they knew he was serious.

'A counter-offensive?' David said.

'I don't believe it,' Kanin said.

'No kidding,' the doctor said. 'It's the truth. All hell's broke loose out there.'

'That's ridiculous,' Kanin said.

'No, it's fact,' the doctor said. 'At least eight known Panzer divisions have smashed through the 8th Corps line, and parachutists are dropping all over the place. As far as we can make out, some of the 1st Army's forward positions have also been overrun: south of Monschau, near Vianden, around Luxemburg. We're moving out right now. We're following the 21st Army Group. They've been deployed to hold a general line from Liege to Louvain, with patrols along the west bank of the Meuse, between Liege and Dinant. They'll have to protect the river. They'll have to prevent the Germans from crossing. In short, they'll have to prevent the Germans from marching straight back into Brussels.'

There was the sound of cracking glass. They all jerked their heads towards Rachel. She was holding the broken tumbler in her hand, the blood staining her fingers.

'*Oh my God!*' Rachel sobbed.

# CHAPTER NINETEEN

THE mist covered the wooded hills, swirled around the grinding convoy, icy and damp, almost blinding, making everything ghostlike. Ahead of the ambulances the tanks roared and lurched forward, smashing through blazing vehicles, exploding German ammunition, the roadblocks made of barbed wire and trees, the dark, smouldering debris. The trucks were behind the ambulances. Shells exploded all around them. The hills erupted in smoke and spewing earth, trees collapsing and burning.

'Where are we going?' Kanin shouted.

'Oh my God!' Rachel hissed.

'Stavelot!' David shouted. 'We're linking up with the US 1st! The Germans have taken Stavelot and Malmedy, and we're launching a counter-attack!'

A sudden roar, a blinding light, the whiplash of the explosion; Rachel shrieked as the dirt poured through the truck, her hands over her ears. David cursed and looked out, saw the other trucks behind, black, prehistoric in the mist, the swirling grey of the elements. More shells exploded; the guns were firing from far away: spewing earth and jagged sheets of livid flame, spreading out, disappearing. The air roared, reverberated, ground shrieking, blowing open, trees splitting and spitting and igniting into red-yellow flames. The truck howled and bounced roughly, crashed over some fallen trees, lurched forward, throwing everyone together, cursing and groaning. David looked out again. The mist hazed the wooded hills.

Shadows swooped down and coiled through the greyness, were devoured by the crackling fires.

Another roar, another blast, dirt and stones in a whirlwind, white light and heat, then subsiding, the truck lurching on. 'God, *the noise!*' Rachel hissed. She had her hands on her ears. She was leaning slightly forward, the canvas flapping behind her, Kanin sitting close beside her, drinking Scotch, the metal flask gleaming dully. Rachel shook her head, hair dishevelled, green eyes blinking, glanced wildly around her for a moment, grabbed Kanin's left shoulder. Another roar, whipping air, dust and stones swirling outside. 'The *noise!*' Rachel hissed. 'Oh my God! *Why on earth don't we get there?*' Kanin patted her knee. He passed her the metal flask. She put it to her lips and drank deeply, wiped her lips with one hand. The truck shrieked and sank down, tilted sideways to the right, sending bodies tumbling into one another, men and women together. David pulled himself upright. Someone cursed, someone laughed. He glanced around at the nurses and medics, at Rachel and Kanin. The truck roared, the wheels screeched. The ground exploded and swirled around them. The truck shuddered until the wheels found the earth, pushed it forward again.

'A close one,' someone said.

'Oh my God!' Rachel hissed.

'Death,' Kanin quoted, 'takes us piecemeal, not at a gulp.'

One of the medics laughed sardonically. Kanin grinned and drank some Scotch. Rachel shivered and then collapsed against his shoulder, let his free arm encircle her. The high whistle of a shell. Eyes went up and closed briefly. The shell passed overhead, exploded somewhere on the hill, dirt and stones raining down upon the truck as it shook on the broken road. David felt almost numb. The cold was eating at his bones. Another roar, swirling dust, Rachel's eyes, his ears ringing then clearing. He shook his head and blinked, saw white faces in the gloom; the eyes were sunken with depression and fatigue, the mouths slack, ringed with dust. More explosions: heat and light, swirling dust and freezing cold. David hugged himself, stamped his booted feet, let his ears ring and clear.

Rachel. Dear God. He wondered if she would make it. They had travelled all night, first to Louvain, then Liège, crossing the river Meuse in the dawn, seeing mist on the water. The noise, the confusion. The men marching across the bridge. Rachel's eyes reflecting flares illuminating the greyness, drinking in the aftermath of previous battles: the banks of the river, that charnelhouse silence; on scorched earth old helmets and weapons, the mangled machinery. He had seen her shaking then – the revelation of her dread – body quivering like a string on a bow, pulled taut to the breaking point. Now he licked his dry lips, saw her huddled against Kanin, shrinking, getting smaller every minute, preparing to disappear. David felt a great sympathy. It swept out to her and Kanin. He saw the glint of the flask in the gloom and he hoped it would help.

The truck lurched from left to right, engine screeching, wheels spinning, jolted to a halt, suddenly roared, crawled forward again. The tanks rumbled up ahead. They made a harsh, metallic clatter. More explosions, more shells whistling overhead, the hills catastrophic. Rachel jerked away from Kanin, put her knuckles in her mouth. Kanin screwed the top back on the flask, put the flask in his pocket. He was wearing combat clothes, seemed too bulky, out of place; slightly drunk, he was ridiculously calm as he pulled out his notebook. David watched him, amused. Kanin scribbled, unperturbed. Rachel sat up, took her knuckles from her mouth, stared at Kanin with wild eyes. 'Jesus Christ,' she said. Kanin raised his right eyebrow. The shell whistled and roared, the noise spreading out, crushing them, someone screaming and then the fierce heat, the white light and the awesome blast.

On the floor, looking up, a nurse sprawling across him, David blinked and saw Rachel's green eyes, glazed with panic, now elsewhere. David gulped and shook his head, felt the Sten gun in his hand. 'Was it us?' someone said. 'No it wasn't. Dear God, those poor bastards.' The nurse pushed herself from David, looking down at him, smiling; she had dark hair and she brushed it from her face with long, delicate fingers. Very cosy,' she said. Someone shrieked and she quivered, turned her head as David climbed to his feet, adjusting his clothing. The truck had stopped; he heard screaming and bawling. Looking out, he saw the truck just behind them, now blazing, a furnace. '*Oh my God!*' Was it Rachel? 'What a mess.' That was Kanin. In front of David, the medics were jumping out, running towards the inferno. David saw the dark-haired nurse. Blazing silhouettes danced about her. They were shrieking – not shrieking, something else: demented animals dying. David jumped out of the truck. Icy cold and dense mist. The screaming, the shrieking, high-pitched and unearthly, the burning men writhing and rolling around the larger inferno.

'She can't take it,' Kanin said. He was standing beside David. He was scribbling in his notebook and his hazel eyes were flitting here and there while more shells fell about them.

'Rachel?'

'Rachel. I don't know that she'll last. She's been with the Army since D-Day; now she's reaching her limit.'

David glanced back at the truck. He saw Rachel inside. A flash of blonde hair, shifting eyes; the shadowed body was shivering. He had to look away. He saw the medics at work: on their knees, above the stretchers, strapping down the twitching bodies, the stench of burnt flesh in their nostrils, the inferno behind them. Other men rushed back and forth, waving hands, bawling orders, dragging bodies to the sides of the road, trying to•comfort the wounded. They didn't have much time. They had to get the road cleared. Both the wounded and the dead were put into the ambulances, then the first half of the column moved forward, away from the blazing truck.

David watched the blaze receding. The dark mist diffused the flames. More shells were raining down on the wooded slopes, the smoke filled with bright flickerings. The mist swirled before his eyes. Burning vehicles lined the road. The remaining trucks were creeping around the inferno, then racing to catch up. David sighed and sat down. He was sitting beside the dark-haired nurse. When he smiled at her she didn't smile back: her eyes were focused on Rachel. 'Some nurse,' she whispered, her eyes still focused on Rachel. 'She didn't even get out of this truck; she just sat here and sweated.' David glanced across at Rachel, felt the cleansing ache of pity: she was leaning against Kanin, her head on his shoulder, Kanin's thick arm encircling her neck, fingers stroking her face.

'She's exhausted,' David said. 'She's been through an awful lot.' The nurse looked at him, tried to comprehend him, as the truck lumbered on.

The explosions were now behind them, turned to dulled, distant rumblings, finally became faint reverberations, then faded away. The convoy kept going, trucks growling, tanks clattering, rolling down out of the densely-wooded hills towards the mist-covered lowlands. Fresh sounds: deep and distant. The rhythmic pounding of big guns. David pulled up the canvas and glanced out of the truck, saw the mist swirling over the dark fields, clumps of trees, far below. More than mist: smoke. The smoke drifted in grey clouds, moving leisurely, ominously, away from the small, far-off houses. Then a muffled, rolling thunder; silvery flashes through the murk; minute, criss-crossing lines of yellow flame in those smoke-smothered fields.

'Malmedy,' someone said. 'Them fucking Krauts have got it back. Stavelot's about five miles away, and they've got that as well.'

David kept looking down. The fields were coming up to meet him. The smoke swirled and glided through the mist, the spotty plague of the shellholes. Then more smoke; convulsive. A black cloud spitting flames: yellow darts shooting out, disappearing, the bass rumbling of guns. David looked down and saw them. They recoiled and exploded. They belched flame and smoke, the dust billowed around them, and the gun crews were dwarfed by their presence, minute, almost negligible. Kanin's flask glinting dully. A quick glance from Rachel. David noticed and then turned away as the truck travelled downhill. They were levelling out above the fields. The guns' thunder enveloped them. The fields rolled back through dense mist and smoke, disappeared in a grey haze.

Distant fire: that was Malmedy. They weren't going to Stavelot. David looked and saw the flat, disrupted fields, the trees scorched, the ground smouldering. The mist, the swirling smoke. Looking deeper: the tanks; moving out from the batteries of allied guns, heading straight for the distant town. The guns roared again: US 1st Army field guns; 155-mm shells curving down towards Malmedy. Then a dull answering fire. A muffled rumbling from the haze. The tanks spreading out, ant-like, in silence, before the whole field went mad. Soaring pillars of dirt. Swirling columns of smoke. Shooting upward, then out, huge umbrellas, then raining back down again. The noise was insane. It seemed to split the sky apart. The flat field kept exploding, the squat tanks kept advancing, a whirlwind lashed trees and hedgerows: all this lay there before him.

The convoy rolled downhill, reached ground level, moved onward, not in need of directions or instructions, guided in by the bedlam. The tanks split and fanned out, lumbered over the rough terrain, formed a wall of steel behind the gun batteries, their own guns facing Malmedy. The ambulances did like-wise: they spread out behind the tanks, the drivers and medics jumping down to join the milling tank crews. Then the trucks followed suit. They drove through the choking dust. They stopped with a jolt, engines whining to silence, while the earth beneath their wheels shook and grumbled, protesting the holocaust.

David jumped out of the truck. The mist was dense and very cold. He shivered; was surrounded by doctors and nurses and medics. Then Kanin jumped out. The guns roared as he hit the ground: demoniac, a cosmos exploding, huge planets colliding. Kanin winked and turned back. He reached up for Rachel's hand. Glancing out, seeing dark, screaming sky, Rachel trembled and jumped down. The guns roared, reverberated. Shrieking metal, shouting men. The smoke swam through the mist, swooped and glided, men and women dissolving. Rachel coughed and embraced herself, saw David and smiled. Without mockery her smile was redundant: all pain and confusion. David nodded and glanced at Kanin. The hip flask was not in sight. Kanin grinned, took his notebook from his pocket, bit his pencil with strong teeth. The guns roared again. Metal shrieked, the smoke swirled. The men unloaded the trucks, the paraphernalia of surgery, the tents springing up mysteriously as they did so, men bawling, guns thundering.

David watched it, intrigued. It had never ceased to fascinate him. Men were running to and fro, tugging canvas, pulling ropes, the tents billowing out and rising with the wind, growing taut, standing upright. Rachel watched it as well. The guns roared and she twitched. The smoke swirled around the nurses and medics as they moved the equipment in. Rachel bit her lower lip, glanced at Kanin and shivered. David walked up as she said, 'I need a drink. Just give me a drink.' Kanin gave her the hip flask. Rachel had a stiff drink. She passed the flask back, looked at David, said, 'Sorry ... Dear God.' The massed guns roared again. Rachel twitched, bit her lip. She stared at David, at Kanin, glanced across at the working nurses, shivered again, straightened up, rushed towards the first tent. Another roar of the guns. The smoke obscured the tent briefly. When it cleared they saw Rachel inside, laying blankets on stretchers.

'She won't stop,' David said.

'That won't help,' Kanin said. 'She can't wipe the blood off her hands. She smells blood in her sleep.'

'We could report it,' David said.

'What's the use?' Kanin said. 'She'll deny it and the Army, being desperate, will gladly accept it.'

They walked towards the roaring guns, felt the ground shaking under them, saw the huge barrels belching smoke and flame, shadows waving around them. The noise was beyond belief: catastrophic, ear-splitting, exploding, rolling over their heads, spreading out like a giant fist. They were self-propelled field guns, shaped like tanks, on steel tracks; the men running around them were filthy, wore helmets and battle gear. The men bawled, the guns roared; the barrels jerked and recoiled; then fierce yellow flame, swirling smoke, shrieking metal, more shouting. The flat field stretched out before them, black with mud, pocked with shellholes, littered with helmets and broken, discarded weapons; not too far away a smouldering half-track, further on a deserted jeep. Spread across it were the tanks, moving forward, growing smaller, disappearing into dark smoke and mist, the ground erupting between them. There was something unreal about it; denying noise, it was dreamlike. Behind the tanks were the British and American infantry, crouching low, weaving left and right. More geysering earth; the rolling thunder of the guns; men would spin away from mushrooming smoke, their limbs flapping, collapsing. The mist swallowed the tanks; the soldiers gradually vapourized. Desolation: still forms on the flat field, the mist settling over them.

The silence was brief. Within the mist: winking lights. The muffled thunder of enemy guns, the muted flickering of burning buildings, then brighter flame and smoke in the distant haze, the rhythmic dance of explosions. The allied guns returned the fire. Massive thunder; a whirlwind. Dirt and stones swirled through the air, whipped their faces and hands, stuck to skin, settled down on their shoulders, the noise echoing viciously. David blinked and looked at Kanin. The guns roared again instantly. Kanin grimaced and scribbled something in his notebook, glanced across the wide field. David looked and saw mist, the smoke rising from the dead, the helmets and rifles and shellholes: a too brief desolation. More explosions, more noise. A moving fire in the mist. The mist parted as the burning tank emerged, minute shadows around it. The tank slewed to the left. Shuddering, it stopped. From the furnace of the turret a dark form, limbs frantic, on fire. This thing rolled off the tank. The tank shuddered, exploded. Other figures started running from the mist, the ground erupting between them.

'They're coming back!' someone bawled.

'Not *again*!' someone added. David turned and saw the white face of a gunner, his eyes ringed with mud. The gunner took off his helmet, threw it angrily on the ground. Leaning against the gun, he put his head in his hands, glanced at David, then shook with desperation. 'Jesus Christ,' he said softly.

The soldiers made their retreat, first hazy, then clear, running out of the mist and swirling smoke, the fires winking behind them. Exhausted, grimy, many covered in blood, they collapsed to the ground behind the guns, shook their heads, coughed and retched. The tanks followed them from the mist. Some were smoking and burning. A few stopped and the men clambered out, not always on time: the tanks shuddering, exploding, jagged flame, then the black, smouldering pyres. Thunderous noise, swirling dust: the guns tried to give protection. David covered his ears with his hands, watched the soldiers returning. They poured in around the guns, faces filthy, helmets missing, dropped to their knees, threw their heads back, gasped for breath, then collapsed. Kanin wandered amongst them. He knelt down to talk to them. Looking up, David saw the retreating tanks, coming out of the smokey mist.

' – *too much! We can't take it!*'

But they had to take it, had to regroup and go back, moving out a few hours later, behind the tanks, into the mist, the flames winking in the distance, the ground erupting between them, the bedlam of the guns front and rear, a brain-crushing cacophony. The wounded stayed behind, filled the hospital tents; and while the guns roared, while the earth swirled and howled, more wounded poured in. David saw the blood and bone, the gaping wounds, the dismembered limbs, heard the whimpering, the groaning, the gargling as men choked on their own blood. Night came and the mist deepened. The belching guns split the darkness. In the tents, the lamps swinging above their heads, the surgeons worked without sleep.

David helped as best he could, carried blankets and stretchers, limping slightly, his leg not quite healed, wondering what he was doing there. In truth, he was observing: Rachel's smock soaked with blood; the green eyes above the pale cheeks; the hands no longer steady at their work, moving frantically, blindly. It was all too much for her. He would have to protect her. His own pain had now been placed in perspective, was of little importance.

Another day: more blood; the guns belching and thundering; the tanks heading out towards Malmedy, the men running behind them. Advance and retreat: the answering fire of the German guns; through the drifting haze of mist and dark smoke the flickering flames of the burning town. Then the wounded returning, sometimes crawling, sometimes carried, soaked in blood, pouring blood, white bone flashing, eyes scorched into blindness. They stumbled towards the tents, were helped in by the medics, fell gasping to the stretchers, threw up, stared at nothing with wide eyes. The cooling hands of the nurses, the green tears in Rachel's eyes, then the guns roared again, the world exploded . . . one more night, one more day.

He didn't know how she could stand it. Her latent strength held him in thrall. He saw Kanin reaching out to stroke her head, her head jerking away. That was Rachel: no more. It was someone lost and broken. David worked with the dead and the dying, saw her shivering, frail form. A brief rest: exhaustion. Rachel crouched low, eyes blinking. Kanin walked between the stretchers, above the blood and the broken bones, passed the bins with the amputated limbs, put his hand out to stroke her. Rachel twitched and turned away. 'How much more? *Oh my God!*' The lamp swinging above her head cast a bright light, made dark swarming shadows. Then the guns roared again. They heard the droning of the planes. The planes had come from behind the allied lines and were flying towards Malmedy. 'That's it,' Rachel said. 'Bomb the bastards! Give it to them!' Kanin sighed and stood up and walked away, waving one hand at David.

'She's going to crack,' Kanin said.

'We'll look after her,' David said.

'That might not be possible,' Kanin said.

'We can try,' David said.

They both went outside. Looking up, they saw the planes. Flying low, they were hazy in the grey sky, seemed monstrous, unreal. They flew across the cheering men, disappeared over Malmedy: flame and smoke, the ground shaking, rolling thunder from the mist; the black clouds from the death and destruction formed a bleak new horizon. The men cheered, waved their hands, suddenly ran to and fro, picked up helmets and weapons and ammunition as the tanks clattered forward. Then the aircraft returned, flying low, in salute, headed back towards the airfield at Brussels, inviolable, untouched.

Bedlam and chaos: the guns belching and thundering; the tanks rumbling out into the fields with the soldiers behind them. They headed straight for Malmedy, towards the mist and the smoke, the field howling and exploding amongst them, the men spinning and falling. David watched it, intrigued; he felt calm, academic. He had changed and he knew it was for the better: he could now ride the whirlwind. The tanks weaved left and right. Some trailed smoke, some exploded. The mist eventually swallowed the others, plus the soldiers behind them. A final run of explosions. The ground soaring, then subsiding. A sudden roar and an ambulance lurched forward, heading straight for the littered field.

'Rachel!' It was Kanin. David jerked his head around. He saw Rachel climbing into a half-track, Kanin walking towards her. 'Where the hell are you going?'

Rachel looked down from the half-track, brushed the hair from her forehead; the hand, when it came down from her face, was visibly shaking. Looking down, she licked her lips. The dark-haired nurse was beside her. Behind them, in the back of the half-track, were three or four medics.

'We've broken in,' Rachel said. 'The troops are fighting in the streets of Malmedy. We have to have people over there to attend to the wounded. We have ambulances following.'

She glanced briefly at the nurse beside her, licked her lips, her eyes blinking, sighed, her body shivering with fatigue, then looked down at Kanin. Kanin glanced across at David, shrugged his shoulders, waved his notebook. David nodded and they both got in the half-track, David holding his Sten gun. 'Let's go!' someone bawled. The half-track roared into life. Kicking up mud and stones, bouncing over the rough terrain, it passed the mud-begrimed trucks, the men lolling beneath the guns, rumbled past the still smoking gun barrels and headed into the misty field.

Rachel didn't say a word. She held the white cap on her head. The half-track bounced up and down, weaved around the littered shellholes, travelled steadily into the swirling smoke and mist, passed scorched trees and dead bodies. A flash of white through the murk, the silence broken by nearby shouting: looking hard they could see the other medics, crouched low, working desperately. The half-track didn't stop; its back wheels churned the mud up. They passed blazing tanks, skeletal buildings, the black, smouldering trees. The mist and smoke covered all; the air was icy cold. Through the murk they could see diffused flames, a yellow haze in the distance. Rachel shivered and hugged herself. Kanin watched her, started scribbling. David, now watching them both, felt an uplifting grief. He saw the curve of Rachel's breasts, dominating her thin body; beyond them, far ahead, through the mist and swirling smoke, were the brightening flames of gutted Malmedy.

The half-track kept going. Up ahead: bursts of gunfire. Beyond the mist and the thinning clouds of smoke: a hazed light spreading out. David held his Sten gun tightly. Rachel's green eyes, bright with fear. He felt crushed by his love, raised on high: a voluptuous transcendence. Rachel suddenly turned towards him. She reached out and touched his face. Her green eyes very big, a jade glittering, demented, she said, 'Oh God, poor boy, please forgive me, it's not what I wanted.' Then guns roared up ahead. Rachel twitched and turned away. David looked up and saw Kanin's face, his calm smile, understanding.

David wanted to say something. He wanted to share some secret joy. He looked beyond Kanin's head, saw the swirling smoke thinning, saw the flames, the shadowy outlines of houses, heard mortars, machine-guns. The half-track raced on. They saw streets lined with rubble. They heard gunfire, saw soldiers, shadows racing through the mist, the grey murk illuminated by the fires as they raced into Malmedy.

The town was being cleared. Allied tanks blocked off the streets. The soldiers clambered over rubble, darted in and out of doorways, were at one, in that smokey-dark haze, with the bewildered civilians. More explosions: sliding mortar, the dust rising and spitting sparks; soldiers bawling, firing weapons, running forward, falling down, rolling over. The half-track stopped amongst them, was in fact stopped by debris, the driver looking down, cursing loudly, waving everyone out.

David saw the dark-haired nurse. She smiled bleakly and jumped out. She was followed by three medics, then by Rachel, her green eyes wide with dread. David and Kanin followed. Along the street a machine-gun roared; looking along the street they saw the ruins, the rubble rising and falling. Here the smoke was really dust; the dust was settling and the mist was thinning. The soldiers advanced through the town, the fighting moved further away, as they unloaded their equipment from the half-track and set up a first-aid post.

The town was cleared and secured. The promised ambulances arrived eventually. By the next day the hospital was operating inside the battered town hall. David worked beside Rachel. His wounded leg pained him little. Through the windows, beyond Rachel's head, he could see the hazed hills. Inside it was different: blood and bone, tortured flesh; a low murmuring defining mass pain, the final gasps of the dying. Kanin interviewed the victims. He scribbled constantly in his notebook. Watching Rachel, sometimes touching her lightly, he showed a father's concern. Rachel seemed to be oblivious. Her eyes had turned to focus inward. Her hands fluttering over blood and scorched skin, she worked fiercely, obsessively. Kanin's hand brushed her lightly. David knew what Kanin meant. Now close to the end of her tether, she could break without warning. David felt a great anguish, an even greater supporting love, and working close by her side, sharing pain and death with her, he understood that whatever might happen, her frightened soul had renewed him.

The battle raged far away. The allies were pushing the Germans back. It was not without cost and the trucks brought more wounded into Malmedy. The medics worked night and day. They snatched sleep when they could. By day the mist clung to the town; the mid-December winds froze them. David looked up at the sky, saw clouds drifting, increasing; he held his hand up and felt the ice, thought of Christmas at home. The next day Rachel spoke. She stood beside him at the window. They watched allied planes flying overhead, their wings glinting in pale sun.

'I feel dead,' Rachel said.

A choked sob as she rushed away. When he next saw her, she was working, folding up blankets and sheets, working fiercely, obsessively. His heart went out to her, shared her pain, her nameless dread, and he walked up and gently touched her cheek, heard the breath of a sigh.

The following day they moved again, rolled laboriously out of Malmedy, following the Army, heading up into the hills, deeper into the Ardennes. The cold was biting and numbing. The mist glided around their heads. Rachel shivered and put her head on Kanin's shoulder, closed her eyes, bit her lower lip. David understood her anguish, felt the need to protect her. Glancing around, he saw the dark-haired nurse, her face weary, smile haunted. The convoy headed for Hotton, rumbled through the deepening mist, past discarded jeeps and tanks and half-tracks, beneath the barren, scorched trees. David held his right hand up. The icy air turned it to stone. A single flower, very light, almost warm, melted over his palm.

His heart froze: it was snow.

# CHAPTER TWENTY

WHITE world, white sky: wollen caps and white camouflage; the snow dazzling, drifting over itself, the men speckling albescent fields. The white hills rolled towards the river, the men in camouflage blending with them: all white, earth and sky, the snow falling in silence, the black branch of a tree shaking loose, a white powder descending.

The road was different: it was sludge; the tanks and half-tracks had churned it up; it was now a black line snaking back through a colourless haze. Other black spots: the trees, the gutted shells of bombed houses, the steel litter of discarded Army vehicles, now mangled, destroyed.

An apposite world: black and white.

David knelt by the roadside, blew warm air between his hands, felt the wool of the cap around his ears, his ears stinging with cold. He was not alone behind the hedgerow, between the roadside and the truck: Rachel and Kanin were both there; the dark-haired nurse, the medics. They were all kneeling and shivering, all wearing snow camouflage, the snow blending with the white of their outfits, covering faces and hands. Far away the big guns roared: a muffled thunder, reverberating. Rachel twitched and reached out for Kanin's hand, glanced at David with stricken eyes. David smiled, rocked a little, brushed some snow from his shoulders, finally raised his eyes and gazed above the hedgerow at that clear, white expanse.

The rolling hills draped in snow, a white dazzle, quiet and dreamlike; on the snow the black specks of the weapons of the camouflaged men. The men were spread across the fields, countless men, moving forward, the only sound the distant thunder of the guns beyond the still unseen river. Cumulous clouds: white as snow. The sun glinting: on the snow. The snow languidly, incessantly drifting across its own gleaming surface. David blinked and looked again. The black spots climbed the hill. Over the hill, where the guns were now roaring, was the Ourthe and its frozen banks.

'Too easy,' Kanin said.

'They're just waiting,' David said. 'And we should have had that air support by now. What the hell are they doing?'

He turned and glanced at Rachel. She was huddled against Kanin, body shivering, her knuckles in her mouth, staring down at her booted feet. David wanted to talk to her, touch her, hold her gently; he felt a strange grief and exultation, pain and pleasure combined. The snow drifted around her feet, settled down on her shoulders, melted slowly on her cold cheeks and hands, the taut ridge of her knuckles. He couldn't talk to her. There was nothing left to say. She was running away from them all, retreating into a private world.

In truth, she was cracking; she couldn't last a lot longer. If they didn't get her out of here soon, she would just fall apart. There had been too much too often – too much blood, too much death; four weeks in the hell of the Ardennes was too much for anyone. They had not stopped for Christmas; on New Year's Day they had been bombed; after that: more engagements, exploding shells, screaming men; trucks blazing, wheels spinning in the mud ... then the fierce, freezing snow. It was too much for Rachel: her hands shook, her lips trembled; in the brief spells between each engagement she would huddle up, shivering. They couldn't break her isolation, couldn't persuade her to ask for leave; she would just shake her head and turn away, lose herself in more work. David and Kanin could only watch, both despairing at her tenacity: huddled up in the freezing truck, tending the wounded in exploding fields, eyes wild, crawling through mud and snow, the guns roaring around her. They knew she couldn't last much longer, that any day now she would crack, and they had both agreed that once across the river they would have to report her. Rachel, whether she liked it or not, needed treatment and rest.

A distant, staccato roaring. Rachel twitched and bit her lip. David looked above the hedgerow, saw the white hills, the black specks, then explosions, snow soaring, curving out, falling down, the dark, boiling smoke rising up between the camouflaged men. It was all very dreamlike, almost pretty, rather graceful, the snow soaring to the sky, falling down, a white rain over puffs of smoke. Death: far removed; a distant pageant of snow and flame, the black specks spreading out, moving up, without names, in great numbers. Then the increasing noise, the muffled rhythm of exploding shells, the snow spinning and streaming across the hills, the black specks in a white haze. It didn't seem bad. It never looked bad from a distance: the muffled roaring, snow swirling, cascading over dark smoke and black ants.

'All right,' the doctor said. 'We'll take the truck along that road. We'll go straight along the side of the field until we get to the river. The ambulances will follow later. They'll attend to the field as they go. Meanwhile, we'll go straight to the town and set up a first-aid post. That's it; let's move out.'

They climbed into the truck. Kanin helped Rachel up. She glanced once across the field, surveyed the shellholes on the hills, the upturned earth desecrating the whiteness, then she twitched and sat down. The dark-haired nurse followed her, no longer smiling, fists clenched, looking up as David climbed in behind her, her eyes darting away again. Too much, David thought. He heard the roaring of the guns. He sat down as the truck roared into life, its wheels churning up mud and snow.

They drove along the road, running parallel to the field, turned right and went through an opened gate, bounced down onto a narrow track. It was just wide enough for the truck, black with sludge and upturned mud, already flattened by the wheels of the jeeps and half-tracks, the tanks and heavy guns and supply transport. The field was spread out to their right, rolling gently downhill; there were thousands of footprints in the snow, leading towards that last hill. More explosions: much closer. David turned and looked ahead. The field ran down to the base of the hill where the shellholes began. Black scabs on the whiteness. Drifting smoke, swirling snow. The noise increased, became a constant, rhythmic thunder, the snow exploding in yellow flames. The snow soared up and out, spiralled lazily, rained down, covered the white-suited men on the hill, blew across the grey smoke.

The truck bounced along the track, the field spreading out beside it: glittering whiteness, snow kicked up by boots, the gnarled limb of a tree. The guns roared, the shells exploded. The hill approached and grew larger. The dark specks were now visibly men, shadows caught in a blizzard. Dressed in white they were hazy, unreal, part of the snow; framed by trees or the ugly black shellholes, they would suddenly stand out. They were struggling up the slope, the shells exploding in their midst: the earth roaring, the snow geysering skyward, the men spinning and falling. More explosions, cracking rifles; the vicious chatter of a machine-gun; bullets stitching jagged lines across the snow; the sounds of screaming and bawling. Rachel licked her lips, glanced at Kanin, then at David. The men swarmed across the brow of the hill, disappeared down the other side. Rachel groaned, bit her knuckles. The earth roared, the snow swirled. The approaching slope was littered with bodies, burning trees, smouldering shellholes. The snow melted and turned to steam. The steam rose from the dead soldiers. More explosions and the snow soared and swirled and rained over the prone forms: the dead and the wounded.

'Damn them!' the doctor bawled. 'Where's the air support?'

They drove alongside the hill, the truck roaring, struggling upward, its wheels slipping and sliding in the snow, the driver changing gears, cursing. The truck stopped, shuddered violently. The dark-haired nurse groaned, '*God!*' The truck roared and jerked forward again – into chaos and bedlam. A screeching shell, a blinding thunder; white light and swirling snow. Someone screamed and then they slammed into each other, the snow howling around them. The truck stopped, roared again. The driver cursed, someone whimpered. David shook his head and saw the dark-haired nurse, her brown eyes streaming tears. He opened his mouth to speak. Blinding light, hellish din. Streams of snow and yellow fire and black mud, the sky spinning and roaring. David struggled to sit up. He felt the shuddering of the truck. He saw an arm, then a leg, bodies tangled, snow and mud falling over them. Another roar:

swirling whiteness; the truck shuddered, crept forward; more explosions, blazing air, howling earth, then they were through it and climbing.

They disentangled themselves. The truck was climbing the winding track. To their right the white breast of the hill was a nightmare of smoke and flames. The swirling snow was like a blizzard. The explosions tore through the climbing men. The men hid behind the trees, darted out, ran uphill, rolled back down again. The guns roared, richocheted: fans of flame, falling bodies. David looked up at the grey, empty sky, saw no sign of the planes. The truck continued climbing. The truck curved around the hill. More explosions, the dark-haired nurse sobbing, a sudden whirlwind of snow and mud. David cleared it from his eyes, blinked repeatedly, saw Rachel: a taut face, green eyes ringed with snow, staring inward for shelter. Poor Rachel. The noise. The searing light overhead, jagged, spreading out, heat and bedlam, then the whole world exploding.

A scream, tumbling bodies, the truck roaring and screeching, rocking violently, sliding back, turning over, snow swirling and hissing.

Kanin's face and then darkness.

Numbed, suffocating, David coughed snow and blinked, raised his head, saw the truck overturned, white forms crawling around it. He spat more snow from his mouth, shook his head, cleared his eyes, heard the thunder of the guns, the screeching shells, the jagged roar of explosions. ' – come on! Let's get going!' Looking up, he saw the doctor, now standing, pointing up through the blizzard, face lined with exhaustion. David got to his knees, groped around for his Sten gun; finding it, he climbed to his feet, felt his wounded leg throbbing. A shell whined overhead. More than one machine-gun chattered. He saw the dark-haired nurse sobbing and shaking, someone slapping her face. Rachel. Where was Rachel? The snow swirled around the truck. ' – come on! Take your gear! Let's get going!' The doctor shouted, kept climbing, a dark form in the white haze, other shadows, the medics, just behind him, all struggling in deep snow. Then Kanin, turning back, reaching down to grab at Rachel, stumbling, almost falling against her, finally pulling her up. The guns roared, the hill erupted. A medic guided the dark-haired nurse. They climbed up through the trees and David followed, whipped by fierce wind and snow.

The noise beyond the hill grew louder; the hill itself was levelling out. The exploding shells tore the trees apart, filled the air with scorched debris. David hurried to catch up; fighting the snow, his legs ached. The guns thundered and the smoke swirled all around him, the wind whipping the snow up. He passed the medic and the dark-haired nurse. The nurse was wiping her tearful eyes. With the medical bags over her shoulder, she seemed bulky, inhuman. Another roar, another explosion. The snow howled and swept across them. David rushed ahead and caught up with Rachel, saw the dread in her green eyes. Not Rachel: someone else. Rachel gone and in need of rebirth. David felt a great love, a new conviction, as he stumbled ahead.

Then a sudden, shocking bedlam. A silvery light through the gloom. Looking down, he saw the gorge, the flowing river, the battered town on the far side.

'Damn it!' the doctor shouted. 'Where's the air support? Those thick, thoughtless bastards!'

The walls of the gorge were very steep. The Germans held the far side. The first British and American troops had reached the river, but were now being butchered. Steep walls, almost vertical; a hail of bullets poured down upon them; the allied soldiers spun around, threw their arms up, fell into the river. David studied the rushing water. It was rough and filled with ice. The allied guns lashed the Germans, machine-guns and mortars, and snow exploded from the wall of the gorge and rained down on the river. David looked at the river. He saw gleaming slabs of ice. Between the slabs of ice, drifting, were the dead, also drifting, then sinking.

'Oh my God!' Rachel said. She was leaning against Kanin. They were both looking down the steep slope, at the men clinging to it. The men were inching down slowly, firing weapons, waving wildly, being covered, unsuccessfully, by the guns along the brow of the hills. 'We've got to get *down* there!' Rachel said. 'Oh my God, it's *impossible*!' They saw the far bank exploding, spitting snow and shrieking Germans, the men kicking and falling through the air, splashing into the river. Rachel shuddered and turned away. The dark-haired nurse came up beside her. They all stood there with the doctors and medics, gazing down at that white hell.

'Let's go,' the doctor said.

'Go where?' David said. 'There's no point in going down now. It won't do any good.'

'Those men down there are wounded.'

'That's right,' David said. 'And we can't afford to have your medics wounded. We'll have to wait till the river's crossed.'

The allied troops swarmed down the slope, were cut to pieces by the German guns, the snow spitting and exploding around them, spiralling over the gorge. Nevertheless, the men went down, sliding down, rolling down, a great many flying out in exploding whiteness, plunging into the river. The huge slabs of ice glittered. A white powder filled the air. Down on the bank, spreading along the gorge wall, the soldiers set up more mortars. The mortars boomed, machine-guns roared. The far wall became smoke and flame. Bodies flew out from the rocks, the spraying snow, went spinning down to the water. More troops swarmed down the wall, clung to shrubbery and rocks, poured out along the banks of the river, jerked demented-ly, fell in. The water was now filled with dead men; they drifted along with the glittering ice. Grenades thrown from both sides, falling short, made the water convulsive.

The noise was hideous; catastrophic: it echoed up and down the gorge. The exploding snow was like a dense, silvery mist, falling over the fighting men. Rachel's wild eyes drank it in. Kanin stood there scribbling notes. David saw Rachel shiver-ing, a fatigue beyond the physical, then he looked down and watched the mounting carnage. It was hellish; inhuman. The men fought and died like ants. The two walls of the gorge were exploding in white snow and black earth. It rained over the milling men. They rushed about, their guns spitting. More men were falling off both the walls, plunging into the water. If not dead, they would freeze to death. The water carried them away. They turned slowly, drifting past the other men, now waist-deep, wading forward. They held their weapons above their heads. The water spit and danced around them. Some screamed and plunged under the surface, but the others kept going. Grenades exploded, guns roared; the water hissed and boiled around them. Blown apart, stitched by bullets, they kept going, finally swarmed up the far bank.

The entrenched Germans were now distracted, had to focus on their own side, dropped hand grenades, poured gunfire on the men clambering up the sheer wall. Yellow fire, boiling smoke, the snow exploding and swirling wildly; nevertheless the climbing men clung to the rock, inched their way up the gorge wall. Many cried out and fell, tumbled down, bounced off shrubs, flew out above the snow-covered river, plunged down through the drifting ice; others simply kept going, hurling grenades, firing weapons, ducked back as the Germans slithered down, their limbs flapping in death. Glittering ice, white snow; the black, littered river; men screaming, sailing out through the air, the world exploding around them. It went on much too long. Time stood still for the horror. The dead were strewn about the gorge, drifted languidly, sank slowly . . . but eventually the Germans were cleared from the far bank, retreated back towards the town.

'All right,' David said. 'Let's go.'

At what point did it finish? Certainly not at the wounded. They were clinging to the walls of the gorge, were stretched out by the river. Eyes dulled, bodies twitching; freezing cold, pouring sweat: here a man with no jaw, there a man with smashed legs, somewhere else a man clutching his stomach lest it slop down his thighs. Kanin watched and took notes. Rachel sobbed and administered care. The dark-haired nurse, in a trance, her eyes dry, worked with equal despair. David knelt there and watched them. He kept his eyes on the far bank. Reassured that there were no lurking Germans, he gazed down at the river.

A temporary bridge had been placed across it. Half-tracks rumbled across the bridge. Along the gorge, to the right of the bridge, he could see the small town. The charred walls rose from the snow, filled with holes, exposed beams; yellow flames flickered under black smoke; the guns roared, shells exploded. It didn't end at the wounded. The fighting continued amongst the ruins. The river flowed, the ice glittered, bodies drifted, the fresh snow settling over them.

'Damn them!' the doctor hissed, sweating over a bloody man. 'The bastards! The dumb, mindless bastards! They didn't give us that air support!'

They crossed the river shortly after, huddled up in a half-track, crouching low while the guns roared and hammered, as the air screamed about them. The dark-haired nurse bowed her head, hid her face in her hands. Rachel chewed at the knuckles of her right fist, the green eyes seeking clemency. Smoke: crackling flames. A blazing house drifted past them. Rachel looked straight at David, didn't see him, her eyes fixed on nothing. Shouting voices, roaring guns. The smoke thickened, swirled around them. 'Jesus Christ, oh my God,' Rachel murmured, looking down at her feet. An explosion: sliding rubble. The half-track ground to a halt. The back dropped down with a clang, and Rachel twitched as the doctor jumped out. 'Here we go,' Kanin said. 'Pour not water on a drowning mouse.' He jumped down and Rachel looked up and blinked: a gun roared and she shivered. The dark-haired nurse got out. She helped them pass the bags down. She looked at Rachel, smiled bleakly, took her hand, helped her out of the half-track. David followed her down, heard the guns, the hand grenades. Rachel turned around, blinked, said, 'Jesus Christ. Oh my God. Where's my bag?' A medic handed her the bag. She started slinging it over her shoulder. A sudden shriek, an awful roar, the ground erupting: earth and snow like a giant fist.

Darkness, wheeling stars, a shocking swoop through inner space: David retched and shook his head and rolled over, saw the sky above drifting snow. Sitting up, he saw Rachel, on her knees, her hands outspread, looking down at blood and bone on her smock, the grey tripe of exploded brains. Rachel screamed and shook her head. Another roar, the swirling earth. David jumped up, saw Kanin reaching forward, pulling Rachel away. She was screaming, falling back. Kanin caught her in his arms. A medic lay at her feet, his brain exposed, a bloody stump where his head had been. More explosions, machine-guns, the noise deafening, nearby, bullets stitching the snow all around them, ricocheting off broken walls. Rachel screamed and wriggled backward, tried to kick the bloody head, the wall behind her exploding, showering Kanin, the snow leaping and spitting. A medic grunted, jerked away; a flash of blood and then he fell, Rachel screaming and wriggling beside him, Kanin trying to smother her.

David turned, feeling dazed, saw the soldiers coming back, allied soldiers, being pushed back by the Germans, moving backwards and firing. '*Inside!*' His own voice? He pushed the dark-haired nurse away. '*In that house!*' He pushed the dark-haired nurse again, waved his hand at the nearest door. The nurse glanced all around her, looking dazed, agitated; saw the door in the house closest to them and started to run. Then the soldiers were all around them, crouching low, moving backwards, some flinging their arms up and falling, most of them bawling. The nurse disappeared inside. David turned to the medics. The guns roared, the snow swirled all around them as they fought through the soldiers. David looked down, saw Rachel; then white light and heat; a roaring, a shattering cacophony, and he found himself crawling. White snow: sun reflecting. More snow: a white haze. Snow dancing and spitting and swirling, bullets whistling overhead. David crawled up to Kanin, saw him smothering Rachel, her legs kicking, hands beating the snow, Kanin suddenly slapping her. More soldiers: pounding feet. Screaming men, roaring guns. David jumped up as Kanin grabbed Rachel, helped to drag her away. The shriek of ricocheting bullets: the grey wall spitting concrete. They dragged Rachel across the street, through the door, collapsed inside the house.

Rachel lay there in the rubble. She was sobbing and shaking. Looking up, her eyes were empty as the moon, seeing nothing but darkness. David cursed and glanced around, feeling rage, a bright fury, saw three medics, the stunned, dark-haired nurse, Kanin crawling towards Rachel. A crashing sound, the nurse screaming. David turned and saw the German, on his knees, looking up, quite amazed as David raised his Sten gun, let it roar in his hands. The nurse screamed again. The German writhed in spitting dust. David kicked him down and rushed to the door, saw more Germans, kept shooting. They scattered and spun. The gun roared and reverberated. The nurse screamed and David stepped back inside, kept his eyes on the door. Glancing down, he saw Rachel. 'Those goddamned bastards!' Kanin bawled. He was kneeling above Rachel, who was shivering, staring up at the ceiling. '*Where the hell is that air support?*' David went back to the door. Roaring guns, more explosions. Looking out, he saw shadowy figures in a whirl-wind of mud and snow. David fired, watched them falling; fired again as they retreated. Stepping out, he saw the Yanks and the Brits, pouring back to the street. David stepped back inside. The allied troops rushed past the door. David looked down and heard Rachel groaning, saw the blood on her legs.

'Oh my God,' David said.

The battle raged in the street as David knelt beside Kanin. They pulled Rachel's skirt up, saw the blood, the torn flesh of the bullet holes. Kanin sighed and David groaned. The dark-haired nurse knelt beside them. She studied the wounds, winced, shook her head, and then opened her medical kit.

'We need the doctor,' she said. 'I can only give her immediate aid. I can bandage her and give her an anaesthetic, but we must get a doctor.'

'The doctor's dead,' Kanin said. 'The doctor bought it in the street.'

'Then you better find another one,' the nurse said. 'I can't hold her for long.'

David cursed and stood up. He felt a blind, choking fury. Looking down, he saw that Rachel's eyes were closed, that she was breathing more evenly. David cursed and kicked some rubble. The fury boiled up and devoured him. 'All right,' he said. 'Move her over here. Put her under the stairs.' Kanin sighed and stood up. The nurse tended to Rachel. Kanin reached out and squeezed David's shoulder: 'You better go,' he said quietly. David nodded and looked down. Rachel's face was deathly pale. David cursed and walked out of the house and heard the roaring of guns.

The troops had pushed the Germans back. The major battle was beyond the town. David saw a tank grinding through the snow, its gun moving from left to right. British soldiers were massed behind it. They were jumping in and out of doorways. The snow fell on the rubble, on the charred, smouldering beams, on the debris of weapons and machines, on the still, frozen dead.

David went to find a doctor. He followed the troops along the street. He saw an ambulance at the end of the town, the medics moving around it. Further off, the guns roared. He heard the mortars, the hand grenades. He felt rage, a deep, lacerating grief, an almost shattering pain. The soldiers ran back and forth, ducking in and out of doorways; there were shots as they finished off the snipers, perhaps murdered the wounded. David didn't give a damn. He simply had to protect Rachel. He heard a droning in the sky above the river, saw the soldiers look up. David turned back towards the river. More troops were pouring across the bridge. Above their heads, flying low, were the aircraft that had turned up too late.

'Fucking typical,' a soldier said. 'Mother's Air Force. What's the good of them now?'

David turned his back to them, started walking towards the ambulance, saw the men looking up, their eyes widening, knew that something was wrong. Then he heard the sudden roar. '*Fucking Jesus!*' someone shrieked. The street behind him exploded, a wall of sound, an earthquake, the ground shuddering, the plane roaring down and up, another taking its place.

David fell automatically, disbelieving, outraged, felt the hammering of the road beneath his face, the awesome blast of the bombs. The noise was deafening, demoniac, spreading out, crashing down, splitting earth and sky, making him numb, reverberating, continuing. He started rolling towards a wall, saw it cracking apart, collapsing; rolled away as it crashed to the snow, became dark dust and powder. He was jolted, felt pain. He shook his head and sat up: leaping flames, swirling dust, his ears ringing, the ground shaking beneath him.

'Stupid bastards!' someone bawled. A man kneeling, fist shaking. 'The stupid fuckers think we're the Germans! Stupid bastards! The arseholes!'

A plane roared down and up. Blinding light, sudden deafness. The noise rushed back when David glanced up, crawled through dark clouds of dust. He spat mud from his mouth, heard a roar, felt the blast, rolled over, hit a wall, shook his head, climbed back up to his feet. The planes roared down and up. The whole street was exploding: immense flames, white and yellow, tinged with blue, dark with smoke, racing outwards and up, devouring walls, the walls crumbling and sliding. David stood there and raged. He shook his fist at the sky. The planes roared down and up, dropping bombs, their guns roaring and chattering. David saw the explosions. He saw the running men spinning. He thought of Kanin and Rachel in that house ... a swooping fear, then he ran.

Dead bodies and craters; walls growling and collapsing; soldiers writhing in the snow, trapped in rubble, trying to scream, the noise drowning them. The planes coming in again; David running, looking up; the planes roaring above him, then away: the whole street going crazy. A catastrophic brute force: ballooning fire and swirling snow; the world spinning, a white umbrella above, the smoke billowing under it. David flew, catapulted, saw the earth and the sky, an explosion without and within, light and darkness: oblivion.

He awakened. Where was he? He remembered and stood up. There was silence, what he thought was a silence, then a groaning, a whimpering. David looked along the street: falling dust, drifting smoke; on the road, in the craters and around them, the scorched, smouldering bodies. David saw it and remembered: a cold dread, a churning nausea. He stood up, stumbled over the rubble, ran past the dead and the dying.

His lungs burned, his body ached. Through the white snow, the scorched earth. David ran, feeling panic and fear, an incandescent despair. He tripped, almost fell, felt the pain in his wounded leg, cursed, feeling clumsy and old, reached the door of the house. He stopped, saw the front wall. What remained of the front wall. He blinked, felt reluctance, a brief refusal to believe, then he stepped across the rubble in the doorway and went into the house.

Devastation. Death. The nurse's dark hair in the dust. A white hand, fingers outstretched, dismembered, lying under some bricks. Then he saw the medics. The collapsing front wall had crushed them. No movement: the dust settling down, on their legs, close by Kanin's head. David felt hypnotized. He accepted the pain and let it shake him. The reality: Kanin's head without a face, the eyes staring from stripped bone. David shook and turned around. He saw Rachel beneath the stairs. He saw the rise of her breasts, heard her murmuring, and he went over towards her.

He knelt beside her, stroked her forehead. She glanced up, green eyes flickering. The snow fell through a hole in the roof, on her face, on her hands. She looked up at him, thinking. He saw the light of recognition. One hand was raised to gently stroke his cheek, then she forced a small smile.

'What a good boy you are,' she said.

David sighed and stood up. He put a blanket around her. Stepping outside, he saw the drifting dust, settling down over silence. The medics came soon enough. They took Rachel away for good. They rolled her onto a stretcher, carried her outside to the ambulance, let her reach up to touch David's cheek, slid her in, closed the doors. David watched them drive away. He felt a deep, healing pain. She would live and that's all that really mattered; they would not meet again.

He turned back towards the town, saw the ruins, the falling snow. Sitting down, he let the snow fall on his face, on his hands, on his body. It was cold, but he felt warm. He saw the dark, smouldering debris. The smoke drifted up and blended with the snow, settled down, filled the shellholes. White world, white sky: he felt cleansed and made whole. He felt hope, an intimation of peace, and it was something to cling to . . . Beyond that was the possible.

# PART FIVE: SKY

# CHAPTER TWENTY-ONE

FACING his father-in-law once more, David felt a well remembered discomfort. The major-general was sitting again behind a cluttered desk, his head now framed by a window that overlooked the ruins of Bremen, his grey eyes less sardonic than before, but still cool and perceptive. The ruins behind him were dark and jagged. A fine dust blew through the air. In the distance, from somewhere in the conquered town, was the sound of gunfire.

'It's the docks,' the major-general said. 'They're still fighting in the dock area. The whole of Bremen is in our hands, but some idiots are trying to hold out in the dock area. We'll soon have them flushed out, and the Russians will soon be in Berlin. So, how are you, David?'

David picked up his coffee. His hand was shaking slightly. He put the coffee to his lips and it was hot, but it made him feel better.

'I'm fine,' he said. 'My leg still hurts me occasionally. Not badly, but enough to make me twitch. Apart from that, I feel fine.'

The major-general sighed. 'That was a bad wound you had. Still, you didn't actually *lose* the leg, so it could have been worse.'

'Yes,' David said. 'All I have is a slight limp. I won't be playing rugby anymore, but I got off quite lightly.'

'I must say, I was impressed,' the major-general said, folding his hands under his chin and smiling a little. 'I had a full report on the engagement; it was not an easy one by any means. The whole commando performed a remarkable feat, and you acquitted yourself admirably. I believe you're now up for a commendation.'

'Yes,' David said. His smile was slightly self-mocking. When he thought back on Port-en-Bessin, it was not with great pride.

'So,' the major-general said, 'at least you proved yourself to yourself.'

'Did I?' David said.

'Well, didn't you, David? You were engaged in one of the worst operations one could possibly imagine, and you came through it all with flying colours. That surely proves something.'

'It proves I was lucky,' David said.

The major-general sighed, raised his large hands, said nothing; simply gazed around the room as if resigned. David just smiled: he was still a civilian, not a soldier; he had marched to Port-en-Bessin conscious only of chaos and a fear that stripped away all illusions. That's all there was to it; all else had been accidental. He thought of Robert and Pip Hunter, of Sergeant Cowie and Corporal Brown, of the noise and the smoke and the blood, and he felt it was meaningless. What force had driven him? It was the force that feared death. It was an instinct for survival that overrode all more honourable considerations. What was the commendation for? For his courage? For his leadership? The very words, given the nature of this war, were almost tragically farcical. He had run forward blindly, had shot and been shot at. His only memory of this war would be one of confusion, a stumbling through chaos and noise to a final exhaustion. David had survived ... had survived by sheer chance. Better soldiers than himself – Sergeant Cowie, Corporal Brown – had died as accidentally as he had lived: that's what being a soldier meant.

'You still don't think you're a soldier?'

'No,' David said.

'You just don't want to believe it,' the general said.

'Yes. Perhaps you're right.'

The major-general sighed. 'And what on earth were you doing in Brussels? I know I told you to take your time getting back, but I didn't mean *that* long.'

David thought about Rachel, felt a deep, healing pain, a wholeness that had not been there before, a new strength at his centre. He had loved and been loved and in the end that love was lost – yet what mattered was not what had been lost, but what had finally been gained. He thought of the banks of the Ourthe, the snow falling on the pontoon bridge, the ambulance disappearing across the bridge, taking Rachel away. He hadn't felt sad when it happened, had felt only a cleansing pain, a sense of loss that brought with it the knowledge that his debts had been paid. He had owed Rachel that much, possibly owed her much more, but could now rest assured that she would live and would one day recover. He thought of her mockery and despair, her singular refusal to let him hold her, her collapse into a manifest terror that would not let her go. It had been that all along: a latent fear, a suppressed revulsion; too much blood, too much pain, too much death, all in too brief a time. And what had he learnt from her? That love need not possess; that love, which could hurt and destroy, could also heal and make whole. Yes, Rachel had made him whole. Her despair and strength had given him faith. He wouldn't see her again – she didn't want it and he accepted it – but he knew that he could now face the future without fearing the past.

David looked at the major-general. The grey eyes were unrevealing. David wondered what his father-in-law would think if he knew about Rachel. The major-general would not be pleased; it would be beyond his understanding. Knowing this, David thought it expedient to say nothing about it.

'I went with a journalist,' he said. 'We travelled around with a medical unit. It was a field unit; I wanted to see the war . . . what my bad leg would keep me from.'

'And you got trapped in the Ardennes?'

'Yes,' David said.

'Well,' the major-general said, folding his large hands, 'in that case you saw the war all right. It will all soon be over.'

'What's happening exactly?' David asked.

'Germany's finished,' the major-general said. 'The whole country is collapsing. At this very moment we're closing in on Hamburg, and the Canadians are encircling Oldenburg. South-east of Hamburg, the 2nd Army and the US 82nd Airborne Division are preparing to cross the Rhine, drive on to Lubeck, and once there make contact with the Russians. The liquidation of the Ruhr has been completed. The Elbe has been crossed. Dortmund, Dusseldorf, Frankfurt, Stuttgart, Frieburg, Nuremburg and the Danube Valley have all been captured. In a few days the 7th Army should be in control of Munich and in touch with the Russians, thereby closing the back door on the German forces in Italy. The western frontier of Czechoslovakia is being sealed off, leaving the Germans no hope of escape from the advancing Russians. As for their fellow Russians, they have completed the encirclement of Berlin and are fighting in its streets this very moment. In the south, the US 3rd and detachments of the 7th are pressing on towards Bohemia and Austria, and are also overrunning Bavaria. In Italy, the allies are pursuing the Germans as they attempt a retreat across the Po; also, we have just received word that about one hour ago Mussolini and his mistress were summarily executed by partisans in a village called Giuliano di Messegere. Hitler has lost his last ally. Berlin's surrender is a matter of days. It is finally all over, David – and I'm sure you feel pleased.'

David didn't smile. He could think only of the destruction. He had been flown in to Essen from the hospital in Brussels, and had travelled from there to Bremen by jeep, along the choked, dusty roads. Now he thought of that journey; it had not been very pleasant. He would not easily forget the soldiers marching along the lanes and the total devastation all around them: the shattered, flattened towns, the awesome mountains of rubble, the endless columns of refugees streaming the other way with terror and despair in their eyes. Carts piled with furniture; ragged children and black-shawled crones; the thousands of German prisoners in the compounds that stretched back to the skyline. The sky itself had been grey and gloomy, the very air had been choked with dust; the dust fell upon the ruins, upon the massed refugees, upon the tanks and half-tracks and jeeps and bren-gun carriers, upon the soldiers with the rifles and bayonets and machine-guns, upon the ruins, the desolate, endless ruins that had once been so beautiful. It did not look like Germany; it did not look like anything: it was the landscape of a nightmare, a shocking dark dream, and it filled him once more with the conviction that civilization had died here. David didn't want to forget it. He felt it was something worth remembering. He had yet to discover if what they were doing was right, if the end justified the means, if finally, when the guns ceased their firing, the results would be worthwhile.

'Why was I transferred here?' David asked. 'Will I be working with you?'

'You can't fight with that leg,' the major-general said. 'And no, you won't be working with me.'

'Military Intelligence?'

'Yes,' the major-general said. 'But not against the Germans. It's a job that might be of special interest ... We think we've found Katherine's killer.'

The shock was considerable, making David a little dizzy; he sat up and looked straight at the major-general, his heart fluttering ambiguously. Excitement? Dread? The lust for vengeance, the fear of facing it? David sat there and looked at his father-in-law, felt the past rushing back at him. It was what he had wanted, first with hatred, then with grief. He thought of Rachel, of what she had told him, wondered if it were possible. *It will do you no good. It will just eat you up.* David burned, tried to keep himself calm, saw the ruins through the window. The major-general's eyes were veiled. They did not reveal emotion. David wondered what his father-in-law was feeling, if he ever felt anything. As for himself, what did he feel? His fluttering heart spoke of confusion. He thought of Katherine, felt the past rushing back, and knew he had to accept it ...

'Did you hear me, David?'

'Yes,' David said, 'I heard you.'

'You must try to control yourself, David. These things must be faced.'

Had he not faced it enough? Had it not forced him to live? He had lived with his hatred, had found strength through rage, had paid off a debt and buried shame, but now he still had to face it. Of course he had thought about it; had thought often about Katherine. Most particularly in the hospital, before Rachel and Kanin, numbed by shock and anaesthetics and loss of blood, he had thought about all of it. The days had been long then. The nights had seemed endless. Awakening to pain, suddenly dazed by the needle, wheeled in and out of the operating theatre, he had thought it would never end. And so he had thought of Katherine, had suffered her visitations: she had come in the night and in the hazed dream of his days to remind him of what he had lost – and of how he had failed her. It had not been soothing; had been close to unbearable. Without Rachel he might not have survived, and to her he was grateful ... Beloved Katherine and Rachel: two sides of the same coin. He had loved them, had learnt of shame and pride, but it still hadn't ended.

'Katherine's killer?' David said.

'Yes,' the major-general said. 'We haven't exactly found him, but at least we think we know who he is – and we want him tracked down.'

'We?'

'That's what I said. I meant myself and the Americans. They want him because they think he has a high body count and is also involved in various other crimes; I want him for reasons obvious to us both. Their man is a GI, an experienced staff-sergeant. Since there are reasons for thinking he might also be Katherine's killer, I want you to help them in the search.'

The major-general's eyes were veiled; the flat greyness revealed nothing. David looked down at his coffee, searched deep within himself, wondering what divided the man from the beast and bordered civilization. Two sides of the same coin: himself and Katherine's killer. Had the killer ever felt the sort of doubt that now filled David's thoughts? The doubt was very real. It made him study his own reflection; made him look at his anger, his curiosity, his dry excitement, and try to define just what he meant.

What-did he really want? Was it pure, primitive vengeance? Was it something that base, or was it the need to comprehend an alien world? The killer was David's opposite: he represented the hidden self; he epitomized the war, the dichotomy in Man, the contradiction between what he had come from and what he could be. Given this, he intrigued David; beside the rage was the need to know ... but somewhere between the two was the beast: the primal instinct for vengeance. David didn't want that; he wanted to be above such pettiness. He wanted to see the killer's face, to see the mystery unravelled, but he still wasn't sure of his own motives, of his 'civilized' reasoning. A man's reason could be self-deceiving, an abstraction designed to justify, a means of denying one's own nature and inviting destruction. Was it vengeance or curiosity? Was it hatred or the need to learn? Thinking of this, David no longer knew why he wanted to find this man.

'Why me?' he said.

'It seems logical,' the major-general said. 'You have a personal interest in the matter. That interest, combined with your natural intelligence and curiosity, qualifies you admirably for the task.'

'No,' David said. 'I'm not qualified at all. I'm too involved in the matter to think coherently about it. I'm not sure I could handle it emotionally. I'm not sure I should do it.'

'Really?' the major-general said. 'Why, David, you surprise me! I thought you loved my daughter ... and I certainly thought you would have wanted to find her murderer.'

'I want him found,' David said. 'I'm not sure I should do it myself. I thought you would have understood that ... that it's not quite that simple.'

He wanted to say it might be painful, that his own motives might be suspect, but such sentiments seemed very out of place in his father-in-law's presence. He was suspicious of the major-general, had always been so; he didn't know what was behind those grey eyes, and this made him uneasy. David felt hot and cold. His fluttering heart made him feel weak. The past, and every hurt that lurked within it, was now rushing around him.

'I'm confused,' the major-general said. 'I am offering you Katherine's murderer. I am saying to you: Go out and find him ... and you don't want to do it.'

'I want him found,' David repeated. 'I'm just not sure I want to find him. I'm not sure I should be the one to hunt him ... I just want him caught.'

The major-general sipped his coffee. The guns rumbled beyond the window. The major-general's head was framed by the ruins and the bleak, smokey sky.

'You have no curiosity about this man? You do not think about him?'

David had thought about him, had rarely stopped thinking about him; he had tried to put a face to the ghost that had murdered then disappeared. Where had he come from? Where had he gone? What did he feel and live by, and what did he look like? David was haunted by the man, was obsessed by his unknown nature; in his sleep he would see that dark figure looming over her broken form. Yes, he was curious, was driven by the need to know ... if the killer still lived, if he was mad or coldly sane, if he suffered, felt remorse, sought forgiveness, or if he just didn't care. It was important to know. It might reveal the dividing line: that line between the man and the beast, between himself and his own sins.

'It's more than curiosity,' he said. 'I want him found and put away. I don't want it to become a personal vendetta – and that's what you're suggesting.'

The major-general smiled bleakly. 'I won't deny that,' he said. 'But is it really such a crime to want revenge? I would have thought it quite natural.'

'It's not a crime,' David said, 'nor is it natural. I would rather not do it.'

The major-general sighed, drummed his fingers on his coffee cup. He glanced up at the large map on the wall and then turned back to David.

'You're idealistic,' he said. 'Your idealism confuses you. My daughter, your wife, is not the only concern in this matter.'

'Isn't she?'

'No.' The major-general seemed almost curt. 'You think it's too personal. For you and I, it probably is. But this man must be found for reasons far beyond our personal feelings. You will do it, David. It doesn't concern only you. It concerns every soldier in the allied armies. This man must be stopped.'

The major-general stood up, went and opened the office door. David turned and saw another man walk in: an American Army lieutenant. The lieutenant nodded and sat down. He stared at David with some interest. The major-general went back to his desk and sat down and waved one hand.

'Lieutenant Morrell of American Intelligence,' he said briefly. 'He already knows who you are, David.'

The American smiled and shook David's hand. 'Pleased to meet you,' he said. 'I believe you're going to help us find this man. We could do with the help.'

'You're not alone,' the major-general said, looking at David. 'The Americans are already on his trail, but they *do* need assistance.'

'He moves around a lot,' the American said, opening his attaché case. 'We hear about him from all over the place, and he seems to be travelling fast.' He took some papers from the attaché case, laid them out on the desk, took his cap off, ran his fingers through his hair, gave David a friendly smile. 'He's all over Germany,' he said. 'First he's here and then he's there. He's either in front of, or behind, the allied lines – and he's very elusive.' He smiled again at David. 'We're doing the best we can,' he said. 'But my jurisdiction only extends to the American sectors ... which gives me some headaches.' He glanced briefly at the major-general, sighed, looked at his papers. 'This character, he goes where he wants, and that's why we need you.' He looked directly at David. 'We'd like you to cover the British sectors; we want you to move as fast as possible. This man is a maniac and he's got to be stopped at all costs. We don't care who catches him.'

The guns rumbled in the distance. A fine dust blew through the window. It fell on the major-general's hair and on the hands on the desk.

'His name's Stryker,' the lieutenant said. 'Staff-sergeant Stryker. I want you to study this ID pic and keep it for reference.'

He passed the photograph to David. David felt a bleak panic. He was burning, quite suddenly dissolving into something like dread. The lieutenant stared at him. He felt the presence of the major-general. He had the urge to stand up and walk out, but he just couldn't do it. David looked at the picture. He saw intelligent, dark eyes. He saw full, sensuous lips that were at odds with the rough, boxer's features. Apart from that, the man looked normal, one of a million GIs. David felt an acute disappointment that made him ashamed of himself.

'That's him,' the lieutenant said. 'He's quite a strange character. Now please put that picture in your pocket and try not to lose it.'

David did as he was told. The lieutenant picked up some papers. He glanced at them casually, then he looked directly at David.

'We don't know much about him. We know he comes from Chicago. Chicago's a rough city, and Stryker comes from one of the roughest areas. We're vague on his childhood. We know his mother died young. His father died when the kid was six, and then Stryker went to live with his uncle. This uncle was a lush – that's what you'd call a drunkard. He drank a lot and he was booked a few times for sex offences against minors. This could be important; it could explain something about our Stryker. Stryker's pretty damned peculiar himself, and it might come from uncle. The uncle worked in the stockyards. The kid naturally followed him in there. He left school at seventeen and he worked in the slaughterhouse and he stayed there until the army got him. That's ten years in the slaughterhouse. It's a very long time. For a man, it's a rough place to be; for a boy, indescribable. We don't know what he was like in there ... they're just numbers in there. We can assume it was a brutal education in more ways than one: the slaughterhouse breeds psychotics.'

A slaughterhouse, David thought. What's it like in a slaughterhouse? Not quite like Oxford or Cambridge: no boats on the river. The slaughterhouse breeds psychotics. Is it the blood? The shrieking animals? They don't teach such things at Oxford or Cambridge ... A dialectic of death.

'He joined the army at twenty-seven. He's thirty-two now. At first he was a pretty good soldier, if a bit wild at times. He tended to be insubordinate. When he drank he'd start fighting. He did a stretch in the Stockade for hitting an officer – but that's not a particularly unusual occurrence. Apart from that, he was pretty good, was in fact a natural soldier: intelligent, quick-witted, exceptionally good on the firing range, and a natural at tactical problems and leadership. He got his stripes quickly – more so given his nature: by the time he made sergeant he had a long record of offences, most notably for insubordination and brawling ... so he must have been good. Then, in 1943, he went to Italy and some things started happening.'

He's intelligent, David thought. He's not educated, but he's intelligent. What happens to intelligence when it's trapped and has no space to roam in? I must try to remember this.

'He made staff-sergeant,' the lieutenant said. 'He made staff-sergeant with Patton. He saw a lot of rough action during the Italian campaign, and his record as a fighting soldier was exemplary. Then these things started happening: his minor offences became worse. His commander heard rumours of black-marketeering, of beatings and intimidation, of sexual offences against girls in the captured Italian towns. The rumours grew worse, took on lurid overtones ... what had at first been thought of as a bit of minor graft was now shaping up as organized looting and possible rape. His commander became disturbed. He had good reason to be. More and more of his men were being convicted of graft: of stealing penicillin and cigarettes and liquor; of protecting collaborators and releasing German prisoners; of recruiting young girls and turning them out on the streets ... The commander was disturbed. Stryker's name kept cropping up. The commander ordered an investigation and a lot of heads rolled, but they found nothing definite on Stryker. Still, they remained suspicious. The men who hadn't talked were scared. And although Stryker escaped, they did pick up some stories that were strange enough to make them want to keep a check on him.'

Stryker, David thought. He has a name and a face. He has a history and a definite personality. He is not yet a killer.

'The word was picked up in the brothels. All the prostitutes knew him. Apparently they remembered because he had never been known to have intercourse. Stryker wanted fellating. He wanted the girls down on their knees. At least one girl volunteered to let him nick her with a knife, and a couple of others were beaten up. No rape was confirmed. I mean rape of the mouth. Even that and we might have had Stryker, but a whore makes no witness ... Stryker survived the investigation, was

327

shipped back to America, and shortly after was relocated to London as part of the invasion force.'

The lieutenant dropped one of the sheets. He picked up another. He smiled at David and continued to speak in his mild, pleasant tone.

'In Stryker's company, based just outside London, there was a certain Corporal Boletti who worked for the PX. Boletti, a regular soldier with an exemplary record, started stealing from the stores on a grand scale. The MPs got wind of it. They held off at first. He had such a good record, they just couldn't understand it, so they gave him a warning and kept their eyes on him. Boletti didn't stop. He got worse every week. He drove the stuff out of camp in a supply truck, and he took a lot of it. They didn't know this till after. They only knew the stuff was missing. They warned Boletti again, and when he didn't stop they knew he was frightened. Stryker's name came up again. They checked out, but no one talked. Boletti got a six-month stretch, was returned to his company, and then was killed when on sniper patrol with Stryker.'

'Is that so unusual?' David said.

'No, it's not,' the lieutenant said. 'However, another person killed on that patrol was a particularly efficient soldier called Corporal Bliss. Now, it seems that Stryker had a notable hatred for this corporal, and that this caused a great deal of animosity between him and one Sergeant Kline. According to some of the men from that barracks, Kline actually accused Stryker of having deliberately engineered the deaths of Bliss and Boletti. This was true. Kline confirmed it in hospital. The same evening that Kline made his accusation to Stryker – adding, in front of most of the men, that he was going to put in a report, not only about that incident but about certain other offences, including the possible murder of one Captain Mann – that very same evening there was a mysterious explosion beneath the washroom of Stryker's own barracks. Kline was in that washroom at the time. Stryker had apparently only just left the barracks. Kline wasn't killed immediately – though he certainly should have been – but quite a few of the other men were burnt to death. From that moment on, Stryker just disappeared, taking with him a private called Kantaylis, whom he dominated totally. Subsequent investigation of the under-side of the barracks produced pieces of an explosive device.'

'And Kline gave you all this information?' David said.

'Yes,' the lieutenant said. 'Nearly all his bones had been broken, he had lost an arm and a leg, his lungs had been punctured, and he was suffering from first-degree burns – but he asked for the MPs. I went to see him instead. He was wrapped up like a mummy. He told me that Boletti had been stealing for Stryker ... that Stryker had him terrified and would beat him up if he refused. He said Stryker was good at that. He said he could do it without leaving marks. He said that Stryker badly beat Bliss and Boletti just before they were killed. He said he made them middle-men during a sniper patrol and that he withheld covering fire until they were dead. Another member of that patrol, a Private Yurick, confirmed this information.'

'And Captain Mann?'

'It checked. Captain Mann, a good officer, was shot in the back in St. Lo when advancing upon some Germans straight ahead. No one in that area recalled seeing him turn around, but he was found facing our side of the street. Kline swore that Stryker killed him. He didn't see it, but he was sure. Apparently this Captain, also, had been about to report Stryker on some very heavy charges indeed. Now that good Captain is dead ... and Kline, he died a few days after I saw him – but he did sign a statement first.'

He's a killer, David thought. He has shape and dimension. He's not a ghost in my nightmares; he has a name and a face and he kills. I must bear this in mind.

'That brings me back to London,' the lieutenant said softly, looking at David and flushing slightly. 'In short, to your wife.'

'Go on,' David said.

'I was investigating Stryker. I went back through all his movements. I checked out all that happened in any area he had been over the specific period he had been there. When I was covering his London period I came across two cases that struck me as particularly interesting. One involved your wife, the other involved a GI corporal, and both of them involved a GI staff-sergeant. The first thing I came across was the report put in by a Corporal Shaun O'Hara. The corporal stated that he had met up with a GI staff-sergeant who called himself Wallace; that they had spent the night drinking together; that they had gone to a room with two prostitutes; and that the staff-sergeant, after beating and kicking the two prostitutes, did the same to the corporal and stole his wallet into the bargain. I subsequently located and interviewed Corporal O'Hara, and some interesting details emerged. Among them: that the staff-sergeant had told him that he once worked in the Chicago stockyards; that the staff-sergeant seemed to be obsessed with blood and killing; and finally, that the staff-sergeant had not had intercourse with his prostitute, but instead had made her fellate him on her knees. It was immediately after this that he attacked them all.'

David closed his eyes. A cold revulsion slid through him. He thought of Katherine in the park with this man, and the horror was total. He wanted to weep, knew immediately that he would not, thought of Rachel, of the strength she had given him, and then settled down. It didn't matter what was said: the words could only recall the past. What mattered was not the failed past, but the more hopeful future. David thought about Rachel. In her need he had not failed her. Knowing this, he could now face any nightmare that was placed down before him.

The lieutenant had stopped talking. He glanced across at the major-general. There was no discernible response, so he turned back to David, flushing slightly.

'My wife,' David said.

'Yes,' the lieutenant said, looking relieved. 'I read the report on your wife in our headquarters in London and followed the case up immediately. Your wife was seen with a GI staff-sergeant the night she was murdered. As you know, it was in the Allied Forces Club. A few of the customers recognized him, but none of them knew him by name. He had been there before and his pattern rarely varied: he would drink steadily and quietly, rarely speak to any men, but often leave the premises with a woman. The barman said that a couple of times this staff-sergeant had been forced into a conversation that necessitated him giving his name – and that each time this happened, the name he had given had been different. Among the names used by the staff-sergeant were Kelly, Scott, Thomson ... and Wallace. And that night, this particular staff-sergeant left the Allied Forces Club with your wife.'

The lieutenant stopped talking again. He studied David with some care. David shuddered, but did not feel the dread that might once have destroyed him. He glanced at the major-general. He saw the hands on the desk trembling. He looked up as the grey eyes turned away from him, hiding their grief.

David was startled. He felt near to tears. He wanted to reach over and touch the general's face and beg his forgiveness.

Then he saw it all clearly. He saw the fallacy of both their lives. Trapped by class and the myths of their culture, they had both sinned the same way. David looked at the major-general. He saw the grey eyes wet with tears. The major-general had suffered, but his shame had not allowed him to release it ... *What you say is romanticism. The reality is somewhat different. You see life through individuals when in fact you should be looking at numbers* ... Could the major-general have shown his grief? Could any man refute his own life? What weakness would he have seen in the contradiction between belief and reality? Yet Katherine's death had forced the issue. He must have seen his own world tumbling. He had based his life on self-deceiving logic, and her murder had shattered it ... *They only think they are unique. The individual is nothing. Men are numbers and they move to a pattern that is always set for them* ... What pattern in Katherine's death? What logic could condone it? What creed built on politics and numbers could survive individual loss? The general's daughter could be no number. The state of fatherhood destroyed philosophy. In the end all that mattered was the love that was gained and then lost. The rule of numbers was a fallacy. The individual must hold dominion. The death of Katherine had proved to them both that love must be expressed.

David stared at the major-general, saw the tears in his grey eyes. He thought of his own love for Katherine, of how he had feared it, of how Rachel had forced him to express it and finally live with it. Rachel had saved his life, had set him free from his prison; she had showed him that his feelings were as valid as his reason, and that reason alone would not suffice to control natural chaos. The major-general had learnt this also: his daughter's death had destroyed his history. Now, in the revelation of his grief, the truth was taking its measure.

David felt a rush of sympathy. He wanted to comfort the major-general. He wanted to tell him that the grief should be accepted without shame or self-punishment. Yet what could he say? What could soften the lesson? Let the major-general wipe his eyes dry as the final grief cured him.

'Can I continue?' the lieutenant said.

David blinked and stared at him. The lieutenant's face was young and sensitive. He seemed bothered by what he had to say, and David sympathized with him.

'Yes,' David said.

'Alright. Examination of your wife's body revealed that no sexual intercourse had taken place – that no sexual intimacy of any kind ... apart from ... the semi-undressing of your wife, had taken place. It therefore seems that the staff-sergeant took your wife into that park for no purpose other than to kill her. Sex didn't come into it.'

David didn't say anything. He felt the shame of his ignorance. He glanced across at the general's wet eyes and felt the guilt of his blindness. The major-general was in pain. He was trying to hide it, but it showed. David wondered at the extraordinary self-punishment that such discipline bred.

The lieutenant had stopped talking. He looked carefully at David. He was obviously embarrassed, and he dropped his eyes briefly to the floor.

'Go on,' David said.

'Alright. A relatively simple check revealed that staff-sergeant Stryker had been on a pass that weekend. Assuming he went to London, the only train he could have gotten was the same train that Corporal O'Hara used. He told O'Hara he was called Wallace – the same name he had once used in the Forces Club. He also told O'Hara that he came from Chicago and that he had worked in the stockyards. Finally, he told O'Hara that he had been with Patton in Italy; and, according to

O'Hara, he had the ribbons to prove it. Given this, that staff-sergeant Wallace was definitely Stryker.'

Stryker, David thought. He has a name and a face. He came out of the slaughterhouse and devastated my life and disappeared to construct a larger nightmare. What motivated this man? What sort of personal loss had shaped him? What did he want beyond his impulse for obscure, dreadful vengeance? And surely that was it: the rent flesh was retribution; it was repayment for something denied, a perverse affirmation. Dear God, oh my Katherine. Why did your path cross with his? And why did I let my own cowardice drive you into his murderous embrace?

David didn't move a muscle. His fists were clenched in his lap. He saw his weakness, which had driven her to her death, and he sensed he had conquered it. He had to find this man Stryker. In a sense this man had punished him. He had forced him, in the most vicious manner, to look at the truth. Katherine had gone with him; had done so of her free will. Stryker had obviously felt something inside her that David himself had missed. David now had to accept it: he had failed her and she had died. She had died because the killer had promised what it was she most needed. David had to find Stryker. He had to view the face of truth. He had to see his own hidden self revealed and made brutally manifest.

David glanced at the major-general. The grey eyes were not accusing. David felt a new warmth and he smiled, then looked at the lieutenant.

'So you came back to Europe,' he said.

'Yes,' the lieutenant said. 'We've got to find this Stryker. He's moving around a lot, so it won't be that easy – but, no matter how, we've got to find him. A few things to note ... This Stryker, six foot tall and as strong as an ox, is incapable of normal sexual intercourse. He got his satisfaction from a mild sexual sadism that obviously offered diminishing returns. The sadism increased. The sex itself became secondary. Somewhere along the line – and I think it first happened with your wife – even his form of sex was not enough and the killing replaced it. Investigation of Stryker's movements during his stay in the camp near Paris revealed that he hideously tortured and then killed two female collaborators after pretending that he was taking them away for questioning. This happened in the town of Domfront – and Private Kantaylis was with him. An FFI man on the scene at the time claimed that Stryker, prior to taking the two girls away, let the townspeople maul and kill four suspected male collaborators. The girls were later discovered in the basement of the hotel; the wine stock was missing. Not long after, a similar case was found in an empty café in the Porte Saint Denis. A German prostitute, mistress of a French collaborator, she had been badly mutilated, probably after torture, and then killed. In both cases there was no sign of sexual intimacy, either oral or otherwise. As for the missing wine stock in Domfront, I mentioned it specifically because it lends support to Stryker's other crimes: the tracing of Stryker's movements on the night the German prostitute was murdered led back to a certain Madame Boullard. Madame Boullard is in fact the madam of an expensive Parisian brothel and was known to have had dealings with Stryker. A search of her premises revealed a large stock of American PX liquor, cigarettes, food *and* penicillin. Subsequent investigations have revealed that Stryker had been dealing extensively in these items since his earliest days in France. It also seems likely that he organized, for money, passports for French collaborators, the escape of German prisoners, and the blackmailing and intimidation of his fellow servicemen. He's now somewhere in Germany. We have an incomplete record of his movements. But we have to follow him and capture him before he goes completely insane.'

David stared at the lieutenant. The lieutenant's eyes were very bright. The lieutenant had revealed the shape of the nightmare, and now David was in it. He had wanted the killer caught. He had not wanted to see his face. Now he wanted to see him, to know him, and to bring him to justice. What manner of man was this? What drove such a creature? How different was his world from David's that it led to such darkness? David now had to know. He had to know because of Katherine. He would turn up every stone in the rubble of Germany until Stryker's secret was revealed.

334

David looked at the major-general. The grey eyes were not commanding. Veiled, but with a strange, haunted honour, they were giving him the choice.

'I'll find him,' David said.

# CHAPTER TWENTY-TWO

THE black ruins of Germany became a natural backdrop to the increasingly demented nature of Stryker's activities. Now part of Stryker's nightmare, dissolving into his personality, David moved back and forth across the land and felt the earth slide away from him. The man had a name and face. He had a fathomless hunger. He travelled through the levelled towns and the chaos of the collapse as if obsessed by the need to find clear sky. David shared this obsession: he wanted to find a bright space, wanted to go to the end of the widespread destruction and find a sky unsullied by smoke. The smoke seemed to be everywhere. It fell over the shattered towns. It blew along the dusty streets, drifted over the piled rubble, and coiled slowly around the heads of the refugees who filled the choked, blasted roads. The names of the towns became interchangeable. The towns themselves were nightmare landscapes. Behind the broken walls, beneath the charred rafters, the dead had been buried. David saw it and was held by it. It surrounded him on all sides. It represented Stryker, his lust for destruction, and Stryker was himself a part of it, living in it and by it ...

'Ja, mein Herr, he was called Stryker. He was an American staff-sergeant. He came here in an ambulance with a corporal, and he looted the village. This man was very brutal. He was carrying a sub-machine-gun. There are few of us left and he lined us all up and if anyone argued he beat them. There were no soldiers here. All the soldiers had moved on. This man

336

asked for watches, for jewellery and antiques, and then he took all the wine in the cellars. The corporal was with him. The corporal seemed a little kinder. He made us fill the ambulance up with all the things they were stealing, but did not seem to enjoy it all that much. I think he was frightened. He was frightened of the staff-sergeant. The staff-sergeant laughed when he beat us, and he threatened to kill us. We are tired, mein Herr. We are tired and mostly old. We live in the ruins and this staff-sergeant took what we had left. Then he departed. He took two of the young girls with him. They drove off in the ambulance and we never saw the two girls again. I think he was mad, mein Herr.'

The desolation increased. The broken walls clawed at the sky. The sky itself was dark and foreboding, pressing down on the ruins. David followed Stryker's trail. It led deeper into Germany. It meandered back and forth across the land, disappeared, reappeared again. It led to mounting destruction. The planes forever roared overhead. The big guns constantly thundered in the distance, beyond the receding horizon. Stryker was part of it. His presence permeated all. His shadow lay across the eyes of the thousands of marching prisoners, the hungry children in the rubble, the dead deserters hanging down from the lamp-posts, turning slowly and languidly. David felt it all around him, felt himself dissolving into it. He touched the photograph of the man with dark eyes and watched his bleak, shifting progress ...

'They were found in a field. They're both sixteen years of age. They had started to decompose, so they must have been there for some time. Two girls. Both German. They were both cut to ribbons. This butcher can peel the flesh from the bone, and he's pretty precise. We didn't know who they were. I really appreciate you telling us. We'll have to get in touch with their parents, but we won't tell the truth. There was no sex at all. Both virgins, throats clean. He just cut them up and left them there, and we found them much later. It must have taken a long time; I think they suffered a lot. A local farmer said he saw them in the field, the girls flat on their backs. He didn't think anything of it. He thought the soldiers were going to screw them. Around here a farmer doesn't mix with soldiers, so he just walked away. That might have been wise. That man was luckier than he knew. He said he saw an army ambulance by the road, and that it later went north. I hope you find him, lieutenant.'

The planes roared overhead. The guns thundered in the distance. The horizon was forever receding and was smokey and grey. David followed Stryker's trail. He was haunted by Stryker's presence. He felt Stryker looming larger and surrounding him and drawing him in. The army dead lay in the ditches. The tanks and half-tracks filled the roads. The dust boiled up in huge, swirling clouds and fell down on the refugees. The refugees fled from the gunfire. They fled from mounting ruins. They were old men and women and children and babies in swaddling clothes. Their eyes were large and luminous. They had pale, translucent hands. Their hands wove arabesques in the air, the wild tracery of terror. David had to fight through them. They were all going the other way. He looked down and saw the shawls on their heads, the black caps, the brown dust. Stryker lived off these spectres. He picked them clean and moved on. He was the scavenger within the holocaust and he followed the wreckage ...

'His name was Kantaylis. The staff-sergeant called him that. He was thin and very pale and he didn't want to do it but he did. The staff-sergeant made him. He was sobbing, but he did it. When he shot them the staff-sergeant laughed and inspected the sick bay. He was looking for penicillin. We said we couldn't get any; we said there was a shortage and that soldiers had been dying for the lack of it. He just laughed at this. It seemed to amuse him. He said he could well understand that, and he asked for some drugs. We had to show him the dispensary. He took everything we had. He forced us at gunpoint to load up the ambulance and then he ordered us back into the sick bay. He wanted to know if we'd report it. Someone stupidly said yes. He told the other one, Kantaylis, to kill us and then he walked out. Kantaylis didn't want to do it. You could tell he was scared. I think he was crying, but he finally squeezed the trigger and everyone was killed except me. Kantaylis didn't check the bodies. I think he just ran out of there. I woke up in a hospital and I just couldn't believe it had happened. That was an army sick bay, sir. This guy came in in an ambulance. He had a pass, so the roadblocks let him through, and then he just damned well slaughtered us. He was big. He laughed a lot. He seemed a little bit crazy. The other one, Kantaylis, he was frightened, was too scared to argue. Anyway, they got away. They took a lot of drugs with them. I think they sell them. I think that's what they do. I don't want to remember, sir.'

It stripped David to the bone. The revelations bled him dry. He crisscrossed the land and the wheels of his jeep bounced on rubble. What demon impelled Stryker? What dark dream enslaved him? What world that was not seen by David did he view through his eyes? David had to find out, had to see the other side; he had to know what existed beyond his own limited comprehension. This Stryker was intelligent. He was brutally seductive. He had a talent for control and domination that was not commonplace. Stryker pillaged from the defeated, drew his energy from human suffering. What suffering had he located in Katherine and then brutalized? She had gone with him willingly. She had gone to reveal herself. He had analysed her suffering, her need, and had then cut her open. Stryker understood suffering, had experienced it and survived it, had emerged from his own harsh experience as a man blind to pain. Instead of pain he saw weakness; instead of need he saw stupidity. Faced with either he would slip the blade in and find justification. What hell did Stryker see? What nightmares gave him comfort? Stryker travelled through the rubble of Europe as if he were part of it. This desolation was his kingdom; these broken ruins filled his mind. In the terror and the growing despair he would find his fruition. Stryker lived the dream of conquest. He stood alone and wanted power. He was a man who could never return to where the guns would not fire ...

'Yes, mein Herr, he is trading. I dealt with him once. I stink in this camp while that man, that monster, escapes. I met him in Hamburg. We were hiding in the dockyard area. The city had fallen to the British and the dockyards were badly blitzed. We were hiding in a bombed ship. The ship was dry-docked in rubble. The British were patrolling the dockyards and we didn't dare step out. I now wish we had done so. The British are civilized. We were frightened – not because of the British, but because of the Russians. We had heard about this Stryker. He had a widespread reputation. It was said he would do anything for a price, that he was very efficient. I managed to get word to him. There was a chain of command. They were deserters from the American army, the scum of the lower ranks. I finally got to this man Kantaylis – a child really; very frightened. I told him we belonged to the SS and that we wanted moved out. This message was conveyed to Stryker. A meeting was arranged. We met in the ruins of a house near the Town Hall of Hamburg. Stryker lied to me immediately. Naturally I believed him. He said if we surrendered the British would hand us over to the Russians. You understand, mein Herr: the Russians do not like the SS I paid this Stryker with antiques worth thousands of British pounds, and he told us to wait and he would come for us. We waited five days. This Stryker came with a truck. He was to drive us to the edge of the city and then give us passports. I wondered about that. I was stupid not to realize. Still, I was frightened, my men were frightened, and we got in the truck. This Stryker drove us through the city. The truck had a false bottom. I do not know how he got through the patrols, but he managed to do so. The truck finally stopped. This Stryker made us climb out. We found ourselves in a thick wood, and this Stryker had us covered with a BAR. There were four other men with him. One was that Kantaylis. All four of these men had sub-machine-guns and I knew what was happening. I told my men to run. It was night and very dark. The guns opened up and I heard this Stryker laughing and I saw my men falling all around me. Naturally I was hit – I was shot through the legs – but I managed to crawl into the woods and hide myself there. More shots rang out. They were finishing off the wounded. When the truck drove away I crept back and found all my men dead. We belonged to the SS, mein Herr. We had only been doing our duty. We did not deserve what this Stryker did – as I'm sure you'll agree. Next day I was found by the British and interred in this camp. This place is filthy, mein Herr.'

The rubble rose up in dark piles. It fell down and filled the streets. The streets were lined with scorched, gutted houses and irregular broken walls. The walls were filled with shell-holes. There were few rooftops left. The interiors of the houses were blocked up with debris and broken glass. A fine dust blew through the ruins. Its hissing broke the deathly silence. The wooden beams had collapsed and were smouldering and turning the sky grey.

David drove through these ghost towns. He smelt the cordite and the smoke. He was obsessed by the breadth of the destruction, and by Stryker's dark presence. The old ladies queued for soup. The ragged children begged for food. The stooped men dug laboriously at the rubble and hardly looked up. Somewhere the guns thundered. The planes roared overhead. The horizon receded and was then lost in a bleak, smokey haze.

David thought about Stryker. He felt very close to Stryker. He felt Stryker in his blood, in his bones, and he sought out a common ground. What knowledge did Stryker have? What kind of world did he behold? Stryker lived as if divorced from all laws, beyond morality or reasoning. The scavenger within the holocaust. The brute force within the nightmare. Stryker laughed as the living found death and surrendered before him. What world did he inhabit? Was that world David's world? Was Stryker the embodiment of evil or did he simply strip lies away? David wondered about this. He felt threatened by Stryker. Stryker's knife, which had violated Katherine, had forced the truth upon David. Cowardice breathed in disguise. David's fear had worn that mask. Faced with Katherine, with her love and her need, his own courage had failed him. Stryker's courage had not failed him. He had ascertained her needs. Thus encouraged, she had gone to her death, and the guilt lay with David. Now he had to know Stryker. He had to know how he had done it. He had to know what had been hidden from him and then offered to Stryker . . .

'There were a lot of them, mein Herr. Not two and not four. There were a great many of them, mein Herr, and they all carried guns. These men looked like brigands. They arrived in three trucks. These three trucks surrounded an ambulance and the staff-sergeant sat in it. He didn't come out during the operation. A ragged private gave the orders. This private had a strange-sounding name and was thin and quite pale. The staff-sergeant was in the ambulance. He never left it at all. His men spread out through the village and searched all the houses and emerged with the inhabitants' prized possessions and three German soldiers. The soldiers had been hiding there. They belonged to the village. They were children who did not like the Nazis and so we were hiding them. They were made to kneel down in the street. Their hands were tied behind their backs. They remained there while the village was looted and the trucks loaded up. A young girl was raped. We heard her screams from where I stand. The staff-sergeant remained in the ambulance, sometimes spoke to the private. I remember the private well. He was dishevelled and very thin. He wore glasses and he had a wild smile and he liked giving orders. I thought he was mad, mein Herr. The staff-sergeant's face was hidden. He spoke softly and they dragged out the screaming girl and threw her into a truck. Then they shot the boy soldiers. The staff-sergeant gave the order. They kept them kneeling on the ground with their hands behind their backs and the ragged private shot them in the head and then the trucks drove away. We never saw the girl again. The Canadian Army found her body. I am told that she was badly mutilated and that her throat had been slashed. Not two men and not four, mein Herr. More like twenty or thirty.'

David drove through shattered Germany. He drove deeper into Hell. The ruins cast their broken shadows on the rubble and gave no sign of ending. He drove along the dusty roads. He passed the tanks and the half-tracks. The marching soldiers formed endless dark columns that stretched out to the smokey sky. The roaring planes had thinned out. The distant guns were less constant. The refugees were increasing in numbers, a swollen flood of despair. David looked at them with wonder. He saw the silent, flattened towns. He thought of Stryker moving somewhere out ahead, criss-crossing the broken land. What was Stryker doing now? What fresh atrocity would spring to light? What kind of army did Stryker presume to lead and what end was envisaged? The sullen landscape gave no answers. The jagged ruins told no tales. In that bleak and quite awesome desolation Stryker found his protection. He was at one with this destruction. His ambitions paralleled it. He inhabited this ultimate collapse as if it might be all his. Yet what could he want here? Could he conceive that it must end? Did he imagine that he would go on forever, removed from the future? Stryker's madness was futile. He would short-circuit himself. He would finally come back to the beginning of what he had started. The stench of death was Stryker's world. The sound of pain was his reality. Beyond that he did not stop to think – and he would return to it. Stryker's circle was shrinking. His every venture denied the future. He would finally stop before his own reflection and see death in his own eyes ...

'This is Berlin, lieutenant. You must understand Berlin. You must understand what happened in Berlin when it fell to the Russians. We were very bad in Russia. Our SS troops were dreadful. They raped and pillaged and committed mass murder on a scale beyond the bounds of the conceivable. We therefore feared the Russians. We knew what they would do. We knew that with the fall of Berlin their revenge would be terrible. A great terror filled the city. There were rumours of orgies. Stories came through of mass rape and murder by the advancing Soviet troops. Berlin became hysterical. It was a city of women. We had two million women and only seven hundred thousand men – most of the men either under eighteen or over sixty years old. A city of women, mein Herr. Berlin was terrified of rape. So great was this terror, the possibility of suicide became the only glimmer of hope ... I was a doctor, you understand. I was close to this hysteria. Like all doctors in Berlin I was besieged by many patients, all begging for poison prescriptions. At first I wouldn't prescribe it – the demand was too great – then, I admit it, I started selling to more prosperous patients ... The city was dying, mein Herr. My thoughts were only of self-survival. God forgive me this brief aberration, but that's what I did ... Then I met your Herr Stryker. He came right into Berlin. He was alone and he wore civilian clothes and he carried a pistol. I admit, I was amazed. The Soviets had not yet reached the outskirts. Yet this

American walked up to my clinic and knocked on the front door. We came to an arrangement. American dollars changed hands. He supplied me with thousands of KCB capsules – the most powerful and most popular poison in Berlin at the time. He came to see me once or twice. He supplied thousands of these tablets. He disappeared before the Russians arrived, and I have not seen him since. The hysteria had not been groundless. There was an orgy of mass rape. There were thousands of female suicides in the city and I sold all my capsules … They must release me, mein Herr. My aberration was merciful. I have lost all my money and the Americans will now give me to the Russians. Why me and not Stryker?'

Berlin was a charnel-house. The dead littered the streets. The bodies of young Wehrmacht troops still hung from the lamp-posts. A grey pall covered the city. Every third house was in ruins. The city smouldered and stank and fell down, and the rubble was mountainous. David drove through it slowly. He was stopped many times. He saw the Russians and they did not look like rapists – they swopped smiles with the allies. David tried to find Stryker. He passed the dazed, reeling victims. He saw the suicides dragged from the cold Havel River, saw the dead women lying in the rubble, their wrists slashed and bloody. It didn't seem credible. The massive city had died. Berlin as it had been was no more: it was pulverized rubbish. Stryker knew it and had used it. He had made his contribution. In the dead eyes of the faces on the streets he had left his dark mark. What could he hope to gain? Where could he hope to go? If the ruins of Europe now protected him, they must soon fall around him. David wanted to find Stryker. He wanted the source of the destruction. He wanted to know if what had happened was inevitable or if a cure could be found. Civilization had been murdered. It was panting in its death throes. It might never be reborn and it had died because of what men had done. These were ordinary men. Stryker might be ordinary too. The face of evil in the photograph had looked commonplace, but had not revealed what it was thinking. What made Stryker run? Where was Stryker running now? Berlin no longer needed poison capsules, so a change was in order. David tried to work it out. He couldn't stop thinking about it. Berlin lay in rubble, Adolf Hitler was dead, the dream of the Third Reich had crumbled, and nothing was left. What was left for Stryker? How much further could he go? The dead hung from the lamp-posts, the dust settled on the ruins, and the silence that ends all vain dreams had fallen over all Europe. The war was at an end. All that stood had been destroyed. The remaining walls would soon fall to the dirt, leaving nowhere to hide . . .

'She is ten years of age. She told me about it. She told me once and she hasn't spoken since and I don't want to force her. She comes from the Pankow district. The Reds were particularly bad there. She lived there with her mother and two sisters, one nine, one eleven. The Russians entered the area. They were drunk and very fierce. They raped and murdered and plundered, and no one could stop them. The Russians came into her home. At first there were three of them. They grabbed one of her sisters, the eleven year old, and started dragging her into the street. Her mother tried to stop them. She was beaten and kicked. They stuffed rags in her mouth and then the three of them raped her and then one of them brained her with a rifle. The children had to watch all this. The eldest girl got hysterical. She was beaten, then the Russians left the house and some more soon came in. They took Ilse and her sister. They left the nine year old alone. They dragged them into the street and put them into a truck with some women old enough to be their mothers. They stayed there all night. They were raped repeatedly. When the eleven year old sister got hysterical, they dragged her away. Ilse never saw her again. When the Russians left, she crawled back home. She was bleeding profusely when she got there, but her remaining sister was alright. They left home that night. They tried to find the American lines. They blundered into more Russians and the nightmare started over again. This time the nine year old was raped; when they had finished, they stabbed her. Ilse herself had been knocked unconscious, and they must have forgotten her. When she recovered, she couldn't walk. She lay there for many hours. She was crying, but no one came near her and she thought she was dying . . . Then the Americans came. She thinks they came in three trucks. There was a staff-sergeant with an ambulance and he picked her up and put her inside it. This man got in the back with her. She claims he was very gentle. He said he couldn't fix her wounds, but he covered her in a blanket and gave her some tablets to kill the pain. She was in the ambulance all day. She says it travelled around a lot. She didn't know where they were going, but then it stopped and she heard the sound of gunfire. The staff-sergeant jumped out. He was carrying a gun and some grenades. Ilse got out of the stretcher, looked through the ambulance door, and saw that the three trucks had also stopped. A full-scale battle was going on. The American soldiers were fighting some Russians. These Americans were not dressed like normal soldiers – they wore a mixture of uniforms. Ilse thought they looked ragged. She says they seemed to enjoy the fighting: apparently they were drinking and laughing and slapping each other's backs ... They soon defeated the Russians. They took two Red Army women prisoners. They put them into a truck and Ilse swears she heard the women screaming terribly. Ilse stayed at the door of the ambulance. By this time it was night again. She saw the staff-sergeant emerge from a truck with one of the two women prisoners. This woman was naked. She was being prodded with a gun. The staff-sergeant made her walk to some trees near the clearing, and once there he made her lie down. Then the staff-sergeant tied her up. He tied her hands and her feet. Ilse thinks he stuffed a rag in her mouth, and then he took out a knife. Another man soon walked over. He was small and very thin. Ilse says he held the woman down on the ground while the staff-sergeant cut her. The woman wriggled a lot. Ilse thought she was trying to scream. She thought the staff-sergeant was stabbing her with the knife, but she couldn't be sure ... Nevertheless, she was terrified. She crept back to the stretcher. She heard the other soldiers laughing and shouting, and she thought they were drunk. Then the staff-sergeant returned. He got back into the ambulance. They moved off again and Ilse pretended to sleep, and the staff-sergeant just stroked her hair and wiped sweat from her forehead. She says he was very gentle. She says he didn't say a word. Some time later, the ambulance stopped again and he carried her outside. They were at a British military hospital.

The staff-sergeant took her in. He left her with a male nurse in reception and then he walked out ... She hasn't seen him since. She has lost the power of speech. She is ten years of age and I don't want her disturbed any further. No, lieutenant, you can't talk to her.'

Berlin smouldered and died. The revelations stripped David naked. He drove out of Berlin and his hands on the steering wheel were sweaty. The barbarity had no limits. The brutality was mindless. A man chops a woman to pieces and then strokes the fevered brow of a frightened child. What was this war for? Would its contradictions be resolved? Would Stryker, would the violence, be appeased when the guns ceased to fire? Stryker sheltered in the ruins. The ruins stretched across Europe. Beneath the rubble, behind the scorched broken walls, a great anguish was present. Stryker lived for and by it. He had been shaped and moulded by it. It was possible that now he would never cease to need it: would find no peace calling from the mundane; would be trapped by his own creed. The revelation stripped David naked. It left nothing between him and Stryker. He suddenly saw that this Stryker, with his seeming invincibility, had in fact become trapped by his own nature and could now not escape.

He would find the man called Stryker. He would see the killer's face. He would find him because Europe had been leveled and must now be rebuilt. The ruins would fall upon Stryker. They would leave him exposed. The war had joined all men in a circle, and that circle was closing. Where could Stryker go? Where could he possibly hide? All of Europe was now filled with the stateless and dispossessed, and the barriers of a very suspicious peace were springing up overnight. All exits had been blocked. Every citizen was being numbered. The wardens themselves were now imprisoned and there was no escape route. David drove past the ruins. He drove beneath the smokey sky. He didn't know where Stryker was, but he knew that Stryker couldn't stay hidden. The circle was shrinking. The massed armies were closing in. Stryker now stood in the middle – and he wouldn't get out ...

'I do not know his name, mein Herr. I had no intention of asking. This man, he did not come alone; he came with a regiment. Perhaps I exaggerate: three trucks, about forty men. There was an American army ambulance, and the leader, the big man, drove this and stepped out to a bodyguard. He had a laugh that was frightening. His second-in-command was a ragged private. This private had glasses and grinned like the inmate of an asylum. The forty men all had guns. They simply took over the town. There was an American patrol protecting the town, but they shot them all dead. We simply could not believe it. These were Americans killing Americans. They killed them, then they stripped them of their weapons and watches and money. It was a terrible thing to see. It was worse than watching the SS. We could do nothing about it – we had the ruins and no food – and they simply took over the whole town and stole what they could find ... They all seemed a little crazy. They drank a lot and raped some girls. The staff-sergeant took one of the girls and locked her up in the ambulance. He did not indulge in rape. He was more interested in our valuables. I asked him what he meant – we had little enough to offer – and he led me to one of the trucks and made me look in. I saw a great many paintings – superb paintings, *beautiful* paintings! Then he led me away again, made me line up with the other citizens. His men were drinking and getting a little crazier, but I think they were frightened of him. He asked us what we could offer. We said we only had the wine. It was a wine that the Germans had stolen from France – an extremely rare vintage. He made us bring it all up. He made us put it in the trucks. We did this under gunpoint and then we were ordered back to the wall. The Americans got back in the trucks. They were drunk and laughing a lot. They suddenly sprayed the whole street with machine-guns, and we scattered and hid ... When we emerged, they had gone. They were heading for Celle. They never returned, and the girl was never heard of again.'

David drove towards Celle. Every road led towards Celle. He had heard about the camp close to Celle, about that ultimate horror. Why would Stryker go there? Was the darkest pit his shelter? Did the stench above the air of Belsen-Bergen resolve all his traumas? David drove past the ruins. He saw the widespread desolation. He saw the mountains of rubble

nd the charred, broken walls and the dust that blew around
he crushed people who stumbled in debris. The stench of
leath was in the air. It was a stench that Stryker knew. Like
he bloated fly drawn to the dung heap, Stryker might like
he taste of it.

And then suddenly David despised him. The mystery of
Stryker was resolved. No romance about Stryker's bleak history
could release him from guilt. Stryker wasn't a child. The child
had died long ago. No matter what the child might then have
suffered, it no longer existed. Stryker was now a man. He was
a man of gross appetites. Perverse, homicidal, doubtless close
to insane, he was nevertheless a man amongst men and as such
was a constant threat. His suffering could not justify him. His
thwarted energy could not absolve him. Beyond morality,
numbed to feeling, probably warped by his own ignorance, he
was nevertheless a blind, destructive force that now had to be
topped. Katherine's death didn't matter. David's anguish was
beside the point. What mattered was that Stryker was a threat
o decent men, and that decent men must be protected.

David drove towards Celle. From Celle he drove to Belsen-
Bergen. He now knew why he had to find Stryker, and he
drove without doubts.

# CHAPTER TWENTY-THREE

STRYKER knew about David. He had known about him for weeks. He had known that he was being pursued, and he had checked the man out. Lieutenant Holmyard was a Limey. He had once been a Marine Commando. He had been wounded in action and transferred to Military Intelligence. Stryker knew about him. Stryker knew he was being followed. He knew that this lieutenant had been chasing him for weeks, and that he seemed to be obsessed with the matter. Stryker grinned. He wondered what the lieutenant was like. Kantaylis had told him that he was young, and that he walked with a slight limp. Port-en-Bessin, Stryker thought. That was a pretty rough show. He must have been a pretty fair soljer to have come out of that lot. Stryker yawned and got out of bed. He glanced around the luxurious room. He scratched himself and walked across the carpet and went into the bathroom. Why the obsession? he thought. He turned on the bath taps. Who is this fuckin Limey lieutenant and why does he want me? Stryker watched the bath fill up, poured some Eau de Cologne in. Stryker worried about his skin because he wanted it to stay soft and white. He climbed into the bath, lay back in the water. It was warm and it came up to his chest and made him feel good.

He knew why the lieutenant wanted him. The lieutenant represented the Army. He represented the forces of Law and Order and was doing their work. But something about him disturbed Stryker. He did not seem like the others. The others had treated it as just another job – had been lazy and easily distracted – but this lieutenant was different.

'He seems obsessed,' Kantaylis had said. 'That's the word I got on him. He's been following us from Bremen and he hardly ever stops to eat or sleep. He seems totally determined.'

Kantaylis really amused Stryker. He had started getting scared. He had blinked behind his glasses and grinned dumbly and begged Stryker to move on. But Stryker wasn't moving. He was staying right here in the château. He had everything he wanted, he owned the whole town, and he wasn't going to run any more.

Stryker washed himself. He was nervous about his penis. He pulled the foreskin back and examined it and then washed it carefully. He did the same with his testicles. He treated them very gently. When that was done he slowly cleaned his anus, probing deeply, meticulously. He then washed himself all over. He got out of the bath to do so. He filled the basin up with a clear, icy water and he splashed it on his chest, arms and legs. He washed under his armpits. He applied Eau de Cologne. He also applied it to the back of his neck, to his throat, behind his ears. Stryker studied his physique. He studied muscles and stomach. He was pleased by what he saw and he smiled and then powdered his testicles.

He walks with a limp, he thought. That means he can't move fast. I must have a look at his face . . . so I must bear that in mind.

Stryker saw his own face. He saw the fathomless eyes. He saw the dark, swirling depths of a world beyond his own comprehension. A sudden claustrophobia seized him. He felt a sharp, fleeting panic. It passed away and then he felt almost luminous, aware of himself.

He went back to the bedroom. He was thinking about the lieutenant. He wondered what the lieutenant knew about him, how much he had picked up. It wouldn't be too difficult. Stryker's army had been everywhere. Stryker liked to have a certain notoriety, so he hadn't been subtle. The lieutenant therefore knew. That explained the long chase. That explained the circling journey from Bremen to Dortmund, from Dusseldorf to Leipzig, from Magdeburg to Hamburg to Berlin to Hanover, and then, in the lieutenant's relentless manner, back to Berlin again. The lieutenant was getting closer. He had *always* been drawing closer . . . and Kantaylis was tracking him right now, because Kantaylis was frightened.

Stryker snorted and started dressing. He was getting fed up with Kantaylis. Stryker had taught him everything he knew, and now the kid was just blowing it. He was having nightmares all the time. He sometimes cried when he killed. He kept talking about the lieutenant who was following them, and he seemed truly frightened. It was not a pleasing sight. It filled Stryker with revulsion. He had often thought of dumping the kid, of maybe blowing his brains out.

Stryker put on his jock strap. He tucked himself in carefully. He put on his trousers, then his socks and his shoes, and then he put on his shirt and tie. Finally he put on his medals. He had an awful lot of them. He had taken them from the Americans he had killed, and he felt very proud of them.

Stryker inspected himself. He adjusted his peaked cap. Satisfied, he strapped on his pistols and walked from the room.

It was a 17th Century château. It was large and very cold. It had been owned by a Prussian aristocrat, but Stryker had killed him. The château stood on a small hill. The hill ran down to the town. The town was patrolled by Stryker's men, and the townspeople worked for him. Stryker knew his politics. He knew you couldn't push them too far. He let them go about their business as long as that did not entail leaving town. Stryker stopped them right there. He let no one leave the town. He had threatened that if anyone left, there would be some reprisals. The Krauts knew about reprisals – they had practised it enough – and the townspeople, knowing about Stryker and his men, knew he meant every word he said. Apart from that, they weren't bothered. The soldiers didn't rape or fight. If they wanted some pleasure, Stryker sent them elsewhere; his own girls he brought to the château. Stryker's girls never emerged. Stryker never talked about them. Only Kantaylis, who was going insane, had been allowed in the cellars.

Stryker stood in the baronial hall. A bomb had shattered the high roof. The floor was still covered in rubble, but the roof had been fixed. The townspeople had done it. They had been amazed at Stryker's treasure. The hall was piled with paintings and antiques and boxes of silverware. The Germans had pillaged it from the French. Stryker had pillaged it from both. He would stay here until the hall was full, and then he would trade in it. After that, he didn't know. He hardly ever thought about it. He liked it in the château and the future was too far away.

'Morning, General,' some of the men said.

'Morning, men,' Stryker said. 'Watch your bayonets don't scrape them fucking paintings. That shit's worth a fortune.'

'I like that one,' a soldier said. 'The one with the big tits.'

'That's a Goya,' Stryker said. 'Worth a fortune. Don't go jerking off near it.'

The soldier laughed. He was filthy and unshaven. He wore a British Commando jacket, a pair of American GI trousers, and had a battered Nazi helmet on his head. His belt was strung with grenades. There was a knife behind his gaiter. He was carrying a German machine-pistol, and he knew how to use it.

'We tripping today, General?' he said. 'We goin' out for some fun, sir?'

'No,' Stryker said. 'A quiet day today. I'm waiting for Kantaylis to get back and give me some news.'

'When are we moving out, General?'

'I don't know,' Stryker said. 'I like it in this town. I like the set-up. Why the hell should we leave?'

'Because they'll find us,' the soldier said. 'Because they'll have our guts for garters. The word's bound to get out about this town, and then they'll come looking.'

'Fuck them,' Stryker said. 'We'll beat them off.'

'We can't do that forever.'

Stryker didn't reply. The future didn't exist for him. He had lost the future somewhere in the past and now he just didn't think of it. What Stryker wanted was freedom. He wanted the heat of the moment. He wanted the white eyes in the dark of the cellar, the fear that released him. Stryker had changed a lot. He didn't know it, but he had changed. He no longer liked the moon and the stars; he liked the dark, enclosed spaces. His own knife hypnotized him. The shredded flesh was his sustenance. In the cellar, with the wine and the other great paintings, Stryker practised his own bloody art. He was

353

master of his domain. He had no past nor future. He had the town and the château on the hill, and nothing else mattered.

Stryker went to the large kitchen. The Bürgermeister's wife was there. Once jolly and plump, she was now thin and nervous, and she laid out the table for Stryker. The general had a good appetite. He was a big, strapping man. He had said he was a general and she didn't have cause to disbelieve him. Now she gave him ham and eggs. She put some milk on the table. He drank the milk and then asked for some more and didn't look at her once.

Stryker thought of the lieutenant. He wondered what the lieutenant was like. He wondered why the lieutenant was so persistent in trying to find him. Such persistence was unusual. More so in these times. It was dangerous to travel through the towns and the sniper's sharp eyepiece. This lieutenant wanted Stryker. He obviously wanted him a great deal. There had to be a reason beyond duty, and that reason teased Stryker. Did he know this lieutenant? Had their paths crossed indirectly? Why did the lieutenant traverse the whole country with his obsessional need to find Stryker? The general thought about it. He glanced down at his medals. They glinted on his neatly pressed uniform and they gave him some comfort.

He thought about the lieutenant. He wondered what he looked like. He thought it strange that of all the men who were trying to find him, this lieutenant should be the one to fill his dreams. Stryker was used to being pursued. He knew the whole army was after him. He therefore felt it strange that both he and Kantaylis should have picked up a feeling about this particular man. Kantaylis was frightened. Stryker's response was very different. He wasn't frightened, he was totally fascinated, and he wanted to see him. It was strange to feel that. It went against his own reasoning. He had enjoyed the perverse thrill of being wanted and pursued, but that simple satisfaction had since passed. He knew he was a wanted man. He knew the army was after him. He had eluded them so far, knew he could do it again, but was driven by the need for confrontation.

He couldn't understand that. He only knew it was true. He had gone beyond reason to find some ultimate, binding truth;

and now, when there was little left to conquer, he wanted to blow it. That's what life was all about. It was going as far as you could go. It was building what you needed and then destroying it and starting again.

Stryker finished his breakfast. He did not look at the woman. He pushed the plate aside and stood up and walked out of the kitchen. A man came towards him, a fat, dishevelled sergeant. He walked past the paintings that were stacked up in the hall, and he carried a sub-machine-gun in his right hand.

'Morning, General,' he said.

'It's a morning,' Stryker said. 'What's happening down there in the town? Any trouble last night?'

'No trouble,' the sergeant said. 'It was as boring as diarrhoea. But the men are getting a little bit restless. I think we've been here too long.'

'I like it here,' Stryker said.

'It's been a month,' the sergeant said. 'That's roughly twenty-eight days too long. We shouldn't stay in one place.'

'Why not?' Stryker said. 'Where the fuck else can we go? The war's over, sergeant, it's all finished. They'll soon start getting organized.'

'Right,' the sergeant said. 'That's what I want to talk about. The men are getting restless and a little bit nervous because they think the army's gonna move in soon. The war's ended. We won't be able to roam freely. We can't take those three fucking trucks out and pass unobserved. The men wanna break up. They all want to go their own way. They're mostly tough monkies so they know how to take care of themselves. I think we should let them do it. I think we should break up today. There's talk of some lieutenant who's getting very close, and the men don't want to wait till that happens.'

'I'm staying here,' Stryker said.

'What the fuck for?' the sergeant said.

'Because I didn't work my ass off for nothing. Because everything I own is here.'

'You mean the paintings?'

'That's right. I mean the paintings. They're worth over a million fucking dollars, and I'm not gonna lose them.'

'You'll never get them out,' the sergeant said.

'I won't try to get them out. I'll keep them here and I'll go out myself and pass the good news around.'

'Great,' the sergeant said. 'And who's gonna guard them for you? These boys, they wanna cut out today, and even you won't be stopping them.'

'I'll use Kantaylis,' Stryker said.

'You must be kidding,' the sergeant said. 'That fucking kid's crazy as a coon on a griddle, and there's no way you can leave him alone.'

'He'll do what I say,' Stryker said.

'If he can,' the sergeant said. 'But I don't see him controlling this town when there's no one else here.'

'I'm not leaving,' Stryker said. 'I don't care who fucking goes. I'm not leaving until I've sold this stuff, and that's all there is to it.'

'You're crazy,' the sergeant said. 'You must be as crazy as that Kantaylis. The army's bound to come here, they'll just drag you out, and then they'll stick you in the Stockade for life. To stay here is just crazy.'

'I'm staying,' Stryker said.

'You're fucking crazy,' the sergeant said. 'You can't hold off the whole fucking army. Even you must know that.'

Stryker didn't say anything. There wasn't anything he could say. He didn't know himself why he was staying, so he couldn't explain it. Yet he definitely was staying. He just didn't want to leave. He knew it was suicidal, but he couldn't resist the coming confrontation. This decision intrigued Stryker. It had been made outside himself. As if controlled by some force beyond himself, he could not think in logical terms.

Stryker felt he had a destiny. He had felt that all along. Compelled to catch the moon, to tear down all that blocked him, he had lived with a passion that transcended all mundane imperatives. Stryker didn't want existence. He wanted a fierce, shocking clarity. He wanted everything that life could not offer if lived in a normal sense. Stryker wanted freedom. He wanted ultimate intensity. He wanted the power of that awesome self-awareness that had always eluded him. Stryker just couldn't stop. He had to go beyond the normal. Between the intensity of the nightmare and the calmer light of day he would always be forced to choose the nightmare.

What made him want to stay here? What could possibly be achieved? He could not hold the château if faced with the guns of the army. Surrender was out of the question. Stryker never surrendered. He therefore knew in the back of his mind that his options were closed. If he stayed he would die. He knew that very clearly. He knew it and yet he would stay, and the mystery would tease him.

'I'm staying,' Stryker said.

'Okay,' the sergeant said. 'You wanna commit suicide, go ahead. We're all leaving right now.'

'Adios,' Stryker said.

'I'll tell the boys you sent best wishes.'

'Just take them fucking hooligans and go. A bunch of shit, the whole lot of them.'

'You're gonna die, Stryker.'

'I don't know what that means.'

'Okay, Stryker. That's it, then. I'll see you.'

'Just fuck off. Get going.'

The sergeant turned and walked away. Stryker stood in the enormous hall. The stacked paintings were all around him and they dazzled his eyes with the beauty and terror of the centuries. They meant nothing to Stryker. He didn't know who had painted them. They formed a world of foreign places and a riot of colour, and he wondered just how much they were worth. No matter: they were his. This whole château was his dominion. It held everything he owned: all the paintings and antiques, all the watches and jewellery and money, all the charnel-house dreams and experiments ... the wealth down in the cellar.

Stryker thought about that. He thought of how their eyes had widened. He thought of how the flesh had peeled off to reveal the white bone beneath. There was truth in the cellar. Down there he had found reality. It was a brief and quite blinding reality, but it offered him new life. This was Stryker's dominion. It had no past nor future. In the kingdom of Stryker there was no movement backward or forward: simply startling immediacy.

No, he wouldn't leave. It would be impossible to leave. All the webbed lines of his life had been leading to this place, to the screams of the dying in the cellar, to that fierce incandescence. Stryker knew it had to end. He almost wanted it to end. He had gone about as far as he could go and there was only one mystery left.

Stryker walked out to the patio. The morning sky was grey. He looked up and the clouds were like lead, drifting backward and forward. Not for me, Stryker thought. No more backward or forward. No fucking grey sky to depress me; no rain to torment me. Stryker shivered a little. He felt sluggish and unreal. There was rain in the air, and with it the distinct stench of death. He thought of the camp not far away. He had heard stories about it. Even Stryker, with his knowledge of the cellar, had found them hard to believe. Of course it was understandable. Only lone acts were criminal. Do anything by numbers and it became a simple matter of politics.

Stryker gazed down the hill. The earth was pocked with shellholes. The hill had once consisted of gardens, but was now just a wasteland. Stryker saw his men below. They were milling about in the road. They were putting their booty into the trucks, and shouting loudly and drinking. Stryker knew what they would do: they would head back for France; they would drive until blocked by the army, and then they would split up. He knew what would happen then: there would be arguments over the booty. The winners would take all and disappear into the desolation of Europe.

Power, Stryker thought. That's the only thing we crave. Power based on wealth and security, at no matter the cost.

Yet even that was not enough. At least not for Stryker. Now purged by blood and fire, by the screams in the cellar, by the artistry of the knife in the flesh, he had come to the void. Impelled by gross appetites, enslaved by the need for clarity, he had gone beyond all normal self-indulgence and was still not relieved. Every need led to another. Each sated hunger was regained. The lust for a fierce, transcendent freedom had led to diminishing returns. Stryker boiled with his frustration. He felt explosive with baulked energy. His new need for that ultimate release made all logic redundant.

He heard someone on the patio. It was the thin, grey-haired woman. She was setting a jug of milk and a glass on the white, wrought-iron table. She glanced nervously at Stryker. He was offered a trembling smile. A fucking Kraut, Stryker thought. Another ageing German whore. They oughta put her in that camp with all the Jews and make her eat her own vomit. He stared silently at the woman. He had never spoken a kind word to her. He had simply dragged her from the Bürgermeister's home and turned her into his housekeeper. Her fat husband hadn't argued. He had bowed and bitten his nails. He had watched Stryker leave with his wife, and his cheeks had been flushed. Now the woman bowed slightly. Her dark eyes fluttered nervously. She wanted to get away from the general, but she didn't dare move.

'You're dismissed,' the general said.

'Mein Herr?'

'You're dismissed. I don't want you around here anymore. Go back to your husband.'

She didn't comprehend. Stryker pointed to the town. 'Out!' he said. 'Get the fuck out! Take your cunt back to Daddy!'

The woman bowed and rushed away, her skirts swirling on the marble patio. Stryker poured some milk into the glass and walked back to the stone wall. He drank some of the milk. It was cold and made him feel good. He looked down the hill at the men who were massed on the road. They had finished loading the trucks, were now climbing up into them, some fighting and rolling in the dirt to applause and loud cheers. A bunch of animals, Stryker thought. A bunch of unimaginative pigs. Fill their bellies with food, stuff their pockets with dollar bills, and you had the fuckers body and soul. He looked down the hill with interest. The fighting men were pulled apart. They climbed into a truck, the few remaining men followed them, the trucks roared into life and drove away, leaving nothing but clouds of dust.

Stryker looked at the empty road. It ran past the small town. The clouds of dust spiralled above it, then subsided in silence.

Stryker couldn't leave his kingdom. He couldn't leave his gathered wealth. He would now never sell it, would not benefit

359

from it, but he couldn't leave what it represented. This was Stryker's dominion. It was what he had become. It was a treasure-house filled with what had always been withheld, a charnel-house offering a brief peace. Stryker couldn't let it go. What he needed now enslaved him. His whole past had been obliterated and no envisaged future could sustain him. What more could he do? Where else could he go? Not back to Chicago, to that crushing anonymity, and not into the Stockade for life. No, he had to stay here. His options were all closed. He had to find that ultimate release beyond the blade and the stripped bone.

Stryker looked down below. He saw a jeep in the distance. It came along the road, turned into the driveway, and climbed up the hill and finally stopped beneath the patio wall. Kantaylis climbed out. He was ragged and dusty. He was wearing a regular uniform and his helmet seemed too big for his head. He glanced up and saw Stryker. His eyes blinked behind the glasses. He grinned crazily and waved one hand in greeting and then walked up the steps. He stopped in front of Stryker. His whole body seemed to twitch. He glanced around him and licked at his lips and he seemed quite exhausted.

'Where *is* everyone?' he said.

'Never mind,' Stryker said. 'What did you find out about the lieutenant? Where is the cunt now?'

'He's in Celle,' Kantaylis said. 'Apparently he's going to the camp at Belsen. He wants to see the commander at the camp. He thinks he might have heard something.'

'Do you think he has?' Stryker said.

'Yes, I think he has. I think he was told there's some soljers on the loose and that they're based in the general vicinity. I think he's heard at least that.'

Kantaylis glanced around him. He couldn't see a soldier anywhere. The grey walls of the château rose above him, silent and desolate. Kantaylis was exhausted. He wanted to lie down and sleep. The very thought of sleep filled him with fear, made him think of the nightmares. He blinked and looked at Styker, tried to keep himself from shaking. He was coming apart and he knew it, but he just couldn't stop it.

'What's he like?' Stryker said.

'Who?'

'This lieutenant.'

'I don't know,' Kantaylis said. 'I mean, he's young and too damned quiet. He never talks unless he wants to ask a question, but those questions are sharp. He frightens me, Stryker. He just won't give up on this. I don't know why, but he just wants to get us; it's a fucking obsession.'

'What's he look like?' Stryker said.

'What d'ya mean, what's he look like? Dark hair, brown eyes, pale face, pretty slim. He looks like a million other fucking people. I don't know what you mean.'

'Does he look like a soljer?'

'Not a regular soljer, no. He looks sort of intellectual, you know? Not a regular soljer.'

'He's worked fucking hard to find us.'

'Yeah, you're right there. It doesn't make sense because no one else really gives a fuck – everyone's just waiting to be shipped home.'

'I wonder why,' Stryker said.

'I don't care,' Kantaylis said. 'I just wanna get the hell out of here. I just wanna get away from all these men and try to disappear quietly. It's all over, Stryker. We can't hide out much longer. That lieutenant's gonna find us pretty soon, and he'll bring some support. We gotta go now.'

Stryker didn't want to go. He badly needed a confrontation. The ruins had closed in all around him and now he felt throttled. He had to face this lieutenant, had to make him call the shots. He could not do it alone, but he knew that he must now put an end to it . . . and this lieutenant would help him.

Stryker didn't understand it. He just sensed the swirling darkness. It was closing in about him and it offered that ultimate release. Stryker had to have that. He had tried everything else. He had imprisoned his loins, searched for freedom through violence, and found nothing beyond the blade except the void. Stryker wanted to finish it. He wanted total consummation. He would find his penultimate peace, and this lieutenant would help him.

'Where *is* everyone?' Kantaylis said.

'They're all gone,' Stryker said.

361

'Gone?'

'Yes, gone. Kaput. You won't see them again.'

Kantaylis seemed bewildered. His bewilderment gave way to fear. The light flashed off his glasses as he blinked and glanced wildly around him.

'I'm scared,' he said to Stryker. 'I gotta get out of here. I don't wanna be here when he comes. Let's leave, Stryker. *Now*.'

Stryker stared down at Kantaylis. He seemed small and terribly frail. He had always been skinny, but now his bones rattled when he walked. The kid was finished. He was numbed by shock and dread. He had been to the cellar, had been forced to watch Stryker, and had never quite recovered from the experience. Kantaylis had nightmares. His hands shook and he couldn't eat. He sometimes jibbered like a man in a trance, wiping spit from his hands. Kantaylis was finished. He would not last much longer. He walked on the crutches of fear, and those crutches were breaking.

'Okay,' Stryker said. 'Go get some sleep. I'll wake you in a couple of hours, and then we'll both leave.'

The kid nodded dumbly. He licked his lips and blinked his eyes. The anguish of hope filled his features and made them more human. He walked back across the patio, disappeared inside the château. The silence fell back around Stryker and increased his awareness.

Stryker looked at the grey sky. It shadowed the shattered town. It was going to rain and Stryker didn't want to feel the rain again. Kantaylis was finished. He couldn't possibly hold out. He had been a good kid and he shouldn't be made to suffer his future. Stryker waited for some time. The shadows raced across the land. The stench of death clung to the air, drifting in from the distant camp. There was no sound of gunfire. There were no planes in the sky. Stryker studied this final desolation and then went back inside.

The kid had earned his peace. He deserved more than he would get. They would capture him and punish him and break him and cast him aside. Stryker didn't want that. He didn't think the kid deserved it. He didn't want the kid to have to endure what he himself had endured. Stryker smiled at old memories. The paintings glowed all around him. He thought fondly of the kid as he took out his pistol and walked up the stairs to the bedroom.

Kantaylis lay on his bed. He was curled up on his side. He had a thumb in his mouth and one hand was covering his right ear. He looked like an adolescent, had the innocence of a child. Stryker held his head lightly, put the gun to his temple, and then, with a sigh of regret, he blew the kid's brains out.

# CHAPTER TWENTY-FOUR

THAT he had missed the worst of Belsen did little to diminish David's shock. The lines of crematoriums were still filled with charred bones, the uncovered mass graves still offered up their ghastly stench, and the gallows, though devoid of hanging men, were still redolent of recent horrors. David couldn't ignore it. Death permeated the very air. The British 2nd Army was trying to move the inmates out, but hundreds still littered the compounds. These things were living skeletons. Their huge eyes recalled the nightmare. They were dying from tuberculosis and typhus and typhoid, from starvation and gastroenteritis and indescribable brutality. Their throats fluttered when they tried to speak. Their hands rarely left their sides. They stretched out in the sun before the huts that had imprisoned them, wandered slowly back and forth past the gas chambers, the furnaces, the open graves. David felt a great shame. It consumed his own pain. The revealed heart of the rotting Nazi corpse made his own grief superfluous.

'When we arrived,' the brigadier said, 'there were 56,000 inmates still alive. The shock of freedom was too much for some of them, and others simply wasted away. The typhus and typhoid and sundry other diseases are killing many more every day. It is impossible to estimate at the moment just how many thousands were exterminated in this camp alone, but my medical officer has estimated that of the present survivors, about 13,000 will die in the near future. You understand what I'm saying, lieutenant? I'm saying we're very busy here. We've heard about your Stryker, but we can't take the time to go after him.'

'You don't understand, sir. This man is a killer. He leads a gang of hooligans and cut-throats and they go on rampages. They rape and pillage. They trade in badly needed drugs. They've left a trail of dead across Germany, and they've got to be stopped.'

'I understand, lieutenant. I appreciate your concern. From what I hear this bunch are quite crazy, but that still doesn't matter. I have my hands full. I have the dead and the dying. I'm trying to fight disease and malnutrition and deprivation, and I'm short of both men and supplies. Given this, your Mr Stryker is insignificant.'

David knew what he meant. The camp outside was hell. It was a nightmare created by Man, and now men had to handle it. What was Stryker beside this? Who could spare the time for him? In the gorge of the aftermath, Stryker was one evil amongst many.

Yet David still wanted Stryker. The reasons were personal and all-embracing. He had lived too long with Stryker, had endured his hideous wake, and could no longer cast him aside. David wanted to stop Stryker, wanted to stop what he represented. He no longer had doubts about Stryker, but he had to affirm himself. Stryker could not be excused; his personal history was immaterial: what mattered was not what he might have been, but what he now was. Stryker was beyond redemption – his every action removed him further – and if the dead lay in Belsen, if the dying cried for water, it could not detract from what he had done. Stryker had to be stopped. David had to do it personally. He had to affirm his own beliefs or suffer doubt once again.

'I take your point, sir,' David said. 'I can't believe what I saw out there. But I don't need your involvement in this matter; I just need some assistance.'

'What assistance?' the brigadier said.

'Information,' David said. 'I need to know where this man's been seen and what he's been up to.'

The brigadier smiled wearily, folded his hands beneath his

chin, gazed out through the window at the smoke coiling up t
the grey sky.

'They're burning the dead,' he said.

'Yes,' David said.

'You seem very determined, lieutenant.'

'Yes, sir. I am.'

'But you're in the Royal Marine Commando ... that seem
strange. Why on earth are you following this man?'

'It's a temporary transfer, sir.'

'For personal reasons?'

'Yes, sir.'

'I see,' the brigadier said. 'Say no more.' He sighed, stroke
his chin, gazed at David in a thoughtful manner. 'Well,' h
said slowly, 'this Stryker chap is really quite a character.'

'Yes,' David said.

'I must confess that, for reasons which I'm sure you appre
ciate, lieutenant, I didn't have too much interest in him
However, my adjutant, who *has* become increasingly disturbe
by his activities, has been keeping a close check on his move
ments ... In fact, I think he knows where he is.'

The brigadier picked up a telephone and asked someone t
locate the adjutant. When he had finished, he put the telephon
back down, slumped wearily in his chair, folded his hand
under his chin and studied David. The brigadier had blac
hair turning grey, a round, pleasant face.

'What age are you, lieutenant?' he asked.

'Twenty-five, sir.'

'And what's it like for a twenty-five year old to come to
place like Belsen-Bergen?'

'To be frank, sir, I find it rather shattering.'

'There are a lot of camps like this. We're finding more ever
day. I confess that even as a soldier of some experience, I fin
them to be almost beyond my comprehension. There is wa
and there is war. I've seen some bad things in my time. . . . Bu
I've never seen anything like this, and I find I can't sleep a
nights.'

David knew what he meant. Beyond the horror was th
insanity. No logic, no dialectic nor system, could make thi
camp comprehensible. Belsen-Bergen was the sum of numbers

the fruit of logistical thought; it was an arrant display of what could happen when the names became numbers. A number has no identity; it exists for and by the system. Without names, without identity, human beings become digits in a system that sees nothing but statistics. What morality is then required? Why the need for human feelings? No brother and sister, no husband and wife, no mother and child need exist to raise distracting emotions ... just the numbers, the statistics, the simple addition and subtraction: so many transported, so many incinerated, subtract from the total, check what's left ... the statistics improved.

To murder human beings is a crime – against morality, against God – but to simply lose numbers is to take refuge in a system whose one aim is logistical efficiency. Here, in Belsen, they hadn't murdered human beings, had hardly seen or recognized such; they had simply worked with numbers, had checked their totals and then subtracted, had known nothing but the pleasure of efficiency, the system, that dream built on numbers and equations, with no names to corrupt it ... The major-general had been wrong. His military thinking had been remiss. The death of Katherine had proved to him that numbers would not ease human suffering. What mattered was the individual. More: individual rights. The military consciousness, the totalitarian mind, would always fail to acknowledge this.

What happens when men are numbers? The beast growls and runs amok. Divorced from pride, from self-identity, from any shared source of feeling, the man looks upon his fellows without seeing his reflection in their eyes. Nameless, without a face, himself a number lost in statistics, he can only accept the system for what it is and abide by its terms: obedience, efficiency, the general good above personal need, seeing nothing but the overall view, the results based on logistics. He accepts it or he revolts; either way he is dehumanized. His awareness of his fellows is destroyed, and all feelings die with it.

Stryker was such a man. Similar men had run Belsen. They were men made or broken by the system ... and they only saw numbers.

The office door opened and David stood up and came to

attention as the adjutant walked in. The adjutant was tall and thin, his face weary and pale, and he nodded at David and shook his hand.

'Lieutenant Holmyard?' he said.

'Yes, sir,' David said.

'I've heard about you,' the adjutant said. 'You seem very determined. I assume you're here looking for this Stryker chap.'

'Yes, sir. I believe he's in the area.'

'I *know* he's in the area,' the adjutant said. 'In fact I think I know precisely where he is. Step up to the map here.'

David stepped up to the map. 'There,' the adjutant said, his index finger falling on a name slightly north-west of Belsen. 'It's a small town,' the adjutant said. 'A *very* small town. Stryker's gang have been appearing and then promptly disappearing, but their tracks always led back to there. I only guessed this a few days ago. They made quite a few raids. These raids were scattered all around this area, but we didn't know where they were coming from. I worked it out a few days ago. I knew it had to be in this area. I checked it out and I heard a few rumours that were almost bizarre. There's a large château in that town – in fact it dominates the town. Rumour has it that this gang of American deserters had taken over the château and were controlling the whole town beneath it. As you know, these soldiers are crazy. They loot and they kill. It therefore seems likely that control of the town would not be beyond the bounds of possibility. Their leader is a staff-sergeant. He's obviously crazy as well. He wears a lot of stolen medals and has two pistols strapped around his waist – rather like Patton.'

'That's Stryker,' David said.

'No doubt,' the adjutant said. 'Anyway, apparently, inside that château, this Stryker has an enormous collection of valuable antiques and paintings. As you know, during the occupation the Nazis engaged in wholesale looting of the art treasures of Europe. Not long ago, in the salt mines of Altaussee, near Salzburg, the Americans discovered a very large collection of such works. In this immense underground gallery, which was the depot for a proposed Hitler museum for Linz, his home

368

town, were paintings by Rembrandt, Brueghel, Titian, Rubens, Tintoretto, Van Dyck, Caravaggio and Michelangelo. It had been Hitler's intention, in the event of losing the war, to turn the whole gallery into a sort of artistic *Gotterdammerung* – in short, to blow everything to hell. However, the Americans, after wresting control of the mines from the SS, decided to transport many of the treasures to Munich, prior to redistribution of the masterpieces back to their original galleries and museums. Consequently, escorted by two half-tracks, a convoy filled with these treasures made the journey from Austria to Munich ... Now this convoy was prepared for marauding SS troops, what it was *not* prepared for was marauding Americans. They were attacked by such a gang. They lost two of their trucks. One can but assume that the paintings from those trucks are now up in that château with Stryker.'

The adjutant looked at David. His dark eyebrows were raised. David gazed through the window, at the smoke rising slowly, and felt numbed by this fresh revelation. Where did Stryker end? What more could he want? He thought of Stryker in the château with his wealth of pillaged culture, ignorant of its spiritual value, enamoured with power. Stryker had his own dominion. He had his kingdom on earth. It was a kingdom based on ignorance and resentment, on the need to affirm himself. How innocent was the criminal? How guilty was the warden? Stryker sought affirmation in the only way he knew, just as David, in his own way, sought it also. The differences between them was accidental. It was the accident of birth. If their parallel lives had been reversed, David might now be the hunted one. In the end all men were brothers. The guilt of one lay with the other. But also, in the end, the transgressor must be stopped lest destruction ran rampant on earth. Stryker had tried to affirm himself. In doing so he had become a criminal. Because of that, no matter his own reasons, he would have to be banished.

'He has the paintings,' the adjutant said. 'Those paintings must be saved. If you want this man Stryker you must get him without losing the paintings.'

'What if he won't come out?' David said.

'You think he won't come out?'

369

'I think he's crazy,' David said. 'He wasn't before but he is now. He's crazy and he's quite unpredictable, so he may not come out.'

'Are you telling me you think he'll actually *fight* you?'

'Yes, I think he might. I think he's crazy enough not to surrender – to make us take him by force.'

'You can't fire on the château. I won't let you do that. You can take some men with rifles and try to pick him off, but I won't let you go there with grenades or mortars or machine-guns.'

'Fair enough,' David said.

'Not yet,' the adjutant said. 'You only fire at this Stryker. You ensure that no bullets are fired inside the château, that no accidental damage is done. You know him better than I. You say he's quite crazy. He might therefore threaten to destroy the paintings – and if he does, you back off.'

'And then?' David said.

'I don't know,' the adjutant said. 'We might have to let him go. If we do, we will certainly have a lot to answer for – but the need to preserve the paintings is more crucial. Stryker's trail may be bloody, but it's largely innocuous against the total devastation of Europe. Those paintings, lieutenant, and all the other pillaged masterpieces, have enormous emotional and spiritual value to the countries we've liberated; for this reason, General Eisenhower himself has expressed grave concern that as many as possible be saved. You can't storm the château. Stryker isn't worth that much. You can try to get him personally, but if he threatens the paintings, you must back off and let him escape. Is that understood?'

David thought about it. It was an exquisite irony. He remembered what the major-general had said about Monte Cassino. It was all a matter of values. Something always had to be sacrificed. And in this case, where the values had by necessity been reversed, he knew that the adjutant was right: Stryker wasn't worth that much.

'Yes, sir,' he said.

The adjutant smiled, glanced across at the brigadier. The brigadier removed his chapped hands from his chin and spread them out on the dusty desk before him.

'I'll lend you four men,' he said. 'You can't have more than that. The war's over and I don't think it's fair to risk more than we have to. They'll be experienced men. You'll have no fears on that count. If anything happens to the paintings we will hold you responsible. I think that's fair, don't you?'

'Yes, sir. That's quite fair.'

David left with the adjutant. They walked into the compound. A dark smoke billowed up from a mass grave, disappeared in the grey sky. David couldn't ignore the silence. It was the silence of death. He thought of the crematoriums, of the gallows and the gas chambers, of the torture and the murder and the degradation, and he felt a slight nausea. He tried to ignore the inmates. Their glowing eyes were pursuing him. He could not ignore the bones beneath their flesh, the scars from burnings and whippings.

What had led to this nightmare? What rebuilding would redeem it? In the long history of man there had never been a hell that could match it. The dream of power had no boundaries; it refuted all morality. As with Stryker, the dream of the Reich had sprung out of brute hunger. Such a hunger was inhuman. Nothing gained would satisfy it. It would transcend all reason to the point where it would choke on its own bile.

'It's terrible,' David said.

'Yes, it's terrible,' the adjutant said. 'Wait here. See as little as possible. I'll be back with your men.'

David stood by the jeep. He saw as little as possible. He saw too much to take in at once, and he felt his heart beating. A pair of huge eyes swam towards him. The eyes shone from a skeleton's head. A tongue drooped down from parched, trembling lips while translucent hands waved. The man was trying to speak. His throat offered a strangled rattling. His huge eyes held a cosmos of despair, then he gave up and disappeared.

David started to shake. He took hold of the jeep. The stench of death was in the air all around him, drifting in with the black smoke. What was Stryker beside this? He represented what it was. He was the brute force that had willed it and encouraged its rank, putrid growth. Stryker waited in his château. The dead were scattered throughout Europe. Here and now, at the heart of the monstrous desecration, that brute force would have to be stopped. David let go of the jeep. He touched his pistol with one hand. He would do what he now had to do . . . without doubts or regret.

He heard the footsteps coming towards him. He looked up and saw the adjutant. The four soldiers behind him had rifles and were looking resentful.

'Here they are,' the adjutant said, pointing languidly at the four men. 'Corporal Forbes, Corporal Wortley, Private Webb and Private Shaw. They're all experienced men. I've explained the job to them. The ball's in your court now, lieutenant, and the best of luck to you.'

He shook David's hand, nodded briefly and walked off. David looked at the men, noticed their lack of enthusiasm, and was relieved when Corporal Forbes made a gesture.

'Is this our jeep, sir?'

'Yes,' David said.

'You want me to drive?'

'Yes.'

'All right, lads, get in.'

The men climbed into the jeep. Their rifles rattled as they sat down. David sat in the front beside Corporal Forbes, then the jeep roared into life and they moved off. They drove past the crematoriums, past the haunting, empty gallows; they passed a long row of corpses, a wavering line of living skeletons, turned the corner at the end of the gas chambers and went through the main gates. David touched his pistol lightly. The barbed wire passed by his head. He saw the smoke rising up to the grey sky from the mass graves below.

'What's he like, sir?' Forbes said.

'Who?' David said.

'This man Stryker. This man we're going after. What kind of man is he?'

'He's a killer,' David said. 'He's killed an awful lot of people. He has a gang of deserters and they murder and rape, and they've looted to an extraordinary degree.'

'The gang's gone,' the corporal said. 'The adjutant told me to tell you that. While you were waiting for us a woman appeared at the main gate and told us that the gang had all gone. She was the Bürgermei wife. She'd been a prisoner in the château. She said gang had all gone and that they weren't coming bac knew about the gang, sir. There were a lot of rumours about them. I knew about this Stryker as well. It's what he's like that concerns me.'

'I'm relieved about the gang. That should make it a lot easier. As for Stryker, he's undoubtedly mad. Expect just about anything.'

'He's still there,' the corporal said. 'The woman said he was still there. Of course he could have left by now, but she said the general was still in the château. They all think he's a general.'

The camp fell far behind them. The forested hills rose above them. The trees shadowed the road and whipped past and the men watched for snipers.

'I wish he'd gone,' the corporal said. 'I must confess, I wish he'd gone. I don't like coming out on an action now the bleedin' war's over. There's still snipers about. If they don't get us, your man might. I've fought for four years and I don't fancy getting shot now.'

'I'm sorry,' David said.

'Oh, it's not your fault, sir. I'm just saying that I don't like this Stryker for dragging us out like this.'

'He might have gone,' David said. 'He might have left after the men. I don't think he would want to travel with them and make himself noticeable.'

'I hope so,' the corporal said. 'I sincerely hope so. Let the bleedin' Americans look after him ... I'd rather not get shot now.'

David didn't reply. He watched the shifting grey sky. He saw the shadows of the trees on the road as the forests whipped past. He wondered what Stryker was like, had a feeling about him. He was certain that Stryker was waiting for him, though he didn't know why. It was just a feeling he had. He did not understand it. He only knew that he knew Stryker, that he was living and breathing Stryker, that in the miles he had covered through the rubble of Germany he had picked up an instinct for Stryker, a mysterious awareness. Stryker swam through his veins, pulsated in his brain; Stryker permeated his very existence and would not let him go. He would find Stryker for Katherine, for Rachel, for all the dead. He would find him because he knew that he was waiting in the dark of the château.

'This man,' the corporal said. 'What's he doing here? Why's he still in the château?'

'I don't know,' David said. 'I just don't know.'

'Does he know we're coming for him?'

'I think so,' David said.

'Then it doesn't make sense,' the corporal said. 'He can't stay there forever.'

'No,' David said. 'He can't stay there forever. But he has a lot of art treasures and antiques in there, and it's possible that he needs time to pack them up.'

'You mean for selling?'

'That's right.'

'He must want the money bad.'

'Possibly,' David said. 'He's taken a lot of chances to get it. And he's killed a lot of people in the process. ... He hasn't too much to lose.'

'You mean they'll have him for murder.'

'That and a lot more. They'll either hang him or give him a life sentence. So what has he to lose?'

'A life sentence or death: that's some choice.'

'This man won't want a life sentence.'

They fell silent after that. The high forests fell behind them. The ground flattened out and the ruins reappeared and the awesome desolation of the conquered fell about them once more. The sky above was etched in charcoal. The shattered houses cast black shadows. The shadows fell across the rubble in the roads and touched the heads of the people. These people were quiet, were either young or very old, seemed like spectres in some formless midnight dream, engaged in nothing but waiting. What were they waiting for? What desperate hope filled their eyes? Their whole country was in ruins, was a dust-covered wasteland, and they waited for the men to return and tell them what they might do. The children waited for their fathers. The women waited for their husbands. These fathers and husbands were now marching to captivity, and a great

374

many would never return. They would vanish into Russia, would die in Siberia; the resurrection must now seem inconceivable to those left behind. All of Germany had been flattened. The silent ruins spoke of the dead. The day's passing revealed only emptiness, a vast, anguished void.

'This is it,' Corporal Forbes said.

David came out of his reverie. The jeep was gradually slowing down. They were on a dusty road and the town fell to their left and the torn earth climbing up to their right led straight to the château. The jeep came to a halt. Some people stood by the roadside. They were lining up and waiting for the soldiers and looking up at the château.

David followed their searching eyes. He saw the château surmounting the hill. It spread along the brow of the hill and was surrounded by grey sky. The slope had once been filled with trees. The trees were now a mass of debris. The flower-beds and gardens were now upturned and littered with shell-holes. The château was very quiet. It was gloomy and mysterious. The grey sky swam beyond the gabled rooftops which cast long, shifting shadows. There was no movement up there. The château offered only silence. David wondered where Stryker might be, if he was watching them right now . . .

The Germans stood by the roadside. There were children and old people. David waved to an old man nearby and the man shuffled toward him. He stopped in front of David, held his hat in his hands. He had a haggard, emaciated face and he licked his lips nervously.

'Ja, mein Herr?' he said.

'You speak English?'

'Ja.'

'Is the general still up in the chateau?'

'Ja, mein Herr, he is.'

'Where is he?'

The old man shrugged. 'Who knows, mein Herr? He did not leave. He is somewhere up there. I cannot say where.'

'You haven't seen him at all?'

'Nein.'

'No movement up there?'

'Nein.'

'And the troops have all gone?'

'Ja, mein Herr.'

'Danke.' David turned to the corporal. 'What do you think?' he said. 'There's not much cover up there.'

The corporal shrugged. 'I don't know,' he said. 'There's only one way to find out, sir . . . and that's to go up.'

'Right,' David said. He turned to the men behind him. 'Okay,' he said, 'we're going straight up. Get ready for anything.'

The men glanced at the château. They didn't want to die now. They had been through the war and escaped, so they couldn't be blamed. They grimaced at David. David pulled out his pistol. The men pulled the bolts on their rifles as the jeep started moving.

The corporal drove along the road. He turned into the driveway. The jeep started climbing up the steep gravel drive and they all kept their eyes on the château. David saw the gabled rooftops, the grey sky drifting above them; his eyes roamed down the massive front walls and then stopped at the windows. The glass had been broken. Tattered curtains flapped loosely. There were no lights in the room, and that elongated darkness revealed nothing. The jeep kept climbing. It started leveling out. The walls of the patio swung towards them, revealing the front door. It was wide and formed an arch. Marble columns surrounded it. The large wooden doors were wide open; inside it was dark. The patio walls kept swinging towards them, very grey, rather ornate. All grey: the towering walls, the low clouds, the bleak sky drifting over their heads.

David suddenly felt set free. He suddenly knew it had been worth it. He thought of Belsen, of the charred bones and furnaces, and he knew there was justice. This war was a just war; though hideous, it had been necessary. The destruction of Europe was a high price to pay, but the possibility of a future had been saved. What alternative had there been? What future could have sprang from Belsen? If now there was doubt and uncertainty, at least hope remained. The Nazi dream was a madness. Like Stryker, it had lived to kill. And like Stryker, like that madman in the château, it had no hopeful future. The war had been worth fighting. The pursuit of Stryker had been necessary. David knew it, sensed it, let the revelation warm him, felt a giddy, intoxicating excitement, the healing touch of true freedom. Nothing mattered any more: not the shame, not the guilt. He could face Stryker, the devil, Hell itself, but would look back with pride.

The jeep exploded beneath him.

# CHAPTER TWENTY-FIVE

DAVID saw the soaring earth, the noise shattering his senses, was picked up and shaken and hurled sideways, the ground rushing towards him. He closed his eyes and felt the blast, thumped the ground and rolled away, saw the jeep rising up and turning over and tipping the men out. The noise of the blast was still echoing; the falling soil rained down upon him. The savage roar of a machine-gun lashed the air and Private Shaw started dancing. ' – *over here!*' Wortley waving. ' – *Jesus Christ!*' The smoke swirling. Shaw jack-knifed, coughed blood and fell down as the other guns roared. David cursed and crawled forward, glanced around for his pistol. Bullets ricocheted off the upturned jeep and kicked dirt up around him. Beyond the jeep was the patio. Behind the jeep were Forbes and Wortley. Private Webb was hanging out of the jeep, his head covered in blood. David blinked, heard the roaring, smelt cordite and smoke, let the hammering of the guns jolt him awake, wondered how it had happened.

' – *fucking machine-gun!*' Wortley screamed. ' – *fucker mined the bleedin' drive! – machine-gun behind that low wall and it's got us pinned down!*'

David sat up, saw his pistol: on the ground beside Private Shaw. The private was lying flat on his back with his arms and legs outstretched. David slithered towards him. The machine-gun roared viciously. David glanced at the patio, saw the barrel of the gun spitting down at him. Forbes and Wortley continued firing. Private Shaw was pumping blood. David snatched at his pistol, got it, jumped back, then stood up behind Wortley and Forbes and looked up at the château.

The machine-gun was on the patio. The man firing it was behind the wall. At that moment David knew only one thing: that soldier was Stryker.

'Fucking cunt!' Wortley bawled. He took aim and fired a shot. The gun roared and he spat on the ground and glanced bitterly at David. 'The fucking drive ... *mined the drive!*'

The distant machine-gun roared. Wortley cursed and dropped down. The ground around them erupted in lines of leaping earth, bullets ricocheting off the upturned jeep and making Private Webb twitch. The jeep was lying on its side. Webb was hanging across a back seat, his arms dangling down towards the ground, his smashed head dripping blood. David saw brain and bone. Beyond this mess he saw the château. There was movement behind the patio wall, then a roar, spitting earth.

'Damn him!' Wortley bawled. 'Why now? *What the hell are we doing here?*'

Forbes and Wortley continued firing, reloaded, fired again, and were answered by a brief, mocking laugh, the machine-gun's fierce roaring. Bullets ricocheted off the jeep; Private Webb's body twitched. David glanced around the jeep and saw the battle-scarred lawn that climbed gently towards the wall of the patio. The machine-gun roared again; bullets whined and ricocheted. David saw Private Shaw, lying stretched out on the ground, his body twitching and pouring fresh blood as more bullets stitched into him. Then David felt the anger, boiling up, negating reason, and he looked up at the patio, at the roaring machine-gun, and knew that it had to stop here, that he must put an end to it.

Forbes fired and reloaded. Wortley cursed and kept firing. The roar of the machine-gun continued, the jeep shrieking and shuddering.

'*We're pinned down!*' Wortley bawled. '*We can't move! What the hell can we do?*'

The roaring guns were deafening. The earth danced around the jeep. Bullets ricocheted, screamed off through the air, stitched the two twitching bodies. David almost choked with rage. He heard the guns and felt murderous. He looked across the lawn, saw the shellholes, the debris, saw a long hedgerow bordering the far side. It ran the length of the whole lawn, stopped just short of the patio; if he got over there, he could use it for cover and then they could take Stryker from both sides. David studied the sloping lawn. It ran uphill to the patio. It was wide, but if Forbes gave them cover, he and Wortley could make it.

Forbes and Wortley fired their rifles. The machine-gun roared back. Bullets thudded into the grass, whined off the jeep, ricocheted all around them. David tapped Forbes on the shoulder. The corporal jerked his head around. ' – *over there!*' David shouted. '*Across the lawn! Give me covering fire!*' The corporal nodded and continued firing. David nodded at Wortley. Wortley glanced across the lawn, looked at David, shook his head understandingly.

'*Now!*' David screamed.

They burst out from behind the jeep. Forbes was firing up at the patio. The roaring of the machine-gun had stopped to leave a lingering echo. David heard his own footsteps, saw the shellholes, raced around them; his chest was burning and he caught a glimpse of Wortley, to his left, about twelve feet away. Then a roar, silvery light, an awful shriek and boiling earth, the blast rocking him and throwing him sideways, seeing Wortley in flight. David crashed into the ground, was winded briefly, body aching, spat dirt and rolled towards the hedgerow, the earth still raining over him. Forbes firing, machine-gun roaring; the dying sibilance of the explosion. David rolled into the hedge and crawled beneath it, ears ringing, head spinning. He spat more dirt from his mouth, smacked his head with one hand. Mine, he thought. The bastard mined the lawn. Then he heard Wortley screaming.

The machine-gun had stopped. Wortley's screaming split the silence. David looked across the lawn and saw Wortley stretched out near a shellhole. He was scorched, his clothes in tatters. Both his legs were a terrible mess. He was lying on his back, his body shuddering and jerking, screaming and hammering the earth with his fists, his wide eyes staring at nothing.

'Don't move!' David shouted.

'*Jesus Christ! Oh my God!*' Wortley screamed and hammered the earth with his fists, trying to wriggle with useless legs.

'Don't move!' David shouted. 'He's mined the whole lawn!'

'*Jesus Christ! Oh my God!*' Wortley screamed and shuddered violently. 'Jesus Christ! Someone kill me! My legs ... *Jesus Christ, where's my legs?*'

Wortley screamed and Forbes kept firing. There was no sound from the patio. David knew that Stryker wanted him to go out there, and he felt a great rage. That bastard, he thought. Damn his hide, the rotten bastard. He saw Wortley lying stretched out on the lawn, body shuddering, mouth dribbling.

'Don't move!' David shouted. 'The other mines!'

Then the machine-gun roared. The earth erupted around Wortley. The bullets stitched a line along the twitching man, but they didn't go too close. Wortley yelped and wriggled away. His eyes widened, his head jerked. He moved again and the bullets moved closer, forcing him sideways. David couldn't believe it. The machine-gun roared, Wortley wriggled. Then David realized that Stryker could have killed Wortley with one burst, that he was not aiming for him, that he was methodically forcing Wortley towards the other mines by firing closer each time.

'You bastard!' David bawled.

'*Jesus, no!*' Wortley screamed.

David jumped to his feet, saw Forbes racing from behind the jeep, then the ground beneath Wortley erupted and tore him apart. The noise, the raining earth ... David was picked up and hurled away ... spinning stars, the painful ringing in his ears, then the roaring machine-gun. David blinked and looked up, saw the grey sky, Forbes running, Wortley's remains dropping back to earth, a dull thud in the showering dirt. David knelt down and fired. The pistol bucked in his hand. He saw the winking of the machine-gun on the patio, heard the roar, saw Forbes falling. David got up and ran. He didn't think about the mines. He saw Forbes with his knees on the ground, head flung back, flopping forward. David ran across to him, almost reached him, glanced up, saw the hand-grenade sailing through the air, a stark, timeless suspension. Stryker?

381

Was that Stryker? Standing up on the patio ... ? David dropped to the ground, felt the blast, heard the explosion, rolled away from it. The dirt rained down and subsided, the roar echoing, reverberating; there was silence, the sound of running footsteps, running back towards the château.

David jumped to his feet, felt dizzy, a little nauseous, saw a figure racing back towards the château, then stumbled over towards Forbes. The corporal was dead. His face was buried in the gravel path. David glanced back and saw Webb hanging out of the jeep, the other dead man close by, the scattered remains of Wortley on the sloping lawn. He couldn't quite believe it. He looked up at the patio. It was empty, the machine-gun barrel drooping, a chilling silence beyond it.

David holstered his pistol, picked up Forbes' semi-automatic rifle. He felt rage, an obliterating fury, plus a dawning confusion ... Why had Stryker spared him? He could have killed David with ease ... He looked up at the château, the shadowed walls, the grey sky, suddenly realized that Stryker had deliberately spared him and was luring him inside ... A sport: that was it. Stryker was playing with him. David shivered and felt the touch of madness; emanations of mystery. Then the rage returned and shook him. His beating heart drove him forward. He raced up the gravel path, clambered over the stone wall, and stood, quite exposed, on the patio, looking up at the château.

There was no sign of movement. Curtains flapped in the windows. A sudden roar and David saw the gun winking from a window, the earth spitting and whining around him, coaxing him sideways. The roaring stopped, returned to silence. David stood where he was. He saw movement from a third-storey window, then the gun roared again. The wall behind him exploded, raining concrete and powder, then the ground to his left started spitting, coaxing him sideways. David felt wild with rage. He had never felt like that before. The roaring stopped and he looked up at the château and knew that Stryker was teasing him. David cursed and grabbed the machine-gun. It was pointing down at the lawn. David jerked it around and then knelt down behind it, aimed up at the dark, mocking window, let the gun roar and shudder. H watched the bricks disintegrating. He swung the gun from left to right. He was screaming, spraying the windows and wall, his body shaking with fury.

There was no response. David finally stopped firing. The barrel dropped to the ground as David stood up and tried to control himself. He looked up at the château. He heard a distant, mocking laugh. A sudden roar, the gun winking from the window, the tiles exploding around him. David wanted to scream. He almost raised his fist and shook it. Instead he picked up the semi-automatic and loped away from the bullets. The machine-gun stopped roaring. David headed across the patio. The machine-gun roared again, the bullets stitching the tiles around him, but David knew that Stryker wasn't trying to hit him, that the gun was just teasing him.

Why?

He didn't know. He kept running and reached the front door. He stopped by the side of the door, pressed his back to the wall. The machine-gun stopped roaring. David stood there a long time. He felt the presence of Stryker above him, still up there by the window.

David looked across the patio. He saw the machine-gun against the wall. Beyond the wall was the lawn, the upturned jeep, the four still, broken men. David felt the rage again. He remembered firing on the chateau. He remembered what the adjutant had said, and his cheeks burned with shame ... Stryker was teasing him, goading him, deliberately trying to madden him; and he, like a fool, had fallen for it, had given in to a mindless rage ... Now he tried to control himself. He took a deep breath and glanced up. He saw a hand reaching out, saw the grenade dropping down, and he gasped and jumped in through the door and threw himself at the floor.

The porch exploded behind him, a cataclysmic bellowing, echoing wildly and beating about his head as he rolled on the floor. He felt the whiplash of the explosion, heard the hissing and swirling, a rainfall of powder and stones as he climbed to his feet. More noise: the rush of boots. Looking up: a darting figure. High above him: a bannister, a lot of doors, a dark statue, the gun aiming not at David but above him, then roaring and bucking. David hit the floor again, rolled away, touched the stairs, saw the bullets stitching the wall above the front door, a black drum exploding.

David couldn't believe it. The flames roared across the walls. Yellow, ringed with smoke, racing outward and down, they engulfed the front door, the large windows on either side, hissed and crackled and roared along the floor: a furnace blocking his exit. The drum was hanging above the door. It was pouring burning gasoline. The flames shot out and splashed along the walls and filled the hall with a fierce heat.

David felt a jolt of dread, glanced around the huge hall, was relieved, if mystified, to see no paintings or precious antiques. Then the sound of racing boots. David glanced up to his left. He saw the bannister, the running figure behind it, passing doors, disappearing. David choked in the smoke. He saw the crackling, hissing flames. He stood up, now surrendering to rage, and raced up the curved stairs.

'Stryker!' he shouted. 'Damn you, Stryker! Come out here and face me!'

Was that laughter? He wasn't sure. The possibility was bad enough. David cursed and kept running up the stairs, felt the heat, heard the crackling flames. Then a clicking. Another roar. David felt the fearsome blast. He was punched in the spine and thrown forward, the stairs exploding behind him. His head hit the carpet, world roaring, wood flying, smoke and powder filling his nostrils, the whole staircase shaking. David blinked and glanced back down. He saw space where the stairs had been. Below that space, a good twenty feet down, the tiled floor of the hall ...

'Damn you, Stryker! *Come out!*'

He crawled up the remaining stairs, glanced along the open landing, saw the doors along the wall to his left, the blazing hall to his right. David quivered with rage, felt humiliated and stricken, felt the heat, heard the crackling of the flames, smelt the smoke, saw the furnace ... The paintings ... Dear God ... The yellow flames licked up the walls. David suddenly felt divorced from himself, consumed by rage and despair. He cursed and stood up. The landing stretched out before him. He held the semi-automatic in his hands and walked past the closed doors.

*'Come out, Stryker! Let's finish it!'*

Was that laughter? It was laughter. The sound was mocking, disembodied ... David stopped and tried to hear it again, heard the hissing and crackling. He glanced down at the baronial hall. The front walls were a mass of flames. The gasoline had poured across the tiles and turned them into a sea of fire. David couldn't believe it. It was beyond his comprehension ... the mindlessness, the barbarity and gross extravagance, the destruction of centuries ... The smoke rose up and choked him. He walked slowly along the hall ... No, not destruction; something else: by Stryker's terms ... a with-holding.

David came to an open door. He knew that Stryker had escaped through there. He listened, heard nothing but the crackling flames behind him, the snapping of wood within fire ... Not destruction: a with-holding. Stryker was keeping what he had gained. If he had to go now, he would make sure his whole world went with him ... David stood outside the room. The door was partially open. He listened, heard the crackling of the flames, smelt the smoke drifting closer ... Stryker wanted to take it with him. He would die in his own kingdom. He had lured David in because he didn't intend ever coming out ... he had decided to end it.

David felt the world dissolving. It melted around him and disappeared. There was flame and a rising tide of smoke and a feeling of timelessness. The landing was filled with shadows, black gargoyles, darting shapes. There was David and Stryker and the furnace that might swallow them both ... An open door: silence. The smoke swirled, the flames danced. David felt Stryker out, felt him deep within himself, that latent being lurking within, forever promising omnipotence. Stryker had lured him in. There was no possibility of refusal. David now had to finish the osmosis that had started with birth.

He kicked the door open, rushed in, saw the movement, fired, heard the roaring of his gun, saw more movement, kept firing. The noise was catastrophic, a murderous roaring, a screaming, someone laughing and glass shattering and exploding and flying at David. In the darkness: a bright winking. His gun roaring: barrel flashing. He saw the figures disappearing, the mirrors disintegrating all around him, all mirrors, the whole room lined with mirrors, himself multiplied endlessly. David cursed and stopped firing. The raining glass slashed his face. He covered his eyes and let the flying glass subside, heard oblique, mocking laughter ... Then silence. Drifting smoke. David cursed and surveyed himself: his own image multiplied and now fractured, a bizarre, jigsaw being.

David rushed to the other door. It led into another room. David raced in and gasped and stepped back and then stared down in horror.

A young man lay on the bed. He was curled up like a child. He had a thumb in his mouth and his brains were splashed across the white pillow.

David almost retched. He shook his head and controlled himself. A private, he thought. Very thin. That must be Kantaylis ... Then he saw the explosive primer ... The stairs, he thought; that bastard ... He wiped blood from his face and stepped in, saw antique chairs and tables. He blinked, licked his lips. His face was stinging and pouring blood. He saw two more doors, two other rooms, wondered which one to go through ... Labyrinths. Life's illusions. Stryker's mockery and ultimate lesson ... David stood there and listened, heard crackling, smelt the smoke coming towards him ... You and I, Stryker. Finish it ... The smoke swirled in around him. He stepped forward, then stopped, looked at both doors, hearing nothing from either ... Then a further dissolving. The smoke and the flames below. His rage, a pure rage, devoid of hatred, illuminating and strengthening.

Something dropped on the floor behind him. An unmistakeable, thudding sound. David threw himself forward to the floor, felt the blast, heard the roaring. A grenade, he thought. Christ. The blast crushed him and shook him, whipped him, lashed his arms, bit his legs, disappeared, leaving pain ... No time; must ignore it ... He rolled around and pressed the trigger, the gun roaring, jolting up both his arms, his back stinging and bleeding. Shrapnel: the grenade. He saw the room he had just left: smoke swirling, walls scarred, floorboards smashed, more mirrors cracking and disintegrating.

David jumped and ran back in. He glanced around and then

386

rushed out. The flames leapt up the walls, filled the hall, the heat and smoke sweeping over him. Then footsteps and he turned. A moving figure and he fired. The gun roared, the bullets stitching the walls along the dark, smokey landing ... A game: he had disappeared. The drifting echo of laughter ... David ran along the landing, past the rising wall of flames, saw an open door, didn't hesitate, no longer thinking or caring.

He tripped and fell over. The landing exploded behind him. He rolled away, was slapped away by the blast, the wood and plaster cascading. No Stryker: swirling smoke. He jumped up and shook his head, saw the tripwire across the doorway, running out to the detonator ... Stupid; should have known ... Hearing footsteps, he jumped up, rushed out through the room's second door: another dark-shadowed corridor. David stopped, saw more doors. One was open: this endless game ... The corridor was long, very quiet, all the doors closed but one ... He dissolved. Hypnotized. A slow walk down to death. Possibly not that; something else: the revelation of harmony ...

David stepped forward slowly. He heard the echo of his footsteps. He floated out of himself and looked down and saw the child in the silence ... Somewhere smoke and crackling flames. Somewhere else the hunting fugitive. All the doors closed but one, a dark room, an invitation or trick ... David walked along the corridor. He approached the door with care. He stopped, listened, kicked it open, rushed in and found ... nothing.

'Damn you, Stryker! *Where are you?*'

The sound of laughter, gentle mockery, floating nearby, far away, distorted, disembodied, without direction, along the corridor ... which way? David walked back to the door. He saw the slow drift of smoke. He glanced out, turned his head left and right, saw no movement at either end. Eventually he stepped out, went towards the unexplored end, walking slowly, his gun at the ready, checking all the closed doors ... A riddle of space. Conundrums. Stryker's ultimate maze ... You and I, David ... That's what it meant. All hands joined at the crossroads.

David reached the end of the corridor. Steps led down to a

large drawing room: antique furniture, rich drapes, the sheltered past, history spinning within itself. David stood there and surveyed it, saw the shadows, the hiding places. He held his gun up, very steady, his eyes scanning the gloom.

'All right, Stryker! Where are you?'

Something heavy crashed behind him. He whirled around and pressed the trigger. Too late: he saw the steel drum rolling towards him, the gasoline pouring out. His own bullets did the job. The drum exploded into flames. The flames roared and rushed along the narrow corridor and swept over David. He screamed and fell back, tumbled down into the drawing room, rolled away as the flames poured down after him, raced over the carpets. David screamed and kept rolling, his body burning, wrapped in pain. He kept rolling until his clothes had turned to ash, then jumped up and kept running. The flames roared and filled the room, found the curtains and devoured them, jumped up, bright and hissing, to the ceiling, threw a black smoke back down. David reached the far door. A wall of heat pushed him out. He heard a roar and the flames rushed around him, and he slammed the door shut.

One thought: Stryker. He stumbled forward wrapped in pain, his skin blistered and bleeding, whiplashed: pure anguish and nausea. Then footsteps. And amazement: he still had his gun. He jerked it up and it roared and then stopped, the smoke drifting in silence.

*'Damn you, Stryker! Let's finish it!'*

David ran along the corridor. It led into a ballroom. He saw stacked chairs and tables and chandeliers, a vast space, hybrid silence. Then movement, a roaring gun, catastrophic, reverberating, the wall exploding above David, sweeping over him, bullets whining and thudding. David dived behind some chairs, felt the pain, his burning body, cried out, like a child, unafraid, picked his gun up and fired. He heard a laugh, crashing chairs, looked up, saw a dark form, racing across the entrance to the room, disappearing again. David fired, the gun roared, his blistered shoulder exploding; he saw the far wall breaking up and spitting plaster, saw the large window shattering. Then he saw the grenade. He watched its flight, almost smiled: it fell amongst the chairs to his left, quite deliberately teasing him. The chairs exploded and blew apart, spiralled slowly, fell back down, crashed through the smoke and into other chairs, pieces falling on David. He just got up and ran. He wanted to end it right now. He rushed across the dance floor, lost in space, wrapped in pain, and then scrambled through the chairs at the other side and crashed into the wall.

One thought: Where's Stryker? He looked left and then right. No Stryker; just a long, patterned wall ... another door in the middle.

David groaned and started shivering. He slid along the patterned wall. He heard footsteps, looked out, saw a room, another door now left open. David stumbled across the room. His blistered fingers gripped the gun. No time, no abstractions, no concepts: just a ghost to be hunted. He went through the other door. Another room, a further door. The door was open and he saw the tripwire stretched across the dark carpet. He smiled as his body burned. He stepped over the tripwire. He walked into another room, saw large windows, a balcony: grey sky. He was at the back of the château. The flames hadn't come this far. He stepped out onto the balcony and looked down, saw the gardens ... and Stryker.

Stryker was in the garden. He was crouched behind a machine-gun. The gun roared and David dropped behind the wall and it exploded above him. He started crawling across the floor. His burning body was wrapped in pain. He knew nothing but the pain, the open door, leading down to the garden. David wept and kept crawling. He heard the roaring of the machine-gun. Plaster flew off the wall and fell over him, scorching his open wounds. David yelped and kept crawling. He struggled through the open door. Once through, he scrambled back to his feet, shook his head, stood there swaying.

One thought: Must see Stryker ...

David stumbled down the stairs. They were narrow and very dark. They turned back upon themselves, plunged down steeply, opened out to a grey space. He was in a conservatory. It overlooked the enormous gardens. He saw Stryker outside, not far away, crouched behind the machine-gun. The glass made Stryker blurry. David saw the swinging machine-gun. He started running as the gun started roaring, the glass exploding above him. David felt the pain and screamed. The shattered glass poured down and slashed him. David stumbled and fell, felt the pain, saw his blood on the broken glass. He screamed out Stryker's name. The gun roared, more glass exploded. David crawled towards the door of the conservatory, slashed by glass, showered by falling wood.

'*Damn you, Stryker! You bastard!*'

David jumped up and ran, crashed through the conservatory door, burst into a grey light, cold air, an almost riveting silence ... He stopped. Where was Stryker? He saw the deserted machine-gun. Then laughter and the sound of running feet ... to the left, towards the château. David turned around and fired. His blistered hands twitched with pain. He looked along the conservatory, saw the bleak walls of the château soaring up above a roofed-in verandah ... a door swinging inside it.

David didn't stop to think. He ran towards the verandah. He felt weak, felt the blood pouring out, felt the cuts and the blisters. A fierce pain and nausea. All pain; wrapped in pain. Beyond the pain, divorced from history and future, the livid need to find Stryker ... David saw the verandah, very close, coming closer ... saw the door, swinging slowly back and forth, hinges squeaking in protest. He ran up to the steps. The pain whipped him and blinded him. He raised his gun and jumped up the steps – and then his bad leg gave in.

A darting pain and David fell. He flopped across the verandah floor. Cursing, his leg useless, he crawled forward, his eyes fixed on the swinging door ... Then he saw the black wire. It was fixed to an explosive charge. The wire coiled from the explosive charge back through the door ... Beyond the door: a crouched figure.

Detonator, he thought.

A roar and then a scream. A wall of flame and white light. A sudden vacuum, spinning over, crashing down, a shocking inrushing pressure. David's body exploded. Wood and concrete rained upon him. Pain, an all embracing sheet of agony, falling over and blinding him ... Smashed. Suffocated. Choking dust and crushing debris ... His ears roaring, then ringing, then whistling ... a dying sibilance: darkness.

One thought: I want Stryker.

No pain. No more feeling. David crawled from the rubble. His burnt fingers clawed at the ground as he hauled himself forward. The rubble slid off his body. He spat the dust from his throat. Then a fall, tumbling down the verandah steps, rolling over the powdered grass. David lay on his back. He saw the grey sky above him. And now curious, feeling no more than that, he looked up at the verandah.

Stryker was standing there. He had his hands on his pistols. He seemed enormous, his shadow elongated, the château rising above him. He didn't move for some time. He made no sound at all. David lay there and listened to the breeze blowing gently around him.

Then finally there was movement. Stryker jumped down to the garden. He walked slowly, leisurely through the grass and then gazed down at David. David tried to sit up. He moved a little and then fell back. He gasped and tried to reach for his gun, but he couldn't feel anything. Giving in, he looked up. Stryker towered high above him. His eyes were very deep, extremely dark, quite intense, and they glittered with a veiled, distant humour: the acceptance of loss.

'You're some soljer,' he said.

# CHAPTER TWENTY-SIX

STRYKER knelt down. He put his arms beneath David. He picked David up and held him close to his chest while David felt a great lassitude falling over him. Stryker held him with ease. He might have been carrying a child. David saw the grey sky high above him, the clouds drifting and turning. Then he looked at Stryker's face. The brown eyes were strangely fathomless. Stryker grinned and David saw his own reflection, twice reflected in darkness. He dissolved into that darkness. He floated in and out again. He licked his lips, saw the world spinning slowly, then surrendered to Stryker's arms.

Stryker carried him into the château. David's eyes drank in the paintings. He saw the Rembrandts and the Brueghels and the Titians and the Rubens, and they glowed with an extraordinary beauty that embraced and enraptured him. Stryker carried him across a lobby. They passed the wealth of the ages. Varnished tables radiated the seductive tints of dark amber and jade. David felt a sublime stillness. He heard the echo of Stryker's footsteps. Stryker's shadow danced and slid along the walls, over velvet and satin.

David felt the strong arms. He felt the heat from Stryker's chest. He glanced up and saw the handsome, battered features gliding under a domed roof. A grey light poured through the roof. It beamed down over Stryker. Stryker's head moved through drifting motes of dust and benign, soothing colours. David sank into lassitude. He felt the peace of a cathedral. He looked up to see an arch of grey stone, then a darkness enveloped him.

Stryker carried him down the steps. A purifying chill rose up. David saw the mossy stones gliding past him, a green glint in the growing gloom. The cold slapped him awake. He felt weak but aware. He saw the shadows flickering over Stryker's face, the stone ceiling above him.

They kept moving down the steps. Stryker didn't say a word. They passed candles that flickered in wrought iron attached to the walls. Stryker carried David down. David felt himself dissolving. He felt light and he started floating up and then he drifted back down again. He was still in Stryker's arms, felt an extraordinary lassitude. They reached the bottom and he saw a cavernous cellar, spreading back into deeper gloom.

Stryker walked across the cellar. David lay still in his arms. David glanced around and saw the stone walls, the green moss, the dark shadows. Stryker laid him down gently. He put him down on the stone floor. David felt the cold creeping through his clothes and reaching out for his bones.

Then David saw the paintings. They were stacked up all around him. They glowed with the magic of the ages in the flickering candlelight. David felt himself dissolving. He dissolved into the paintings. He was surrounded by, and revelled in, the splendour, and then he emerged again. He felt totally at peace, quite removed from himself. Stryker knelt down on the stones and David looked up to see his dark eyes.

'You're all done,' Stryker said.

The voice was quite placid, sounded strangely disembodied, and it echoed with an ethereal lilt through the cellar's vast caverns. David listened carefully. He heard the silence returning. He saw the candles flickering over the paintings and making them glow. It was the wealth of the ages: the soul of man set free. David looked around and felt a great peace ... then he saw the slumped bodies.

'I know,' David said.

Stryker sighed sadly. David looked at the paintings. He looked down them until they touched the floor and there he saw the slumped bodies. They were scattered before the paintings. They all lay in grotesque positions. Their clothes lay beside them, and he saw the glint of bone beneath stripped flesh. David studied them a long time. The mutilations were appalling. The stones beneath them were stained with dried blood, but the bodies were clean. There were sacks fixed to the walls; these sacks were stained also. David studied the sacks a long time and he knew what was in them.

'Why?' David said.

Stryker sighed and smiled a little. He seemed hazy and unreal. He glanced across at the white, contorted bodies and his dark eyes were fathomless. He studied the bodies a long time. He finally gazed back down at David. David saw himself reflected in Stryker's eyes, receding back into darkness.

'I cleaned them out,' Stryker said. 'I opened them up and cleaned them out. I don't know why ... I just had to do it. The stench of death is all gone now.'

He gazed steadily at David. There were no depths to his eyes. There were depths, but they led into a void that offered nothing but silence. David lay there and looked at him.

'It's all corruption,' Stryker said. 'It's all filth and stupidity. I couldn't breathe for the stench, I couldn't see for the filth, and I had to dig down and drag it out. I just had to do that.'

David glanced across the cellar. His eyes were close to the stone floor. The candles cast flickering shadows on the walls, on the paintings, on the stripped flesh and bone beneath the beauty of man's quest for the absolute. David thought it was a dream. He saw the phantoms in the paintings. The colours dazzled him and drew him towards them, and then he returned again. He saw the shadows on the floor. They shivered over the stone slabs. They crept over the bodies and licked at the eyes that stared up and gazed blindly at the candles.

David looked at Stryker. He tried to see Stryker's madness. He saw nothing but the fathomless eyes, the darkness leading to nowhere.

'You're dying,' Stryker said.

'Why?' David said.

'How does it feel?' Stryker said.

'I don't know,' David said.

Stryker sighed again. He seemed almost disappointed. He

glanced casually around the cellar and then he looked back down at David.

'I had to do it,' he said. 'It was the only thing left to do. I tried everything else and it failed, and that's all there was left. Thing is, I was frustrated. You probably understand, lieutenant. I had everything going inside, but it couldn't get out. You know what it's like, lieutenant. It's like being suffocated. You're going crazy and you have to get it out, so you have to do something. Fuck it, it wasn't easy. It was hard as fucking hell. I'd wake nights and look at the stars and I'd feel suffocated ... I had to get out, lieutenant. I had to do something drastic. I felt like I was gonna explode and I had to do something ... What were they in the end? They were nothing but shit. It's nothing to do with them – it's what we are; it's what we're all full of ... I had to clean the air, lieutenant. I had to clear away the stench. I went into it as deep as I could go, and came up feeling better.'

Stryker sighed again, glanced across at the heaped bodies. The white bone was glinting in the candlelight under the paintings. The cellar was very quiet. A tap dripped in the distance. The black shadows danced and writhed on the walls, across the barrels of wine.

'It's all done,' Stryker said.

David followed Stryker's gaze. He saw the shadowed, glowing paintings. He saw the stripped bone and the slashed throats beneath, and they, too, seemed like paintings.

It's a dream, David thought. It had always been a dream ... the smokey rooms of Oxford, the boats on the river, the tangled web of Katherine's dark hair, the green wildness in Rachel's eyes ... David felt a great peace. He saw the linear earth. All the tangents of his life had joined together in a healing simplicity ... Katherine and Rachel. His own absorbtion in Stryker. The two sides of the same coin were revealed and were seen to be apposite. We live and are wounded. We wound when we seek to heal. The blind would lead the blind into hell, but they would always return ... David felt a great peace. It was what they had always wanted. He and Stryker, two sides of the same coin, were now finding their resting place.

'You're a mess,' Stryker said.

'Feel weak,' David said.

'It's your chest,' Stryker said. 'Blown to hell. You won't feel it much longer.'

There were no questions now. The night resolved its own silence. The tap dripping in the distance would continue when his hearing had gone. David blinked his tired eyes, felt the drying of his throat. He looked at Stryker as his centre drained out of him, soothing his passions.

'It never lasted,' Stryker said. 'I thought it would, but it never did. I only did it 'cause I needed something special, but it always escaped me. You know what I mean, lieutenant. There's always something you can't have. It's always there, but it's always just out of reach and you never quite see it . . . I didn't know what it was. I just knew I had to get it. I couldn't sleep and I couldn't think straight, and I didn't trust no one. They don't think like that, lieutenant. All the rest: they're just shit. They drink and they piss and they play fucking cards, and you just have to open them up and see what goes on inside . . . There's nothing inside, lieutenant. There's just the shit and the piss. They're just bags to hold what they eat and drink, and there's nothing else to them. That disappointed me, lieutenant. I'd been cheated again. I thought there was a mystery to unravel . . . and that mystery was blood and bone.'

David lay on the hard stone. The cold ate at his bones. His whole centre was collapsing and dissolving and floating away from him. He blinked his eyes and licked his lips. He stared straight up at Stryker. The dark eyes looking down revealed nothing but the void of their history.

David felt a great sadness. He did not feel any pain. He looked at Stryker, at the dark brown of his eyes, and he just felt the sadness. He wanted to reach up to Stryker. He wanted to touch Stryker's madness. He wanted to know that what had happened to Katherine had not been preordained.

'You killed Katherine,' David said.

'Did I?' Stryker said.

'Yes,' David said. 'You killed Katherine.'

'I didn't know that. Who's Katherine?'

David looked at Stryker's eyes. He saw the dark, shifting

void. The void led David into the park in the still, moonlit darkness. A slight breeze shook the trees. The stars glittered in the sky. They shone down on Katherine's hair, into Stryker's brown eyes, through the window onto David's sleeping face. David dreamt of Monte Cassino. Katherine reached out towards him. Stryker entered her embrace and she was lost in his need to possess her. David tossed in his bed. Katherine's face floated past him. He reached out and then he drew his hand back as Stryker stepped in between them. The moonlit blade glittered. It knew not what it entered. It searched blindly for the all revealing truth and found the flesh that knew just that. David cried out in his sleep. Katherine cried out and fell. Stryker turned and walked back into darkness and emerged to the cellar.

'Who's Katherine?' he said.

David stared at the brown eyes. He tried to touch Stryker's madness. He saw nothing but the unrevealing depths, a hint of incomprehension.

'She was my wife,' David said.

'But you're English,' Stryker said.

'You killed her in London,' David said.

'I don't remember. Who was she?'

David closed his eyes. He felt peaceful and remote. He saw the harbour of Port-en-Bessin, the ruins of Europe, the pyres of Belsen, then Katherine and Rachel and Stryker: the cellar's dark, bloody secret ... It didn't matter: it had happened. Life retained its contradictions. What mattered was that the chance had been given, that the lives had been lived. David felt a great peace. It was the peace of understanding. He had lived just to learn that he must die and that he need not regret it ... He opened his eyes again. The tap dripped in the distance. Stryker's brown eyes above the breathing lips offered no sign of shame.

'I'm thirsty,' David said.

'Don't worry about it,' Stryker said. 'It's not gonna last all that long. It'll all soon be over.'

He looked intently at David. He did not seem like a madman. He reached down, wiped the sweat from David's forehead, wiped his hand on his trousers.

'I cleared the hall out,' Stryker said. 'I cleared it out before you got here. I knew you were coming and I didn't want my valuables ruined. It was a bitch of a job.'

David glanced across the cellar. He saw the shadows on the paintings. The paintings glowed with the imagery of the ages while the dead eyes stared up at them. David felt very calm. The stripped bone held no horrors. He looked up and saw Stryker looking down, the brown eyes unrevealing.

'So that's it,' Stryker said.

'That's what?' David said.

'That's why you've been following me all this time ... It must have been a long time ago.'

'When you killed her?'

'That's right.'

'Yes. A long time ago.'

'Where did I do it?' Stryker said.

'Never mind,' David said.

He wanted to deny Stryker something. Stryker knew it and grinned. David coughed and Stryker loosened his tie and then opened his shirt.

'Is that better?' he said.

'Yes, that's better,' David said.

'I'm not normally so considerate,' Stryker said, 'but I think you're a special case.'

David didn't smile. He simply studied Stryker's face. He wondered what he would find in the map of an experience that had led to this cellar in Europe: to the silence of death ... Stryker's face refused to show him. It offered nothing exceptional. It was one of a million other faces: a parchment of flesh and bone.

'Why did you stay?' David said.

'I wanted to meet you,' Stryker said. 'No one else has ever wanted me that much, so I just had to meet you. It was stupid. I knew that. It just didn't make sense. But I just had to know why you'd come. It just fucking intrigued me.'

'Yes,' David said. 'Stupid.'

'That's right, it was stupid. This whole of fucking life is just stupid. It just doesn't make sense.'

David felt himself drifting. He drifted out of himself. He rose up and looked down at himself and saw Stryker above him. The shadows fell over Stryker. His shadow fell over David. David licked his lips and blinked his tired eyes and glanced across at the paintings. The paintings transformed the cellar. Their life glowed above the dead. The dead lay in a bloodless repose, now cleansed of their debris. A tap dripped in the distance. It made a hollow, splashing sound. The sound filled out the gaps in human breathing and would go on forever.

'You can't get away,' David said.

'I know that,' Stryker said. 'I knew that as soon as the war ended. Now I'm trapped in this hole.'

'Why don't you give up?'

'Give me one good fucking reason.'

'They might let you off with a life sentence.'

'That's no fucking reason.'

Stryker glanced around the cellar. His eyes roamed across the paintings; they dropped down and studied the bodies on the floor and then they looked back at David.

'I've done it all,' Stryker said. 'I've gone as far as I can go. I tried everything and everything failed me, and that's all there is to it. Where do I go from here? What the fuck can I do? I crawled through the fucking shit and out again, and I still can't find anything ... I might get off with life? That's one life far too long. I can hardly stand the stench of it now; I don't want time to think about it ... I've got imagination, lieutenant. That's something I've always had. That's a pretty rare commodity, lieutenant, but it comes at a high cost. The dull shits, they don't think. They don't have no ambitions. You and me, we can't stop till we're satisfied; we don't figure the cost ... You intrigued me, lieutenant. You just wouldn't fucking stop. That's something I gotta respect, and I tell you that straight. I'm sorry about your wife. I can't remember her at all. But I tell you, I think it was fate: you and me had this meeting ... You understand, lieutenant. I can tell you understand. You're a man who understands imagination, how it won't let you rest. That's why you followed me, lieutenant. That's why I had to kill your wife. That's why we're both down in this cellar with the stiffs and the paintings ... A man feels what he feels. He has to follow those feelings. He has to follow them or else give them up – and the shits, they all do that. But we're not like that, lieutenant. You and me, we know the score. A man has imagination and it won't let him him rest, and he has to search it through to the end or else let it defeat him. I searched it through, lieutenant. I found that life was blood and bone. That wasn't enough of an answer, but there's nothing else left.'

Stryker stared at the paintings. The candles glowed around them. The yellow flames flickered in the gloom, beneath the cellar's domed roof. It was cold in the cellar. David felt cold all over. He felt tired and disconnected from himself, floating up and back down again. He looked up at Stryker's face, saw the shadows across his eyes. The eyes were dark, and the shadows made them darker, as if disappearing.

Stryker licked his upper lip. He studied the wealth of the ages. He looked at what had always been with-held, and he wanted to keep it. Yet he knew that he couldn't keep it, that there was nothing he could do with it. He could leave it and return to anonymity, which was worse than his fevered dreams. Stryker looked down at David. He saw the lieutenant looking up. His eyes, a deep brown, were going darker, receding to nothing. Stryker suddenly saw himself. The dying man's eyes were fathomless. Stryker saw the swirling depths of a world beyond his own comprehension. A sudden claustrophobia seized him. He felt a sharp, fleeting pain. It passed away and he knew that he was free to walk into his kingdom.

'What now?' David said.

'You're dying,' Stryker said.

'I know,' David said. 'I didn't mean that. What about you?'

'What's it like?' Stryker said.

'What?' David said.

'Dying.'

'I don't know,' David said. 'Am I dying? Who are you?'

Stryker didn't reply. He was glancing around the cellar. It was quiet and he heard the tap dripping and saw dark shadows gliding. It was weird in the cellar. He thought the cellar was mysterious: the dead eyes were staring up at the paintings which glowed in the candlelight. Stryker looked at the lieutenant. The lieutenant's mouth closed and opened.

The lieutenant looked into Stryker's eyes, and Stryker saw his reflection.

'I'm staying here,' Stryker said. 'I won't let it all go. I wanna keep my medals and paintings. I can't stand to be touched.'

He wiped the sweat from David's forehead. David licked his dry lips. Stryker sighed and stood up while David shivered with cold and looked around him ... The paintings glowing in the candlelight. The stripped bone and dead eyes. Katherine smiling, Rachel weeping, white world and white sky; the peace that transcended the mundane and offered abundance ... David drained out of himself. His bleeding body was weightless. He was sweating and numbed by the cold as he looked up at Stryker.

'Brothers,' David said.

'What?' Stryker said.

'All pointless,' David said. 'Too ridiculous. Too hungry for small things.'

'Hang on,' Stryker said. 'Hang on, kid. It won't be long now.'

Stryker stood in the shadows. He seemed tall and far-away. He gazed around him as if in a trance, pistols strapped to his waist. David saw the gleaming medals. They flashed brightly when Stryker moved. He saw Stryker unbuckling his belt and holding up the twin holsters. David looked at the pistols. They cast shadows on the walls. The shadows fell across the paintings, but did not disguise their ravishing beauty. Stryker looked at the pistols. David thought he was smiling. Stryker placed the pistols gently on the floor and then he stood up again.

'Won all,' David said.

'What?' Stryker said.

'Nothing,' David said. 'What's the time? When are we leaving?'

Stryker studied the cellar. He thought of the bombed cathedrals. He looked at the stripped bone on the floor, knew it couldn't last longer. Then he took off his clothes. He did it calmly and methodically. David watched the clothes dropping to the floor, then he looked up at Stryker. The paintings glowed behind his head. The bone and flesh was at his feet.

He stood naked in the cellar's damp chill, his white body half-shadowed. David kept looking at him. I now know what to do. Katherine's face and the rubble of Europe and I want a cold drink. Stryker walked across the floor. He took something from a table. He came back and knelt down beside David, and the candlelit knife gleamed.

'It's clean,' Stryker said.

David looked at the long blade. It was turning in the air and it glittered across Stryker's eyes.

'I'm thirsty,' David said.

'Not for long,' Stryker said. 'I'd give you some wine, but it's valuable and I don't want to waste it.'

He put the knife down. It lay beside David's head. David tried to turn his head but he couldn't, so he looked at the paintings. He surveyed a dark radiance. His drunken eyes drank it in. He thought of Katherine and the hope that was Rachel and the ashes of Belsen. 'I feel thirsty,' he said. 'I think I said I feel thirsty.' He looked up and saw Stryker's naked body standing close to the wall. Stryker looked like a gladiator. The stripped bone lay all around him. He was close to the paintings and he turned on a tap near the wall. I'm thirsty, David thought. I want to know when we're leaving. He heard the gentle splash of water and he looked across and saw Stryker shadowed. The shadows made him black and white. The deeper shadows surrounded him. The deeper shadows swooped around the large cellar and filled it with phantoms. Stryker splashed himself with water. It's all clear to me, Katherine. David blinked and gazed across the dark cellar: yellow candlelight flickering. He saw Stryker with some soap. Stryker soaped his whole body. Picking up a long scrubbing brush, he scrubbed himself until he was raw. David watched him with interest. We're such ritualistic creatures. Stryker eventually stopped scrubbing, drenched himself in the water, stepped away and took hold of his penis. He pulled back the foreskin. He soaped himself carefully. He washed the soap off, put more soap on a finger, and then carefully, obsessively, cleaned his anus. The shadows fell over him. He seemed tall and far-away. He turned off the tap, there was silence, then he picked up a towel.

'No fear,' David said.

'What?' Stryker said.

'Don't care,' David said. 'Makes no difference. Might be possible this way.'

Stryker walked across to David. His naked body was shining. He was drying himself vigorously with the towel as he looked down at David. David thought he seemed tall. I don't mind, I'm just thirsty. David looked up as Stryker dried himself, his muscles rippling in candlelight.

'I'm clean,' Stryker said. 'They won't find me unclean. The one thing I can't stand is filth. Fuck them all. They won't find it.'

'I'm thirsty,' David said.

'Yeah, I know,' Stryker said.

'What time is it? I think it's getting dark. I want to know when we're leaving.'

Stryker finished drying himself. He dropped the towel to the floor. He walked over to the table and returned with a small jar of powder. David tried to turn his head. He found his head couldn't move. He turned his eyes and then saw the glowing paintings, glowing over the stripped bones. David felt a great sadness. He felt calm and at peace. I know I should have accepted what I am and it would have been easier. The glowing paintings filled his vision. He saw the imagery of the ages. He turned his eyes up and looked at Stryker who was looking down at him.

'Forgive,' David said.

'Fucking great,' Stryker said.

'No resentment,' David said. 'Should have known. It's a lie to be not.'

Stryker powdered himself. He was meticulous about his testicles. The tap dripped through the silence of the cellar, the shadows, the paintings. David blinked and looked at Stryker, saw him powdering his anus. Stryker went back to the table and left a dark void, a silence: seductive ...

David drifted away slowly. Rising up, he saw himself. Within and beyond his frail shell he saw the dream of his history. He was here and he was there. He saw the life in Stryker's shadow. He lay still and saw the swimming, domed roof, shattered brick, the grey streaming sky ... Katherine and Rachel. First love, then understanding. Two sides of the same coin revealed: the lieutenant and Stryker. Grey stone and grey sky. Was it grey stone or sky? The major-general's grey eyes and the grief that was locked up inside him ... It was love. David felt it. David felt a great peace. Robert stood up and the sea soared behind him and the forest fires smoked. David licked his dry lips. He looked up and saw Stryker. Stryker seemed very tall and far-away, and his white body rippled.

'I take care of myself,' he said.

'It was an accident,' David said.

'It's the filth and the stench,' Stryker said. 'I can't stand all that shit.'

'I'm thirsty,' David said.

'Yeah, I know,' Stryker said.

'Why?' David said.

'I'm real clean. I can't stand to be filthy.'

Stryker knelt beside David. He picked up the gleaming knife. The thin blade cut a line across his eyes, illuminating the nothing. Stryker waved the knife slowly. The blade obviously entranced him. He looked at David and a grin split his face as David longed for a drink ... I should have stepped forth and told her ... The blade glittered before his eyes ... I needed courage and that's where I failed, though it wasn't important ... Stryker sat down beside him. He crossed his legs and looked at David. The paintings glowed with their melancholy ardour behind Stryker's dark head.

'I wanna tell you,' Stryker said.

'Why?' David said.

'I can't stand the filth and the stench and I won't let them find it.' Stryker looked down at David. He knew that David understood. 'When they find me I'll be drained fucking clean, and that's all that's important.' Stryker slashed his own left wrist. David saw the bright blood. He thought the blood was the colour of the paintings that glowed on the wall. 'That's a start,' Stryker said. 'It's not much, but it's enough. I'd like to scour my insides like I did with the others, but at least I'm fucking doing what I can.' Stryker slashed his other wrist:

the knife red, slicked with blood. The blade gleamed through the blood in the candlelight flickering overhead. 'Fucking Jesus,' Stryker said. 'Smarts a bitch. You just wouldn't believe it.' The knife clattered to the floor. The noise echoed throughout the cellar. The deep silence returned and emphasized the sullen dripping of the distant tap. 'Red,' David said. 'Fucking right,' Stryker said. David saw Stryker's hands in the air, the white wrists red with blood. 'The paintings,' David said. The paintings framed Stryker's hands. They pulsated in the candlelit gloom and receded to darkness.

David closed his tired eyes. He saw the dark, swirling cosmos. He sensed the paintings glowing dimly all around him, looming over the bloody wrists. I must not accept this. He licked his lips and coughed a little. Immense value to the peoples of Europe and they have to be saved. David licked his lips and sighed. He opened his eyes, but saw little. Floating up and then drifting down again, hearing blood dripping slowly. It was over. It had ended. David felt a great sadness. He thought of Stryker and the paintings in the cellar, the tragic need to affirm. I won. And he lost. I will win and he will lose. David lay there and drifted in the darkness, knowing what he must do. Death would not have dominion. The long night would not triumph. David smiled and spiralled out of himself and felt a cold, clean conviction.

'Yes,' David said.

'Fucking Jesus,' Stryker said.

Stryker looked down and saw David's eyes closing quietly in shadow. Stryker snorted and grinned wildly. He wondered what it was like. The paintings glowed all around him and he saw the red floor beneath his wrists. Stryker felt a bit light-headed. He felt as if he was floating. I'm clean and they won't find no filth and that's all that's important. The shadows swooped around the cellar. The slashed flesh revealed the bone. Dig as deep as you can go and pull it out and there's nothing worth having. Stryker snorted and grinned wildly. The tap dripped in the distance. The dripping echoed throughout the vast silence and surrounded the cosmos. Stryker saw the glowing paintings. He saw the flickering yellow flames. He saw the darkness of the cavernous cellar as he fell across

David. He lay there a long time. He let himself drift away. The revelation of silence stripped him bare and left nothing to cling to.

'Fuck you all,' Stryker said.

# CHAPTER TWENTY-SEVEN

DAVID opened his eyes. He knew that Stryker was dead. Looking up, he saw the stone roof of the cellar, a grey tendril of smoke. Fuck you too, David thought. He felt pain and that meant life. Stryker now lay across him, his arms outstretched, his wrists dripping blood.

David blinked and glanced around him. He heard the dripping of the distant tap. He saw the candles flickering over the paintings, saw a thin, drifting smoke. Pain: must be saved. Beyond the pain: must save the paintings. Fuck you, David thought, trying to smile, you will not win it all.

He welcomed the pain. It whipped his nerves and gave him life. He gasped and raised a hand and grabbed Stryker and pulled the corpse off him. Stryker was very heavy. He slid from David with reluctance. He rolled over and his head thumped the floor and then he stared at the ceiling. David blinked and looked at Stryker. Stryker's frozen lips were smiling. David saw the smoke drifting across the paintings, then he started to crawl.

He crawled across the cellar. The paintings glowed all around him. The candles flickered over the paintings, over the dead eyes staring upwards, over David as he crawled on the floor, his body blistered and bloody. Pain: must transcend it. Death: must not admit it. David crawled towards the steps, feeling pain, smelling smoke, breathing harshly and muttering incantations and transcending his mortal self.

The smoke drifted down the steps. The stone was cold to his touch. David glanced back at the cellar, at Stryker, and then he pulled himself up. The cold air stung his wounds. He felt intensely unreal. He saw the mossy stones, a green glint in the gloom, and he sobbed and kept going. Pain: must transcend it. Death: must not admit it. David crawled up the steps, felt the pain, let it whip him, coughed and bit his lips and tasted blood, let his flesh shred and shriek.

One thought: Must show Stryker.

He refused to give in. He had to see the boundless sky. He saw the stone steps curving up above his head, the grey smoke drifting down. David thought of the paintings. He felt a fierce, driving rage. He thought of Katherine and Rachel and the funeral pyres of Belsen, and his fingers gripped the earth between the stones as he pulled himself up. His blistered body, his shredding skin; looking back, a trail of blood. The candles flickering over the paintings and the dead eyes on the floor, casting shadows on the stones and on Stryker, that dark, huddled form.

David smiled and turned away. He kept crawling up the steps. The candles flickered on the walls, illuminated the green moss, and then a grey light poured down on waves of heat and spread out in a silvery haze. David shuddered and fought the pain. His fingers clawed at the last step. The blisters burst and his fingers turned to fire as he hauled himself forward. A wall of heat engulfed him. A grey smoke poured around him. He gasped and then choked and dropped his head and then looked up again.

The paintings here were moving. They drifted backwards and forwards. He saw the Rembrandts and the Brueghels and the Titians moving through the grey smoke. David blinked and tried to focus. He was at the back of the château. He saw the paintings gliding through the swirling smoke and then he saw the men carrying them. It was the civilians from the town below. They were rescuing the stolen treasures. David sighed and rolled onto his back and looked up and smiled gratefully.

Farewell, Stryker. I won.

There was a domed roof high above. The roof was shattered and he saw the sky. The smoke swirled in the air above his eyes and poured out through that jagged hole. David studied the grey sky. Footsteps rushed around his head. The men were shouting in German, and he heard them rushing down to the cellar. David felt a great relief. It turned to joy and filled his being. He blinked and saw a circle of faces, felt the hands sliding under him.

The Germans picked David up. They carried him out of the blazing château. He saw the encircling faces, felt the hands beneath his body, gazed up at the smoke, the bobbing paintings, the immense, sultry sky. They carried him around to the front lawn, laid him down on a blanket. He was surrounded by the paintings already stacked up on the lawn, was seduced and made whole by the splendour, by the hands on his fevered brow.

David felt a great peace. He heard the men shouting in German. They were rushing back and forth, carrying paintings, denying Stryker his victory. David lay there and smiled. He felt himself drifting away. He saw the low wall of the patio, the smoke swirling around the men, saw the flames leaping up the château walls, heard the crackling and hissing. Yellow flames and crimson sparks. The black smoke, the grey sky. David drifted away, the voices fading, the flames receding; rose up and glanced back and saw himself lying still on the blasted lawn. His fellow-men were all around him. The stacked paintings enriched the light. The château burned and the flames rose on high and then were lost in the boundless sky.

No more pain, David thought. We need the pain to make us live. We are hopeful and the dark nights destroy us to make us return. These are accidents; no more. We will the wounds to solve our problems. Reaching out, we touch the tips of the flames to reaffirm that we burn. I am: that I am. You are: that I will be. In the dark nights we touch and find grief and then awaken renewed. Katherine. Rachel. I see, therefore you are. Love and its ultimate commitment: what is known can't be lost . . .

David closed his tired eyes. He felt drained and at peace. He sensed the paintings glowing dimly in that darkness filled with gaunt ruins and rubble. The smoke rose from the mass graves. The refugees choked the roads. The roads ran back to the sea and the grey waves washed over the decks. Katherine's dark, flowing hair. The darker skein of the river. He bought peaches and cream and saw the boats on the river and blue sky. Rachel's smile: the green tears. A flower of snow in his palm. A destructive, ecstatic renewal with the guns roaring fiercely. He felt joy, then transcendence. Stryker living and dying. He saw the living rising out of the dead and populating the barren earth. David smiled at the nothing. People passing on their way. Drifting out into white world, white sky, unknown feeling; beyond it, vaulting over the nothing, something just out of reach: possibility ... freedom.

'Yes!' David said.

## THE END